Toni and Addie Go Viral

Also by Melissa Marr

A COURSE IN MAGIC

Remedial Magic
Reluctant Witch

Toni and Addie Go Viral

Melissa Marr

x

B
BRAMBLE

Tor Publishing Group
New York

TONI AND ADDIE GO VIRAL

Copyright © 2025 by Melissa Marr

A Bramble Book
Published by Tom Doherty Associates / Tor Publishing Group
120 Broadway
New York, NY 10271

www.torpublishinggroup.com

Bramble™ is a trademark of Macmillan Publishing Group, LLC.

EU Representative: Macmillan Publishers Ireland Ltd, 1st Floor, The Liffey Trust Centre, 117–126 Sheriff Street Upper, Dublin 1, DO1 YC43

Library of Congress Cataloging-in-Publication Data

Names: Marr, Melissa author
Title: Toni and Addie go viral / Melissa Marr.
Description: First edition. | New York : Bramble, Tor Publishing Group, 2025.
Identifiers: LCCN 2025013480 | ISBN 9781250364890 trade paperback | ISBN 9781250364906 ebook
Subjects: LCGFT: Lesbian fiction | Romance fiction | Novels
Classification: LCC PS3613.A76872 T66 2025 | DDC 813/.6—dc23/eng/20250411
LC record available at https://lccn.loc.gov/2025013480

Our books may be purchased in bulk for specialty retail/wholesale, literacy, corporate/premium, educational, and subscription box use. Please contact MacmillanSpecialMarkets@macmillan.com.

First Edition: 2025

Printed in the United States of America

10 9 8 7 6 5 4 3 2 1

To Amber. You are the stability when I am flailing, the laughter I need in my blues, and the strength in my weak days. If younger me heard I'd be happy to put a ring on anyone's hand and promise to be *faithful forever*, I'd have laughed. I'm so glad you proved me wrong.

SPILLING THE TEA ON THE BIGGEST STORIES IN CELEBRITY AND ENTERTAINMENT NEWS

From secret relationship to viral wedding, the Darbyshire romance is either a brilliant playbook or a pending catastrophe. Either way, we'll be here to share the scoop!

Hot new author Toni Darbyshire just made every other proposal this year (century?) look boring. The author of *The Whitechapel Widow* (which Universal grabbed in a hotly contested bidding war) wowed the lady of her dreams by penning a blockbuster hit about a Victorian detective named after her paramour. And how do you follow up such an opening volley? You sell it to the studio, pull strings to get your girlfriend the role, and top it off with a surprise wedding.

Modern Victorian Brides?

Ingenue Adelaine Stewart was recently cast in the adaptation of her new wife's book—and at a Victorian ball to celebrate the book's success the two tied the knot in an elaborate "costume" wedding. The twist? A real reverend! The author wore a custom tailcoat in a ladies' cut and the actress wore a lovely 1892 dress. From invisible to married in mere months, this couple knows how to make a statement.

More:

Boston Weddings

Fashion Forward—By Looking Back

Hottest New Book Trend? Or Just Another Passing Fancy?

Chapter 1

Addie

"I know I have my badge somewhere. Just hold on. . . ." Addie darted a look at the middle-aged man working there as she dug through her tote bag. A lidless pen, a tube of coral lipstick, several environmentally friendly straws, a few hair clips, a cloth napkin: she piled it all on the desk haphazardly. She paused, debating this persona. *Too far?*

She really wanted to get in, though. *Desperate times call for awkward moments. . . .* She pulled out a container with a menstrual cup in it.

"Would you hold my cup? Please. I don't want it to fall on the floor since I need to put it . . . you know." She gestured at her crotch and then looked up, giving him her widest eyes. "Never too safe, right?"

The man looked at her with the same appalled look she'd been aiming for. "You know what," he said in a pained voice, "there's a crowd building up behind you, and you seem like a nice young woman. Why don't you just go ahead?"

Channel woodland animals and ingenues, she reminded herself before her victory glee appeared in her eyes and ruined everything. *Be sweet! Be clueless!*

He crossed his arms over his chest, and she realized she was still holding the cup out.

"Are you sure?" Wide, innocent eyes again. She took a long

tendril of the honey-blond highlights in her bland brown hair and twined it around her finger. Lost-damsel-in-the-woods hair always seemed to work.

He scribbled something on a badge, held it out, and gestured her forward. "Enjoy the conference, miss. Don't lose this one."

Adelaine shoved all her many items back into her bag. A part of her hated playing these games, but a larger part of her liked being able to buy groceries. Paying to get into the lectures would mean that buying food wouldn't be possible. Someday when she landed a real gig, a big role, she'd pay her fair way into everything. She'd pay *other* people's way.

First, though, she had research to do. There was an order to things—Step 1: research; Step 2: get the role; Step 3: be fabulous. Repeat. Repeat. Repeat. And then she would have her career dreams met.

On to Step 1!

Addie fell into the flow of attendees, switching from "ingenue" to "just another academic at a conference." She twisted the fall of hair that reached her low back into a hasty braid, and then clipped it up into a headache-causing bun.

Maybe it's time to cut it.

Hair aside, she'd dressed for this part, though, and Lady of Shalott hair wasn't a fit. *Think academic.* Over her own jeans, she had added a basic colored blouse she'd picked up at a thrift store and a smart but well-worn sweater. Not *too* frumpy, but beige enough that she thought she'd blend. Her usual style was too much, too notice-me, for this venue, and as with any role, she was dressed in character.

Today's role was Young Academic.

When she spotted a conference handout on a table, she snatched it up and scanned it until she found *her.* Dr. Darbyshire was the real goal, the research Addie needed but in human form instead of a book or video. Addie had read one of Darbyshire's articles when she was researching for a role, and while she wouldn't say she'd fangirled—

because really, who fangirled a professor?—Addie knew "fangirl" was pretty much on the mark. Any quotes, social media references, and one brief conference video, Addie had collected all of them in a laptop folder labeled THE PROFESSOR SAYS. Dr. Darbyshire was a handful of years older than Addie's twenty-seven years, but she was poised, polished, her life together, and she made history seem interesting. So Addie wasn't going to miss a chance to hear her speak.

Addie skimmed the panel listing, looking for Dr. Darbyshire's talk.

ROOM: BALLROOM B
"FRIENDS AND SECRET LOVERS: LESBIAN
RELATIONSHIPS IN THE VICTORIAN ERA"
—DR. ANTONIA DARBYSHIRE

Addie didn't bother reading the description. She had exactly four minutes to get to the ballroom and slip into an unobtrusive seat. Addie was going to learn how to be a convincing Victorian, and she was going to get a role in the upcoming Victorian stage production of *Dracula* that posited that Mina and Lucy were the true romantic couple in the tale and retold the entire story from their point of view.

Addie followed several serious-looking women in blazers and trousers into the room. She glanced at her own thrift-store clothes. With her jeans, she still looked remarkably American—which she was—but she didn't want to look it. Her one exception to her common style of dress was the enormous opal ring she wore on her right hand. It had been her grandmother's, and upon pronouncing Addie's mother "too fickle to marry," Gran had put it on Addie's hand. And there it stayed.

Who knew people wore trousers and skirts to a lecture like this?

Addie slipped into a seat in the back row along the aisle. It meant she could lean out slightly and look at Dr. Darbyshire if she needed. Or wanted. It was only a few moments before Addie did just that, taking in the woman at the front of the crowd.

Fangirling the professor . . .

The professor was thirty-two, according to her online biography. She was slightly older than Addie *and* taller than Addie's five feet four inches, but not by too much. She was also exactly the sort of woman to make Addie's usual ADD hit hyperfixation.

It's not obsessing if she's a teacher and I need to learn. That was Addie's answer, and she was sticking to it. It was even mostly true. She'd discovered the professor in her research, and the fact that she was stunning was just a bonus.

Dr. Darbyshire had a commanding presence, as if she were hoping for trouble so she could show off her muscles. Her pose was a power stance, feet slightly spread as if bracing for something. There were curves hidden under her blazer, hinted at by the flared bottom of the jacket, and as the professor turned to say something to an attendee, the angle made clear that she had a swimmer's body. *Lean and strong.* Addie stared at her, appreciating the way her short hair toed a line between professional cut and statement cut.

But then Dr. Darbyshire said, "We are running out of seats, so let's begin." She paused, her voice rich in that honey and whisky way that great blues singers had, before teasing, "That way any of you who find my lecture tedious can slip away and leave empty seats for the latecomers. . . ."

A ripple of laughter greeted her words, and Addie grinned at the sheer arrogance in that statement, as if the professor were daring them to find the talk boring but also absolutely certain they wouldn't.

Arrogance.

Athletic body.

Husky voice.

Addie had been half-smitten after watching a shaky video that didn't do justice to Dr. Darbyshire's presence. Seeing the woman in person was enough to tempt even a rational person—and Addie wasn't renowned for her common sense.

Trying to stare in "studious" not "smitten," Addie pulled out her notebook and pen and took more notes than she probably needed, but Dr. Darbyshire was Addie's secret weapon. With her knowledge, Addie could understand the Victorians. Knowledge. Killing the role. Acclaim. Bigger roles. Respect. It was a whole thing. A plan.

Over the next fifty minutes, Addie wrote down enough information to flesh out the persona she needed for the role. Dr. Darbyshire made the information in dry books come to life. She was a gifted teacher.

If I had teachers like her, I'd have gone to college forever....

After the professor answered the last question, Addie stayed in her seat as the crowd thinned. People stepped over her, and Addie tried to convince her feet to follow. What was she going to do? Walk up and ask Dr. Darbyshire out? Call it a research lunch?

Bad idea, Ads.

But the more Addie looked at the perfect column of Dr. Darbyshire's throat and listened to her husky voice answer questions for the people gathered around her, the more the thought of talking to Toni Darbyshire, of asking for advice, was increasingly seeming like a perfectly sound plan. Of course, Adelaine was certain that any plan she created that seemed "perfectly sound" was ill-advised. She knew herself. Impulsivity typically led to trouble for her.

Addie stared at the professor a bit longer.

She's a professor. Professors like answering questions.

Finally, Addie stood up and started forward. She had questions. Plus, it was only polite to say "thank you" for the great information.

And she's talking about women like us. That's another reason to ask advice on a Victorian-influenced lesbian play . . . or maybe casually ask if she's single.

Adelaine knew better. She was a committed romantic, dreaming of forever, saving her heart—and other parts—for the right woman. A serious history professor who lived on the other side of the ocean was not going to fall for Addie on a conference trip. And Addie wasn't going to be all "free love" like her parents. She might have moved temporarily to Scotland on a whim; she might even pick roles on a whim or adopt personalities to playact. But when it came to relationships, she was a one-woman kind of person, the marrying kind, the commitment kind.

Then Dr. Darbyshire looked up, catching Addie's gaze briefly.

Maybe I could just say thank you. . . .

Head throbbing from the weight of her hair, Addie reached back and unclipped her braid. It fell like Rapunzel's rope. She took several more steps forward.

Saying thank you for being such a wealth of information was fine, right? And if the professor was responsive, maybe a little flirting and—

A stunning brunette in a plain but very well-fitting dress walked up to Dr. Darbyshire.

"We still on for tonight?" asked the woman. "Or are you standing me up?"

The professor laughed. "As if."

"Uh-huh. I see that research glimmer in your eye. Someone asked a question that got you thinking. . . ." The brunette grinned. "Can I trust you to meet me there or will I need to leave my meetings early to pull you out of your laptop?"

Dr. Darbyshire put her hand to her heart. "Emily, I swear I will be on time. Early, even."

The brunette, Emily, nodded. "Lady's Hand. Seven."

"Yes, dear."

And Addie's heart sank far more than it should've. The professor had a girlfriend that her biography online didn't mention, and the girlfriend was six shades of sexy.

It wasn't as if there was a real chance of a relationship with the confident professor anyway. They would have an ocean between them come Monday. And Addie wasn't the sort to let her lust lead her away from The Big Plan: true love, monogamy, and growing old together. She also wasn't willing to let lust lead her away from her career goals, which meant returning to her life in LA where the film jobs were, not moving to the East Coast where Dr. Darbyshire lived. Unlike her parents, Addie had a clear life path in both career and relationship goals, and she would find a way to achieve all of it.

Addie pivoted and walked away from the idea of trying to talk to Dr. Darbyshire after the panel. She wasn't a home wrecker. Maybe some other time she could ask Dr. Darbyshire questions about the Victorians, but right then, she was too emotional to try to approach her.

Chapter 2

Toni

Toni paused at the bottom of the uneven steps into The Lady's Hand to take in the sight of several dozen patrons surreptitiously looking at her. She couldn't complain. She was a stranger here, and a lot of bars catered to regulars.

"Mind yourself," a woman behind her muttered. "Some of us trying to get a drink."

"Sorry." Toni stepped to the side, feeling like a weight slid a little off her shoulders at the distinct pub smell. Hints of smoke and liquor, perfumes and sweat, and it was inside a Scottish lesbian-friendly pub.

Tonight, Toni needed the familiar comfort of a woman-centered space. Her father had managed to reach out from beyond the grave and ruin things. She'd had a great turnout for her talk, and then a steak with colleagues. It should've been an excellent day, but then she received news far worse than she'd feared.

Thank your stars you're already dead, Dad.

If he hadn't been, Toni would be flying back to the States tonight to plant her fist in his face. Violence wouldn't solve this problem, but it would make her smile. Her temper was still a work in progress, despite years of effort. Unfortunately, the old grifter was dead, and so he was impossible to punch.

More's the pity.

After dropping her rain jacket on an empty chair at a table, Toni made her way to the bar. At first glance, the stone-walled basement space felt like any generic bar, but this particular bar had the honor of being a newly opened lesbian bar, which felt remarkably hopeful. In an era where such bars were an endangered species, the opening of a *new* one was exciting.

The bartender, a forty-something woman with teal hair and generous curves, came over. "Evening. Menu?"

Toni slid a credit card across the weathered wood of the bar and said, "No menu. Talisker, regular, *not* a special cask."

A day might come when she could splurge on one of the Talisker top-tier whiskies, but not for the foreseeable future. At least the good whisky was cheaper here than back home. And though she was typically not a huge drinker, tonight Toni needed a metaphorical shot of Novocain.

The bartender's gaze slid over Toni, and she pretended not to notice. She knew she looked like a million other nondescript women. Brown hair, brown eyes, spent too much time at the gym, and had a chip on her shoulder that she wore with pride. Not quite sporting an undercut, but hair short enough to make a statement. Not *extremely* masc but definitely not femme. The labels had changed since Toni came out in high school, but the long and the short of it was that no one looked at her and thought she was anything other than what she was.

She took care of herself, and she made no excuses for her tendency to walk out of most bars with company. Most women weren't surprised that she didn't stick around. Toni wasn't the staying kind, intentionally so, but she made a point not to imply otherwise.

Or leave with anyone wearing a ring.

Or bi-curious.

Or hoping to U-Haul.

Her interests were simple: no strings, no heartbreaks, no home-breaking.

Sex was like any other appetite. She fed it, but it didn't define her.

Tonight, however, she knew she looked tired enough and felt lousy enough that she would likely leave alone. Toni had glimpsed her reflection in the mirrored pillars of the hotel lobby. *Bone tired. And soggy from the light rain outside.*

Whatever the bartender mistakenly gleaned from Toni's weary face softened her expression, though. She nodded and grabbed a bottle. "Coming right up."

Toni exhaled. Talking wasn't high on her skills list tonight. She just wanted a few drinks to silence the feral rage that rolled under her skin. Every fucking time it felt like things were turned the right direction, reality snuck up and slapped her down.

That man hits from beyond the grave.

This week was intended to be a turning point toward victory. Present at a respected conference. Accept the new job. Build a name . . . she'd worked toward this new future for a decade already. She'd overcome her roots, or at least left them buried in small town nowhere that she would never again visit—especially since she was going to have to move her mother closer to her.

Toni had her hooks in a tenure track position already. Her career was on solid ground. Her health was good. All of her financial woes *had been* sorted out. This week was to be the start of the dream, but the specter of her dead father had to fuck everything up.

"Passing through?" the bartender asked as she slid the overfilled glass to Toni.

"Just here for the weekend." Toni paused, seeing a generous double shot instead of the single shot she'd expected. She lifted the glass and said, "Thank you."

"You looked like you could use it."

"You're not wrong." Toni smothered a laugh that was half cry, half rage. Confession wasn't going to do a thing to plug the gaping money shortage in her life, so she switched gears. "I'm meeting someone. No food, just a drink. Can I order her drink now?"

The bartender nodded, looking a bit less friendly. "What'll it be?"

Toni ordered her bestie's drink.

"We don't generally bring them out. Come get it when she arrives."

"Thanks." Toni settled the tab, and then she took her own glass to the table alongside the wall.

This wasn't the way she'd hoped to spend her night at The Lady's Hand. When she'd added the bar to her plans, she was hoping for a strings-free evening with someone who was not living close enough to Toni's new place to think that a hookup would turn into anything permanent. Maybe it was crass, but relationships were right there alongside family reunions and "team building exercises" on the list of things she had zero interest in trying.

No rings. No marriage. That's where her own mother went wrong. Once a woman started thinking that anyone's promises of love were real, disaster was sure to follow. Better to avoid the nonsense. Late night hotel rooms, no last names, and vanish by morning.

Women are better for my liver than whisky is, too.

Toni took in the bar's options. Dim light illuminated a decent sized crowd of female-presenting people, nonbinary people, masc lesbians, one Hey Mamas lesbian who was eyeing Toni like she was competition, and a number of what her Aunt Patty used to call the "lipstick ladies" back when Toni was a girl not yet aware that wanting to stare at those painted mouths was about kissing, not about wanting lipstick of her own. There were newer terms, politically proper terms, but every so often, Patty's voice crept into Toni's mind like a salve.

"It's okay to stare at them." Aunt Patty patted Toni's hand. *"No matter who you are, no matter what you do, don't doubt yourself."*

"Dad says I'm a freak."

Aunt Patty made a sound that might've been a word swallowed back. "My brother is a drunken, lying fool. The only good thing he ever did was help create you."

Sometimes, Toni wished she could turn back time to those moments with Patty, who had been a rock through Toni's childhood and rough teen years. Instead, Toni was on her own now, without the calming voice of her aunt or the occasional supporting words of her mother. Her mom wasn't physically gone, but she was more likely to call Toni the wrong name than she was to recognize Toni lately.

I've got this, Aunt Patty. I do. I'll look after Mom and myself, too.

Toni pushed maudlin thoughts away as Emily slid into the chair across from her.

"Sorry I'm late." Emily settled into her seat with the sort of graceful elegance that Toni could never mimic. She was the delicate crane next to Toni's stomping owl—and truthfully, she was as close as Toni would ever get to love. Em was like a sister, and that was the only sort of emotional entanglement Toni was willing to accept.

"No worries. I just got here." Toni gestured at her partially empty glass as Em went into a colorful story about an editor who had a stain on his shirt that made her feel like it was a Rorschach test the whole conversation.

Emily paused as the bartender brought over the glass of wine Toni had ordered and a second glass for Toni that she hadn't ordered. Table service was not the norm over here, so the gesture was particularly kind. Apparently, Toni looked like she needed a refill.

"Talisker?" the bartender asked.

Toni fumbled for her wallet, but the woman simply smiled and gave a shake of her head. "On the house."

"You are a goddess," Toni said.

The bartender smiled and left. Emily gave her a look.

"What?" Toni muttered as she slid the glass of white toward her oldest friend.

Emily raised one brow. "Bartenders here don't bring drinks out to you *or* buy you drinks."

"Maybe it's boredom."

Emily rolled her eyes, and Toni cracked a smile. The bartender had that sexy older woman thing going on, but she also seemed like a talker, and Toni wasn't sure she could manage that—thanks to the news she'd just received. She'd have to . . . Who the fuck knew? She had no idea how to fix the debt now on her plate.

When the bartender was gone, Toni said, "It's worse than I

thought, Em. I'm going to head home tomorrow and see if I have any options. I have a few things I can suggest to the department, maybe I can add an extra class and sign up early for teaching summer sessions. If I had to, I could rent my guest bedroom and—"

"How bad?"

"Here." Toni opened her bag and withdrew a stack of pages. She slid them toward Emily. She could recite them by heart even if she hadn't printed the email and read and reread it. The words on the top—from the attorney's office—covered the crux of things.

Ms. Darbyshire,

I have concluded my investigation, and I regret to inform you that your late father convinced Mrs. Darbyshire to sign the documents. Upon his death, payments halted. There now exists a lien on the house. Should you sell the property, the appraised value will be enough to pay off all but the $200,000 lien Mr. Darbyshire incurred; however, the lien on the house prohibits the sale of asset; it must be paid before you can close any sale on the house.

Toni put her hand on the top page for a second. "The letter goes on. Short version: I hate my dad."

"Longer version?"

Toni took a long drink before answering. "I told you that Mom's memory slips are getting worse. I found a decent memory care residence near me, and I was going to sell her house to offset the cost not covered by her insurance, but selling her house to pay for it no longer works because of *him.* And because in her situation, she was not aware that she had bills to pay. The house sale is on hold, but I cannot move there without quitting my job and losing *my* town house. Oh, and he downgraded their insurance, so it only covers part of a stay at a decent place. His gambling and whatever get-rich-scheme he was in at the end has left her in a pile of debt that I need to sort out—all while figuring out how to afford a safe place for her."

Emily took a fortifying sip before prompting, "So . . . what's the plan?"

"Fuck if I know." Toni let her gaze dart around the bar. This should have been a good night. This should have been a good trip. Instead, she was drowning in email from the new facility where she was moving her mother, emptying her emergency account for a down payment for that, and parsing legal letters.

The conference where Toni had been presenting the last of the papers from her dissertation no longer felt as exciting as it had when she'd boarded her flight to Edinburgh.

"We'll sort it out," Emily said yet again. "You have a tenure track position and—"

"Two hundred *thousand*, Em. Plus the cost of the care facility. Not exactly junior faculty salary. Between student loan payments, mortgage, repairs to the car, food, and utilities . . . I am at *almost* enough to pay for memory care if I still live like a grad student. How do I pay her debt, too?" Toni looked at her best friend and exhaled loudly. "Sorry to ruin our weekend. This is my crisis, not yours."

"*Psh.* We're sisters in all but blood," Emily said, echoing a mantra they'd taken turns uttering over the years. The timing of the gap between Bologna Book Fair and the London Book Fair had matched up with Toni's event, and they'd decided to make a celebratory girls' trip and head to London after Edinburgh, but that plan was about to be nixed.

"I have no more savings, Em. I used everything on the down payment to get my new place in DC and to pay the first few months for Mom's stay in her new care facility. It's not even an *ideal* place. It's good, but nowhere near me, and I can't even afford it now. I have two months. Two fucking months, so what am I going to do? How do I pay for the rest of her care? I can try to get a second job . . . and . . ." She shook her head.

"I have an idea . . . but you might hate it." Emily swirled the last of her drink.

"More than I hate being broke? Or Mom moving to some sketchier place or living with me before the year's end?"

"Maybe . . ." Emily stalled.

Emily Haide had been Toni's dearest friend since they were ten and attending the same summer camp. This weekend, they were to be celebrating both Emily's position at an excellent Manhattan literary agency and Toni's tenure track position. They had done it, achieved their goals, managed their dreams.

And my dad still fucked it up, even from beyond the grave.

"Hit me."

"Victorian murder mystery. I was talking to an editor at one of the Big Four Houses, and the word is that they are all hungry after that Regency that hit. 'Fresh' in publishing is really only two steps to the left, so Victorian instead of Regency would have them salivating. If you want to be the be to answer my prayers, write me a book. You have the history chops—"

"I *teach,* Em."

"Which means you write academic papers all the time. You finished a PhD dissertation. Those are as long as a novel, just add more murder and sex."

Toni laughed. Her dissertation wasn't short on either murder or sex, and Emily knew it. Admittedly, Toni had tried her hand at writing books during the ramen days of grad school. She'd started a half dozen that ultimately were shelved—and one that wasn't.

Toni started, "So here's the thing—"

"What was your major in uni?" Emily interrupted, cutting her confession off with a tap of a finger on her cherry-red lips. "That's right. Double major. History and . . ."

"English." Toni flipped off her best friend.

"Look. I just spent the week in Bologna seeing what's selling, hearing what people are seeking, and I think you could pull this off."

Toni took a deep breath before adding, "I maybe already have . . .

something. It's not what I would usually . . . I mean, I didn't bring it up because of your job, and it's embarrassing for faculty who ought to be focused and—"

"Hold on." Emily stared at her until Toni started to squirm. "You wrote something, and you didn't tell me?"

"Sort of," Toni hedged.

Emily made a "go on" gesture.

"I was drowning when Mom got sick, and I just couldn't focus on another academic thing. It's just something I wrote for myself." Toni gulped her drink like an awkward college kid discovering booze. She was a grown-ass woman, and Emily was her dearest friend, so squirming was silly. "It's a book about a Victorian detective. Lesbian. Avoiding marriage and solving crimes."

"Yummy."

Toni laughed. "She's a bit more my taste than yours, Em."

Emily pouted exaggeratedly. "So she looks like your dream lady?"

"More or less. Not quite as curvy as my taste. More statuesque Boudica than naked, clever Lady Godiva. And in Victorian widow's dress."

Emily paused, nodded. "Okay, visual acquired. I have the character, the setting, and . . . where are the *pages*, Toni?"

Toni took a deep breath. "Fiction is more intimidating than academia. If I send a paper out, they critique my research or my methodology, and I can revise. It's—"

"Agent, dear," Emily interrupted. "I know how intimidating it can be." She reached out and squeezed Toni's wrist. "If it's good, though, it's a start to filling that hole that the debt is creating. Let me see it."

Toni was sure of her teaching and sure of her academic papers. She was sure she was a trustworthy friend and a loyal daughter. Hell, she was sure of her prowess in bed. She wasn't sure of her fiction writing skills, though.

"It was just a thing I did to recharge when I was sick of classes and worried, so if it sucks, you'll tell me . . . right?" Toni looked at her best friend and hated herself just a little for feeling like a coward.

Emily tossed back her wine. "Email it to me tonight."

"But if it's awful, you'll—"

"Toni, I love you like the sister I wished I had, but we both know I won't burn my career pitching a book that's not going to build my reputation." Emily smiled with her professional smile, one that made sensible people flinch and made Toni relax. Emily added, "If your book is terrible, I'll tell you."

Toni sighed. "If it isn't, though . . ."

"If it *isn't*, I'll sell it, and you'll have something to put a dent in that debt of yours. At the least we can get a five- to fifteen-thousand-dollar deal to cover some more time at the facility for your mom. Even an average deal would help, right?"

Toni nodded, feeling more unsure than she was used to around Emily. "I want brutal honesty, though. Don't be nice because you like me."

"Ob-viously," Emily said in an exaggerated drawl before laughing.

They had few secrets and even less judgment, but Toni had heard the stories of people doing ridiculous things to get the attention of an agent. One man had followed Emily into the ladies' room at the airport, and it was best not to even think about the panic that they'd been through when some enterprising fool sent a vial of what looked like blood along with her pitch for a vampire book.

"I don't want to take advantage of you," Toni said.

Emily laughed louder. "You might be one of the few women here thinking that."

Toni sent a wide-spanning glare around the pub. She didn't often play the stereotypically overprotective sibling, but she relished it when she could. Unlike her, Em *was* a relationship person, and while Toni didn't understand it, she would defend Emily's virtue at the hint of a frown.

She also felt awkward as hell right now. Mixing business and friendship was a terrible idea. She grabbed Emily's arm. "Nothing will change if you hate it, you know?"

"Dumbass." Emily gave her a doting smile. "Of course I

know. . . . are we still on for breakfast? Or I can grab a train to London if you're sure you're headed home . . . ?"

"I need to go back. I hate to abandon you, and it would be amazing if my scribbles made money, but what are the odds of that?" Toni scoffed. "Unlike my dear departed deadbeat of a dad, I live in the real world. So I need to talk to the department chair. Try to get something in motion."

Emily sighed. "I'm extra sorry I missed our dinner now. I'll come down to DC to see you when we're both back."

"You could stay now and have another drink," Toni suggested.

"Nope. I'm clearing my desk so when you send me the book tonight, I can read it and sell—"

"Maybe sell," Toni interjected.

Emily laughed. "Sweetie, you can write, and you know the era. I am already optimistic, so I'm going into it thinking positive enough for both of us." She leaned in and brushed a kiss on Toni's head. "Trust Auntie Em."

"We're the same age," Toni pointed out.

"Technically . . . now, go play. I expect to hear about whatever you're going to do once I leave to ease that . . . mood." Emily gave her an exaggerated brow wiggle that made Toni laugh despite everything. "Then I expect a book in my inbox, Ms. Darbyshire, or I'll be pounding on your hotel door."

"Yes, dear," Toni agreed.

Then Emily left, and Toni realized that she no longer had any intention of rushing back to her hotel room. Hope was a powerful drug.

Chapter 3

Toni

Toni was fairly sure that whisky wasn't the answer, and she wasn't about to get excited about a *maybe* book deal. It was a pie-in-the-sky plan, as her mother used to call such things.

Wouldn't Lilian have loved it if it worked? If I did something so like him, *and it panned out?*

A bitter sting hit Toni then, the odd feeling of mourning someone who wasn't dead. The Lilian Darbyshire Toni knew and argued with made fewer and fewer appearances these days. There were moments when Toni saw her mother, and they knew each other, and everything felt normal—or as normal as it could be. They'd never been close, but that didn't change the sense that Toni wanted them to be.

And it's too late, now.

As much as Toni had longed for the sense of friendship she saw people build with their parents, she'd never have that. Her grifter father was dead, and her mother was lost to an illness that made her disconnected from reality. Knowing the impossibility didn't undo that gnawing desire to be that kind of connected. Aunt Patty was the only one who had ever accepted Toni, and she was long gone, too.

Leaving me in this mess all alone. Although in fairness, Patty had cleaned up after her brother for so long that it was probably a blessing that she wasn't here to see the mess he'd left for Toni—or to see how lost Toni's mother was.

Lilian Darbyshire was a woman whose dreams of fame were cut short by an accidental pregnancy in her mid-thirties and a quick marriage to a man who traded on cons his whole life. She'd had a career about to blossom, until him, until the pregnancy. And she'd been fool enough to love him so much that she surrendered her own dreams.

Like so many women throughout history.

He'd loved her in his way. Toni could see that now. It was just that his way of loving was no good for anyone. Not his wife. Not his daughter. Not his sister. Not even the countless mistresses he took. He was a charmer, but charm wasn't the same as substance or hard work.

If there was a racetrack in the afterlife, Anthony Darbyshire was sidling up to some gullible mark with a plan.

Or he was still being conned out of his last set of winnings.

And back here in the land of the living, his widow was likely yelling at someone for letting him know where she'd stashed her money. That was the peculiarity of Lilian's memory slips. They weren't always the sort that made her fall into her bad years with her husband, but most of the times with him were so similar in the yo-yo of their fortunes that Lilian's sense of what she thought was "now" were good moments in a range of bad to worse to decent years.

And all of them were with her con man husband exasperating her.

And people wonder why I avoid relationships.

The curious part of her parents' marriage, to Toni, at least, was that no matter what the timeline was in Lilian's reality, she always had an underlying fond exasperation, as if she found her husband's haplessness with money endearing. No matter that she'd had to surrender dreams of a singing career, and then later drop out of college as an older adult.

All because of him.

No matter what plan Lil had had to turn her life around, to build something stable, Anthony Darbyshire found a way to ruin it.

Growing up in the mess of his mistakes hadn't felt "endearing" to Toni, and her years with her Aunt Patty—when her parents were too broke to look after their only child—were really the only ones that had offered any semblance of stability. Now? Now Patty was gone, and Toni's dad was gone, and the adult version of Toni had to figure out how to fix the latest catastrophe on hand.

Honestly, the fact that she was more inclined to academia and workaholic tendencies than addiction and destruction felt like it was a victory—even if more than a few therapists called her workaholic path another kind of addiction. She never gambled. She didn't smoke or use drugs. She strictly limited shopping, drinking, or excess.

There was one exception to her rules.

Just the one.

From her teen years until recently, Toni had coped with feeling lost or overwhelmed by bed-hopping like it was an Olympic sport. Her therapist spent more than a few sessions trying to get Toni to address her commitment fears, but it wasn't a huge mystery. Her mom trusted her dad, and look where she was now. That was a fate Toni would never endorse.

Better to count on herself—and find a bit of comfort in willing women.

Her gaze drifted over the people here again, hunting for the one she'd bed and forget next. Her gaze jumped right past the desperate-eyed ones with visions of U-Hauls dancing in their minds.

Toni wasn't interested in *forever*. She was only interested in *for tonight*.

She skipped the coupled-up women, including the one with the body language that spoke of discontent. Rebounds were fine, but only after they were single. The tall woman in overalls was a maybe. So was the primly dressed one shooting bold looks her way. Women in all their shapes and sizes were amazing. Toni had only a few simple rules: No hookups with colleagues. No "I'm bi-curious and can my husband join" women. No students. No one already in a relationship.

What Toni needed was a simple, no strings, no complications temporary connection with a woman who wouldn't walk away thinking that one night meant anything, and she'd had to put that urge on hold too often during her dissertation and job hunt. She was well overdue for . . .

Well, hello, there.

A real-life Lady Godiva, complete with both the near-nakedness and the waterfall of hair, stood in the doorway to the bar. She wore a thick braid of golden-brown hair that reached clear down to her hip. She was shivering, probably because she was wearing what looked like a Victorian nightdress and not much else. Pristine white cotton with a ruffle at the ankles, it was a shapeless sort of thing—but it was illuminated by the fire in the pub, and Toni was far from the only woman noticing the stranger's hourglass figure . . . and obvious lack of a bra. She could also see that the stranger had Victorian drawers under her nightdress, and those were made of thicker fabric, enough that Toni couldn't tell if they were historically accurate.

Is she actually wearing historic drawers?

The Victorians were thought to be prudish, but historic drawers were akin to modern lingerie. *Crotchless.* It was practical, of course. Their dresses were heavy things, and being able to use the toilet was a challenge in such dresses.

That didn't explain why a modern woman would wear such drawers, though.

Is this woman wearing crotchless Victorian drawers? Surely not.

Toni wanted to know, wanted to investigate the matter. Lesbian in historical garb? Yes, please. She looked like Toni's fantasy come to life.

The woman's gaze zeroed in on Toni like an invitation, and Toni was on her feet and across the pub before the thought fully settled. If the stranger was going to turn her gaze toward Toni, there was zero reason to ignore her. The woman was one of Toni's favorite types—slightly shorter than her, fit enough that she'd be willing to go hiking or to the gym, and obviously possessing at least a passing interest in history, according to her attire. And the fact that she was busty wasn't exactly a deterrent. Toni was always a little extra pleased when her lovers possessed a sort of pin-up girl set of curves.

More than a few people were looking at the new woman like she was a lost damsel, but Toni was certain that they were thinking more villainous than heroic thoughts.

Not that I wasn't looking at her like a dessert in convincingly historical boots.

The stranger shivered.

And though Toni wasn't sure if it was a chill or nerves, she slipped her blazer off and held it out. "Here."

The woman stared at her.

"You shivered." Toni's gaze dropped to the woman's chest, despite her best efforts. It was a chest that deserved extra looks, and up close, the dark areolas around pert inviting nipples were making Toni extra sure that she deserved an award for not staring. The stranger had glorious breasts.

The woman clutched the blazer to her chest like a shield but didn't put it on. "Who are you?" she whispered.

"Antonia. *Toni.*" Toni took her blazer back and helped the woman into it. The sleeves hung over her hands, covering the large fire opal ring on her right middle finger.

When she pulled the front of the blazer closed and buttoned it, the woman stared up at her. "I'm Lady Adelaine Stewart."

"Lady? Is there a costume ball nearby, Miss Stewart?" Toni teased. "You seem to have missed the evening gown. . . ."

"I was rehearsing," Adelaine said, sounding more serious for a moment. "Stage production."

"Ah." Toni glanced around the pub. No one was watching them now, likely presuming that the not-quite-dressed woman was here to meet Toni, since Miss Stewart had stared directly at her upon arrival—and Toni had gone to her side like she'd been summoned.

I don't think I know her.

Surely it was a coincidence. Her table was likely just the first place the stranger's glance had fallen. *I wouldn't forget someone like her!* Toni might have bedded the occasional woman whose name she couldn't recall, but she didn't forget the shape of a woman's body—especially a shape like this.

"Did you mean to wander into *this* bar, Miss Stewart?"

"I did." She looked around, wide-eyed. "But . . ."

Miss Stewart looked as if she were on the verge of a swoon. She was obviously quite committed to her persona.

"Do you need an escort to a car? Or train?" Toni offered.

"No. I am here." She straightened her shoulders, and Toni briefly cursed her decision to button the blazer. "With you, in fact."

At a guess, Toni would say Adelaine was only a number of years younger than her own thirty-two years. *Mid to late twenties?* She had soft hands, the sort that looked like she'd never seen hard work, and impeccable posture. She was shorter than Toni, softer in some indefinably vulnerable way, and had the sort of mouth that was made for gasps of surprise.

In all, she was a Victorian historian's perfect thirst trap.

A flicker of familiarity hit Toni. Had they met before? Toni hadn't spent much time in Scotland. This was only her second trip. Maybe Miss Stewart was a type? Maybe she was a conference attendee? Toni tried to recall all the people she'd spoken to that day, the faces in the seats, and she couldn't place Miss Stewart there.

"Do you live here?" Toni asked. "In Scotland?"

"Yes," Miss Stewart said. "Why?"

"I was wondering if we'd met before," Toni admitted. She didn't exactly phrase it as a question, but she pointed out, "You seemed to be looking at me when you walked in."

"Who wouldn't be looking at you?" Adelaine's response was a non-answer, but then she stepped closer and stared up at Toni through her lashes. "Can I trust you? You look like I can trust you."

"I'll protect you, Miss Stewart." Toni offered her an elbow this time. Her anti-relationship stance might be tested by Adelaine if they lived nearer one another. *Thank goodness for an ocean between us!* She smiled at Adelaine and prompted, "So, this is a local play . . . ?"

Adelaine paused. "Maybe. Would you find me a convincing Victorian damsel?"

"I'm not your average judge, I fear," Toni said with a small smile. "I'm a Victorianist by trade."

"So I would have to be *perfect* to convince you, wouldn't I?" Adelaine's character slipped slightly then, and Toni liked her a touch more.

"Indeed," Toni murmured.

"Shall I be perfect for you, Miss Darbyshire?"

Toni ignored the unfamiliar flutter in her stomach and challenged, "Impress me, Miss Stewart. Maybe you'll earn a reward."

Adelaine's answering trill of laughter made Toni suspect for the first time that the younger woman was not quite as innocent as the character she'd adopted, but then she fluttered her eyes and that flicker of wickedness vanished.

Adelaine held Toni's gaze and asked, "Would *you* like to play pretend with me, Lady Victorianist?"

In answer, Toni pulled out a chair for her. "I fear that your virtue could be imperiled. . . ."

"If I'm convincing enough," Adelaine murmured as she pulled the incredibly thick braid of hair over her shoulder. If it were loosened, she could hide the fact that she had no bra under her thin nightie. "That could be a risk coming here, I suppose."

"It could." Toni itched to reach out and use that braid as leverage to pull Adelaine nearer. She wondered briefly if the hair had been loose on her trip here. If not, Adelaine had been vulnerable as she traveled. Toni felt a wave of anxiety at the thought of such risks. Hopefully, Adelaine had braided it just before she entered the pub.

Adelaine unbuttoned the jacket as she leaned forward. It gapped enough to see the curve of her cleavage but no more. "Surely, you can keep me safe."

"From everyone but me," Toni assured her. "I fear I'm not a great supporter of any plans to preserve your innocence."

Adelaine's wicked smile returned in a flash. "Oh, thank goodness, I wasn't sure when you covered me up so quickly."

And Toni decided that her evening—hell, her entire month—suddenly looked a lot better. It had been a long minute since she had a woman in her bed. In her teens and twenties, a steady stream of women had been the norm, but as she passed thirty, her dissertation, job apps, and family drama had been all-consuming.

"Are you unattached then?" Toni asked.

"Does that matter?"

"It *does*," Toni admitted. That was a trait she wouldn't share with her namesake. Unlike her father, Toni had a strict "no catting around with other people's wives or girlfriends" stance.

If Adelaine wanted to role-play, Toni was willing to go along with it, but she had rules that had to be addressed first. *No married women* was number one.

"I am, regrettably, single," Adelaine began, holding up the hand with the antique fire opal ring. "I have my future engagement ring, but for now, I wear it on the opposite hand. And you?"

"I am single, not even a ring in waiting. In fact, I have—" Toni was going to add that she was permanently single, but she was saved from answering by the bartender stopping at the table. The table service that had seemed sweet earlier, now felt awkward.

"Quite the revolving door," the bartender teased.

Adelaine frowned slightly and looked down to her lap where her hands were politely folded, and Toni muffled a terse word at her reaction. Maybe the bartender was trying to look out for Adelaine, but it wasn't like Toni had been there with a date earlier.

"Not that it's anyone's business, but the woman who was here was a childhood friend, not a date," Toni said, sounding sharp enough that the bartender flinched.

"Would you like a drink, love?" the bartender asked, whisking away Emily's wineglass and Toni's empty highball glass.

"Lemonade?" Adelaine asked in a shaky voice, not quite looking up.

"No actual lemonade here. Lemon drop? Or hard lemonade?" the bartender asked.

Adelaine looked at Toni, who was oddly charmed by the gesture.

Toni sized her up and decided she looked more like the sort of woman who preferred a fussy umbrella drink than swilling something out of a longneck bottle. "Lemon drop sounds good. Another Talisker for me, too."

Once the bartender left, Toni tucked her foot under the bottom rung of Adelaine's chair and pulled the chair closer.

Startled, Adelaine put a hand on Toni's knee and let out a squeak of sound that shouldn't be as adorable as it was.

Toni took a breath before reminding herself that whatever else was happening, Adelaine would be here in Scotland next week, and Toni would be back in her condo in Northern Virginia.

"So, first time here?"

"Yes." Adelaine's voice was quiet. "Is it obvious?"

Toni reached forward and put a finger under her chin, tilting her head upward so she was looking at Toni again. "Hey? Everyone was a baby gay once. First time going out like this can be scary as fuck. . . ."

Adelaine gasped, hand covering her mouth.

Toni had a flicker of a suspicion that there was a part of this persona that was actually true. Gently, she said, "You're safe with me. Unless you're looking for something unsafe, but if that's the case, you need to tell me that, Adelaine."

"Addie. You may call me Addie."

"Addie." Toni smiled. "Tell me about you."

"American in Scotland. I'm working on a local stage production. . . ." She shrugged. "Terrible impulse control. You?"

"American in Scotland for the week. I teach." Toni caught her eye before adding, "I'm a fan of beautiful women with bad impulse control."

Addie giggled.

"Your drinks," said the voice behind Toni.

Without hesitation, Addie smiled up at the returning bartender. She lifted her drink as soon as it was released and drained half the glass.

The teal-haired bartender exchanged a surprised look with Toni before shaking her head and walking away. Either Addie was a heavy drinker or would be soon on her way to tipsy. Toni wasn't sure which was worse.

Toni shook her head at what she was about to say. She wasn't in the business of policing other people's bad habits, but she wasn't interested in either leaving a vulnerable woman alone or handling a drunk. All she said was, "If you need liquid courage for whatever you're thinking . . . maybe you should reconsider doing it."

"Did you ever want something so badly that you wanted to ignore reason?" Addie asked. "Sometimes it's easier to play a role or toss back a drink. . . ."

Toni took a swallow of her single malt and eyed her companion. "So play a role, Miss Stewart. I'm game. Tell me about your *character*. Married? Job?"

Addie visibly straightened, lowered her gaze demurely, and slipped into her role again. "I live with a relative. He is my chaperone, but I stole away while he was indisposed." Addie took another drink. "No job, obviously. I'm not that sort of woman. Do *you* work?"

Toni nodded. "I teach."

"And your employer lets you dress so . . ."

Toni quirked her brow. "So?"

"Provocatively," Addie whispered.

Whatever else Addie was, she was bolder than she looked.

Toni took another look at the curves outlined by thin cotton. "No more so than a damsel in her nightdress."

When Addie said nothing, Toni asked, "So, Miss Stewart, what are looking for tonight? You're in your nightdress in a pub. That's a dangerous move."

Toni watched her, wondering exactly how committed she was to her playacting and deciding after a brief moment that she needed to know that answer.

Addie stared at Toni with a boldness that Toni wasn't going to ignore. "I'm an innocent in a vampire play where the lead finds herself seduced by another woman. My character wants to be a little bit debauched before she's married off or put on a shelf for being unmarriageable."

"I see." Toni reminded herself that she was leaving for home in a day. What harm could come of an ill-advised night if they were about to have an ocean between them? Toni wasn't a huge fan of role-play typically, but . . . when in Scotland. "And what do *you* want?"

"You." Addie's voice quavered.

So Toni reached out and pulled Addie even closer. From this angle, Toni's blazer did little to cover the pert nipples that stood like an invitation under the sheer white cotton of the nightdress Addie wore. "I am a fan of all sorts of wickedness, my lovely Miss Stewart. If you're asking if I'm interested, the answer is yes. So what would you do next if you were writing this stage play of yours? No consequences. No price to pay."

Addie took several deep breaths, nodded to herself.

Toni felt like the air was crackling.

Addie was watching her. Her lips parted, and she looked Toni over with unmistakable albeit tipsy interest. For a moment, Toni thought about the long list of women in pubs or parties in the past, and she felt a flicker of self-doubt. This woman made Toni want to be chivalrous, gentle, any manner of irrational reactions that were out of place for someone playacting in a bar on a rainy night in Edinburgh.

One-night stands happen, Toni reminded herself. *It's Addie's choice here, too. We're in public, and she's likely nowhere near as innocent as she acts.* Intellectually, Toni knew better than to act like this was a big deal, but her traitorous heart sped as Addie stared at her.

When Addie licked her lips, Toni was ready to scoop her up in her arms like the Victorian damsel she was pretending to be.

Toni's voice was rough as she prompted, "Adelaine?"

For another moment, they were silent, and then Addie crawled into Toni's lap. She sat sideways, legs tightly together. In the firelight, those lovely legs were defined silhouettes in her cotton nightdress, and as much as a dress that reached to her ankles ought not be so sexy, it was. *She* was.

Toni quickly reappraised her situation and wrapped an arm around Addie's waist. It was harmless flirtation, right?

Adelaine settled herself in Toni's arms with a sigh. "You make me want to be decadent, Toni. I feel scandalous already. I am barely dressed and in your arms. Such things aren't acceptable in these days."

"Are the 1800s so very strict?" Toni teased.

"I am a woman of means, and there are expectations. . . ." Addie sounded quite convincing. "I am expected to marry, to let a man of my family's choosing touch me, but I want . . . something else."

Toni encouraged Addie, "Tell me what you're looking for."

"I have always wanted to kiss a woman, to feel *wanted* by a woman such as yourself," Addie whispered in Toni's ear. "Will you make me feel wanted?"

Toni opened her mouth to answer, but Addie pressed her lips to Toni's in an awkward kiss.

For a moment, Toni couldn't respond, thinking about her other rules. She didn't make a habit of bedding baby gays; they tended to imprint like newly hatched ducklings, which led to notions of commitments—and the underlying rule that had created all the rest was that Toni didn't do complicated.

But it very quickly became apparent that if this woman had kissed anyone in her life, it was not often. There was plenty of passion, but not a lot of experience.

It's just a kiss. Everyone deserves a proper kiss.

Just one kiss.

Toni took control, guiding their kiss, and after a moment, Addie followed her lead. When Toni's hand tightened on her hip, Addie's lips parted in a gasp, and Toni deepened their kiss.

Addie's hand slid into Toni's hair and gripped as if Toni were considering stopping.

But when Toni's thumb grazed the underside of Addie's breast, Addie jumped up, a vision with wide eyes and kiss-stung lips. She crossed her arms over her chest.

Addie blinked her eyes and stared at her. "There are *people* in here."

Toni tossed a handful of bills onto the table. "Let's go."

Addie let out a little noise of protest, but she followed Toni outside.

"Do you live nearby?" Toni asked, hating how brusque she sounded.

"No."

They stood quietly for a moment before Addie said, "I'm sorry I was so rude. I've never . . . and there were people *watching* us."

"Fair." Toni eyed the small garden in the next lot. There was a gate, a locked gate, but someone hadn't fastened it thoroughly. "Come on."

Addie paused. "Just so you know, Adelaine is my *real* name. Adelaine Stewart."

"Toni's really my name, too." She didn't add her surname. She wasn't keen on sharing that. For a moment, she frowned, thinking that Addie might have already *said* her surname, but that didn't make sense. How would she know Toni's name?

Had they met? Toni glanced at her again. She had a few fuzzy details about women in her past, but there was no way she'd forget having Addie in her arms before this.

Toni opened the gate enough for them to slip into the garden and took Addie's hand. She pulled Addie behind her. "Is this scandalous enough for you?"

"Not yet." Addie's voice shook, but she squeezed Toni's hand tightly.

"It's private-ish," Toni offered. "Unless you want to go somewhere—"

Addie lurched into her for another kiss, cutting off the question, and pressed her braless chest against Toni. The jacket was now pressed to the sides, and Addie's pebbled nipples against Toni's thin blouse were a welcome reminder that Addie wore no bra.

Toni's hands landed on Addie's narrow waist, and she slid her thumbs upward to caress the line of her ribs. Eventually Toni's hands moved upward, thumbs grazing Addie's nipples.

When Addie pulled back, her pupils were blown wide. She glanced down at Toni's hands and said, "More, please. More touching."

Toni decided that this was where they were going to be staying. "Are your drawers period-accurate, Addie? I've been wondering that since you walked in," Toni said, crowding the woman closer to the shadows of the hedge.

Addie nodded once. "I think so. . . ."

Toni closed her eyes, leaning her head against Addie's for a moment. "Now is when you tell me you want to go home or . . . say yes."

"Toni . . ." Addie reached out with one shaking hand and curled it around Toni's hip.

"Going? Staying?" Toni felt like her voice had been rolled over gravel with how rough the words felt in her mouth.

"Kiss me, please?"

Toni lowered her mouth to Addie's, tasting the tart lemon still on her tongue, but she kept her hands carefully still. She needed a solid yes before going anywhere that was going to be too far or too fast, and she still hadn't sussed out what was character and what was real.

When Addie let out a little whimpering noise, Toni pulled back. "Answer, Addie. Are you staying here with me or going?"

Toni stepped back slightly. She might be more than a little tipsy, too, but she wasn't going to coerce Addie into anything.

Addie stepped forward, raised her hands so they were flat on Toni's collarbones. Addie's voice was barely a whisper when she asked, "What would staying mean?"

Toni swallowed a sigh. Addie, apparently, was either truly committed to her persona or genuinely innocent. She was also eager. Her hands smoothed over Toni's chest, like she was trying to memorize the shape of Toni's torso as they spoke.

"Whatever you want." Toni didn't hide her own moan as Addie's fleeting touch paused to cup Toni's breasts.

"Would you kiss me more?" Addie whispered.

"Yes."

"And touch me some . . ." Addie swallowed visibly.

"Do you want me to?" Toni asked, feeling more awkward than she was accustomed to feeling in hookups. She held Addie's gaze. "What *you* want is what I need to know here, Addie."

"I want you to"—she took Toni's hand and moved it to the juncture of her thighs in a very clear answer—"let me know if my undergarments are historical enough. Touch me *there*."

A slow smile came over Toni at the request. "It would be my pleasure."

She stepped closer and nudged Addie's legs apart so that Toni's leg was between them.

As Addie reached out to touch Toni's breast again, Toni caught her wrist. "Be a good girl, Lady Adelaine. You said you wanted me to touch you, so I need you to follow the rules now." She directed Addie's hand to the wrought-iron fence that was still visible in the hedge behind her. "Both hands on there now."

Addie whimpered softly. She wrapped her other hand around the metal. "Yes, Toni."

Toni kissed Addie's breasts, now at easy mouth-level, through the thin nightdress. Addie's thighs clamped harder around Toni's leg. She arched backward, breasts jutting out like an invitation.

"Such a good girl you are. . . ." Toni mouthed her nipples through the barrier of that white nightdress.

"Please," Addie whispered, as if she didn't have the words to know what she wanted. "Toni, please."

"I have you." Toni stared down at her. There was something more erotic about the wet circles on the thin white cotton, and Toni felt her own pulse speed as she looked at the sight before her. Along the street, voices carried, and that made their hidden moment more arousing somehow.

"Like a regular Victorian maiden about to be debauched in the garden," she whispered, pinching one of Addie's nipples.

"Yes, please," Addie begged, tilting her head back.

Toni suckled her throat before whispering, "Shall I slide my hands into those delicate drawers or kneel here in front of you? Toss one of those pretty legs over my shoulder?"

Addie was shaking, grinding herself against Toni's leg. "Hands. I'm not ready to . . . I've never—"

"As you wish." Toni was a little surprised that Addie was apparently *that* inexperienced, and every rule Toni had about baby gays screamed into her mind, but within forty-eight hours, Toni would be back in the States. She wanted, *needed,* to give Addie something to remember.

First times ought to be exciting or special.

And I can't give her special.

Toni bunched up the cotton nightdress and held Addie's gaze. "Hold this for me, Lady Adelaine?"

Addie went wide-eyed enough that Toni stepped back and asked again, "Would you rather I stop completely?"

"N-no." Addie grabbed the cotton in one hand, clutching it in a tight fist and exposing her drawers. She pressed back against the fence. "I want . . . *more.* I want you to touch me."

As Toni trailed her hand to the juncture of Addie's legs, pausing at the place where her now-damp leg had been, she let out an appreciative noise of her own at the damp material there. She parted the opening on the almost criminally accurate drawers. They were slit from bum to button, and Toni said a silent prayer of thanks to whatever costumer made these as she stroked Addie's slick skin.

Addie was already trembling, and several moments later, Toni murmured, "Bend your knees just a little, love, so you can let me in."

When Addie complied, Toni slid two fingers inside the slick warmth of Addie's body.

Addie clenched around her and made a sound that sent a flood of warmth through Toni's own body.

After several moments, Toni shifted her hand so her thumb could press and stroke Adelaine's swollen clit while her fingers continued to thrust inside. The only sounds were Addie's whimpers and Toni's own deepened breathing. There was nothing quite as satisfying as having a beautiful woman quivering under her touch.

"Such a very good girl, Addie," Toni told her.

"I've never"—Addie moaned—"been in a garden."

Toni chuckled. "Are you a wicked girl, then, Adelaine? Wicked in the garden, writhing on my hand like you want to come?"

"Yes. Please yes." Addie's legs were shaking. Her whole body was trembling, and whatever she was saying was more noise than words. "I've never . . . and this . . . oh my . . ."

She wasn't holding on to the railing now. Adelaine wrapped her arms around Toni, clutching like she needed to get closer or be held up.

"Such a good, wicked girl," Toni whispered. "Let go, love. Just let go."

By the time Adelaine reached climax, Toni was holding her entire weight up, one arm around her waist, and pressing her back against the fence. Addie had both arms fisting Toni's shirt so fiercely that Toni suspected it would tear.

Afterward, once Addie's breathing started to calm, she whispered, "Should . . . I mean, *may* I . . ."

Toni unfastened her trousers and shoved them far enough down that her far-more-modern underwear were exposed. "No convenient crotchless underwear, I'm afraid."

Adelaine angled her hand so she could reach under the scrap of cloth. Her nails were longer than Toni would prefer, but tonight, a little pain seemed like a fine price to pay for an unusual but incredible encounter.

Maybe I undervalued role-play. . . .

Unlike Toni's perhaps-too-fast approach, Addie explored as if she wasn't quite sure what she was doing.

"Just like you'd touch yourself, Addie," Toni murmured. "Maybe a little gentler so you don't scratch me. Do you want me to touch you again? At the same time? Reward you for how good you're going to make me feel . . ."

The noise Addie made was hungry, and her hands were far from tender.

When Addie said nothing, though, Toni suggested, "Come back to my hotel, Lady Stewart. Let me have you in my bed for tonight."

Unexpectedly, Addie froze. She jerked her hand away from Toni. "I can't . . . this was a *mistake.*"

Then she darted under Toni's arm, spun on her delicate boot heel, and fled, clutching Toni's blazer closed over her damp cotton nightie.

"Damn it." Toni jerked up her trousers and stumbled following after her, but by the time she got outside, Addie—and Toni's best blazer—were long gone.

Chapter 4

Toni

Toni had been just this side of tipsy, and after a few minutes of standing in the rain looking for Adelaine, Toni headed back to the hotel. She wasn't about to go back to the bar or pace the rainy streets.

I hope she's okay.

Toni would never be a person people whispered about like they did her father—or her mother. Neither the trouble nor "that poor woman." Chin up, steps steady, she made her way to her hotel room.

No beautiful Victorian damsels in the lobby.

Toni paused, considering a drink, but lobby bars at a conference felt like desperation, and even the flicker of hope that Addie was a conference attendee felt dangerous. If she had been a student, Toni would have never touched her.

She said she was a stage actor. It was all an act.

Despite herself, Toni still looked around as she walked through the hotel.

No beautiful Victorian damsels in the elevator.

Toni smothered a sigh and went to her room. Inside, she flopped on her bed and grabbed her laptop. She was on the verge of searching online for "Adelaine Stewart" and "Addie Stewart" and even "Victorian plays" near the address of the bar. Addie was a convincing Victorian.

"What am I even doing?" Toni muttered.

A fleeting encounter in a garden with a beautiful erratic stranger was not reason to go chasing after her. If anything, it was another reason to go home. Toni didn't chase after women—or get their last names or numbers or emails—even after far more naked encounters. There was no logical reason to chase after *this* woman.

Toni packed everything but her laptop into her bags and cracked a mini-bottle from the hotel room fridge. The price of hotel liquor was absurd, but in that moment—dangerously in debt, fixated on a stranger she'd never see again, and imagining the magic of a ten- or even fifteen-thousand-dollar book deal—Toni wanted one more drink in her system as she sent the manuscript to Emily.

She opened an email, attached the book, and typed out: "If you hate it, just delete this email. Will not make it to breakfast after all." Then she jabbed SEND.

What if it worked? What if I sold a book?

The thought of it working was irrational, but Toni had enough of her father's dreamer genes to let herself imagine it for a moment. A solid deal. Maybe enough to cover a year of her mom's care. Maybe enough to mean that Toni could just focus on her teaching career for one year.

Maybe if I found Addie, tomorrow we could celeb—

Toni stopped herself. There was no reason to think of Addie. She was a woman at a bar. Toni would never see her again.

But if I looked her up . . .

The temptation was undeniable. Toni typed in Addie's name and found a page with a headshot and stage credits. There was a contact page, social media links, but the urge to send a quick email changed nothing. *I just need to know she got home safely.*

From: History Toni
To: Addie

I tried to find you after the bar. Tell me you're home safely.

Toni

Ignoring a twinge of regret, Toni clicked on a flight change email. She needed to go home, far away from the maddening temptation to see Addie again. A few clicks later, Toni was scheduled to fly home within a few short hours.

She forwarded her itinerary to Emily with a "got to go. Sorry about London." Anything that made her consider commitment was a thing that meant it was time to run. Her desire to see Addie was not something she could allow to take root.

Then Toni fell asleep dreaming about wonderful what-ifs: What if she sold a book? What if she ran into Addie again somewhere? She honestly wasn't sure which was more daunting—or exciting.

After a blurry morning, Toni hopped a short flight from Edinburgh to London. She didn't buy in-flight Wi-Fi and search for more information on Addie Stewart. Instead, Toni had napped briefly in-flight. Currently she was navigating the stygian ring of hell that most people called Heathrow Airport while trying to get to her ringing phone without dropping her coffee.

That was Emily's ringtone, or Toni would've ignored it. "Em?"

"You're going to want to sit down," Emily said without preamble as Toni answered.

Toni shifted her phone to the other hand, steered her hand luggage around a family with an assortment of kids, and said, "Airport. No sitting."

"Do you have a minute?"

"Yes, headed to the gate." Toni tried to keep her voice light, no despair, no panic. No breathlessness—despite the inability of people in airports to navigate with any modicum of common sense. "What's up?" Toni wasn't running, per se, but traversing the connection at Heathrow made her feel like she should be. For a nation that seemed to pride itself on being sensible, the Brits hadn't figured out how to make an airport efficient—or maybe the airport was fine. Maybe it was the casual meander of the thousands of travelers who all seemed to need to step directly into Toni's path.

"I read your book on the train to London—"

"Is it awful?" Toni interrupted as she dodged a senior with a cane that she was swinging more like a golf club than a walking aid. "How far did you get?"

"All of it. Damn you, Toni. As a friend I want to tell you to talk to other agents. I want to be nonaggressive, but as an agent, *grrr*, I want to lock you down and make sure no one else can ever talk to you." Emily laughed almost awkwardly. "I *loved* the book. All of it. Even the ridiculous title."

Toni snorted a laugh. "You're sweet, Em. *The Whitechapel Widow* was a joke title."

"I am not laughing. I am trying to walk a line between being a selfish agent and giving you sound friend advice. There are more seasoned agents that you could talk to—"

"Nope. I'm not interested in anyone else, Emily. I'm not starting a new career. I don't want to deal with any of this. I want to give it to you, and if it's worth anything, you sell it. Get me whatever you can. That's it." Toni saw her gate up ahead and picked up speed. "I trust you. You know me and cope with my trust issues and hermit tendencies. Just . . . sell it if you can."

When Emily was silent, Toni thought she'd disconnected. "Em? Are you still—"

"When do you board?" Emily asked.

"Now."

"Do you want to think about this in-flight? Splurge on in-flight Wi-Fi. I can send you some thoughts on the market, editors, film agents. Options. Other agents to at least consider . . ."

There was an odd tone in her voice, but Toni chalked it up to worry over letting her down, so she said, "I trust *you*, Emily Haide. Whatever you can get for the book is cool. I just need realistic time to revise it, hopefully enough so it doesn't interfere with my job at the university . . . I mean, if anyone even wants it."

Emily made a choked laugh sound. "It'll sell, and if you're sure . . ."

"One sec." Toni showed the gate agent her ticket and passport. Then she joined the masses boarding the cramped flight. "Sorry. Boarding."

"Do you want to wait and talk first?" Emily asked. "If you do, that's a valid plan. At the least I need to know if you'll write a sequel. Selling a two-book is likely, and the London Book Fair is a great time to sell a book with buzz."

Toni shoved her carry-on overhead, climbed over the aisle seat, and slumped into her middle seat. Quieter now that she was surrounded, she said, "Two books works. You do your magic. Honestly, Em, whatever you finagle is great. I just don't want to move Mom to a bad place because I can't afford decent care for her, you know? I was thinking I could sublet or sell my new place, but if you can get something out of the book or out of *two* books, it'll buy me time and maybe let me keep my new place, which really is the best thing I can hope for, right?"

Emily sighed. "I better not hear you telling me you regret this later, Toni. I swear—"

"No regrets." Toni lowered her voice. "Do what you can, and I'll see if there's anything else I can come up with. It's this . . . or juggling jobs and roommates."

"Hang in there. I think this may work out a lot better than you think it will." Emily sounded surer now, confident, and that did a lot to ease Toni's nerves. Then she added, "Safe flight. I'll call you on the other side."

Toni disconnected with a sliver of hope that seemed almost too dear to be real. Someone actually liked the weird middle-of-the-night thing she'd written. Maybe it was just one friend, but that friend was an agent. Emily knew the market and she actually seemed to think there was a publisher out there who might like it enough to want *two* books. If Em's math was right, and there was no reason to think it wasn't, that could be thirty thousand dollars.

It still leaves a lot owed.

But owing one seventy was better than owing two hundred.

After years of listening to Emily talk about publishers with short-sightedness and fickle tastes, Toni wasn't so foolish as to think that meant that there was a deal, but today, a little bit of hope felt like a lot of reason to rejoice.

Most book deals were closer to ten thousand dollars than anything that people thought. A lot of writers were earning less than a professor—and worked just as many hours. Toni's childhood desire to be a writer vanished when the reality of low pay, no health care, and no retirement plans kicked in.

Okay, the dream still existed, but she also had to be practical. She wasn't like her parents, chasing impossible maybes and hopes. The only one who paid her rent was her. The groceries, the utilities, the car repairs? That was all her. So she switched to chasing a career with stability and health care.

Shelve the dream. Focus on the other *dream—teaching.*

The good news was that Toni genuinely loved teaching, and maybe once she had secured tenure, she could write, too. That was the evolved adult version of the dream. Writing was a fine side gig, a way to indulge in the love of words and make some money at it. It wasn't enough to survive on unless she had a well-off spouse or a huge book deal. Lots of writers had the spouse or the day job. The huge deals? Those were pie-in-the-sky dreams.

I'm smarter than that.

Toni had considered self-publishing, which was a perfectly respectable plan, but the pace was brutal, and Toni was afraid that judgmental colleagues would use it to suggest she wasn't serious about teaching. That left either waiting for tenure or self-publishing and hiding her identity.

I'd hate hiding any part of my identity.

The downside of being out since she was a teen was that Toni was of the "no secrets" mindset. If it looked like a closet even because of dubious lighting, squinting, and the like, Toni wanted no part of it. She had no illusions that *The Whitechapel Widow* was literary, but it was a fun detective story—which meant that the name on the cover would definitely be her own. No pseudonym, no hiding, no closets. She didn't live her life or career in closets, so she wanted to approach this the same way.

If anyone publishes it, of course . . .

She almost laughed at her swerve toward arrogance. Every aspiring author knew the odds. The lottery was easier than a writing life, and that was a time-honored truth. Nathaniel Hawthorne's disparaging remark on the "damned mob of scribbling women" still echoed among the literati—cis, straight, white men whose perspective often seemed to be that they had the innate authority to write *any* perspective well. Never mind that the reality of life was different from that seat of privilege. Give a man a pen, and surely, he could tell a more poignant story of a Victorian lesbian's life. *As if.*

Not so different from academia, there, if Toni were honest.

Toni flipped her phone onto airplane mode, turned on her travel playlist, and connected her oversized headphones. Pondering the challenges of academia, publishing, or money wasn't going to do anything but create a spike in arrogance that she had no outlet for in the tiny space of her in-flight seat.

Oh, for a lovely Victorian role-playing woman in historical drawers . . .

With a shake of her head, Toni shoved that thought away and adjusted her headphones to drown out thoughts of Addie and of debt and of limitations. The headphones were too bulky to want to wear walking in the airport, but here in the undersized space of her seat they were perfect.

Block out the world. Block out everything.

No stress. No anxiety.

Another stray thought of Addie filtered into Toni's mind, drawing a reluctant smile with it, and she wished they'd had a slightly longer time together. Addie was a lot flakier than Toni's usual type, and her insistence that she stay in character was strangely charming. Whatever play or role she was exploring meant she'd embraced her

Method acting to the point of convincing a Victorian specialist that she could be the real thing—and *that* was talent.

Idly, Toni thought she could change her main character's name—which had changed at least five other times—to Addie's name as a thank-you of sorts. "Adelaine" was a suitable name for a gorgeous Victorian lady detective on the edge of discovering herself. Maybe someday, she'd even see it and know that she was incredibly memorable.

If it sells . . .

If I get a chance to revise it for a publisher . . .

Doubts started to bubble, and Toni made a silly promise to herself—the sort she used to use to bribe herself when she was younger. If it did sell, she'd change the name to Addie's as a thank-you for the strange encounter in The Lady's Hand.

Chapter 5

Addie

"Ads?" Her roommate stared at her in a far-too-familiar judgmental way, one that said all sorts of sentences that Addie could do without hearing. Eric was Addie's oldest, dearest friend. They were cousins by birth, friends by choice, and roommates by convenience. Currently, that meant a wee flat in Edinburgh, but in a few months, they were headed back to California—not up to San Francisco where her parents now lived, but Los Angeles where she grew up.

"Hi, honey, I'm home," Addie chirped, knowing damn well that no amount of avoidance could head off the inevitable conversation. Her cousin was overprotective on the best of days, overbearing on a few occasions. In fairness, Addie was often more impulsive than a hummingbird on straight sugar, and Eric took their parents' mandate to look after her very seriously.

"Why are you wearing a nightie?" Eric swept a look from toes to nose, no doubt cataloguing the new blazer she was wearing as well as the somewhat scandalous lack of a bra under her very translucent nightie. "And not much else? In public?"

"Method acting." Addie sailed past. "Be out in a moment."

Inside the madness of her bedroom, she temporarily removed the blazer, shucked the nightie, pulled on jeans and a shirt, and then slipped the blazer back on. It smelled like the woman who had been wearing it earlier.

Addie took a deep sniff and sighed. Toni Darbyshire. Dr. Darbyshire. Toni. *Could she be any hotter?* Addie knew that her late awakening meant that she could be a little backward on the dating scene. The time for experimentation had been fumbling with boys, and it had bored her. So she thought she was asexual. She'd dated only men, including a few actors who had seen her as a disposable accessory and one who thought of her as property.

By the time she realized she was a lesbian, she felt awkward at trying to figure out how it all worked with someone she didn't really want to date, so she waited. She tried a few dates, but no one had been that person. So now she was a twentysomething virgin.

What if she had gone back with Toni, what if she'd truly tried to return the pleasure Toni had given her . . . and not known what to do?

Hey, I know you usually teach history, but what about lesbian lessons?

Addie winced at the thought of that conversation. Toni certainly knew how to please a woman. Addie's drawers were still damp. Self-consciously, she shoved both her nightdress and drawers under her blankets. Addie's face burned at the memory. She'd been positively wanton when Toni touched her.

And Toni? She'd been everything Addie could dream of, assertive to the point of dominating but still considerate. She'd made certain that Addie consented to every moment, and Addie had crossed lines that she'd not expected to cross tonight.

Am I still a virgin?

It was a complicated question. Until tonight, the only hand that had traveled there was her own. She'd typically cut things off after a few kisses. She certainly hadn't moved at the speed to which Dr. Darbyshire was accustomed. Admittedly, Addie had thought all she wanted in a relationship was cuddles and sweet words. Tonight was proof that she wasn't asexual, at all.

Demisexual, then?

With the right person, she was fine with a little debauchery in the garden. She brought the hand that had been in Toni's knickers to her lips, wondering just how much further she'd have gone if she'd gone back to Toni's hotel. But then Addie had realized, at a rather awkward moment, that Toni had not offered up her own surname even once. Addie meant nothing to her, and that wasn't what she wanted. Not at all.

Addie washed her hands and then walked into the tiny living room where Eric was waiting.

"Well? Spill."

She flopped onto the sofa. "I know. I know. I didn't get that last role, but I have a real shot at the Mina adaptation, and there was this professor at the history conference . . ."

"So you were researching?" Eric guessed.

"Yes. Mostly." Addie had listened to Toni's talk, and she hadn't actually heard *all* of it because she was caught up in the way Toni moved and the curve of her mouth and . . .

Addie sighed. That was not a safe direction to let her thoughts wander. "She's brilliant, you know. Dr. Darbyshire."

"A professor, huh?" Eric wiggled his brows. "Hot for teacher?" He pointed at the blazer she was currently wearing. "One with passable taste."

Addie rolled her eyes and dodged the implied questions. "She's not *my* teacher. I'd read a few of her articles when I was preparing for auditions. Watched some videos online. Then I saw her talk and took a lot of notes. And tonight, I wanted to see if I was a more convincing Victorian."

Eric gave her The Look, the one that said she was worrying him. He went still enough to pass for a sculpture for a moment, and then asked, "Ads . . . what did you do?"

"I just went to talk to her." Addie silently added, *And let her give me my first ever mind-blowing orgasm with another person.* That was a topic she wasn't ready to ponder. Not now. Not out loud.

"*Mm-hmm.*" Eric made a gesture with his hand like he was beckoning.

"At that lesbian bar that just opened last spring."

"*Without* me?" Eric scowled. "You knew I wanted to go there."

"And we still can. We aren't moving home for a few months yet," Addie reminded him.

She didn't point out that Addie felt like it was different when they went to bars together. People looked at them like they might be a couple, which was the one and only downside to her best friend being a trans man. He was already a man before, but now his outside matched his true self—which was totally awesome for Eric! For her? It created conflicts when people assumed they were together.

"I wanted to meet her as my potential character, assuming I get the role," Addie offered. "I went to the bar as a Victorian."

Eric gave her a quelling look. "Ads, you went in public in a see-through nightdress. Do you not see how that could have gone terribly wrong? If Aunt Marlene knew—"

"But she won't because you don't tell my mom what I do, *right*?" Addie glared at her cousin. He was such a worrier; he was more like Addie's mom than her actual mother was. "And anyhow, Toni was like a knight or a duke or some sort of other dashing hero."

She sniffed the blazer's collar again. She wasn't sure what that cologne was, but she definitely liked it.

"You thought if I was there the professor might think you were straight? Or taken?" Eric guessed.

"Maybe."

"That happened *once*, Ads." Eric sighed, again sounding like he was channeling Marlene Stewart. "I swear, if you'd just call me 'cuz' people would—"

"It doesn't matter. The professor is leaving for her new job in DC, but . . ." Addie hugged a pillow. "I met her. We talked, and she was even more amazing in person, especially . . ." She looked away, cheeks burning at the rest of the thought.

"Did you finally—"

"It's not about sex!" Addie flopped backward, really, really, *really* not wanting to talk about that right now. All she admitted was, "We had a spark. She's amazing."

"Uh-huh." Eric walked to the kitchen and grabbed a half-full bottle of red wine and a pair of glasses. "Did you exchange numbers, email, social media . . . anything?"

"Well, no, but . . ." Eric was staring at her, so Addie simply said, "She's not on social media."

He poured the wine without looking up at her. "And how do we know that already?"

Addie smiled despite herself. "I looked before, when I read her article. She's not online. There are videos of her presenting, her bio at the university, links to a few publications, but there's zero social media."

Addie didn't admit how thoroughly she'd looked, how she tried different iterations of Toni's name, how she searched images—or how she felt defeated by her inability to find anything at all.

"I just felt a spark when I saw her first video, so I wanted to meet her and see . . . ," Addie whispered.

When Eric handed her the wine, Addie continued, "And she felt it, too. She *kissed* me."

She didn't let herself think about what else Toni had done, about how tightly Addie had gripped the fence posts. Her hands still ached from it, and unexpectedly her thighs clenched at the memory.

"So now what?" Eric prompted.

She shrugged. Addie had a Plan—that was always how she thought of it. Uppercase, proper noun. It was a *Plan*. It started with meeting the perfect woman and ended in eternal monogamy with her one true love, because she believed in that despite how she was raised.

Addie own parents weren't married now. They often lived together functionally, but they each had half a duplex. Marlene's town house. Lenny's town house. They lived side by side in the San Francisco area these days. They'd tried marriage—to each other and to others—but they just didn't quite like the "leash of it all."

And Addie loved them. She truly did. She just had always dreamed of something more traditional. Too many Regency romances? Too much tragic Russian literature? Too much classic pop music? Addie wasn't sure why, but she knew what she wanted: true love, the kind that books were written about or songs sung about.

However, her own parents thought she was impaired in some way. They'd even gone as far as taking her to surprise therapy to ask if she had been assaulted. Upon learning she had not been assaulted, Marlene had wailed that she'd raised "a victim of the patriarchy" because Addie was a virgin.

As if "virgin" were a dirty word. . . .

She'd tried to explain asexuality, because that was her first theory. Then she'd tried to explain being demisexual. The idea that a person needed to have feelings to be aroused had made her mother roll her eyes, but the truth of the matter was that Addie only experienced *that* urge when she felt affection and friendship.

Which meant never in my life.

Until tonight.

She'd certainly tried. Addie's goal of getting to know each other—building a foundation, starting with friendship—was at odds with the way most people dated. And she wouldn't say women were *worse*, but sometimes it felt like she only went out with women who were impatient. Second date? Time for a U-Haul and definitely a tumble into bed.

That was all too fast for Addie.

Until Toni.

Toni didn't know her, but Addie felt like she knew Toni. Watching and rewatching videos, reading and rereading Toni's lectures had resulted in a level of interest that Addie had never felt before. She knew it wasn't true, but she felt like she had been getting to know Toni. It had, admittedly, made her feel like maybe she was having an academic version of a celebrity crush—and she half thought her interest would vanish if they met.

Now that Addie had met Toni? That spark of interest had turned into a flame.

Addie had almost gone back to apologize for freaking out. She wanted to explain, but she was unexpectedly unsure if she could do that and resist going much further than she was ready for when Toni didn't know *her*. Addie wanted to be known; she wanted to be loved.

And Toni hadn't even wanted to share her last name.

A chime from her phone made Addie pause, heart aflutter in hope. When she looked at the screen, Addie smothered a squeal.

From: History Toni
To: Addie

I tried to find you after the bar. Tell me you're home safely.

Toni

Addie wasn't sure what to say. Obviously, she was home safely, but she didn't want the conversation to end there. "It's her," she told Eric. "I don't know what to say."

"Ask to meet her for breakfast," Eric suggested.

"That's . . . I don't . . ." Addie wanted to see her, but she also wanted time to think. She wasn't ready to process how she'd reacted to the professor.

Eric sat and waited. "Seriously, Ads? Then what's your plan?"

That, of course, was the dilemma. The conference had ended. There was not a lot of likelihood that Addie would casually bump into Toni. Even though Addie would be moving back to the States soon, they'd be on opposite sides of the country.

Here, they had an ocean between them. There, it was still over two thousand miles of land between them. Half the distance in physical miles was still awfully far apart. And what sort of serious history professor would want a woman who lived off theater gigs that barely paid?

"I'll send a reply, but . . ." Addie was low on a lot of things, but she had ample faith that there was an order to the world. "She lives in Washington, DC, though, so we'll be almost as far apart there as if I stayed here."

Eric nodded.

"But I have a good feeling . . . ," Addie whispered. It was more a hope than anything. Toni had touched her, held her, kissed her. Surely, she'd give some sign that she was as overwhelmed as Addie was.

"Does that mean we're moving to DC?" Eric had been the one to pick Scotland, so by all rights, it was her turn to decide where they moved.

An impulsive streak had her wanting to say yes, but the reality was that if she wanted stage credits, they'd look at Manhattan. If she wanted television or film, she should be in Los Angeles, and that was what she wanted—almost as much as she wanted to find The One. Moving to DC and putting off pursuing her career, all because of one kiss, was ridiculous.

"No. We're going to LA. . . ." Addie hated the burst of logic that seemed to have seeped into her, but she truly did believe that if they were meant to be, they would be.

From: Adelaine
To: History Toni

I am home safely. Are you always so demanding? (I like it.) I've never been so . . . scandalous. I panicked. Want to try again?

Addie

And if all else failed, Addie could see what conferences Toni was presenting at. That's what professors did—they talked about their research at conferences—so Addie was sure she *could* find Toni again if the universe needed a nudge.

Chapter 6
Toni

Two days later, Toni was fumbling on her nightstand for the phone that had been playing soothing rainforest sounds until it started blaring Emily's ringtone.

"Em? Are you okay?"

"Yes."

"Why are you calling at—" She looked at the phone. "—eleven in the morning?" Toni didn't quite pet the surly cat who was now kneading her legs and staring at her, as if daring her to yelp. Her trip away from him, even though he had had a cat sitter, had put her in the very obvious position of penitent owner. Despite her best efforts, she yelped. "Damn it. That hurt, Oscar Wilde."

"Aw, is my sweet monster nearby?" Emily's professional voice gave way to the cajoling tone that Oscar Wilde elicited from otherwise reasonable people. "Tell him his Emmy misses him."

The cat started purring, somehow still shooting glares at Toni.

"Did they all pass?" Toni blurted. "The publishers, I mean . . . did they pass on the book?"

"No." Emily took an audible breath. "We have a four-way situation. Initial offers came in, but I was trying to let you sleep after you growled the first time I called."

"Oh. Right." Toni vaguely recalled trying to answer the phone.

"I'm awake." She reached out to pet Oscar Wilde briefly. Being his human took patience. "Wait. Four-way what?"

"*Auction.* Four editors were competing, but Greta Clayborne wanted it more. She's good, talented, and keeps her hands in the marketing, too."

Toni sat up, unsettling Oscar Wilde. "An auction for *my* book? So several people wanted it?"

"Yes."

Toni stood and made her way to the kitchen, accompanied by Oscar Wilde's loud purrs and louder meowing.

"What was the offer?" Toni's hand tightened on the phone. *Surely, auction meant more than ten thousand, right?*

"It's not the final offer," Emily hedged.

"Lower than ten?" Toni was clearly not fast enough at opening the can of cat food as Oscar Wilde swatted her ankle, making her yelp.

"The first offer was two fifty. Each."

"So five hundred dollars for two b—"

"Sweetie, no. Five hundred *thousand* dollars for two books," Emily corrected gently.

Instead of putting the dish of cat food on the floor, Toni slid down and sat on the floor alongside the cat food. She spilled the food as she leaned on the cupboard. Oscar Wilde gave her a bit of side-eye, but his tail was up, and he was chowing down.

"Say that again." Toni pinched her arm. "The math part."

"The final offer was obviously more." Emily's voice sounded a little strained. A *ding* of an incoming email came over the line. "Greta Clayborne went up to four—"

"Are you serious?" Toni asked, even though this wasn't the sort of thing Emily would joke about, especially right now when Toni was in desperate financial straits. Feeling strangely small, she asked, "You sent them *my* book, though, right? They read the right thing."

"They did. I *told* you it was good."

Toni couldn't speak. There were probably words she ought to

say, things she ought to do, but all she could do was stare at Oscar Wilde.

"Are you okay, sweetie?" Emily sounded worried. "You know this is good, right? You can take care of your mom. You can look after yourself without taking on extra classes. You don't need room-mates or to move out of your new place. You can get Oscar Wilde treats every day."

Toni swallowed back the panic. She felt like the world was a roller coaster lately, her emotions everywhere. "Em? Whoever buys it, let them know the main character's name is Adelaine now. I changed it as a thank-you to my last-minute muse."

Toni leaned back, the cupboard handle pressing into her upper back.

"I'm going to have questions about Adelaine," Emily said lightly.

"You know me. I met someone in a bar, and when I got home, I emailed you the book, and here we are. . . ."

"We? She's there?" Emily sounded more shocked by that than anything else. A three-quarter-million-dollar deal didn't send her into fits, but apparently the thought of Toni having a woman in her home did.

Then again, one of those impossible things had actually happened; the other hadn't.

"No, Em. I'm home with Oscar Wilde." She paused, biting back the snark she had at the tip of her tongue, and said, "I'm serious about the name, though."

Foolish or not, she liked the thought of it. Toni might not do re-lationships, but if she did, Miss Stewart would be the sort of woman she would pursue.

"Okay," Emily said.

"Em? Did you really mean eight hundred thousand . . . ," Toni said, clutching the phone, fearing that she misunderstood and need-ing to hear it once more. "Are you sure?"

"I don't make math mistakes, sweetie. Fifteen percent of that is mine." Emily practically trilled the words. "One hundred twenty.

That's enough to ease the pain of living in New York. All thanks to your fabulous book."

Toni felt like her heart might be beating out of her chest. *Too much too fast.* She got the degree, landed the job, got slammed by debt, and now . . . couldn't wrap her head around the idea of her dream of being an author rescuing her.

"Can they take it back?"

"Not unless you do something remarkably stupid . . . plagiarism or something." Emily scoffed at the thought. "I know you wrote this, though."

"I did." Toni tossed a pillow back onto the sofa. Oscar Wilde knocked them down almost every day. "What if I can't write another book? What if—"

"Can we pause to be happy?" Emily sounded gentle.

Toni closed her eyes, gripping another throw pillow and clutching it to her chest. "Right. Yes . . . this is fine, right? It's all fine." Panic rose up.

I'll screw this up.

"It's *good,* Toni. It's really, really good." Emily spoke in that soft tone that eased the panic of most wild things.

And for a weird flicker of a moment, Toni wished there were someone in her life to tell. The only two people she could tell were her best friend, who was on the phone, and her cat. All told, hers was a pretty lonely life.

Chapter 7

Addie

Addie was staring at her inbox, scrolling through spam and other email that might as well have been spam when Eric popped his head in to her room. "Anything?"

And Addie pretended to misunderstand. "There's an audiobook one that could be something."

"Adelaine." Eric tried to sound paternal, but mostly his version of paternal sounded like the dad who was about to deliver a dad joke.

"No. Toni didn't reply. . . ." Addie closed her laptop. "I'm crushing on her, and she isn't even trying!"

"She might be. Maybe she looked but is afraid to follow you. Maybe she doesn't have an account so how would she follow you? You said she wasn't on social media." Eric came in and pulled her into a hug. "Come on. I'll run lines with you."

Addie grabbed the script. "Better than moping."

By the next day, Addie still had had no contact from Toni. She drafted an email or three, decided that she probably shouldn't send them every time.

She never even told me her full name. Her email didn't include her name either.

The ball was entirely in Toni's court, and Addie hated how powerless it made her feel. She was obsessing over Toni, who had returned to her perfect, orderly life, probably not even thinking about their interlude in the garden.

If it's meant to be . . .

But for all that Addie believed in trusting the universe, she was not sure blind trust was enough this time. She set up search alerts for a series of keywords. If the universe didn't deliver, Addie would find a conference and register.

Task complete, she closed her laptop, gathered the script, and slipped into character. She was going to get the role in *Mina* and be amazing. That she could . . . not necessarily control but definitely influence.

From: History Toni
To: Addie

I flew back to my home in the States. I'm sorry if I made you panic. It was a rough night, and meeting you was a high point. Did your play work out?

Toni

From: Adelaine
To: History Toni

I think I have the role. I'm exhausted, but hopeful.

Addie

From: History Toni
To: Addie

No more going out in nightgowns then?

Toni

From: Adelaine
To: History Toni

Not unless you will be there to keep me safe. ;)

Addie

From: History Toni
To: Addie

We may define safe differently.

Toni

From: Adelaine
To: History Toni

I felt safe with you. No regrets on my side. You?

Addie

From: History Toni
To: Addie

Only that I didn't have a second day there.

Toni

Toni could have meant a million different things, Addie told herself. She did not ask "Where?" or "Why only one more day?" She did not say, "I could visit." There were a lot of thoughts that followed every time Addie reread their email chain, but at the end, she was at a loss for words. What was there to say?

Tell me your last name.

That was the thing Addie wanted to say often, but she was afraid that if she tried to rush her, Toni would vanish entirely. And that was a risk she wasn't willing to take, so she settled on safer topics.

From: Adelaine
To: History Toni

I told you about my work stuff. What's new with you?
Conferences? Teaching anything fun?

Addie

Toni sent her longest reply yet on that topic. Asking her about work seemed to do the trick that nothing else did, so Addie researched a little more and started asking questions for her role. It wasn't exactly a normal way to go about hoping to move toward dating, but *normal* was apparently not how Addie's life worked.

Sooner or later, Addie believed that they would meet again—even if Addie had to fly to DC for a made-up reason or attend another conference.

Chapter 8
Toni

"Lil? Mom?" Toni walked up so she was alongside her mother. Lilian was a petite woman, barely over five feet tall. Thin, delicate like a tiny doll, with soft gray hair that fell to her waist. Toni paid extra to have the caretakers keep Lilian's hair the way she liked it, because the mention of cutting it off had set her mother to wailing.

"Who are you calling 'Mom,' Patty?" Lilian Darbyshire glared at Toni. "Are you calling me old?"

"Not at all." Toni smothered a sigh. Toni's first reaction was often one she had to bite back. They weren't enemies; they just rarely agreed on anything, even the fact that her mother was, in fact, as old as many of the other residents. Her precise age was a matter of argument, as Lilian had always changed her answer. She was in her sixties, though.

"Where are we?" Lil asked, looking around suspiciously. "There are a lot of old people here. Are we visiting someone, Patty?"

"We are." Toni was used to being called "Patty" by now. *Apparently, Aunt Patty was more memorable than Lil's only child.* Occasionally on good days Lil recognized Toni, but those days were rarer and rarer.

They arrived at the front desk, and in quick order, they were buzzed through. Like any good memory care facility, the patients couldn't simply leave. To Toni, that was the biggest asset to a facility.

When they got to Lil's room, Toni opened the door and motioned her mother inside. The room was a bit like a very nice college apartment. She had a sitting room, a bedroom, and a kitchenette. The kitchenette only had a small fridge, table, and chairs. No stove or knives.

"Why are my pictures here?" Lilian walked to a row of photos, all in new plexiglass frames. She looked at her small stereo and the framed album jacket from her one and only chart-topping song.

"You moved in here."

Lilian teared up. "Did Anthony lose the house?"

Toni wanted to admit that yes, he had lost the house, but there was no good in upsetting her mother. "No, Lil. This is like a resort. They prepare all your meals, so you don't have to cook."

Lilian laughed. "I bet Anthony loves that. I don't think I'll ever be a great cook."

"Well, most women won't ever be great singers," Toni rebutted.

"Oh, Patty, I lucked out in the sister-in-law lottery," Lilian said, glancing at Toni and then at the framed record jacket. "So what's new with you? Any pretty young things caught your eye?"

And Toni found it odd that she felt more accepted as Lilian's "sister-in-law" than as herself. Would Lil still ask about dating if she remember that Toni was her daughter? Would she invite her to gossip? Or say she lucked out to be in her family?

"Let's finish getting you unpacked while we talk." Toni had managed to get most of her mother's things squared away, but the clothes were left to handle with Lil's help.

I'm not entirely on my own, Toni amended. The agency—her literary agency—had forwarded part of her advance before the publisher even paid. Emily had made that happen, specifically so Toni could get her mother settled. Close to Toni. The rest, the debt and whatever else, she'd figure out later. The house sale should be closing soon, and the "on signing" check for the deal would come soon.

Everything felt almost okay. Still overwhelming, but okay.

"I know that look, Patty," Lilian said as she perched on her bed and started putting dresses on hangers. She handed each to Toni as she did so. "What's her name?"

"Addie," Toni said. "Her name is Adelaine, but she goes by Addie."

Lil paused and caught Toni's eye. "No husband?"

"You know how I feel about that," Toni said, sharper than she intended.

With a nod, Lil said, "What's so special about this one?"

"She makes me smile. She's vivacious." Toni hung another dress in the closet. The woman loved her clothes.

"She's pretty, too?" Lil prompted. "You always did like the dolled-up ones."

"Maybe I should blame you for that," Toni teased, holding what looked like a silk waterfall of a dress up pointedly.

"I can't catch a man's eye walking around in trousers and men's shirts like you do," Lil countered.

Toni smiled. "Lucky for me, I'm not interested in men."

Lil laughed and then asked, "Did you catch this Adelaine's eye?"

"Of course I did, I'm a Darbyshire." Toni postured like she was elegant, and Lilian giggled. The sound of that laughter eased a pressure in Toni's chest.

It wasn't real, wasn't the mother-daughter relationship Toni used to want, but when Toni was mistaken for Aunt Patty, it was the closest Toni and Lilian ever were.

Chapter 9
Addie

The next month or so was busy enough that Addie didn't have time to lament the lack of further contact from Toni. She landed the role, and life became a flurry of rehearsals and then opening night and nightly shows.

When the show ended, though, everything would change.

"Aunt Marlene sent more apartment listings," Eric called out as Addie came into their apartment.

He was hidden behind a stack of boxes. When he stood, marker in one hand and tape gun in the other, Addie giggled. "You're like one of those prairie dogs or something in a fort of cardboard boxes." She sang, "'Pop goes the weasel.'"

"Haha." Eric gave her the stink eye as he climbed out of his box fort. "Go wash the stage makeup off. I'll grab takeaway."

"Fish and chips, please!" Addie called back as she headed to wash her makeup. She turned back. "Or curry? Or shepherd's pie from that new place or—"

"Missed dinner again?"

"Maybe." Addie hated to admit that she still felt too nervous to eat before a show. So dinner ended up being after ten most nights.

After her shower, Addie pulled on her pajamas and checked her email. There were a host of alerts from her search terms. One after the other started with Toni's name and a book announcement.

Toni Darbyshire's The Whitechapel Widow *was acquired in a four-house bidding war by Greta Clayborne at Tinsley House. The Victorian whodunit about lady detective Adelaine Wight—*

Addie stopped reading. She sat on the edge of her bed and reread the sentence again. And again.

She named a character after me.

She fell backward and let out a "Yeep!" of excitement. Proof. This was proof that the night, their encounter, had meant something significant to Toni, too.

Addie decided to reach out, offer an opening for Toni to confess that she sold a book in a massive deal.

From: Adelaine
To: History Toni

Everything ok over there? You went silent. Hopefully your life is just busy. Not that something went wrong. Either way, let me know you are safe.

Addie

Addie was still sitting there hoping for a reply when she heard the key in the door.

A moment later Eric called out, "Ads? Are you decent?"

"Yes." Her voice was shaking. When Eric came in, she asked, "Will you look at the laptop? Tell me I'm not imagining what I read?"

He took it, skimmed, and turned his attention to her. "I guess you aren't the only one who thought your night was a big deal." He read it again and then handed it back. "What's the plan?"

"I don't know." Addie looked over at her cousin. "I feel like it changes everything . . . or maybe she just liked my name, you know? She still hasn't told me her last name or anything really."

Eric gave her a disbelieving look. "Ads."

"Or maybe she really did *like* me," Addie whispered.

But Addie wasn't sure what there was to do about her discovery. Mostly she wanted to ask Toni about it, but she was back to the fact that she was supposed to not know her last name. And if she admitted that she did, then she'd have to admit that she came to The Lady's Hand looking for Toni in the first place.

Chapter 10

Toni

Early July was lovely in Virginia, despite the humidity. And since fall classes would be starting in a few weeks, Toni thought she'd use the quiet of the Independence Day holiday to move into her office a little early.

And escape thinking about being published.

The deal had been announced, and Toni was in revisions—which was surreal. Having a stranger weigh in on pretty much everything about the book had, in all truth, made it a stronger book. It was still *hers,* but now it had layers of nuance that made the plot stronger. But that didn't mean that revision hadn't been overwhelming. Toni had requested a rush turnaround, and her editor had accommodated that request. So they were onto a second round, tightening and tweaking, now.

In between, she was trying to resist emailing Addie. Today, she failed again.

From: History Toni
To: Addie

I'm completely safe. Work is just exhausting lately. My boss wants me to attend some faux historical event for a work talk and . . . I am not interested. Can you imagine me in a dress? How's the play? Distract me, Addie. I'm up to my eyeballs in work, and I would rather be in a garden with a beautiful woman than staring at papers and wondering why I thought I could do this job.

Toni

Toni wished she could confess what she was really working on, but Addie didn't need to know that the "papers" weren't academic articles or student essays. It was the damnable book. She'd pushed back hard on the request to hold a launch party at Cape Dove. The pictures of the venue made it look incredibly authentic, but Toni was adamant that dresses weren't an option. Ever. The last time she'd worn one was in her teen years. She didn't want to do any of the promo events. She had no interest in talking about her process or ideas. She wanted to teach, and she enjoyed novel-writing—but she was quickly learning that the book-promo events were like committees at the university: a painful necessity.

Today, though, Toni had a book dolly and several boxes of books for her office. Atop it all was a lighter box of office supplies. She had a home office, of course, but she wanted a few odds and ends—sticky notes, notebooks, pens, and the like—and research books at her campus office. She'd been playing with a loose plan to keep the home office for writing and the campus for academics. Compartmentalization was her superpower.

After swiping her crisp new faculty ID card, Toni stood just inside the door of her new building. The history and sociology departments both had offices at Tulip Hall. Luckily, history had the ground-floor offices. Her office was standard fare: nondescript bookshelves, sturdy desk, rolling chair, beige file cabinet. A whiteboard rested on the desk, either a gift or someone had needed the hanger it once was attached to. The wall there was slightly darker, as if the light had bleached the surrounding paint. She started stacking the boxes on her desk when she heard a gentle knock on her already-open door.

"Dr. Darbyshire!" A man stepped into view. "You're early."

"Dr. Ellis." Toni smiled. "Overeager . . . or worrying that I'd get lost or . . ." She hated the way she had suddenly slipped into graduate-student mode, slightly insecure of her own place. She pulled her shoulders back and amended, "I like to be efficient. Coming in over the holiday seemed efficient."

"That it is!" He held out a hand to shake. "We're glad to have you, and you'll get no complaints from me about wanting efficiency." He chuckled to himself and then added, "I thought I already told you to call me Harold."

"Only if you call me Toni."

"Are you in a rush to unpack those, or want to join an old man for a cup of tea?" Harold asked. "I know my office manager . . . department memory . . . whatever the term is has some things with your name on them."

"Tea breaks are an excellent idea." She stepped into the hall, pulling the door closed behind her and locking it. "I met Gabe already when I picked up my office key and ID badge. He seems to know everything about everything here."

"The building is pretty secure as a rule," Harold said lightly.

"Habit." Toni wasn't quite so trusting as to leave her door unlocked as a matter of habit. She liked that the department head's assistant-secretary–office manager was a man. It spoke to a level of progressiveness she appreciated, but she was still aware that personal safety was always different for a woman—no matter how much she worked out.

"Gabe said you were in Scotland not too long ago. I'll look forward to reading your paper." Harold was obviously an attentive department head if he knew that already. He turned a corner. "Did you find a place locally already?"

"I did. Not close enough to bike, but close enough to run home if I forget lunch."

Harold swiped his card and opened a door to reveal a comfortable lounge. The sofas were overstuffed green seats. Coffee tables and end tables were scattered around. On one side was a row of printers, a long conference table with eight chairs, and a cabinet labeled OFFICE SUPPLIES. On the far wall was a matching cabinet labeled COMMUNAL SNACKS AND COFFEE. On the far back wall there was a sink, refrigerator, and a counter with multiple coffee machines and an electric kettle.

"We have an embarrassment of snacks, coffees, and teas." Harold opened a cabinet. He gestured to a full shelf of teas ranging from basic tea bags to loose tea. "Pick your poison."

Then he went to a counter and flipped on the electric kettle. While it was heating he pulled out two mugs. "Honey? Milk? Cream? Sugar?"

"No, thank you." Toni brought a tin of Assam over and took the tiny silicone manatee-shaped tea infuser Harold held out.

"Gabe thought they were too pun-tastic to resist." Harold smiled and, in case she missed the humor, said, "It's a *manatee* for your *tea*. The others aren't quite as clever, but I appreciate this one."

It hit Toni with a pang that this world made more sense than anything and anywhere else, and she blurted out, "I sold a book."

Harold paused, dropped a tiny Tyrannosaurus Rex into his cup, and poured water into both mugs. "Subject?"

"Fiction, actually." Toni shook her head. She hadn't planned to tell him yet. "I don't want the rest of the department to know."

"Is it scandalous in some way?" Harold took his cup and walked to the sofa.

"Maybe?" Toni followed, at a loss as to how she could explain without sounding far more neurotic than she would like to sound in front of her department chair. She set her cup on a coaster. "I sold it between Scotland and here. I signed the contract, revised it, and . . . it's a real novel *with my name on the cover.*"

He nodded.

"It's historical fiction, a Victorian murder mystery about a lesbian detective," she added.

"You are a Victorianist, and the novel was quite the thing back then," he said supportively. "And your work is on lesbians in the

Victorian era. I feel that I am missing some key detail here, Toni, to explain whatever is prompting the distress in your voice."

She sighed. She had been wrestling with this since she'd said yes to the offer. After more talking to her cat than any rational soul ought to admit, she had figured it out. "If it fails, I'd rather not have an audience. If it succeeds, I'd rather not have derision for writing popular fiction. I want to be regarded as a serious academic, especially as I am junior faculty still."

Harold plucked the T-Rex out of his mug, set it on a tray, and pronounced, "I am not in the habit of sharing anyone's personal business, Toni, but I hope you change your mind. I didn't hire the sort of professor who would write a book that failed. You had your choice of colleges offering you a job. I am well aware of your talent—"

"At lecturing and research," she interjected.

Harold shrugged. "I read your dissertation, and I have read a number of your articles. I think you'll find that I am often quite right about a very large number of things, so why don't we agree that if your book does *well,* I will receive a signed copy of it to display proudly . . . and possibly crow about to the lit department, hmm?"

Toni blinked at him. *Where was the stuffy academic dismissal? The disdain?* She'd braced herself for that, and instead he was looking at her like he'd just double dared her to do something. "Oh."

He chuckled again, sipped his tea, and said, "Tell me more about this book of yours."

Chapter 11
Toni

ONE YEAR LATER

By the time Toni landed at LAX after the last of several tour dates, the battery on her phone was long since dead, and her charging cable was apparently in checked luggage or forgotten in a hotel. She grumbled that she couldn't email Addie earlier as she'd planned.

A year later, they still emailed a few times a week, and Addie had become a sort of haven in Toni's life, a slice of normality, a person who thought of her solely as a professor and a woman. That was why Toni still hadn't told her about the book. They'd shared a lot—things they read or watched, or thoughts on new albums. They talked about dream trips and favorite meals. Addie's was "somewhere beachy" and "dessert before dinner." Toni's were a bit less exciting—hiking spots and a good steak with even better whisky.

Those conversations had become a lifeline. Toni wasn't unhappy with her dual careers, but she was often overwhelmed and felt like a fraud at the best of times.

And tired. Lord, she was tired. *The Whitechapel Widow* had not only sold, but it had sold *really* well. Her colleagues at the university were mostly in the dark. Harold had respected her privacy, and Toni wasn't sure what exactly to say to anyone about her second career.

I think it's a fluke.

I'm not able to meet my deadline for the second book.

Right now, the whole author side of her life was surreal. Toni worked, went to the grocery, and lived a normal life. Then she went to events, where it was as if she were a different person. She traveled from airport to posh hotel to event in sleek black cars; she attended events where fans gushed and asked her to sign her name. It felt like living two lives.

And being an imposter in both.

And then there was Addie. She was the closest Toni had come to a relationship, but Toni still kept a giant part of her life hidden. *So much for not being in any closets,* Toni derided herself. She hid her author life from Addie and from her colleagues, aside from stray conversations with Harold. She didn't talk about her academic life with the publishing. Everything was neatly compartmentalized.

A year after finishing her PhD, Toni now had a normal professorial week, and then a lot of weekend events where she was "moonlighting" as an author. That's what it felt like, a rather Prufrockian state where Toni would lament that she had measured her life in coffee spoons, or she would if anyone knew what the hell she was talking about. Commercial publishing wasn't high on the classic literary references. Sometimes, she almost wished there were someone in her life to talk to over a cup of coffee or glass of whisky. Someone other than her department head, her agent, and her mother, who only retained about a third of what Toni shared on the best days. Someone who was a lot like Addie in those vague fantasies.

I could tell her. *We're definitely friends now.*

And Addie tells me everything.

The reality of juggling two careers was that Toni was bone tired. But the tour had ended, and hopefully after today's meeting, life would be calmer. The producer for the adaptation of the book was excited, and Emily insisted that Toni just had to show up and be cheerful.

Maybe LA would offer a chance for a harmless hookup. Tour certainly hadn't. Reasonable people didn't fuck their fans, and weird as it was to think about most of the time, Toni had fans now. She categorized them the same as students: untouchable.

It's a damn drought. Toni's thoughts drifted again to the last woman she'd touched. *Addie*. A stranger in a bar. A beautiful woman who knew Toni before she was an author. Not a student. Not someone who learned of Toni's existence on the front of a book jacket.

A few times, alone at night, Toni considered inviting Addie to meet up somewhere, but honestly, what would she say? "So I failed to mention that I sold a book for a ridiculous amount of money. I have the cash to send you a ticket to come see me. Interested?" Considering the fact that Toni had hidden the book deal for a *year,* she sincerely doubted Addie would even keep talking to her if she knew.

Plus, emailing a proposition?

The thought of sending an email meant trusting that sweet Adelaine wasn't going to post it online when she found out Toni had more or less lied. Toni's career—either career, actually—wasn't secure enough to withstand that. No, for now, Toni's only recourse was to handle her own self-care and hope there was someone she'd meet who was not at a book event, a studio meeting, or affiliated with her own college.

No sex with students or fans. The mere thought of that was a turnoff. *Talk about unhealthy power dynamics!*

Toni grabbed her carry-on and made her way to the baggage carousel, where Emily was waiting. Her best friend now had a long list of clients vying for attention, but she was still regularly present when Toni needed her.

"I don't understand," Toni said for what seemed like the millionth time this year.

"Which thing?" Emily good-naturedly steered her toward the exit. "Our driver is at the curb."

Toni traipsed along with her. "Why do I need to meet them? I signed the contract. They paid the money."

"Because *regular* people want to have a voice in an adaptation of their books." Emily sighed the sigh of patience nearing the edge.

"I'm regular people." Toni opened the door for Emily.

"No, sweetie, you're an academic." Emily directed her toward the black car.

The waiting driver opened the door and then rolled her bag to the trunk without a word. Lately, cities blurred together into one long line of airports and black cars, coffee cups and room service. Unlike today, everything was usually handled by Eloise—the publicist assigned to Toni's book. Honestly, it was all smoothly managed a good ninety percent of the time. The trade-off was that it meant grading and writing lecture notes on flights and in hotels—and that she was about to be late on delivering the second novel.

Emily slid into the plush seat beside her. "We can do this, a few stock signings, and then you can take a couple weeks at home to just write."

"And teach," Toni added. "I am a teacher first, Em. That's my *degree* and my focus for thirteen years now. I do all this, and it's incredible that people liked the book, but what if the next book flops. I can't screw up the thing I got my PhD to do. . . ."

Especially because I'm stalled on the sequel.

Toni knew she ought to tell Emily that she was going to be late on the book. She knew it as surely as she knew that she'd do better being the quiet awkward author than she would do being herself at the upcoming meeting.

"They've begun casting," Emily said as the car slid into traffic. "We'll see some tapes—"

"And they'll pretend my opinion matters," Toni muttered. That was a part of this world that she hadn't expected: everyone from editors to the film producer asked questions as if they wanted answers, but Toni quickly realized that what they actually wanted was agreement.

We love this cover direction. What do you think?

This festival is an excellent opportunity. Isn't it great that they want you to speak?

I see this with a strong love story. Wouldn't that have been a great addition to the book?

Of course, it wasn't what Toni thought, loved, should have done differently in the book. Saying that out loud, of course, made frowns or awkwardly long silences fill rooms, so now Emily attended to crit-ical things or replied instead of Toni. She'd stepped up in a "manage the author" way.

"The main character won't be straight," Toni reiterated yet again. There were things Toni could adjust, politely ignore, or whatever, but this detail was writ in stone for her. She met Emily's gaze. "If they want to change that, I'll be as loud as—"

"She won't. That detail was in the contract. They can't change that." Emily looked like she needed a drink.

Toni realized that her best friend was nervous. That was unex-pected, and Toni vowed to be nicer this time. "You know I do try to be flexible, right? I've forced myself to be okay with the historical inaccuracies, the events, the damn woman who insisted I needed makeup for that morning show."

Emily winced. "There is a clear statement that goes out now for any media events. No makeup beyond a basic foundation necessary only because of set lights."

Emily and Toni both shuddered a little at the shared memory of someone trying to apply eye makeup to Toni. Gender normative obliviousness was something Toni hadn't been braced for. Academia functioned differently. At academic conferences, no one gave a damn that Toni's only makeup was the occasional lip balm.

"The protagonist's identity was a good clause, Toni. Unless you agree to a change, the character will be true to your vision of her." Emily smiled more naturally now. "If we hadn't had so much inter-est in the rights, that would've been impossible, though. You realize that, I hope."

"I do. I know I have an incredible agent who connected my book to a great film agency who wrote an incredible contract," Toni said, meaning every word of it. "You are an angel to make things work so well for me."

"So play nice today. They want you to meet them so they can crow that they won the book and wow you a little. They are under the illusion that you will feel better if you have a voice in other aspects of the production." Emily stared out at the impassable traffic and looked at her watch again, but she said nothing. There was something about LA that made travel move at a snail's pace. New York was bigger, but LA still held the crown for worst traffic.

"So you're saying it's my own fault I have to meet them?" Toni chuckled. One of the absolute best parts of this surprise career—aside from the money—was time with Emily.

Emily shrugged, but she was grinning now. They'd had lunches in Chicago and New York, and dinners in Philly and Atlanta, and they'd gone to bookstores in all of the above. And the publisher and agency paid for it. That was the part Toni couldn't get her head around. Per diems for food—and whisky—and cars and hotels and . . . it felt wasteful, but this was just a thing that publishers did when they wanted to trot an author around like a prize poodle.

Some people enjoyed it, but for an introvert like Toni it was starting to wear on her. After years of degrees, years working on a dissertation that maybe a dozen people would read in its entirety, all of the attention was nerve-wracking.

"Tell me about things?" Toni prompted.

Emily gave her an unreadable look. "I have an assistant now."

"Fancy."

"Awkward. He accesses my email. My appointments. My clients." Emily made a face. "I didn't realize that . . . but that means that *everything* in my inbox is accessible."

Toni thought back to their very open conversations. "Ouch."

"Yeah." Emily scowled. "And his cologne is disgusting."

Toni smothered a laugh.

"But I don't want to fire him because he smells like a Vegas nightclub," Emily complained. "This is a tough industry, and I don't want to ruin anyone's chances because of a personality clash."

"So talk to the head of the agency and tell them you want to pick your own assistant," Toni suggested. "Seems weird that they would just assign you one."

"My slush pile is immense. Literal hundreds of queries. My

calendar is awful, too. And my email . . . I can't keep up," Emily grumbled.

Toni suggested, "So have Vegas just do slush."

She'd heard about the mixed barrel that was slush. There was gold in there, but finding it took a lot of sifting. Off-loading that would be an asset. Letting someone into your email and schedule? That was different. It required a level of trust. In some ways it was like having a TA helping. The grading assist was great, or maybe it wasn't if they graded harsher or softer than you wanted to grade. At the end of it all, though, it was the professor's—or agent's—name on the line. Full access was too much.

By the time they arrived at the studio lot, they were both more relaxed, and Toni reminded herself that while writing might not be her forever career, working within this industry *was* Emily's forever career. The connections they made, the successes Toni's book had, were things that Emily would carry with her—and some things were possible sooner because Emily had read and loved *The Whitechapel Widow*.

"I'm calling Book Two *The Widow's Curse*," Toni blurted out as the driver parked.

"I like that." Emily met her gaze. "How late do you expect to be delivering it?"

Toni gaped at her as the driver opened Emily's door. "How . . . I didn't say anything!"

Emily laughed out loud. "Sweetie, I've known you since I was wearing braces and acne cream. You dodge the topic every time I mention the sequel, so I already asked Greta for an extra three months."

Then Emily was gliding out of the car, and Toni was left speech-lessly following her. By the time they were met by the producer's assistant—who led them to a room with sparkling water, coffee, tea, and a fruit plate—Toni elbowed Emily. "You know, I couldn't do this without you."

"Oh, I know. I *definitely* know." Emily grabbed a bottle of spar-kling water, watching the producer's assistant hurry off to collect the woman who had taken Toni's words and decided they ought to be a television program.

"Be nice," Emily stressed. She dropped her voice to a whisper and added, "There's a not insignificant chance you'll meet more than the producer. If you can't say something flattering at any point, look at me, and I'll answer. Okay?"

Toni nodded.

"They're going to bring up Cape Dove again. They're quite fond of a period setting for some PR shots. . . ."

"Em." Toni glared. "We've discussed this. I'm not wearing a dress for anyone. They can take their option check back and—"

"Trust me," Em said sternly.

Then the producer was in the room, arms out like she was presenting something. "I'm thrilled to meet with you, Toni. I'm very excited about our show."

And Toni put on her best smile and stood to greet Marcela Gibson, the woman who had turned her book into a show that was going to stream over nine episodes so far.

Chapter 12

Addie

Addie's keys were still in the door when it jerked open, pulling her entire keychain out of her hand.

"Where were you?" Eric was hopping, literally *hopping*. In anyone else it would seem like an affectation, but Eric was the bounciest person she knew.

"Audition." Addie stepped forward into their new apartment in Burbank. They'd been there four months, not quite long enough to stop missing Scotland but long enough to appreciate the distinctly different weather. Addie had even cut off her hip-long hair. Now, it fell to midback, long enough to resist the frizzy curls that humidity would bring but short enough not to get caught in bus seats or strangers' grubby hands.

Eric grabbed her arm and tugged her forward. "June called, like, six times while you were out. Change. Now. Call June."

"June called you?" Addie dropped her things on the half counter that the rental agency had generously called a "kitchen bar."

"Someone had her phone on Do Not Disturb.'" Eric bounced on his toes, rocking forward like he was about to start doing pirouettes, which he had been doing more and more since he'd snagged a role as a backup dancer in a children's show. He was finding his place in the film and television world with an ease she envied.

Shoving that thought away, she looked at her phone. Twelve missed calls. Eight voicemails. Several texts. She skimmed the latter.

"Ho-ly butter-flies." She looked up to meet Eric's wide grin. "They want to talk to me."

"I think the role's yours. Meant to be and *about* to be. She *did* name the character after you . . . ," Eric teased.

"She did. She really, really did." Addie couldn't repress the smile on her face.

She'd read and reread *The Whitechapel Widow* several times. The character, Adelaine Wight, was not really like her—but hundreds of thousands of people read about the Victorian Addie Wight's character. *One she named after me!*

"Shit. I need to be there in an hour!" Addie stripped as she walked, mentally going over her list of things to do.

Look hotter than hot.

Also demure.

Reference the book at least three times, so they know I'm ready.

Try not to ask if they expect there to be any author events like Comic-Con or anything where I will see Toni. Oh. My. Goodness. I'm going to see her for real again! I will! Do I act surprised? Pretend that I didn't realize it was her book?

Addie had no good answers, but she had time to think of them before she saw Toni. First she had to get the role. *Maybe this is the opening I need. . . .*

She fired off a quick email. If Toni didn't admit her surname or book ownership after this, Addie was going to be angry.

From: Adelaine
To: History Toni

Callback for a DREAM role! So excited about this. It's a streaming show starring a sexy Victorian detective with my same name!

Addie

By the time Addie had herself ready enough to feel professional, she had already texted June, her agent, and called a car—not a fancy car like she one day would ride in when she was drawing a good paycheck, but a rideshare.

"Break someone's leg," Eric called from his seat on the sofa as she left their tiny apartment. "And let me know how it goes!"

The nervous chatter that was her stress reliever was on hold as the driver talked about the construction near the airport, teenagers using the rideshare app with sweaty gym clothes, and the price of eggs. When he pulled into the lot, Addie was completely relaxed thanks to the man's ongoing monologue.

"We're here."

"Thanks." She fumbled with her seat belt, feeling suddenly more anxious than she ought to. She wanted this role, wanted it like it was written for her, which it sort of was—although no one but the author herself and Addie knew that. She debated saying something, using insider intel to get the job, but that wasn't her.

Trust the universe.

The driver caught Addie's eye in the rearview mirror. He had that overall sort of mien that said he was impressed, but it was tangled up with "I am trying not to admit I'm impressed." Typical LA. She felt giddy that she might actually deserve that look finally.

The fact that she just took a rideshare to the studio lot and probably looked like every other wannabe actress in the city undercut her sparkle. Once upon a time, that would've stung. After living in Scotland, Addie felt more confident.

Having a character in a bestselling novel named after me didn't hurt my confidence either.

She was greeted by someone from the production team, and then she was whisked through a check-in process to issue her a temporary badge. It was different from any other audition experience in ways that set bumblebees to flight in Adelaine's belly.

By the time she was led to a room—a Victorian styled room—Addie was at a loss. This wasn't just an empty stage to read lines. This was a *set*. The set. Toni's book would come to life here, and there was a real chance that Addie would be on the set.

"The actor we are leaning toward for Colin is already here." A woman in trousers, a cardigan, and sensible shoes led Addie forward to a study where "Colin" waited.

Addie flinched when he turned around. "Hello, Philip."

He nodded at her, but there was a slight tightening around his eyes. "How have you been?"

"Great. I spent the last year in Scotland." Addie had dated exactly two men whom she'd wished she'd never met. He was one of them. They had barely dated, and even if she hadn't figured out who she authentically was, Philip wouldn't have been someone she could see in her future.

"Easier to get roles there, I bet. Less competition." Philip was a bit of an ass even if he liked someone, and he didn't like her. Not now. Not after their breakup. "Especially now that you can be so *woke*. Do they call your sudden lesbian turn woke over there? Or are you *Method acting* for roles?"

"It wasn't sudden," Addie pointed out, hoping she was misunderstanding his jab. "Don't be like this. Please? I'm just being honest about who I am."

"Honest?" Philip sneered. "Cold fish. That's the right label if you want to be honest, Adelaine."

Maybe they're typecasting his role. She stared at him in vague horror that she'd be likely to have to work with him regularly if they were both cast in the show. *How do I get along with him?*

But then the woman swept Addie away from Philip and into another room, where she was given a Victorian dress and told, "We want this to be the 'full effect.'"

Addie nodded. Once the assistant or writer or whatever she was left, Addie stripped. There was no corset, and the small bustle that ought to be under the dress was missing. The dress was obviously from another production, and as Addie tried to situate it, it became abundantly clear that it had been designed for a woman with fuller hips and a smaller bosom.

There obviously were no historically accurate drawers either.

That thought had Addie's cheeks pink, and she felt more confident than she had after meeting "Colin." The woman who went to a shadowed garden with the author was bolder than the mouse that Addie felt like when faced with arrogant men.

"Miss Stewart?" The woman returned, frowning when she realized that the dress didn't work as it was.

"It's okay from the hips down, a little long, but I practiced in awkward skirts when I was in *Mina* overseas." Addie pasted on her I-can-make-it-work smile. "The top is a bit of an issue."

"What if we added a wrap or cloak or . . ." The woman shifted through a hanging rack that had assorted historical pieces on it. "Try this."

She held out a fur jacket that was entirely the wrong style and not right for the character.

"The character is more like . . ." Addie scanned the rack and found a capelet that felt a little more Little Red Riding Hood than Victorian, but it wasn't a notice-me-now fur coat. She pulled it on—and mentally slipped into the character as she walked to the stage.

She remembered the pages well enough that she didn't need to look at the script as they began their scene. This scene, unlike some of the others, was direct from the page. The personas, the words, it was just turned into a script, but Addie remembered it as words in chunks, not in script.

If there was a man more irritating than her cousin, Adelaine had never met him. Colin was a reprobate of the first order. If he couldn't drink or debauch a woman, he was in a foul mood. Having a ward, an unmarried one at that, was impeding his pursuit of pleasure.

"I have decided to double the amount set aside for your dowry, Miss Wight." He was breakfasting, although it was past midday already, and had summoned her as if she were a servant.

"Out of my inheritance, I presume."

"Indeed."

"Wouldn't want to take anything away from your actress-expenses account," she murmured quietly in an aside, as if he might not hear.

He did, of course. Debauchery had done little to damage his health. So far.

Colin lifted his gaze to her, peering across the table. "If you weren't such a prim thing, you would have been properly re-wed by now."

"I was mourning."

"For two years?" He made a noise that was more fit for a horse than a man.

Or a horse's back end, she thought.

"You might recall that my spouse has passed, and my grandmother passed." Addie kept her voice even. She'd been raised by her widowed grandmother. It had led to a somewhat peculiar upbringing—and a tidy inheritance that was stipulated as hers even after marriage. Lord Wight had only added to that inheritance.

"Join me in the library." Colin walked away.

Silently, Addie trailed after Colin. His steps still sounded clearly, despite the muffling of the rug underfoot. The actor, Philip, stomped. He walked deeper into the house, crossing a threshold she rarely had traversed.

The study. Later, when no one was watching, she wanted to look around here. For now, she paused, as if anxious. Maybe the right attitude was anxiety at being in a closed room with a man, but by the end of the pilot they'd be allies. Instead, her delay was intended to be because of grief over Lord Wight's death.

Cousin Colin watched her carefully as he closed the door.

"You will not continue on this way, Miss Wight." Colin poured a drink, one of the several amber-colored liquids on the bar tray. "I have no interest in being trapped at a country estate this often."

"You don't need to be," Addie said, as she always did. "I have a staff, and I can handle my accounts and—"

"*And you are not going to be unsupervised, ruining my reputa-tion.*" Colin scowled at her. "*I gave Lord Wight my word to see to your well-being.*"

"*I feel quite settled, Colin, and your reputation suffers more from your inability to keep your trousers fastened.*" Addie poured herself a drink, though she was still not convinced that she liked the taste of the stuff.

Her frown was easy, as the brown liquid was flat cola . . . ugh. Not even diet cola.

Colin pinched the space between his eyes. "*I am not the villain you think, Addie. As you seem determined to be gauche, I will add that you have an estate, accounts, and you are reasonably attractive. Ensnaring another man ought to be simple.*"

Addie made an indelicate sound and took a sip of the liquid that every man seemed to find delectable. "*I have no need of any man.*"

"*When I accepted this request, it was with the understanding that I would see to making sure that no reprobates would trap you.*"

"*Men like you.*" Addie started pacing the study.

"*There will be a ball in town next week. I have spoken to associ-ates, and you will be dressed in the latest Parisian fashion—*"

"*Parisian, cousin?*" Addie teased. It was praise, indeed, to suggest she was lovely enough to wear the more scandalous dress options.

"*The seamstress will be here momentarily.*" Colin watched Addie as if she might flee.

"*Here? Now?*"

"*Indeed. Within the next month, you will be entertaining offers of matrimony. Your estates and accounts may not be accessible to your future husband, but I am permitted to offer an enticing dowry. I have added a figure from my own accounts as well.*" Colin stared at her. "*Perhaps the joys of the marriage bed will ease your . . . un-pleasant temperament.*"

Addie stared at him, mouth gaping in the least ladylike expres-sion she thought she might have ever had. "*What sort of woman do you think I am to address me in that manner?*"

"I suspect you are a woman who will appreciate blunt speech. Perhaps that was the mistake I made previously, treating you like a proper lady." Colin *finished his drink.* *"You have one month to select your future husband . . . or I will."*

"Colin."

He paused.

"You realize that my late husband and I . . ."

"That the marital partner who preferred men lies moldering in his grave? I do." Colin *shook his head.* *"I may enjoy my drink, and women, but I'm not addled."*

Addie's *eyes teared up.* *"So I'm just to lie with a man as if . . ."* She stopped herself, hands on hips. *"Would you lie with a man even though it is abhorrent to you?"*

Colin walked away.

And Addie was left alone onstage with tears gleaming in her eyes.

The stage required her to emote nuances and details—like the fact that the late Lord Wight was gay and so her first marriage was a sham that enabled them both to pass as straight in a world that was not welcoming to their true selves. Lady Adelaine Wight was through pretending, and by the end of the pilot her cousin would agree to help her—for a fee, of course.

Emoting her distaste for Cousin Colin was easier than anticipated. Philip was a jerk. She'd figured that out after three dates in real life. In the books, Colin was reformed. In the pilot, they became uneasy allies, but her distaste for Philip had her questioning her ability to pull off that particular storyline. It would be a true test of her talent to pretend to like the man who, in real life, simply could not accept her decision to stop dating him. He was an entitled ass, which would make her character's emotions in the initial episodes a little easier on her.

Addie glanced to the side, where Philip stood glaring at her, before looking over at the producer.

"Thank you, Adelaine and Philip." Marcela Gibson came forward to the stage. At her side were two women, but for a moment, all Addie could see was Toni. Here. Now.

Philip came forward again. "Miss Darbyshire. It is a pleasure." He extended a hand toward Toni, who shook it briefly.

"Well done," Toni said. Her gaze only lingered on him for a few seconds. Toni looked at Addie then. "Both of you."

"They're good characters. Acting when they're well-rounded is easier," Addie said, staring at Toni, fearing that she could probably hear Addie's heart beating.

Marcela Gibson, the producer, pulled Philip aside, steering him away from Toni. He resisted, clearly interested in trying to talk to Toni. "I have motivation thoughts about—"

"Write them out, Philip. I can give them to her if you are signed for the role." Marcela's voice carried, and Addie repressed a flicker of hope that he wouldn't be cast in the role. Honestly, though, perhaps she wouldn't be. *Would Toni find it awkward that I'm here?*

Addie turned to leave the stage, too, unsure of the protocol here. Philip had been steered away, so maybe she was to depart, too. No one there knew that she and Toni were friends. *Pen friends? Online friends?* Addie smiled as she thought about the inability to label them.

"Adelaine? Wait, please." Toni's voice was rougher than Addie remembered.

Philip looked back at them and glared, but then he was gone. Hopefully that would be the end of him.

"You didn't say you cut your hair," Toni said, voice lowered now.

"You didn't say quite a few things either," Addie managed to say. Then she added, "So . . . I cut my hair. Not all the way short. Just a bit less like I fell out of a John William Waterhouse painting. Anything *you* forgot to tell *me*?"

Toni chuckled. "You look good. . . . I, umm, wrote a book. I wrote it before we met, but I sold it after that. I didn't know what to say about it."

"Luckily, I do. Your book is *amazing*. I've read it a lot of times." Addie lifted her chin. She was blushing. Her entire face felt flame-hot, but Toni watched her with something that looked like respect.

Toni stared as Addie pulled a long strand forward.

"Your acting was wonderful," said the other woman with Toni, the one who had been at her conference panel in Edinburgh. She held out her hand. "Emily. I'm Toni's agent."

"Addie. Adelaine, actually . . . in real life, not the character, but I am hopeful." Addie smiled even wider. Emily was Toni's *agent,* not her girlfriend. Addie had considered asking about her in the email exchanges, but there was no graceful way to mention the sexy brunette at the conference without admitting to being there in the first place. Toni had said she was single and that was enough. Addie had thought, though, that the pretty brunette was someone Toni had been with intimately. The relief that she wasn't washed over Addie.

"How *lovely* to meet you, Adelaine. I'm Emily Haide," Emily said, glancing at Toni with a look that made Addie absolutely certain that Emily knew something about Addie and Toni.

"Em." Toni's tone was stern enough to make Addie have an unexpected flutter in regions lower than her belly. That commanding voice brought forth memories that were suddenly crystal clear—and exceptionally awkward in the moment.

Well, then . . . Before Addie had much time to ponder her reaction to hearing Toni sound so controlling, Toni flashed her a friendly smile. "I may start to think you have no modern clothes, Adelaine. The last two times I've seen you, you were dressed like you were from another era."

Addie blurted, "Well, I have perfectly sound explanations."

"Sorry about that. Philip tells me he has another callback anyhow," Marcela, the woman who held Addie's career in her hands, said as she rejoined them. "He would love to talk to you if he's cast as Colin."

"Perfectly fine," Emily said when Toni failed to reply.

"I didn't expect to see you here." Toni looked Addie up and down.

"I sent an email." Addie knew damn well her email was likely sitting in Toni's "to read" file, but she *had* sent it.

Marcela looked like someone had just handed her a gift. "You already know Miss Stewart? That's just unexpectedly *wonderful*! How do you know each other?"

Really, what was she to say? Addie bit her lip and looked away.

We kissed in a bar and did more *in a garden, and ever since that night, Toni was the star of every masturbatory fantasy I've enjoyed the past year,* Addie thought, but she said nothing of the sort. Those were not things Addie had shared even with her dearest friend.

Oh, and Toni hid her surname and novel from me the past year while we emailed incessantly, Addie silently continued as she waited for Toni to answer.

Instead, Toni gestured to Addie with a surprising amount of trust and said, "Why don't you explain, Addie?"

"Scotland." She glanced at Toni, feeling like this was a test of some sort. "I was preparing to star in *Mina,* and I believe Dr. Darbyshire was in town for a conference. . . . It's a little vague since that was over a year ago."

A brief look between Emily and Toni made Addie falter. She couldn't recall if Toni had mentioned the conference, and from the suspicious look on Toni's face now, neither could she.

"That's right. We were both in Scotland at the same time for work," Toni agreed. She caught Addie's gaze. "Were you at the conference or . . ."

Deciding to be fearless, Addie admitted, "Just for the one panel."

"Toni's panel?" Emily prompted. Emily and Toni exchanged another quick look.

"Of course. Dr. Darbyshire is an amazing lecturer." Addie sighed—not to intentionally draw Toni's gaze to her chest, but Addie wasn't complaining when that was precisely what happened. Whatever the spark was when they met, it was still there even though they had barely flirted over email the last year.

Right now, though, Addie could feel Toni staring at her, and this time she felt warm for a different reason.

"How fortuitous that you not only know one another, but Adelaine shares the protagonist's name. . . ." Marcela looked between them.

"I named the character after Addie," Toni said after a too-long pause.

Addie realized in that moment that Marcela had put two and two together and come up with a conclusion that wasn't precisely true. *Yet.*

"I want this role," Addie blurted out. "However, my condition is that you respect Dr. Darbyshire's privacy. No one needs to know that she named the character after me. Ever. Or that we knew each other."

Toni gave Addie an inexplicable look, and Addie felt herself blushing. Maybe it was foolish, but she wanted to defend Toni, to be *her* hero, too.

"The role *is* hers, right?" Toni asked. "I'd like it to be hers, if that matters. I know I said I didn't want to be invol—"

"Of course it matters, Toni!" Marcela's wide-eyed expression was enough to make Addie laugh. "That was the plan, but I was going to ask if it would be awkward for—"

"Not at all. She's perfect for the role." Toni gave one nod, as if that was that, and then glanced at her agent. "Emily, can you grab Addie's current phone number? I want to explore the set for a moment." Then she looked at Addie. "Dinner."

"Yes, please." Addie's traitorous body reacted even more viscerally to that commanding tone, and she pressed her lips together tightly before any other words escaped.

"Good." Toni's gaze fastened on her like a wolf spotting a trembling rabbit. Then she pivoted. "Ms. Gibson? Let's explore the set."

"Marcela, please!" The older woman shot a last look at Addie before gesturing. "This way. You have to see the study up close."

Then Toni was striding away with Marcela, and Addie was biting back a sigh. There was something impossibly sexy about power, and Toni had it. She was decisive, and Addie was drawn to that sort of personality in a way that sometimes bothered her.

Addie fumbled for her business card to give Emily.

"I heard about the bar," Emily said, drawing Addie's gaze away from Toni's backside. Toni had a marvelous firm bum.

When Addie said nothing, still pondering the fact that it made zero sense to find a back end attractive, Emily continued, "Don't use her, Adelaine, or I will destroy you, your family, and any chance at a career you might have."

Addie gaped at her, finally registering the conversation. "*What?*"

"She's my sister and my client, and my job is to protect her. If you don't hurt her, we're fine, but if you have an agenda . . ." Emily gave her a harsh once-over.

Unlike Addie's reaction to Toni's brusque tone, Emily's aggressiveness did nothing but piss her off. "I met her in a bar. Beautiful, smart woman. What agenda could I possibly have?"

Aside from convincing her to love me . . .

Emily stared at Addie. "Fair, but maybe it's a new agenda."

"I already auditioned for the role *on my own* because I didn't want her help, even though we've been emailing for a year." Addie shook her head. "She's smart, and sexy, and I didn't know she was a writer when we met, so it wasn't like I was angling for a role or that I need a handout. I think she's amazing, and I want to spend more time getting to know her. That's my secret agenda, Ms. Haide. I like her."

Emily nodded, an approving look appearing suddenly. "Good, because you'll probably have a few events together for promo."

Addie's answering smile felt like it stretched to the sides of her face. "I can't wait." A torrent of words burst out against Addie's best efforts. "And obviously, my interest isn't one-sided. She named Addie after me and just *ordered* me to dinner, and she emails me every week. Is she single?"

"She is and has *always* been single." For a moment, Emily looked like she had more to say, but she gave Addie a look that felt like sympathy and then walked off.

The presumed assistant from earlier popped out from wherever she'd been lurking. "Let's get you changed!"

"Sure." Addie looked up to see Toni staring back at her the same way she had when Addie had walked into the bar in Scotland. *No, this spark definitely isn't one-sided.*

The assistant led Addie back to the room where she could change into her street clothes. "Congrats, Miss Stewart. We'll get in touch about costume-fitting soon, and then go over the details of everything else with your manager."

In a few short minutes, Addie was back in a car headed home, clutching her phone, awaiting a call or text from Toni.

Everything is finally working out!

She had a new role, a new start at something wonderful. Now, she just had to get the woman!

Chapter 13

Toni

Toni stared at the assorted clothes in her hotel closet. She'd brought what she'd dubbed "author clothes," which worked for the meetings and stock signings she had to do, but they felt wrong for a date. This was a *date*. What was she thinking? She didn't date, but it didn't feel like a hookup after she'd named a character after Addie and now she was in the show and—

A tap on her door had Toni panicking, but then she heard Emily's voice. "Open the door."

"What if I'm half-naked?" Toni called back. She dropped the blouse she'd been holding and went to open her hotel room door.

"Unless there's someone in there with you, I don't care." Emily's laugh was the kind of thing that washed away Toni's worst moods. Friends for life. Sisters since childhood. And now, her agent. How in the hell did *that* even happen?

"You better hope no one with mimicry skills ever knocks at your door," Emily teased as she brushed past Toni. She looked over her shoulder. "Did you even look through the peephole?"

"Nope."

Emily glanced at the chaos on Toni's bed. "Did your luggage explode?"

"Maybe." Toni sank into the desk chair that she'd left in the middle of the room earlier. "What am I doing, Em?"

"Having dinner with a beautiful woman you've been emailing for a *year*, apparently, even though you never told me." Emily picked up the one pair of jeans Toni had packed. "Or having a business meeting with the lead actress in your book adaptation?" With her other hand, Emily held up a pair of trousers. "You tell me."

Toni sighed. "So we met at the bar that last night in Scotland."

"I know."

"And we messed around some. . . ." Toni snatched the jeans from Emily. She wasn't going out with Addie in business trousers. "And for the last thirteen months, we talked. A lot. But just on email."

And I lied to her, hid my name, hid the book news.

"Which is weird for you now because she's in the show," Emily guessed.

"No." Toni pulled on the jeans as she weighed how much to confess. Until Addie, Toni had always told Emily everything—from her first fumbling attempt at oral to the time her father's gambling meant a late-night visit from a man with a gun. "So I invited her to my hotel that night."

"And? Was it bad or something? Too drunk to stay awake for you . . . ?"

Toni leveled a glare. "No. She ran away."

"Isn't that usually your signature move?" Emily sorted through Toni's clothes and pulled out a black sleeveless top that Toni typically wore under a blazer or button-up. "Here."

Silently, Toni pulled the top on as her best friend in the world started refolding the remaining clothing on the bed.

"She ran away *instead* of coming to my hotel." Toni squirmed, feeling like a bit of cad in the retelling of that night. "We were in the garden by the bar and then she took off, and I was there with my pants around my knees. And I worried, so I sent an email. . . ."

"Hmmm."

"'Hmmm' what?" Toni wasn't ready to unpack the way she felt, but Emily was never a fan of waiting until Toni was ready.

"You like her," Emily pronounced, staring at Toni as if daring her to disagree. "Tell me why."

"She's sexy—"

"This is me, sweetie. There are always sexy women willing to fall into your bed or go to the garden with you—" Emily gave Toni a wry grin. "Tell me you'll use that in a book? It sounds like an excellent euphemism."

"Okay, so she strolled into the bar with her hair pulled back in this long braid," Toni said, picturing Addie. "She was dressed in a nearly transparent white cotton nightdress, faux Victorian."

"Sexy, right. You said that."

"No. Victorian sexy. A trembling Lady Godiva. I swear, Em, it was like she was plucked from my dreams. She was obviously afraid, innocent, and . . . she picked *me*. There were a lot of other women, but she met my eyes and stood there trembling." Toni paused at that detail. If Addie had been at the conference, had she sought Toni out?

"Okay, sexy, has good taste, likes history." Emily ticked the list off on her fingers. "Should I be worried?"

"And every time shit got too real this year, I emailed Addie. I didn't tell her what was happening in my life, just . . . she was this safe place for me to be just me. Not a new professor. Not a debut author. Not daughter to a woman who barely remembers my name lately. Just *me*."

Toni and Emily continued folding her clothes. Toni shoved down the unfamiliar flush that Addie had picked her as a protector, that she'd undoubtedly known about the book for a while, that she'd heard Toni speak. She couldn't think about that; it could *change* something precious if she allowed that.

Most women were more apt to see Toni for what she was: a good time with no expectations. Addie looked at her like she was worth *more*. Addie knew her and still looked at her that way. It changed things on some level Toni couldn't explain.

Toni shook her head and snatched a pair of socks up. "Remember doing this when we were kids?"

"Your laundry skills aren't much improved," Emily teased. "And if you bring Addie back here to finish what you started . . ."

"I probably shouldn't," Toni murmured. "Maybe business meeting is better."

"Was she boring to talk to?"

"No." Toni grinned, thinking back to the wicked edge hidden under Addie's innocence. "She was quick-witted. Funny."

"Sexy, funny, likes history, brave—"

"Brave?"

"She walked into a bar half-dressed. That's either brave or stupid," Emily pointed out, not wrongly.

"She definitely had that 'hell with it, I'm going to meet a woman' energy." Toni shook her head. "I was probably like that as a teen. . . ."

How had someone so vivacious and beautiful been able to avoid being caught up by dozens of people? Unless she really wasn't innocent . . . but her reactions were definitely inexperienced. When she'd been attempting to—

Emily poked Toni's shoulder, pulling her into the present. "Sweetie, I mean this in the nicest way, but you're like a bear in need of nourishment after a long hibernation. Your logic for changing your sexual habits is all well and good. As your agent, I'm even grateful that you aren't out there causing a scandal."

Toni stared at her. "Did you just compare me to a *bear*?"

"A *starving* bear," Emily said without even the hint of a smile, even though her eyes sparkled with mischief. "And that lovely creature, the one who wowed you enough to name a character after her, is looking at you like she wants to have you for her main course."

Toni looked at the ceiling, as if praying. Then she poked Emily in the ribs. "All I'm saying is if *you* ever decide to get on one of those dating sites, Miss Haide, I reserve the right to edit your profile. 'Funny lady who likes either a stick and berries or a honeypot. Either welcome so she doesn't turn into a hibernating bear.'"

Emily snorted in laughter. "Too true. I'm not subtle about what I need. Sort of like my best friend *used* to be . . . Remember her?"

"Oh, I remember." Toni sighed. "Damn, Em, I feel like I got suddenly old. I went to a bar last week, and I was talking to this woman. It was going well, and you know what happened?"

"What?"

"She asked if I wanted to go back to her place and *sign her book*." Toni shuddered at the thought of how awkward that could've been. "What do I do, Em? Lead with 'Hi, are you barely literate?' or 'I'm looking for a woman who hates books.' I can't sleep with fans, students, or anyone who might feel pressured or swayed by . . . my job stuff."

"Try 'I'm hoping to hook up and not have you leave your terrible manuscript on the table the next morning,'" Emily commiserated.

They were silent a moment, but then Emily said, "Was Addie the last person you were with?"

"In a manner of speaking," Toni hedged. She turned away and put the last of her clothes in her suitcase.

"Sweetie?" Emily prompted.

"The last I touched, yes." Toni forced herself not to squirm. "She was a bit of a pillow princess, which is fine usually. . . ." Toni sighed loudly. "She had my trousers around my knees, and her hand in my shorts, and then she just left."

"Dear Lord, someone who rejected you *and* left you unsatisfied?" Emily *tsk*ed. "No wonder you obsess over her. You have a case of UST."

"UST? No one says that, Em." Toni rolled her eyes.

"Unresolved sexual tension," Emily singsonged. "Better?"

"Not really." Toni grinned, though. "Still rather unresolved a year later."

"And yet you were chatting with her weekly. . . ."

Toni sighed. "I almost offered her a ticket to fly to LA or meet me on tour. . . . I mean, I had no idea she lived in the States now."

Curiously, Emily asked, "Why didn't you?"

"I was afraid of putting it in writing," Toni confessed. "And I like her. What if she stopped talking to me once she found out about . . ." Toni gestured at the room and Emily. "The job."

Emily rolled her eyes. "You're a writer, not a contract killer."

"I think you underestimate how vulnerable writing makes me feel," Toni said levelly. This was the part she thoroughly failed at. Yes, writing was a dream. It also meant putting your raw heart on the pages and inviting the world to judge you. What if she wrote something that was accidentally revealing? She had one interviewer actually ask if there were "spicy" sex scenes ahead. Not that the Victorians were prudes, despite what the media often portrayed, but her character was single in the book.

"I didn't want to tell her I was a writer and have her read *The Whitechapel Widow*," Toni finally said.

"Well, that ship has sailed."

"No shit. She's going to be the character in front of cameras, Em." Toni stared at her best friend. "We'll end up doing events together."

"Odds are she'll be at the Dove Manor show launch," Emily slipped in casually. "They are looking forward to hosting after you couldn't do a book launch event there."

"There was a conflict—"

"Which you created," Emily countered. "I've known you most of our lives, sweetie, so I can tell when you're trying to con me."

"Em . . ."

"You cashed the checks, and they were for the book *and promotion of it*. So you will put on your big-girl drawers and be charming." Emily's tone was firm.

"I'm not charming," Toni tried.

"Bullshit. Case in point, Adelaine, who has longed for you for a year over email." Emily shook her finger at Toni. "You charmed her."

"But . . . she heard me talk, and maybe she wanted sex or Victorian era consultation and—"

Emily laughed. "Toni, I met her. Trust me, she likes *you*. Real you. If it was just sex, she wouldn't have emailed for a year." She paused and caught Toni's eye. "Did you talk a lot about the Victorians?"

"No. Maybe the occasional question, but . . . no. That wasn't it." Toni couldn't pretend that Addie was interested in that, and they'd never even had phone or video sex—although Toni would've been more than willing—so it wasn't just sex. "She knew about the book, though. She *read* the book. I don't sleep with fans."

"Jesus, Toni. You hadn't even sold it when you were with her." Emily threw up a hand in exasperation. "I swear, it's like you're trying to talk yourself out of sex."

"I'm really not. I just don't want . . . drama," Toni finished weakly.

"Go handle your hibernation issues with your friend who obviously *likes you* enough to stay in touch for an entire *year*." Emily stood and walked toward the door. "Seriously. You're not hard to look at, and she's into you. And you'll be at events here and there, not just Cape Dove. Two problems, one subtle solution."

"Subtle?"

"Friend with benefits," Emily said casually. "It's an easy solution. You aren't her boss. You aren't the one who gave her the role. She likes your book, but she obviously liked *you* first since the books hadn't sold yet. Easy friends with benefits setup."

"*You're* recommending friends with benefits?" Toni echoed. "Is there something you want to confess about your life? That's not a very looking-for-my-one-true-love comment, and you are—"

"Stop." Emily's features were pinched as she looked back. "Sometimes it's about getting what you need right now. Less complicated."

Toni folded her arms over her chest. "Do I need to show up at someone's door with my old baseball bat?"

"No, but thank you, sweetie." Emily's expression relaxed. "Eight A.M. pickup tomorrow. We have a meeting in the restaurant and then stock signings. We'll head to the airport after that. But right now, text Addie."

Emily waved over her shoulder and left.

Toni looked at her phone. It was just dinner. Maybe it would be business. Maybe it would be something else. Not texting her would be stupid, though.

About tonight . . .

Are you bailing now that I know your last name?

Toni paused. She had an opening to avoid potential drama. She should take it. She glanced at her bed, picturing Addie there, imagining her sprawled out naked there. Quick on the heels of that, she imagined no longer emailing. The loss of *that* would be tragic.

Not at all! Do you have any modern clothes?

. . .

None my drawers fit under.

For a moment Toni closed her eyes. *Not a business meeting. Not even a little.*

So don't wear any.

For a moment, Toni thought she'd made a mistake. She started to type an apology.

Then Addie replied.

As you wish. 7PM? Hotel or meet somewhere first?

First? Toni smiled to herself. This was exactly what she needed, and Addie obviously was done pretending to be an inexperienced Victorian maiden—or oblivious to who Toni was. It was time to address both things.

Hotel lobby. I'll have a car waiting.

Chapter 14

Addie

Addie walked into the hotel lobby a good twenty minutes early. Maybe she was overexcited, but she wasn't going to pace her apartment. This was better. The space had that look that screamed "our everything is expensive." Marble floors, ornate crystal chandelier, beautiful chairs that looked exceedingly uncomfortable, and under all of it the scent of expensive colognes. Men in suits, women in dresses or jeans that undoubtedly had a designer label. Sleek sunglasses and real gemstones. West Hollywood hotels were the sort of place that made Addie swear she'd be different if she ever hit it big.

No plastic surgery. No Botox.

No wearing labels I can't afford.

At least I was blessed with a DD cup, so the only breast surgery I'd need would be a reduction.

Her overgenerous breasts were more burden than gift, unfortunately, unless she wanted to star in a *different* sort of film. Nothing wrong with that, of course, but it wasn't exactly a fit for a woman who had no desire to have casual sex, much less sex on film.

Typically, Addie wore loose-fitting tops to downplay her breasts and formfitting jeans, but tonight, she topped her usual jeans that showed off every curve with a whisper-thin blouse that was cut deep in the front, so her cleavage was on display. She wanted Toni to notice her body, but until she saw Toni, Addie had a shawl tossed over her shoulders.

I look like a lost hippie.

The shawl look was fine in Scotland, but here in Toni's expensive hotel, it drew a lot of attention—or maybe it was the tight jeans? Or the hippie hair? Whatever the cause, Addie felt like a bug. People were either looking like they might want to squish her or collect her.

She tried to be casual as she looked around the lobby. Several men stared back at her, and one woman at the desk gave her the assessing stare of "Do you belong here?"

Addie was fairly sure she did not, in fact, belong here. She wasn't a famous writer or actor. *Yet.* She whipped out her phone and texted.

Here early. Traffic wasn't awful for a change.

The three little dots of a message danced over the screen not even twenty seconds later, and the fact that Toni was quick to reply made Addie smile to herself. Maybe Toni would invite her upstairs. Maybe—

I see you.

Addie looked around. Toni wasn't in the lobby, as far as Addie could tell. The sound of an incoming text sounded. Addie glanced down.

Bar.

With a steadying breath, Addie looked over at the lobby bar to find Toni looking back at her. Jeans, black sleeveless top, and another blazer folded over her lap. Ink covered one of her arms from shoulder to wrist, and Addie smothered a sound. Last time, Toni's sleeves touched her wrists. Now, defined muscles on tattooed arms were in full display.

Addie removed her shawl and clutched it as she walked toward Toni. *I dressed for her, so I'm not going to hide.*

Addie's heart thrummed in her chest.

Toni swiveled to watch Addie's approach, and her expression was hungry enough to make Addie want to run toward her. To distract herself from the fact that the woman of her dreams was watching her, Addie studied Toni.

Her cheeks were more defined than Addie remembered them being in Scotland, and her hair was slightly longer. The slight undercut was new, as if Toni had decided to make a statement now that she was an author. Addie's gaze dropped to the hand curled around a glass of what she knew was whisky.

Toni, of course, noticed and grinned as if she could read Addie's mind.

With a slightly faster step, Addie closed the distance as Toni stood to greet her, but Addie wasn't sure what the protocol was here.

"Do I hug or kiss you?" she mused aloud. "After . . . Edinburgh . . . and a year of talking over email, I'm not sure."

Toni laughed like she was startled, but she opened her arms. "Come here. I would've hugged you at the studio, but I was speechless after your performance."

Addie stepped into the circle of Toni's arms. She felt like she might melt. This was right, like finding where she wanted to be.

Then Toni released her, emptied her drink, and added in a huskier voice, "I'll give you what you want, Addie, if you do the same."

Addie flinched. Toni's comment felt very much like a dig at her for freezing back in the garden, and that expression must have shown on her face. The next thing she knew, Toni's hand was cupping her jaw.

"*Not* what you're thinking," Toni said once Addie met her gaze. "You seemed to want some answers earlier, and what *I* want is to have dinner with the beautiful actor about to star in a new show . . . one who failed to tell me she was even auditioning."

"Oh."

Toni leaned in and brushed her lips over Addie's too quickly to even be called a kiss, and then she added, "So I think we have a few things to discuss. Don't you?"

Addie nodded. "I didn't know how to tell you that I knew who you were without risking you vanishing. I laid out openings for you to tell me about the book. You didn't. So I couldn't tell you about the audition for the show about your book without admitting I knew about the book, but . . ." She shrugged

"Today's email was pretty overt." Toni flashed her a grin before she slipped her jacket on and gestured Addie forward.

Addie restrained her impulsivity, folding her hands into tight balls to resist the impulse to touch Toni's arm or hip or bum. She had to remind herself that Toni might have readers nearby, and Addie had to get used to that restriction for herself, too. If the show was a hit—*please let it be a hit*—Addie would have fans of her own.

She kept pace with Toni as they crossed the lobby until Toni paused. "I should've asked if you wanted a drink. . . ."

"No." Addie smiled brightly at her. "I mean, no, I don't, and no, you didn't need to ask. I can speak up to tell you what I want."

"Can you?" Toni shot her a heated glance before she pushed open the door. She looked around at the bellmen and valets, adding lightly, "There's to be a car out here waiting."

Addie spotted a black car with ADDIE WIGHT on the sign in the corner of the window, but she kept looking even as Toni said, "There it is. I hope you don't mind. I put your character name on it in case."

"In case?"

Toni glanced at her. "In case you walked in, and I scared you off, and you wanted to leave. Or in case you were angry that I never told you about the book. . . ."

The driver stepped out as they approached. He walked around the car and nodded. "Evening."

"Hi!" Addie chirped, too brightly, cringing at the bemused smile on Toni's face.

Toni gave the driver a calmer, "Evening." She stood beside the open door, glanced at Addie. "Miss Stewart? After you."

Addie slid into the sleek black leather interior, feeling like an imposter. She slid all the way across, and Toni slid in at her side.

Once the door closed, Toni said, "You don't need to slide over when we take a car. I can walk around."

"Too long to wait," Addie blurted. "When . . . as in there will be other times? This isn't one night, and then I don't see you for another year?"

Toni reached over and took Addie's hand, twining their fingers together, and mused, "So the real you is as unfiltered as I remember from Scotland. In email, you seemed to be more reserved."

Addie looked down. "I edit and reedit before I send. Does it bother you that I'm unfiltered?"

"Not at all." Toni settled back in her seat, still holding on to Addie's hand. "I like a direct woman, especially if a woman plans to be in my bed."

Addie stared at her, noting the quirk of a small smile. Arrogant? Maybe, but Addie was *here* for it. She didn't answer. She simply settled back into the luxurious seat . . . and waited. Toni was calling the shots, and Addie was bracing for being romanced, seduced, and falling in love.

After a year of small talk, she was ready for more. She wanted to tackle everything, talk about everything, share everything. But after several quiet minutes with only the sound of the radio and hum of the wheels, Addie started to worry. It was her superpower. Worry. Self-doubt. Anxiety. It was part of why she loved acting. When she was someone else, she *wasn't* Addie. She was a character, and she liked to go for roles where the characters were confident. That meant she didn't worry—unless she took that kind of role. But so far, she went after roles where she could be bold.

"Addie?"

"Do you have regrets?" Addie whispered.

"When?" Toni frowned like it was the strangest question ever. "Tonight?"

"Now. Then. I don't know. You're really quiet, like maybe you regret ordering me to dinner." Addie pulled her hand away, feeling the loss and hating it, but she didn't want to screw this up by being clingy either.

"Ordering?" Toni echoed.

"It sure sounded like an order," Addie muttered.

"Did you feel like you *had* to say yes?" Toni countered.

"No. I wanted to see you. I just want to know if this was what you want. . . ." Addie glanced over. "So, regrets?"

"Not at all. I'm just tired." Toni gave her a small smile. "I love my jobs, both of them, but—"

"So you're still teaching full-time? You never mention much about it, but you never mentioned your book tours or TV interviews either."

Toni startled. "So you knew the whole time?"

"I went to hear *you* talk at the conference." Addie took a deep breath and then blurted out, "That's why I was in the bar that night. To try to meet you."

Toni turned to face her. "You were at my talk and came to The Lady's Hand to meet *me*?"

"Yes . . ." Addie squirmed. "I wasn't *stalking* you! You were just brilliant, and I was trying to land the role of Mina in a play, and when I found your lecture online, I searched you because you made all that stuff interesting, and I saw you were in Scotland and—"

"You came to the bar because you heard my lecture," Toni clarified. "You weren't a student, though . . . ?"

"Nope. I saw the conference had a lecture on Victorian lesbians, and . . . I was struggling reading the research books. Some of them are so boring! But then I heard you talk, and you had the answers I needed, so much so that I wanted to know more, and I wanted to say thanks. I tried to talk to you after your talk, when you were leaving, but I gave up." Addie took a breath, but her words still tumbled out in a hurry. "Anyhow, I got the role. I used what I learned from your lecture, and from talking to you, and I got the role."

"Not that day, though," Toni said.

Addie sighed. "No, but I wanted to see if I could be Victorian enough, and then you looked at me like . . ."

"Like you're gorgeous," Toni filled in.

Addie didn't look away. "Is that weird that I went to the bar to talk to you?"

"No." Toni was staring at her, an unreadable expression on her face. "The fact that you were excited by my lecture is actually flattering."

"I was also pretty excited by how you worried about me when you saw me," Addie said, half embarrassed by her jumbled confession and half wanting reassurances. "And when I left you there."

"Well, your outfit was . . . incredible, and—"

"You liked it," Addie pronounced proudly.

Toni chuckled. "Yes, but afterward, I needed to be sure you got home safely. I felt guilty that maybe I'd said something or did something to make you leave so abruptly."

"No, like I said in my email, I just freaked out." Addie felt her cheeks heat. "You know, I auditioned in that for *Mina*—"

"In *that*?"

"Well, a dress over it, but I felt brave wearing it because of you, so I wanted that feeling in the audition," Addie admitted. "I wore it for my first audition for your show, too."

Toni laughed. "That's fucking brilliant."

"The drawers are like my lucky panties now." Addie flashed her what she hoped was a beguiling smile. "You changed my life, and I have wanted to see you again so often . . . but I wasn't going to just show up at an event. And you never once said your last name. I didn't want to make you feel awkward."

"That's definitely not what I felt seeing you again." Toni's gaze slid over Addie.

"So what do you feel?"

For a moment, Toni was silent. She stared out the window, and Addie thought she'd gone too far.

But then Toni said, "Ridiculous things." She glanced up at the driver and lowered her voice before saying, "You showed up that night like something out of my fantasies."

Addie's heart dropped a little. *If all Toni liked was my looks . . .*

"And you make me laugh, which I like—possibly *need* these days." Toni glanced at her briefly. Looking away, she added, "And you obviously share an interest in my favorite historical era . . . and you're people-smart. I'm not great at that." She gave a self-deprecating laugh. "I dreamed of selling a book. I thought it would be a tiny deal at most, and no one would care about the author. You were my private haven this last year, you know? The one person who wasn't pressuring me at all. You didn't expect me to be an author or a capable professor or know how to handle interviews."

"But you always seem so confident!" Addie stared at her, baffled that the same woman who confidently held a room of conference attendees in her hand could be insecure. "I heard you lecture in Edinburgh, and you *owned* the room. You were so sure of everything."

The car was stuck in gridlock, and Addie watched Toni look at the other cars but not really see them. She had a contemplative expression.

"I can lecture on history, but I'm anxious at these book events . . . they want to know about my inspiration, my life, and I hate that part. I love writing, and I'm thrilled that readers like the book." She looked back at Addie. "But I am more of an introvert than you might guess. I don't want to talk about my private life"

"I'm not," Addie confessed. "An introvert, I mean."

Toni laughed. "If the show does well, that will be useful. I need to have Emily with me, so I don't say the wrong thing."

Addie wanted to hug Toni, offer to travel with her, whatever it took to make her feel better. "So you're not a big fan of being out in public, then?"

"I know it's weird. If I'd have been on my own, I'd just order room service in the privacy of my room. I feel adrift when people approach me and know who I am."

"Is that what you want? To stay in your room tonight?" Addie moved closer, sliding across the plush leather seat to be closer to Toni.

"I wanted to wine and dine you at an expensive restaurant, Adelaine. Celebrate your new role in what I hear will be an amazing show." Toni's voice was lighter, more natural, as if she was suddenly the woman Addie had met in the bar in Edinburgh. Talking about the show—or maybe about wanting to please Addie—brought back the confidence that talking about book events had evaporated.

"Room service at that hotel is pretty expensive, I bet. You can take me to an expensive in-room meal, or we could get burgers on the beach or walk down to the star walk or you could come to my apartment, and we can make sandwiches." Addie shrugged before reaching out to take Toni's hand again. "Seriously, I don't need fancy things. I'm the same person in real life as in our email . . . okay, maybe more blunt . . . but that's the only difference. I live in LA, Toni. If anything, I ought to be the one tour-guiding for you if we're going out. And traffic this direction sucks anyhow. I'm fine staying in if you want to turn back."

Toni stared intently at her. "You really don't care?"

"As long as I'm with you tonight, I'm happy." Addie took a deep breath before blurting, "I auditioned for the role in part to see you again. You're a hard woman to forget, Toni Darbyshire. I'm here to see you, and if you're happier going somewhere else"—she shrugged—"take me to the lobby bar or wherever you want to go."

Chapter 15
Toni

Toni felt foolish saying it, since walking on the beach had become such a romantic cliché, but she still asked, "What about the beach? You mentioned it in your email, and it's starting to get cold at home, so . . ."

"Santa Monica Pier?"

"Is that a terrible idea? I've never been, and the ocean sounds better than a hotel lobby," Toni admitted.

Toni already felt a bit overwhelmed by the traffic of Los Angeles, and even though she was with someone she'd met before the book sale—literally right before—she was still in Los Angeles, having been on the set of a TV adaptation of her book, and she wasn't entirely sure how to cope. It was all good—exciting, even—but she felt . . . small.

The speed at which her life had changed was daunting at the best of times. She was hella grateful, but it was all so fast, so public, so much attention. And she had not expected any of it. She'd worked on her PhD for years, steadily researching, writing, and revising. Life had been a series of late nights in the library or early mornings finishing grading for her assistantship. And during it all, Toni was invisible. She was just another TA, no one of note.

Flights and interviews and places like LA weren't her usual speed, even now.

"I would like to walk on the beach with you," Toni blurted out, trying not to think about how date-like it was. They'd talked for a year. They were friends. Friends went to the beach. It was a normal thing, a calming thing, like emailing Addie when she felt overwhelmed, but in person.

"You'll have to hold my hand when we walk," Addie teased after a quiet moment. "There are beach rules. If you take a pretty woman to the beach, you must hold her hand at some point."

Toni looked over at her, wondering why this vivacious woman wanted to be with her, but Addie's very serious expression continued as she said, "And we must eat ice cream *before* dinner if we are to have any."

"Dessert first?" Toni clarified.

"California law. I can't make exceptions just because you're a schoolteacher."

Toni smiled. "Well, if that's the law . . ."

She glanced over at Addie and noticed that she also seemed more relaxed now, more than the night they met or earlier in the lobby, and Toni liked that. She wanted to see Addie smile and be the reason for it.

It's a normal friend *thing to want,* she told herself.

The drive to the pier really wasn't any faster than if they had gone to the restaurant, but Toni relaxed more all the same. There was something like a weight that had slid off her shoulders the more she was around Addie. The only things Addie seemed to want were things she'd already had—a romantic interlude—and time with the person she met in Scotland and chatted with online.

"So . . . you failed to mention that you moved back to the States," Toni said once they were out of the car with a plan to get picked back up later.

"Not that long after you sold a book, I think." Addie gave her a look. "Anything you forgot to mention?"

Toni felt briefly chastised. "I wanted a corner of the world where

I was neither professor nor writer. I have been a bit overwhelmed the last year."

"I feel lucky that I was your corner, you know." Addie tucked her hand in the bend of Toni's arm as they strolled along the promenade. "This is about three blocks, car-free, food and shops."

Toni nodded. "I can't believe you knew my name the whole time."

"I didn't know how to bring that up. I did try, though. I told you my full name the night we met. You didn't share yours," Addie pointed out.

"Err, I don't usually share my whole name with women I meet at bars," Toni admitted.

"I figured." Addie looked away, but Toni caught the tense way she held her shoulders.

"You're angry that I didn't tell you?"

"Not that first night . . . it was part of why I left, though. Sex isn't something I take lightly, and you couldn't even tell me your last name. I ran. Later, I was a little disappointed a few times. You *still* didn't even tell me your whole name, even though we talked every week," Addie pointed out. "Did you think about it?"

"I had *two* new careers launching at the same time, and you were in Scotland as far as I knew and—"

"So no?" Addie interrupted.

"Actually, yes." Toni glanced over, feeling like these were the sort of things they probably would've eventually had to discuss, but now, being face-to-face was different. It was a lot easier to control perception in email. In person, there was no dodging awkward topics. "I wanted you to know my name, and about the sale, and I almost emailed to ask about using your first name in the book."

"I almost emailed to ask *why* you used my name," Addie said softly.

"How did you know?"

"I put an alert on your name, and I saw the news on your book deal and . . ." Addie shrugged, like it was no big deal that she had known the very things Toni angsted over confessing. Addie gave her a sheepish smile. "I wasn't trying to be weird. I liked you. I liked your lecture. And I liked what happened when we were . . . when we . . . when you . . ."

"The garden," Toni filled in helpfully.

"Yes." Addie's face reddened. "The garden."

"Me too." Toni gave her a smile before she teased, "Although no one has ever left me with my trousers down before. . . ."

Addie pressed her face against Toni's shoulder, hiding her blush. "I didn't mean to overreact like that. I swear. I was undone, and you weren't even sharing your whole name, and I just felt so exposed."

"She says to the woman whose trousers were at her knees," Toni murmured quietly.

"Fair." Addie giggled. "At least no one saw you like that."

Toni gave her a look. "I guess that was lucky."

They fell into silence as Addie directed them closer to the actual beach and the oceanfront restaurant where they could eat. The restaurant was still a bit fussier than Toni wanted, but the view was gorgeous enough that she honestly didn't care. *Whisky at the beach.* It sounded altogether more relaxing than her best of unwinding attempts most days. *And it matches both of our dream meals . . . which is not an odd thing to remember.* She remembered everything Addie had told her, probably because she'd saved their email exchanges and reread them.

Before they went inside, Addie said quietly, "You know, you were my *first*, Toni. I was terrified of doing something wrong. That was the other reason I ran."

"We've all been there," Toni offered, although in fairness she couldn't remember how long ago it was that she'd been there. "Coming out young like I did and looking more masc meant that every girl who was questioning knew I was safe to hit on, to flirt with, to proposition."

As they were being seated, Toni thought about how different things had been for her overall. She'd been very visibly out in high school, and by then, Lawrence v. Texas had already changed the laws for same-sex relationships. So while gay marriage wasn't legal yet, *being* in a same-sex relationship was not illegal by the time Toni was a teen. That decision brought a level of tolerance that seemed to make every thinking-about-being-a-lesbian woman decide to try easing out of the closet completely, and Toni? Well, she was out and proud, and back then, perfectly happy to be the metaphorical training wheels for plenty of women.

Was that what I was for her, too? Was Addie looking for a set of training wheels?

They took their seats and menus, and Toni weighed whether or not they ought to have a drink. She was pretty sure they both were looking for a sort of repeat of Scotland. And Toni wanted Addie to go into whatever was happening with a clear head.

When the server arrived far too quickly to ask about drinks, Toni said, "We need a minute."

Addie gave her a curious look. "What's up?"

"I'd rather not drink if we're going back to my hotel later. . . ." Toni held Addie's gaze. "This is not me *asking* you to come back, but if we *are* having a drink, we should plan on not drinking much."

Addie nodded. "I'd rather leave the options open."

Whisky or woman? That felt like the choice.

Addie blushed again when the server returned for the drinks order, but she glanced at Toni and ordered a mocktail. Then she added, "If you want to have your whisky, that's okay. You're a lot better at drinking than I am."

After they ordered drinks, Addie leveled an astute stare at Toni. "Drinker in the family?"

"Father."

Addie nodded. "Both my parents drink and . . . other things. It makes me very California-stereotype, though: plenty of baggage thanks to my parents."

"Sounds like I could get away with moving here, then, since I'd need a trailer to carry my family baggage," Toni caught herself admitting. *In for a penny, in for a pound.* "I sold the book because my dad took a second mortgage on my mom's house and then gambled or otherwise pissed it away."

Addie's mouth formed a perfect O for a moment. Then she said, "Ouch."

They paused as the server dropped off drinks.

"My parents are more like a unified pair of hippies." Addie shook her head. "They have a duplex up near San Francisco. He lives in one half, and she's in the other half. Currently, they're dating each other."

"Dating?"

"They've been divorced a few times," Addie said lightly. "From each other but also from other people. They're honestly a train wreck. Can't stay together. Can't stay apart. They think I'm the weird one because I'm not hopping from bed to bed."

Toni was at a loss. "There's a lot to unpack there."

"So my therapists have told me." Addie sipped her brightly colored fizzy drink. "Short version that's relevant to *you*: I don't bed-hop."

For a moment, Toni almost replied with a glib "I do," but she thought better of it. Instead, she replied, "I used to do so, but that changed when work got in the way. Calling in naked isn't really a viable excuse in grad school or for teaching. Sleeping with fans or students? Cringey. I don't want that kind of power dynamic."

"Do I count as a fan?"

"Not unless you're a time traveler." Toni caught Addie's gaze. "I don't want anyone in my bed because of my book. You were willing to be in my arms *before*, when I was a broke-assed new college professor and not *your* professor."

"So I'm grandmothered in?" Addie giggled, covering her mouth with her hand, as if to stop the sound.

Toni cut a look at her. "I think I'm a bit older than you, so I'm not sure about your terminology there."

"I do own historical drawers," Addie said mildly.

"Oh, I remember, Lady Stewart. I definitely remember."

As they chatted, Toni relaxed as much from Addie's exuberance as from the view and the whisky. There was something about her that made Toni feel calmer, freer, and she wanted more of it. *More Addie.* Toni could admit that much to herself. She always wanted more when they talked, even in the short email exchanges.

Honestly, Toni said, "I'm glad I met you."

"Same." Addie looked at the menu and then told Toni, "We ordered food before dessert! Why do I keep breaking rules when I see you?"

Toni chuckled and stopped the server. "Excuse me. Can we order dessert to come before dinner?"

The server smiled. "Of course. Would you like to see the dessert tray? Or just list the options?"

Addie looked to Toni to answer, and Toni reached out and took Addie's hand. "Whatever the lady wants."

The delight in Addie's expression was really all that Toni registered. Whatever she ordered was fine. Toni would have a couple bites, but really, it was about that smile. Addie was exactly the kind of friend Toni needed in her life—someone who lived with joy, someone who was a little silly, a lot impulsive, and absurdly attractive.

Friend with benefits, I hope.

She's perfect.

Chapter 16

Addie

By the time dinner had ended, Addie wondered how someone who seemed so together could be so lost, because that's exactly what Toni was. *Lost.* Not in a majorly impossible-to-fix way, but in a way that made pretty clear that her life had gone off the rails somewhere. Massive trust issues. Workaholic.

How did I talk to her for a year and not know all that?

Addie had to push down her urge to ask what she could do to help. She was a fixer—a trait trained into her by years of dysfunctional parents. She wasn't going to do that with Toni, though. No matter how much she wanted to, Addie was going to think about her own boundaries.

"Beach?" she asked after Toni settled the bill.

Toni nodded. When Toni stood this time, she offered Addie a hand, and Addie felt like a real Victorian lady. Safe. Cherished. Not that she *needed* to be coddled, but it felt nice all the same.

Her phone buzzed. She looked down. *Eric.* A part of her, a part a little too much like her mother, wanted to ignore him. Instead, she asked, "Is it totally inconsiderate to answer this? My cousin probably wants to know about the role and . . ."

"Do you want privacy? I can—"

"Nope." Addie tightened her grip on Toni's hand slightly.

When they were outside, Addie tapped Eric's name and called. "I'm just leaving dinner, but I got it. I got the part."

Eric let out a whoop that Toni obviously heard. "Oooh, maybe you'll see the sexy professor again."

Addie winced. "Maybe."

"I bet you do. They do these panels at Comic-Con and—"

"Let me just be in *this* moment," Addie interrupted, since the woman at her side could hear him.

"This is amazing, Ads. Everything you need. Great show. Hot woman. It's like hitting a lottery," Eric continued. "How are you not freaking out? Why are we not going out and celebrating?"

"Tomorrow."

For a moment, Eric grew quiet. "Are you okay? Use the code word if you're in trouble."

Addie smiled. "I'm fine." Then she lied, "Business dinner right now. Talk later?"

"So, so awesome, cuz." Eric's exuberance was all the proof anyone would need to know they were related.

Addie disconnected.

"Business dinner?" Toni asked with a quirked brow. Her tone was chilly as she asked, "Is that what this is?"

"Nope, but 'strolling along the beach with the sexy professor' would raise questions I don't want to answer in front of you." Addie pulled off her shoes and then tugged Toni closer to the water.

Toni still had on her sensible low boots. "So you talked to your friend about the garden?"

"So you talked to your agent about me?" Addie rebutted.

Toni laughed. "In my defense, Em was my childhood bestie. She's been at my side through crisis after drama after victory. I share everything with her."

"I get that. Eric is my cousin, roommate, and travel buddy." They veered close enough that the crash of waves was louder, almost enough to drown out the drum circle up ahead on the beach. "So yeah,

I mentioned the gorgeous woman who made me feel safe enough and excited enough to give me the first orgasm I had *with* someone."

"You don't filter anything you think, do you?" Toni asked as a woman walking by gave them a look that made it clear she'd overheard.

"Not usually. Is that going to bother you?" Addie held Toni's gaze, feeling uncommonly confrontational in the moment.

"No," Toni said after a pause. "I think it'll land you in some drama if the show succeeds. I travel with Em sometimes because I said what I thought too often, and it caused some problems. I had to see a media-training person."

Addie wanted to hug Toni. "I'm sorry you had to deal with that. I hope you know you can talk to me about that sort of stuff, too. Now that I know, I mean. You could've before because I already did know but . . ." She rested her face on Toni's arm briefly in a hug-like gesture. "I can manage reporters or that sort of thing. It comes with growing up here. But *you're* not one of those, though, so I thought I could be real with you."

"You can." Toni nodded as if she was having an internal conversation or doubts.

It took all of Addie's willpower not to ask prying questions. Turned out, she didn't need to.

A moment later, Toni asked, "So, being real, what are you looking for here? I don't want shit to be awkward, and with the show . . . I mean, if you were already cast in the show when we met I would never have touched you."

"Well, that would suck for me." Addie dug her toes into the sand and stared up at Toni. "I *still* have no regrets, and I wanted to see you again so many times. I thought about video chats, even."

Toni let go of her hand. "I wanted to see you, too. I almost sent you a ticket asking you to meet me. Then I thought back to what a shitstorm that would be if you shared the email."

"I would never!" Addie frowned at the thought of that. "You

have my word. I would never hurt your career—or mine—by going public with anything between us. I can be discreet."

"Same, obviously," Toni said. She squirmed a little. "I don't *date*, though. So . . ."

"Luckily, we're on a business dinner?" Addie teased. She stepped closer and kissed Toni briefly, a butterfly touch of a kiss, before stepping to the edge of the surf and getting her feet wet.

Toni watched her like she was something strange and vaguely unsettling. She obviously had not spent much time at the beach. That was something they'd have to remedy, whether they were friends or more.

"What do *you* want?" Addie asked. "I kinda feel like I need to know that before I can figure out anything. I mean, you're the secretive one here. . . ."

At first Toni just watched her as Addie twirled along the edge of the water once and then walked backward, facing her now-silent date. Addie bit the inside of her lip to keep herself from pelting questions at Toni. She was a self-confessed introvert, and Addie was . . . well, *not*.

"I like all of our email, but I like this tonight, too," Toni said carefully. "Talking and spending time with you in person, wondering if you'll let me kiss you later."

Which, Addie thought, *is the definition of a date.*

Addie thought it seemed wisest not to mention that detail since Toni claimed she didn't date. Maybe she was saying she didn't usually do that? Or maybe she was one of those situationship people who dated but then just didn't call it that? Out of all the little things they'd discussed, this wasn't on the list.

So all Addie said was, "We could do things like this again, including the kissing."

"I liked touching you, too," Toni added in a huskier voice. "In case you had any doubts."

"Yeah?" Addie hated her own insecurity, but there it was. She wasn't sure what Toni thought about that night. It was on the list of things Addie wanted to know, but couldn't figure out how to ask without sounding super needy. Her face flamed as she asked, "Even though I didn't . . . know how to . . . when I . . ."

Toni had no hesitation at all. "Yes. Some women *don't* reciprocate at all, you know."

"Is that what you want?" Addie felt like she'd fallen into a strange world. Lesbians, in general, tended to be more "let's discuss" than the few men she'd dated, but that openness never stopped fascinating her—and, well, she hadn't even thought about dating anyone the last year. There were a few flirtations, but no one had made it to an actual *date*. Her mind had been too full of Toni, waiting for the next email, hoping they'd evolve to talking about big things, like the fact that Toni was the only person to touch Addie intimately or that Toni had named her main character after Addie.

Talk about grand romantic gestures.

Toni stepped closer, not all the way into the surf but moving nearer so she could speak softly and still be heard over the sound of the ocean. "I'm not at all opposed to being touched, Addie, but . . . if you're not ready to do that . . ." Toni paused, like she was trying to find words. "I still take satisfaction in *giving* pleasure. I'm flexible. If all you want is friendship with no sex, I think that sounds good, too. Between my two jobs, I don't have a lot of time with friends. I work. I go to the gym. I mind my monstrous cat, Oscar Wilde, when he's not angry because I had to travel."

"What if I want both? The friendship part and the other part." Addie felt like her face was bright enough to be a beacon even though the sun had set. She stared at Toni and made herself use the actual words. "The friendship and the sex."

Toni smiled. "I'd like that." She looked around then, and in a teasing voice, added, "Not here, though. It's a bit more exposed than that garden."

"So what about a hotel room . . . ?"

"I do happen to have one of those tonight," Toni said. "If you want."

"It's been a *year* of thinking of you," Addie said. "One night. Then nothing for a year. I touched myself to one of your history lectures, Toni. So yes, I definitely want."

The look Toni gave her was half-craving, half-awe. She held out her hand. "Let's go."

Chapter 17

Toni

Addie had pulled her hand free when she slipped out of the car, and Toni had to restrain herself from grabbing it back. *I don't even do PDA. This is ridiculous.* But whether it was absurd or not didn't matter; what mattered was that they weren't touching, and after holding hands in the car and on the beach, Toni was not okay with all these minutes when she was *not* touching Addie. It was ridiculous to be aroused by holding a woman's hand, especially at her age, but there was no other explanation Toni could think of for feeling like this.

By the time Toni led Addie across the lobby, her panic was at war with her libido. Something about Addie made Toni keep confessing things she wouldn't typically share with anyone other than Emily. Talking was different in email. In writing, a kind of distance made it easier to control the narrative, to limit what she confessed and what she kept hidden, but being so open in person was different. That kind of trust was unheard-of for Toni, and she was trying to focus on the good parts, not the panic that kept rising up.

What if she betrays me?

What if she doesn't?

Traditionally, Toni had acquaintances, colleagues, and that one trusted person. Emily. Em was the only family she'd had since Aunt Patty died. She was the only one Toni fully trusted.

When did I start trusting Addie, too?

Toni swallowed her panic as she looked at Addie, who was smiling and keeping pace despite her shorter legs. *Those legs* . . . Toni wouldn't be surprised to discover that the jeans hugging Addie's legs were painted on somehow.

"Do you need me to slow down?" Toni asked.

Addie laughed in such a way that Toni felt like Addie understood her impatience. It was taking an irrational amount of self-control to keep her hands to herself as they crossed the lobby and stood at the elevator bank.

When the elevator doors opened, Toni gestured Addie into the elevator car. "After you."

"Or maybe before me this time," Addie murmured.

Toni shot her a heated look, and Addie gave her the same innocent expression she had over a year ago in the pub. They stood side by side silently as the elevator doors slid open and let several people out.

Addie reached out and slipped her hand under Toni's jacket. There was nothing inappropriate in the gesture. Toni still had on a shirt, but it felt like Addie's palm was searing through the thin fabric.

"Adelaine . . . ," Toni started.

The elevator stopped again. The remaining passengers got out. And Addie stepped in front of Toni, so they were suddenly face-to-face. She stared up at Toni and said, "I want you to be patient with me, tell me what you like, show me what you like. I am not a pillow princess."

Toni's mouth gaped open, but no words came out.

But Addie wasn't done. "I've thought about this *a lot* the last year, and I know what I like with my vibe, but I want to know how to please you, too. I want to learn more about what I like, too. I mean, I know I liked when you told me I was a good girl." Addie laughed self-consciously. "I liked it enough that when you were all brusque at the studio . . ."

When she left the rest of the sentence unspoken, Toni asked, "Enough that what?"

"That if I had to choose between the role and you, I'd have picked you." Addie shrugged.

"I'm not worth surrendering a promising career move," Toni said, sounding harsher than she meant to be.

"I wanted the role because it feels like it was meant for me, but I also wanted it because it was a chance to see you again," Addie said without any apparent artifice. "I want you. I want whatever this electricity is between us. I want our regular conversations throughout the week. There are other roles out there, but no one has ever made me break my no-sex rule until you, Toni. Just you. I want to be your friend, but I *want* you, too, and that's exciting in ways that I don't entirely understand. I thought I just wasn't . . . sexual until you kissed me."

"Oh." Toni's mind couldn't quite keep up with the things she was hearing. A small, very rational part of her knew all the reasons that taking Addie to her bed was a bad idea. *Keep it just friends,* her logic insisted. *No baby gays,* she told herself. *No tangling work with sex.*

Then Addie said, "Since that night, I imagine you saying I'm a good girl when I get myself off. Can we do that?"

And all of Toni's common sense died, left the building, ran fleeing from the wave of lust that surged up. She pulled Addie to her so abruptly that Addie let out a gasp, but she didn't object when Toni lowered her mouth to hers. Instead she parted her lips in invitation.

Toni was the one to whimper when Addie pulled back and said, "Toni . . ."

"What?"

Before Toni could pull her close again, Addie said, "We're here. Your floor."

The elevator doors slid open to reveal the pinched face of a couple who looked like they had caught a glimpse of the antichrist. Maybe it was the sight of anyone kissing, or maybe pockets of homophobia were alive and well, even here in liberal LA. Not as widespread as in some places, but Toni could draw a map of the hot spots for it in the country based on the number of places that dismissed her entire novel because the character was a lesbian. She tried to tell herself, *Some places simply don't love lesbians,* but if the details were reversed, if Toni were reading a book about a het woman, she wouldn't dismiss an entire novel for that one detail.

And while Toni didn't understand the appeal of hetero marriage, she didn't give the heterosexual couple in front of her that lemon-sucking look that the woman standing there was currently sporting.

"Sorry. Excuse us," Addie started to say.

Toni simply shouldered past them, shoving back the rage that threatened to sour her mood. The only downside of Toni looking masc was that no one ever thought Toni *might* be straight. Women who looked like Addie could pass for straight in a pinch, could escape danger or crude remarks. Not that Toni *wanted* to pass, but every so often Toni thought it would be nice to live in a world where she did not get disdainful looks because of how she was born.

"Ugh. It's like they've never considered having sex in an elevator," Addie said, loud enough for them to hear.

A laugh bubbled up, and Toni stopped mid-step and stared at Addie. Foul mood no longer on the horizon. This woman was magical. That was the only explanation.

"Maybe they haven't," Toni managed to say.

"Poor things!" Addie called out as the elevator doors slid closed. She glanced at Toni and added, "Number?"

"What? Number of . . ." Was she asking how often Toni had enjoyed sex in an elevator or—

"Your room number," Addie clarified with another of her giggles. Toni rattled it off.

"For what it's worth, I think about the chance of getting caught when you . . . when we . . ." Addie stammered a little this time, as if her courage had suddenly slipped away as Toni pulled out a room key. She sounded a little breathless when she said, "I can't believe I even did that, you know."

"Maybe we should make a list of things to try," Toni said lightly. She was pretty sure that the scandal of *actually* getting caught would be a big issue for both her careers, but there were plenty of other experiences to try. Addie might be more willing to see Toni if they had a list of things to experience together.

The thought of *not* seeing Addie made Toni's stomach clench.

Toni stopped in front of her room door. "I want to be perfectly clear, Addie. The role is still yours if you walk away. I am not going to sabotage or manipulate you or—"

"I *know*. You're not the casting director, either." Addie took the key card and opened the door. With a direct look and a smirk, she added, "And I still want the role if you don't want me here, but I really, *really* want to get naked with you tonight if that's okay." Addie turned the door handle and motioned, tossing Toni's own gesture back at her, and said, "After you."

The sound of the door closing behind them was unnaturally loud. The room was like a couple dozen others that Toni had slept in over the last year. Nice. Clean. Surprisingly spacious. It felt different somehow, just then, because Addie was in it.

Toni kicked off her shoes, and Addie did the same—except she perched on the edge of Toni's bed to do so.

Toni folded her hands into fists to keep from touching Addie, but her mind was flooding with the desire to kneel there in front of Addie and worship her.

"With two jobs and everything else going on . . . ," Toni started, not quite ready to elaborate more on the drama with her mom or the size of the debt she'd had to clear or the stress of the film deal and travel. Instead, she rushed the next words far more than she usually said anything: "I haven't touched anyone since you."

"*Any*one?"

"Yes."

"Not even yourself?" Addie asked.

"Well . . . yes, but no one *else*." Toni stared at her, thinking that as much as she'd enjoyed the innocent-ingenue persona, Addie was enticing just like this, too. Blunt speech really *was* a turn on for Toni.

"Would you want to give me a demonstration?" Addie asked, holding Toni's gaze even though she was blushing like a virgin at an orgy. She sighed when Toni didn't instantly answer. "I just want to know what you like, but if that's too much . . . Is it wrong to ask? I've thought about what you would like if I touched you. I researched some even."

Toni's mouth went dry, and her voice rasped as she said, "No."

Addie's expression fell.

And Toni quickly added, "No, it's not too much at all."

"Is there anything I can do to put you in the mood?" Addie flashed that wicked smile she revealed every so often, and Toni had the flicker of a thought that she might have met her match.

Toni shucked her shirt, eyes locked on Addie, who was still sitting on the edge of the bed. "That expression helps."

"I could strip you . . . ?" Addie offered in a voice that was not much more than a whisper. Her nerves weren't making her run, but they were still obvious.

Toni held her arms out and gestured at her remaining clothes. "You definitely could."

As Addie stood and stepped closer, Toni saw her hand was shaking. Addie licked her lips as she unfastened Toni's bra with surprisingly quick skill, but Toni could feel the slight tremble in her hands.

That's not why I want her quivering.

So Toni added, "Seeing your body would be *helpful,* too. Be a good girl, and get out of the jeans. . . ."

Addie unfastened her jeans and shoved them down.

Toni's eyes widened slightly when she saw that Addie was naked from the waist down.

"You said not to wear anything under them," Addie murmured, squirming slightly. "So I didn't . . . which is awkward, I guess, since you're the one still wearing jeans and I'm bottomless."

"You're irresistible," Toni pronounced as she unbuttoned her jeans and removed them and her underwear to stand naked in front of Addie.

This feels far more intimate than a hookup, Toni thought. *Is this a mistake?*

"And yet you're not kissing me or doing *anything*," Addie pouted, forcing Toni's attention away from her doubts and fears.

Toni brushed her lips over Addie's as she tangled a hand in Addie's hair, holding her fast although she was not going anywhere. Her free hand outlined the curvaceous line from hip to breast. But Addie pushed Toni away and took a step backward. "Show me."

At that, Toni walked over to the bed and pulled back the duvet and top sheet. She stretched out on the bed and bent one knee. Addie's gaze was laser-focused, and that alone would've been enough to make Toni's body ready and willing.

"I've imagined seeing you naked," Addie whispered.

"And?" Toni patted the mattress beside her.

"My imagination was not this good."

"Come closer. Make yourself comfortable, Addie." She stared at Addie, who was looking at Toni with raw need in her eyes. "Having you beside me would make this a lot more fun for both of us. . . ."

Chapter 18

Addie

At first Addie felt a little silly keeping her shirt on when she was naked from the waist down, but suddenly, Toni was naked and splayed out like an invitation, and every other thought vanished.

Naked woman was the most articulate thought Addie had. *Gorgeous naked woman.*

"You'll see better if you come over here," Toni said, adopting the same tone she had when she was lecturing, confident and instructional.

Addie crawled up the bed to sit beside Toni.

"Sometimes I like a slow, soft touch," Toni said in that professorial voice as her fingers stroked over her bare skin. Addie's gaze was fixed on that roaming hand as Toni stroked the space between her breasts and over her taut stomach.

"I see," Addie whispered.

"You can touch me, too, if you decide you want to," Toni said with a smile. "You don't have to if you're uncomfortable."

Addie nodded, not sure she could actually speak. She watched as Toni's hands moved to the juncture of her thighs. Slow, steady, mesmerizing. Addie *was* uncomfortable, but in more of a craving than in a bad time-to-run-away way.

"Sometimes . . ." Three of Toni's fingers disappeared inside her body. ". . . I want a fast, hard fuck. Do you ever feel like that, Addie? Or was that just that once in the garden that you were impatient?"

Addie reached out to trace the curve of Toni's hip, sighing when Toni arched toward her like an offer. "I don't know what I want yet," Addie whispered. "*You*. I want you."

"Sometimes," Toni said, breathier now. "I just want *everything*."

"Everything?" Addie couldn't look away from Toni's hands. "What's everything?"

"Depends on the woman." Toni chuckled. "Mouths, hands, toys. I liked being outside with you, knowing we could get caught. I liked seeing you holding on to that fence like I'd restrained you. I'd like to have you straddling my face."

"And right now?" Addie whispered.

"Anything you want. I want to watch you fall apart and know it's my doing." Toni's fingers were moving almost leisurely. "What do *you* want, Addie? Sometimes that's the very best thing—knowing how to please your lover, watching them come undone."

Addie reached out as if to stroke Toni but paused. She felt like all the years with no desire had combined in this moment. She might combust if she wasn't careful.

Toni helpfully used her free hand to part her slick lips, and Addie couldn't look away as Toni invited, "This doesn't have to be just a spectator sport, Addie. It *can* be, but if you want to know what I like, I can tell you by the way I moan or beg."

"Do you think I could make you beg?" Addie mused as she moved to half kneel, half sit in the wide-open frame of Toni's legs. Addie trailed her fingers over the defined lines of muscles, easing closer to where she wanted to touch. "If I put my hand . . ." She stared at Toni's thrusting fingers. "*There*."

Toni moved her hand away and took Addie's hand, directing her closer. The wetness on Toni's hand made Addie shiver with longing.

"Do you want to try?" Toni offered. "I bet you can make me beg and writhe under your touch, love."

Addie stared down at Toni's flushed cheeks and slid two fingers inside Toni. She slowly thrusted in and out. "Like this?"

"Yes." Toni spread her legs wider still, like an invitation to be touched. "Such a good girl. Do you like looking, love?"

Addie nodded, unable to tear her gaze away. "And this . . . I like this. Feeling you tense around me."

"Mmmm. Me too. Another finger, Addie."

Addie swallowed a small noise as she added a third finger. She felt Toni's inner walls clench tightly around her suddenly. Addie looked up, mesmerized by Toni's flushed cheeks and lust-heavy eyes.

I did that, Addie marveled. It was a heady thought.

"Are you wet, too, love?" Toni asked.

"Yes."

"That's how I felt touching you in Scotland. Touching you made my body drip with need." Toni suddenly clasped Addie's hip with one damp hand as Addie sped up.

Addie reached out with her free hand to do what Toni had done to her in the garden—circling, rubbing, and pinching Toni's clit. She had wanted to make Toni moan and tremble for a year, imagined it over and over, but seeing Toni rise to meet her touch made even Addie's best fantasies seem mild.

Could I orgasm just from touching her? The pulse between her thighs suggested that she might.

Toni hissed. "What a quick study you are."

Addie paused. "Too much? Was that—"

"Wonderful, Addie. You're wonderful." Toni arched, pressing Addie's fingers deeper inside her in the process. "Faster . . . there's a good girl. Just . . . like . . . that."

She was gorgeous; a thin sheen of sweat seemed like it outlined the ridiculous taut stomach and small but firm breasts. Toni's hips were moving as she rode Addie's hand, and when Toni fell apart under Addie's touch, Addie felt a rush of power like nothing she had ever experienced.

I did that.

She looked down at the satiated look on Toni's face for just a moment as she slid her fingers out of Toni's grasping, pulsing warmth.

For a moment, she left her other hand where it was, pressed against Toni's clit.

The relaxed, open expression on Toni's face was the same expression she'd had briefly when lecturing sometimes, as if everything was right in her world. Not hungry or cautious, not tense or reserved. Open, raw, and completely stunning because of it.

Then Toni looked like she was starting to rebuild a wall. She shifted so Addie was no longer touching her and nudged Addie's knees apart. "Would you like me to touch you or put my mouth—"

"Touch," Addie said quickly. The thought of the *other thing* was daunting still. "Touch this time. I'm not ready for . . . Maybe if we do this again and—"

"That's okay," Toni interrupted as she pushed Addie gently, so she was half kneeling. "There aren't rules."

"I don't want to disappoint you," Addie confessed.

"You aren't. Not at all. Can you stay like this?" Toni asked, staring up at her. "Rise up a little more and part these lovely legs for me?"

Addie adjusted, feeling a little self-conscious about squatting on the bed in front of Toni.

Then Toni sat up and asked, "Can I take this off, love?"

"If you want . . . ," Addie started, but then Toni was kissing her. Her hands were under Addie's shirt, and the thin fabric felt like an obstacle.

Addie tugged her blouse off, and in doing so realized that they were chest to chest. Her brain blanked out slightly at the fact that she had never been bare-chested against another woman.

"Up," Toni ordered. Her hair was mussed, and her lips were kiss-swollen, and Addie was sure she'd never seen anyone more lovely. "On your knees, love."

When Addie moved onto her knees instead of sitting back on her haunches, her breasts were in Toni's face. By the time Toni had her mouth on Addie's breasts and her hand between Addie's thighs, Addie realized why Toni wanted her in this position.

Addie trembled from head to toe from the combined feel of Toni's mouth on her nipples and her hand between Addie's thighs.

Her body was already wet and ready, and unlike the night in the garden, Addie was fairly sure this wouldn't last very long at all. She pushed back her disappointment and within moments, Addie was clutching at Toni and holding on to her for support as her orgasm rolled over her. The noises she made were feral-sounding, and even as she felt herself shudder, she still *wanted*.

But a few minutes later, Toni slid out of bed. "Do you need water or anything?"

Addie watched Toni seemingly reassemble her walls, as if she had to shift into a more reserved version of herself and create distance now. Toni Darbyshire was clearly not at ease with vulnerability, even now after she'd fallen apart under Addie's hands and driven Addie to a shaking mess, even as the room smelled of sweat and sex.

Toni pulled a sheet up over Addie. "It's chilly in here. I can adjust the temp. . . ."

That won't do. If Toni was uncomfortable, she was going to come up with a reason to send Addie away. *I want to be here, with her, in all the ways I can.*

Addie flopped back on the bed, staring at Toni as she returned. "Sooooo . . . you wrote a book after we met. And there's a sequel soon?"

Toni glanced at her and smiled in what looked like relief as they resumed chatting as they had been all night. "In theory. *The Widow's Curse* is what I'm working on between lesson-planning and grading and promo for the first one. I wrote the first book before I met you actually. I sent it to Em that night, and I decided that if it sold, I'd name the protagonist after you."

"Not going to lie, I squealed when I saw it." Addie stretched and stared up at Toni, whose mask of indifference slipped as she watched Addie's bare leg emerge from the sheets. "It felt like that night meant something to you, too."

Toni nodded. It wasn't much of an admission, but it wasn't a refutation either. The truth was that Addie was very used to being the person who wore every emotion on her sleeve, but she wanted to point out that she noticed, that she already knew she wasn't alone in feeling things.

Life was short, so why waste time on hiding?

Instead of replying, Toni walked over to the hotel minibar and uncovered a highball glass. "Drink or . . . ?"

"Water first." Addie sat up and patted the bed. "Am I allowed a drink now that I'm already here in *your* bed?"

Addie accepted the glass of water Toni held out.

"Cheeky thing. Yes, but hydrate first." Toni leaned down and dropped a quick kiss on Addie's mouth.

"You follow a lot of rules, don't you?" Addie asked quietly.

"My father was an alcoholic." Toni held Addie's gaze. "I typically don't have more than two drinks on any day, and *most* days, I don't drink at all."

"I wasn't judging you." Addie took a long drink of water before she said, "So . . . new topic. Old topic, maybe? Your book is amazing. I mean, I'd still be here if not because I think you're smart and incredibly sexy, but . . . I read it several times already—and not just because you named her after me or because of the show."

"It's a good name," Toni deflected.

"It's a really good *book,* and I bet a lot of people loved it. I just felt like I was there. In the 1800s, trying to be me but knowing that I couldn't have it all if I was me. You really made me think about what it was like to be someone like us back then. I wanted *that* Addie to find love, not just avoid marriage but fall in love."

"You and a lot of readers." Toni shook her head. "I do, too, but I think it was more important that she avoid being trapped in a marriage where she had to let a man paw at her because society lied and claimed women have no sex drive. I mean, we weren't even *allowed* to marry other women, and what with the lack of financial rights and legal rights and—"

"I get that," Addie agreed, leaning forward in excitement. "But maybe in *The Widow's Curse,* you can give her hope. Women *did* have relationships. There was Anne Lister, of course."

Toni sighed. "I know, and it would give me something to write about, at least. I mean, I have a mystery, but . . . it's not writing itself like the first one did."

"Pressure." Addie nodded and continued, "I get that. Imagine trying to pull off the role of the character written by the only person you ever—"

"The only one, huh? The only person ever? Not just the only woman?" Toni's brief moment of insecurity over her books was replaced by a look that was far from insecure. History and sex, those were clearly topics Addie could use to chase away Toni's anxiety.

"Two nights in my *entire* life," Addie stressed. "Both with you. Hey, for all I know, it could be like those poor Victorians not knowing for sure if my lover is even good at sex. Maybe you're simply mediocre—"

"Not likely." Toni's husky laugh felt like music.

"How would I know? Maybe I was simply aroused because it had been more than a year since anyone touched me," Addie teased.

"So you need more proof then?"

"That seems like a sound plan." Addie barely had the words out before she muffled her own little squeal of joy as Toni threaded her hand through Addie's hair and kissed her breathless. Toni wasn't the only person to ever *kiss* her, but she was the first to make Addie feel like a simple kiss could melt her bones. Addie felt her body pulse with hunger, as if knowing what could follow had made her crave Toni more.

When Toni pulled back, she asked, "Shall I demonstrate again, Adelaine?"

"Yes, please," Addie whispered. This was it. Everything Addie had wanted. And they were going to see each other regularly at events for the show based on Toni's book. Things were closer to perfect than Addie could have dreamed.

Get the job.

Get the woman.

Done and done.

Nothing was going to go wrong, not now that Toni was in her life.

Chapter 19
Toni

Toni was barely awake when she crawled out of bed the next morning. That was the only excuse she had for looking back at Addie like she was some sort of sleeping princess come to change the ogre's mood. Whatever was happening here wasn't just sex, which was concerning Toni more than a little. She felt . . . safe with Addie. They'd gone to dinner and a walk on the beach, of all things, and as dawn threatened, reality hit hard. Toni was wrestling with how she felt about it, about Addie, about whatever the hell this was.

She's fucking incredible.

She deserves better than me.

If not for the sex, it would be fine. They'd be at the edge of a great friendship. If not for the talking, it would be fine. They'd be at the edge of an excellent hookup without strings. Combining the two felt dangerous.

I could actually fall for her.

Except Toni didn't do relationships. *I told her that, and she still stayed.* Giving that much power to another person was exactly why her mother was miserable and had been for decades. It was why Toni had to find a way to provide for Lilian Darbyshire in her onset of memory loss and widowhood. And unlike her mother, Toni would have no children to save her if she trusted someone.

Not that I'd ask that of a child if I did have one!

Real relationships simply weren't on the table. Ever. They couldn't be. Toni wasn't designed for them, and she had all the proof in the world that love was a lie.

Friends with benefits. That's all this is.

Still, before she could stop herself, Toni leaned down and kissed Addie, who sleepily murmured, "Not saying no, Professor. Just let me sleep bit more first."

Toni pressed her lips tightly together to stop a laugh from escaping. *How I wish* . . . But stock signings and midday flights were all that Toni had on her schedule today.

"Next time, love." Toni glanced at the bedside clock. She was already running late, and she hadn't showered out of fear of waking Addie. That could be awkward, and Toni would rather skip that. This was the problem with the morning after: it was either awkward or Toni had to slip away like a thief who had already stolen the finest jewels.

The idea of seeing Addie again added complications, but they had jokingly—or not?—discussed a few intimate things to try, and Toni was all for playing teacher to the outspoken gorgeous actor currently curled up in her hotel bed. If not Toni, Addie would find someone else to satisfy her recently awakened curiosity, and the thought of *that* made Toni feel like worms were crawling through her belly.

It was just protectiveness, right?

I have no right to be possessive.

Toni brushed the strands of Addie's hair away from her face and reconsidered waking her to say goodbye. That was absurd, though. They had already been becoming friends. Now they were just friends who had amazingly satisfying sex and—

Emily texted again. So far she had texted no less than four times.

Toni discarded the thought of waking Addie and scrawled a note: *You're amazing. Thank you for everything.*

Then she shoved her last-minute items into her carry-on and headed to the door. When she woke with Addie snuggled into her, Toni had legitimately considered blowing off the signings, rescheduling the flight, and taking an extra day in LA.

Completely too far, she told herself as she rolled her bag to the elevator. One night of sex wasn't reason enough to change her routine. Weekends were author time, and weekdays were teaching time. It was how Toni kept things in order.

Where does Addie fit in?

Toni caught a glimpse of herself in the mirrored elevator walls and realized that it was for the best that she had a friend with the makeup skills she lacked. The last thing she wanted was social media photos where she looked even more exhausted than usual.

As Toni stepped into the hotel lobby, the clickety-clack of Emily's shoes sounded like a reprimand. Emily came toward her with a travel cup of coffee in an outstretched hand.

"It's cool enough to drink now," Emily said. "Possibly cold, in fact."

Toni took a long sip, swallowed, and glanced at her best friend as Emily took her carry-on from her.

Emily crinkled her face up. "Sweetie, we need to pause in the gift shop."

"Why?" Toni followed her, sipping her coffee like it was nectar of the gods.

"You smell like sex."

"I washed up," Toni sputtered.

Emily muffled a laugh at Toni's uncharacteristic awkwardness. "I'm glad for you, but I thought maybe we should buy a nice cologne . . . because I'm guessing you don't want to walk into the bookstore smelling like—"

"Fine!" Toni marched into the store, feeling like a child caught breaking rules.

After a few minutes, Emily pointed inside a case in the store. "Let's try that one."

The woman at the display case held it out, and Toni dutifully sniffed.

"Do we like this scent?" Emily asked. "Or at least tolerate it?"

"Fine."

Emily handed over a credit card. "And flowers for room—"

"What?" Toni shook her head. "I don't send flowers, Em."

Emily signed the credit card slip, spritzed the air around Toni's hair and neck lightly, and walked out. Toni trailed after her.

"Sweetie, I love you. You know that," Emily began, her voice dropping into the tone she adopted when cajoling Toni into an interview or other event she knew Toni didn't want to do. "And I'm pretty sure you are at least slightly aware that women . . . *appreciate* your attention."

"Addie did." Toni shrugged. "She just wants a friend and a bit of time with someone with experience, and I'm not exactly able to bed-hop these days. It's just a situationship, Em. We like each other. It's not *dating*." Toni sighed loudly at the blatant look of doubt on her best friend's face. "We're not U-Hauling like every joke about moving in together on the second date."

"I'm not saying you should move in with her on the second date, but if you're a thing—"

"We're not a thing," Toni interjected firmly. "Just because I plan to see her again doesn't mean I'm dating her. We're becoming closer friends."

"Friends," Emily echoed.

"Yep. We email. Now we'll be sometimes naked, but we're just friends," Toni said firmly. No one, even her best friend in the world, needed to know that Toni could develop feelings for Addie if she slowed down long enough.

Not going to happen.

Just to be sure of it, Toni decided she'd swing by the care facility to see her mother when she arrived back in DC—nothing like a careen through whatever year her mom thought it was to remind her that relationships were a terrible plan.

Toni glanced at Emily. "I left her a note. We're cool."

She walked away, rolling her bag behind her until she was outside at the waiting car. Great sex and relaxing conversation was a fine basis for a friendship. Goodness knew that Toni had a few friends who fell in and out of her bed over the years. Surely, one of them was still available.

Maybe that's what I need, see if Leigh is still around. Or Faith.

But even as she thought it, her stomach turned. She opened her own door and got in the car. She didn't need to look up an old friend. She had a new friend—one who was a lot of fun in bed and listened when Toni talked. One who shifted like a chameleon on a stage.

Toni's mind drifted to the second book, and she pulled up a notes app on her phone and started writing down ideas about giving fictional Addie a small romance. That, she could do. She couldn't give one to the real-life Addie, though.

"Great sex and a muse, too?" Emily teased as she climbed into the car.

Toni flipped her agent off and kept writing. This was the most she'd written in weeks. She'd tried—lord, how she'd tried—but her words were as unwilling as her body when she tried exercising the few times she'd been hungover. Technically, Toni supposed the result was still exercise, but it sure as hell wasn't the best exercise.

Today, though, she wrote the whole way to the bookstore before looking up when the car stopped in an underground garage.

"She's good for you," Emily said. "I'm sending her flowers because of that. If nothing else, either getting laid or a relaxing dinner did you the remarkable favor of unsticking your words. I'm sending the bouquet, not you."

Toni shot Emily a glare. "Fine. Just don't say anything sappy."

"'Thanks for the orgasms.'" Emily made air quotes. "Or maybe, 'My agent sends thanks for improving my mood and helping with my deadline.' Too much?"

The driver coughed in what sounded a lot like a smothered laugh as he got out of the car to open Toni's door. She was already out the door and scowling back at Emily.

"I like her," Toni said bluntly. "She's becoming a good friend. Don't write anything that suggests otherwise on the card. Nothing

TONI AND ADDIE GO VIRAL   145

sappy. Nothing dismissive. Don't sign them from me or you. Just . . . whatever."

"You could write something," Emily said. "You are the writer here, after all."

"No. I don't send women flowers."

Then Toni strode off toward the bookstore without waiting for Emily. Toni wasn't about to admit that sending flowers sounded nice—or that she could picture Addie's sound of delight. She'd never sent flowers or even considered doing that. It smacked of relationships. Toni looked over when Emily's telltale clickety-clack heels caught up with her.

"No fucking roses, either. That's the wrong message." Toni ignored the quirk of a repressed smile on Emily's lips. "I mean it. I don't want to hurt her feelings by sending her the wrong message."

"And what message would that be?"

Toni jerked open the store's door and muttered, "That I'm capable of anything other than friendship. You know me, Em. I'm not that sort of woman, and Addie's pretty amazing. She deserves someone wonderful."

And I'm not able to be the kind of person she needs, Toni added silently.

Chapter 20

Addie

When Addie woke up alone with housekeeping knocking at the door, she pulled on the hotel robe and looked around, wondering if Toni was in the lobby or . . . she saw the space where Toni's suitcase had been. No. She'd left.

While I was sleeping.

While the housekeeper came into the room, Addie checked her phone for a text or message. All Toni had left was a note with as much emotional resonance as a grocery receipt: *You're amazing. Thank you for everything.*

Fine, the "amazing" bit was nice.

Addie reread it, as if she'd find more hidden in the words on the scrap of paper. There were none. Nothing on the back. No signature with at least an "XO" or "fondly" or heart. *Nothing.* For a woman whose last grand romantic gesture was naming a character after her, Addie expected more.

Was I wrong about her? About what happened?

Addie felt dirty, especially with the housekeeper giving her a side-eye as she started to empty the trash bin in the room. Awkwardly, Addie wrapped a sheet around herself like a toga.

No luggage.

No anything but Addie's poorly folded clothes and a note.

"Just one minute," Addie said, hastily scooping up her clothes and the note before heading to the bathroom. "I overslept."

No breakfast together. No time for me to grab a shower. No goodbye other than a note.

Toni had left her naked in a room that smelled of sex.

Addie wiped away tears as she dressed, splashed water on her face, and left the room. Maybe Toni hadn't meant to make her feel so sad and rejected, but that didn't change the fact that Addie felt exactly that way. She was as discarded as the empty liquor bottles from the minibar and the used towels on the bathroom sink.

Was that what this was?

I thought we were friends, at least, but friends don't act like this.

Addie kept her chin up as she saw the couple from the night before in the lobby, and she kept her shoulders squared as she walked out of the lobby. So what if she had no baggage? Lots of guests came and went while at hotels. No one knew that she was leaving because her lover left without so much as a goodbye kiss or a promise to see her later.

Tears threatened to fall again, but Addie shoved them down deep to wherever the rest of the rejections went when Addie ignored them. *Maybe I'm just tired.*

Addie realized she might be overreacting. She *was* exhausted. Quickly, she texted, "Safe flight!"

She waited, watching the little dots dance and vanish, dance and vanish. Finally, Toni replied—with a thumbs-up.

Addie's tears fell as she waited for her rideshare driver. By the time the driver pulled up, Addie was full out sobbing and gasping. The man twisted to look back at her and said, "There's lots of fish in the sea. Lots of other roles. Lots of whatever it is you just lost. Don't let the bastards get you down."

She hiccupped in between sobs. "I got the role."

"Well, then, congratulations!" He pulled into traffic. "My grandson gets that way every Christmas and birthday, so much anticipation that no matter if it's exactly what he wanted, he cries until he pukes. Don't you be puking in my car, though."

I thought I got the girl, too.

"I won't." Addie swatted at the rest of her tears, staring at her phone, wondering whether or not she ought to try to say something else. Then in a fit of impulsivity, she deleted Toni's number and turned on an autoresponder on her email. She couldn't text Toni without her number, and Adelaine Stewart wasn't going to make a fool of herself chasing a woman who left without a word or kiss goodbye.

The ball's in your court, Toni, she thought. *If you want me, you know where I am.*

Of course, last time, a full year passed during which Toni hid her name, her career, and even where exactly she lived. They only crossed paths in person because Toni wrote a book and Addie auditioned to play her namesake. Would Toni have invited her to meet up eventually? Had Addie forced things? It hadn't felt that way last night, but maybe Toni was just skilled at hiding her real feelings.

She admitted that she was there that night in Scotland to pick up a woman. That was probably her plan for LA, too. *Just because she said she hadn't been with anyone since then doesn't make it true.*

Addie thought back over every detail, wishing briefly she'd screenshotted their text conversation before deleting Toni's number. Had she misread the situation? Thrown herself at Toni? Was Toni only in bed with her because Addie was conveniently there?

In the morning light, everything looked different. Toni hadn't pursued her. Addie had basically propositioned Toni twice, and Toni had simply accepted what Addie had offered up. *People tell you who they are, and Toni said she was a fan of casual sex. So she accepted. It didn't mean anything other than she liked the way I look.*

Addie was under no illusion that she was unattractive. A woman didn't grow up in LA, of all places, and think she was ugly if she planned to pursue the stage or screen.

With a muffled sob, Addie crumpled up the note, but she still shoved it into her pocket. Even now, she was saving the note Toni left.

Prove me wrong, Addie prayed. *Email. Call. Say something.*

When an enormous bouquet arrived at the apartment the next day, Addie was relieved. She would have to smush the blossoms to wrap her arms around it. For a brief moment, Addie thought she must have overreacted to Toni leaving silently.

Eric buried his face in the blossoms. Not a boring but delicious-smelling rose in sight. Orchids, lilies, and several things Addie couldn't identify populated the enormous bouquet. It was beautiful but not particularly fragrant. "Elegant" was probably the best description—other than "expensive."

Before Eric could grab the tiny white envelope out of the blossoms, Addie plucked the envelope out and opened it. She already knew who had sent it, and she had a surge of hope that there was something *real* in it until she read the note.

It only said THANKS! SEE YOU SOON! TONI

Addie crumpled it up and tossed it at the wall. "If I hadn't deleted her number, I'd say something rude to her right now. *Grrrr.*"

Her cousin walked over and picked up the note. Silently, he read it. "'Thanks'?"

Addie shrugged, but tears welled up.

"Oh, honey." Eric was there, arms around her. "What happened? Did she hurt you? Did you . . ."

"We had sex," Addie blurted out, "And in Scotland we . . . she . . . with her hand."

Eric nodded. "She got you off. Named the character after you. Took you to dinner. Emailed you constantly. And then you fucked?"

"Sort of," Addie hedged.

"You either fucked or didn't, Ads." Eric went over to the sofa and patted the seat. "Come on, cuz."

"We did *that,* but it didn't feel, like . . . just *fucking,*" Addie said, wincing at using that word to describe the night. She flopped down next to him.

"So *sex,* not fucking, and then she vanished and sent that gorgeous bouquet," Eric added.

"Yes, but did you see the note?" Addie let out another muffled scream, and then she told him all about waking up alone and then the text she sent with only a thumbs-up as a reply. And she finished with, "I thought I meant something to her, not just . . . sex. She *thanked* me."

Eric shook his head. "This is what we all went through in high school. 'Did she like me?' 'Was it just sex?' 'Is she actually into me but *also* a dumbass who says stupid things?' You know, you could call and talk to her."

"Can't."

"Because?"

"I sort of deletedhernumber," Addie said so quickly it sounded like one garbled word. She looked over at Eric. "You know my enthusiasm sort of . . ." Addie shrugged.

"Terrifies people who don't understand you," Eric finished with a sigh. "So you deleted her number to keep from texting. Well, she's a fool if she lets you go, Ads."

Addie shrugged. "I'll see her sometime in the next few months. There's this whole event at a historical house with photos and signings, and I was going to show up and wow her if I got the role. Now, it's going to be awkward. I just hoped . . ."

"That she'd call?"

"Or email something," Addie muttered. "Not send a note that could go just as easily to her grandmother or her editor or the showrunner or . . . *anyone.*"

"I can't see how seeing her would work anyhow for anything other than hookups. Doesn't she live in Ohio or something?" Eric shuddered.

"DC, but . . . she writes. Couldn't she move *anywhere*?" Addie thought about it. Sure, Toni had a teaching job, too, but wouldn't she quit that with the book's success? Addie couldn't move just anywhere because of her career, but Toni could.

I'm being foolish. Toni wasn't even sending an actual message or making plans, so why would she *move* across the country for Addie? The whole thing was pointless.

"I've let myself think this is some big romance, but maybe I was just . . . convenient?" Addie whispered.

"Then she's the one losing out," Eric said.

"I feel like I lost." Addie swiped at another stray tear, and Eric pulled her close.

For several moments, they sat there quietly. Then Eric asked, "Are you still doing the show? If you want to hurt her, quit. They'll cast someone less fabulous and—"

"Are you serious? I love the show, the character, the book." Addie glared at Eric. "I'm not going to quit just because the author left without a word and sends impersonal notes that my dentist could send me."

"Ads . . ."

Addie stood up, hands on hips, glaring at her best friend. "Get dressed. I still deserve a celebration dinner with you. This is a great role, and I'm going to kill it."

"You are, cuz. I know it, and she'll see the light," Eric said, sounding remarkably serious, and then he grinned. "How could anyone not love my cousin? We share a lot of DNA, and *I* am fabulous. Ergo, you are *fantabulous.*"

Chapter 21
Toni

Toni was still feeling self-conscious when she got off the plane at Dulles. The signings went great. The show would be fabulous—especially with Addie in the lead. She should be happy.

"Are you sure you don't mind a houseguest?" Emily asked. "I can grab a hotel."

"I have an empty guest room because of you, Em." Toni glared at her. "If not for whatever magic you pulled on the publisher, I'd still be thinking I ought to rent it out, so it's pretty much yours any time you want to visit."

"Does that mean you'll do me a favor?" Emily cajoled.

Toni strode toward the baggage carousel. It seemed silly to check a tiny bag, but Emily had been on the road longer and had checked a bag, so Toni checked hers, too. "Will I hate it?"

"Probably," Emily chirped in her usual cheery way.

"Fine." She waited as they walked the rest of the way to the baggage. She waited as Emily hummed at her side. Finally Toni grumbled, "Are you going to tell me what fresh hell you have planned?"

"I want to go with you to see Lil," Emily said, as if there was any joy in going to see Toni's mercurial mother.

Toni gawped at her for a long moment, until Emily pointed and said, "That's my bag. Would you grab it?"

Mutely, Toni moved through the crowd. Why in the name of

everything remotely reasonable did people crowd up to the carousel like they were starving ducks hoping for a handout? She grabbed the glossy red bag, which weighed just this side of too much. Of course, Toni's perfectly bland black carry-on sized bag was nowhere in sight, so she rolled Emily's to her.

"Why?"

Emily shrugged. "I want to check on her. She's the reason you even shared your *career-changing* book with me. If not for her, I'd still be looking for that book that would put me on the map . . . because *someone* hadn't even told me she wrote a book."

Toni walked away to grab her bag.

When she came back to join Emily, who had dropped her own purse-like bag on top of the cherry red suitcase, Toni said, "I'll need a drink after. I know I don't usually drink more than one day in a week, but . . ."

"You are not an alcoholic if you have a drink twice in a week," Emily said for what was easily the hundredth time in their friendship. She'd been there when Toni wrote out her list of rules way back in their teen years, so she was well aware of the motivations behind each and every one of them.

They were silent as they walked to the parking lot, where Toni had stashed her car for the weekend. She could have had car service, but sometimes Toni just wanted the solace of her own car, her own company, after a weekend of peopling.

"How far away did you park?" Emily grumbled, toting her bright red bag like it weighed more than it did.

"Seriously?" Toni took Emily's bag and glanced at Emily's feet. "If you had the sense to travel in reasonable shoes . . ."

"Tennis shoes and black skirts?" Emily made a pained expression. "Pass."

"You could wear trousers. Jeans. Hell, you could wear leggings or joggers," Toni continued, as if she wasn't aware that Emily had a look that was akin to how she had looked the one time she'd stepped in something gross at the park.

"You are a monster," Emily said with an exaggerated shudder. "These legs take too much work to look this good. I'm not going to cover them with *joggers.*"

They looked at each other and laughed. Here with no witnesses, no work, no anything, they easily fell back into the silliness that got them through their teen years. The fact that Emily was in New York—a short train ride away—was part of why Toni had taken the job in the Washington, DC area instead of another more prestigious position. Emily was and would always be Toni's family of the heart, and the Acela trip between Manhattan and the District was short enough that Vienna College won.

By the time they reached Toni's car, Emily was a little wide-eyed. "Well, *that's* not the car I was expecting."

"It's ridiculous, isn't it?" Toni shoved their bags in the back of her brand-new bright red Jeep Wrangler. "I have *payments.* I was going to buy it outright, but . . . I financed it. I just couldn't write a check that big."

Emily put a hand on Toni's shoulder. "Sweetie, it's your money. You don't owe anyone an explanation."

"I just said I was going to save it all, but my old Ford had *so* many miles, and after it broke down last year, I started thinking about it. Then it had transmission issues a few months ago and . . . it cost less up-front to buy this than fix that and the suspension, and—"

"It's very you." Emily opened the passenger door. "Plus, it matches my luggage!"

Toni went around to her side. She ran a hand along the door quickly before opening it and climbing inside. "Fully manual."

"Says the woman with control issues," Emily replied, sotto voce.

"Not with Addie," Toni confessed in the same quiet voice. She finally admitted the truth she'd been struggling with all day. "I could fall for her, Em."

"Would that be so awful?" Emily asked.

But Toni put the Jeep in gear and headed out of the lot, pointedly not answering. There were two answers—yes, because Addie deserved someone who wanted a relationship, and yes, because just because it felt amazing to let down her walls for a night didn't mean it would always be that way.

"Ask me after we visit Lil," Toni finally said.

The memory care home was outside the city in Reston, but much like in New York, "outside the city" didn't actually mean light traffic. Toni navigated onto the 28, and then onto I-66 westbound. It was on the late side for visiting, what with the time change from LA to DC, but that only meant that Lil would be in her room.

"She still stays up late, as if he'll be home." Toni stared out the window at traffic rather than glance at Emily. She shifted through each gear like the joy of driving the Jeep could help her escape her own panic and anger. "Even after everything, she loves the bastard."

"Not all relationships are like theirs," Emily said for what was likely the five hundredth time. "My parents are still stupidly in love."

Toni slid into a parking spot a few minutes later. The home was close enough to the airport that this was far from the first time she'd made this pit stop. "I warn you: she may not know us. She may think I'm Aunt Patty. She may think we're friends of his come to warn her about him . . . or get money out of her for his debts."

"I am familiar with her health," Emily said gently.

A part of Toni hated anyone seeing her mom like this. She and Lilian had a contentious relationship at the best of times, but that didn't stop Toni from feeling protective. *This is Em, though.* They walked to the front desk and checked in at the visitor log. The woman at the desk, Doris, recognized Toni.

"Did you bring your girlfriend then?" she asked in a friendly voice.

"I'm afraid not. Childhood friend of the family," Toni said. "She wants to visit Lil."

"Lilian is in a mood tonight," the receptionist said. "Threatened one of the nurses for coming around after her husband."

"Perhaps we should switch that one out? Young and pretty was always his type." Toni forced a smile. "Lord only knows why my mother forgave the man so often."

"Well, won't that be an awkward thing to phrase? 'Only old bats on shift with Lil,'" she said with a chortle. "Thank goodness I'm not the one to tell them! I'll mention it to the head gal, and she'll have to find a more delicate phrasing than I would."

She waved them through the locked doors that kept the memory care patients from roaming. The hard reality was that the residents couldn't be trusted not to wander off into danger. That was one of the main reasons that memory care patients couldn't live in the regular senior-living center—and why Lilian couldn't live with Toni. Half the time, Lil didn't know what year it was, so trusting that she wouldn't leave and end up in danger was impossible.

They checked in again with a nurse at a desk on the other side of the door. If not for all the precautions, it might look like a cheerful dormitory. Toni tried to see it as Em would, as she had the first time she toured it. There was a dining hall, living room, a library, a game room, another sitting room, and then there were tiny dorm-style bedrooms.

"It's very nice," Emily said softly at her side.

"I wanted her to be happy . . . well, as happy as she can be," Toni explained, feeling self-conscious over all of it. She shouldn't, not with Em, but she was feeling emotional today.

Of all the facilities Toni toured, this felt the most cheerful—and the least like a prison.

"Lil's in the dining room," the nurse said. "She refuses to eat until her husband calls."

"I'll handle it." Toni took a steadying breath and walked into the room. Her mother sat at a table alone. Tonight was not the best of nights, but at least Lil was semiaware.

"Patty!" She stood to greet Toni, pulling Toni into a hug. Lil's cheeks were tear-damp as she said, "His hussy showed up here. I'm sorry I called you again, but I can't let Antonia see me like this. You know how sensitive that girl is."

Toni winced as her mother pulled back, noticed Emily, and instantly started to fuss with her hair. "Oh, look at me. I'm all in a state, and you bring your girlfriend around. What must you think of me?"

"I think you look lovely, Mrs. Darbyshire, absolutely lovely." Emily accepted the hand Lil extended and shook it. "Patty says so many great things about you."

Toni pulled a chair out for Emily. "Em."

Lil frowned. "Antonia has a little friend with that same name. Cute little thing. Moved in a few blocks away."

"Is that so?" Emily slid into the seat. "Is Antonia your daughter?"

Lilian laughed. "Oh, I'm sure you hear about her all the time from Patty. I swear, Patty is like a second mother to her. The only way people like you can have a child, I suppose."

Toni closed her eyes, counted to five, and then changed the subject. "How was dinner, Lil?"

"Oh, you know I don't hardly eat when I'm worrying over what that man's up to!" Lil laughed.

"I talked to him. He said he was going to stop and buy you flowers before he got here," Toni said. "Why don't we have a bite to eat before he gets here?"

Toni looked over her shoulder, and the staff brought in three plates. There had been several times they'd had to call her here just to get Lil to eat. She was fine mornings and lunch, but dinner could be an ordeal.

"Flowers? Was he betting on the ponies again?" Lil's eyes darkened. "I swear—"

"No. I had a little extra, so I gave it to him," Toni lied, thinking back to all the times she'd seen her aunt pass money to her mother or father over the years. As a kid, she didn't understand it. Patty had showed up with groceries or new shoes for Toni; she'd paid fees so Toni could join this or that sport.

"You're good to us, Patty." Lil smiled. "I swear if God had made me so I liked the ladies, I'd have fallen for you." She laughed like it was an old joke between them, and Toni's heart twinged. Her mother had never really been happy, not for long, not with her husband. Hell, she wasn't happy as a mother either. The only blessing was that her illness seemed to predispose her to thinking she lived in the years when she was happier than not.

They settled into the meal, and then Lil took her bedtime medicine and went off to her room, kissing both "Patty" and Emily on the cheek before walking away with a nurse. Toni felt like her heart was heavier than she could explain. She wanted to be a better person than her father, to never leave anyone feeling the way Lil felt for so much of her life.

What if I'm too much like him?

"She's lucky to have you," Emily said as they left, breaking the silence that had fallen while Toni was lost in her thoughts.

Toni looked over at Emily. "Why did you want to see Lil?"

Emily walked in silence for several moments. "I wanted to be there for you. You mentioned seeing her after a few of your events, and I worry about you."

"Me?"

"Yes, you." Emily gave her a scowl. "Do you not realize that I care about my dearest friend in the world? Or that my friend had a roller coaster of a year?"

Toni scoffed and opened the building door, waving goodbye to the attendant at the front door as she did. Once they were outside, she hip-checked Emily gently. "I don't need you to babysit me."

"Tough. I'm going to be here, and just so you know, I expect you to be here for me, too." Emily rolled her eyes. "I'm not *babysitting* you. I'm being your friend. It's like the adult version of handing you a pad in algebra class."

"That was you," Toni reminded her.

"Exactly, my cycle was a mess, and you had the pad. If not, those new jeans would've looked like they belonged to Carrie." Emily made a face. "Friendship is friendship whether it's being here when

TONI AND ADDIE GO VIRAL   159

you are dealing with Lil or listening to me whine about the fact that I have miserable taste in men *and* women."

Toni shot her an exasperated look. "Fine."

"I'm always going to be here," Emily said. "All the years. Quiet or roller coaster."

"Same." Toni pointed. "Stop being all sappy, and get in the Jeep . . . which I was able to buy because of this roller coaster of a year."

"Good stress is still stress," Emily said lightly. "And you are the loneliest person I know. Maybe if you let someone in, maybe Addie—"

"Seriously? *That*, Em"—Toni pointed back at the building where her mother was—"*that* is what a relationship does to a person. I don't want to trust anyone not to destroy me *or* trap them into looking after me if I . . ."

Toni exhaled and opened Emily's door.

Emily said nothing as she climbed in the Jeep and Toni walked around to the other side. The part Toni didn't say even in her own thoughts was what if instead of being the one who broke someone's heart like her father had, she was the one who ended up locked in her mind not knowing who she was or when it was.

She got into the Jeep and stared straight forward. "I can't risk that, Em. I like Addie too much already. I can't . . . I can't do that, though. I can't end up letting her down or end up trying only to end up like Lil."

"Toni . . ."

"Don't," Toni said harshly. "Please. I don't want her or you or anyone to have to deal with me if I end up like Lil. You are excused. Don't ever feel like you are stuck dealing with it if I do." She glanced over. "This subject is now closed, okay?"

Maybe it was the waver in her voice or the fact that Emily knew there was nothing she could say, but she kept her mouth closed and nodded.

"Don't push about Addie, please?" Toni added. She wanted to explain herself to Addie but in all the things she'd shared, she didn't know what to say about this one.

Addie deserves happiness, and either way I go, I can't give it to her. She's better off without me.

"If that's what you want," Emily said.

"It's for the best." Toni backed out of the parking spot and steered into traffic.

Toni would email Addie later, but right now, she wasn't sure what to say. It sounded awful to admit that her plan was to enjoy the time they had, and then hopefully, they'd drift into platonic friendship so Addie could find someone who could love her the way she deserved.

Even though the thought of anyone else touching Addie makes me want to scream.

Chapter 22

Toni

Of course willpower only went so far. Toni made it a week without emailing Addie, but in the past year, they hadn't once gone more than a week without any conversation. Not since the first email. By rights, it was Addie's turn if the note with flowers counted as a message. They'd taken turns. On the other hand, the last email was Addie telling her about the audition. So when Addie hadn't written at all, Toni finally gave in to the urge to connect and sent her a quick note.

From: History Toni
To: Addie

I'm home safely. Book 2 is going surprisingly well. How is the show?

Toni

From: Addie
To: History Toni

Thank you for your email. I'm on set with limited access to email. If your matter is urgent, please reach out to my manager. Otherwise, I'll respond to you as soon as I'm able.

Thanks.

Adelaine Stewart

From: History Toni
To: Addie

Out of office? It's a bit early to be shooting, isn't it? Do I need to talk to someone about keeping you too busy?

Toni

From: Addie
To: History Toni

Thank you for your email. I'm on set with limited access to email. If your matter is urgent, please reach out to my manager. Otherwise, I'll respond to you as soon as I'm able.

Thanks.

Adelaine Stewart

From: History Toni
To: Addie

I hope it's going well.

Toni

Out-of-office emails were not the response she expected, but Toni decided that she'd respect whatever logic Addie had in not replying. She considered texting, but she'd been the first to email after their night-that-was-not-a-date, and since she was the one who insisted that they weren't going to date, texting too seemed like the wrong move.

Friends text, though, right?

Toni considered it. Often. *Her silence is for the best.* Getting attached to Addie would only complicate whatever friendship they had. If Emily sent an out-of-office, Toni wouldn't text her unless it was urgent, and missing someone wasn't an actual emergency.

If not for knowing that she'd see her at Cape Dove, Toni would likely be more anxious.

The next two months also passed without a single word from Addie, and Toni was both relieved that Addie wasn't being clingy and maybe more than a little let down that Addie hadn't even texted. Toni missed their email exchanges, but she wasn't going to be a hypocrite and demand replies. It was odd, though. Addie had always replied promptly. Toni, admittedly, had not.

But there was neither a text nor an email from Addie.

Not when Emily sent the flowers the day Toni left LA.

Not when Toni sent flowers again on the day the cast was announced.

The announcement of the cast was exciting, and the increased buzz about the book meant that *The Whitechapel Widow* returned to the *New York Times* and *USA Today* bestseller lists.

No texts or emails then, either.

Translation-rights sales kept pouring in, and Toni was starting to admit that maybe she really was an author—especially now that the sequel was zipping along.

Because of Addie's influence.

Toni glanced down at the glossy ad for the show. Like the rest of the promo Toni had seen, Addie was front and center in this one. Her secretive smile vied with her loose fall of hair. The Victorianist in Toni grumbled that her loose hair was historically inaccurate for a well-respected lady. The part of Toni who might *miss* Addie lately simply thought she was a vision of loveliness.

Today was not the time for that thought, though. Emily had called to ease the anxiety that was currently washing over Toni.

"I don't understand, Em." Toni clutched the damnable letter in her hand. "I genuinely would like to visit Cape Dove Manor, but as *me* . . . not as an author. Why can't I skip this? Maybe I could just go up for the day."

"First, you *are* the author," Emily said. It was like a refrain with her.

"Sure but—"

"You are the author of the bestselling book that just got selected as a book-club pick by a famous actor." Emily sounded patient. "The bestselling book with the upcoming show. They want you there because of all of that. You dodged the proposed book launch event there, and I've told you *repeatedly* that this event was required."

Honestly, Emily's soothing tone made Toni relax enough to exhale a little, but she still objected. "I'm not good at peopling, especially on my own."

"Many authors aren't." Emily sighed in that way that made Toni feel a flash of guilt. Then she added, "You're charismatic, Toni. I've seen you lecture and, before that, watched you hook up at almost every bar like it's an art."

"Right . . . That's different." Toni stared at the foil type on the ornate invitation as she paced her living room.

The room was now the sort of space built around the idea of relaxation, stress-reduction, and comfort. Aside from the Jeep, Toni had been exceedingly frugal. She had bought a few new clothes for her increasingly frequent events, and she'd had a decorator do some magic on her home. It was also her writing office and her cave to hide away from her job.

Most of the cash she'd received went to paying off debt, paying for her mom's care, and into a few accounts—one for parsing out now and one retirement account to pay for her own possible memory care one day. Publishing paid on a very weird schedule. *The Whitechapel Widow,* the North American sale, was divided into signing, delivery, hardcover print, paperback reprint. The sequel was all of that, plus a portion on synopsis. So she'd received two hundred thousand dollars for signing the contract—one hundred thousand per book—as well as delivery and print for Book One. Four hundred thousand dollars so far, not counting foreign or film rights.

And maybe that will be the end. There was no way to know. Some authors flopped after the first book. *I could be one of them.*

The money had paid off her mother's debts and the year's memory care for Lilian, with money left over for some clothes for Toni's events and the Jeep. She felt guilty spending it, but . . . Emily had reminded her that there was more to come even without film and foreign rights. She still had checks for paperback and on acceptance of the second book.

And if that's the end, it's enough. I only wanted enough to pay off Lil's debt.

Toni felt guilty for even considering wanting more, as if the ghost of her father was rising up to whisper to her that she ought to try to make one more good bet.

I'm not him.

I could cash out now. Deliver the second book and then go back to my actual plan for life.

Toni paced, even though the serene color palette of her home was specifically chosen to be calming, but Toni had yet to manage talking while angry without moving—or maybe her tendency to move during calls was a result of too many lectures. A moving professor was an engaging professor.

"Sweetie, this is a big deal," Emily said, voice slipping to her manage-the-author tone. "It'll be great for photos. They want to shoot some of you and the star of *your upcoming show.*"

"I hate photos," Toni grumbled. "Addie can do them without me. She's gorgeous. Have you seen the ad in—"

"Toni, the sales numbers are great, and the publisher wants to discuss the next books in the series." Emily sounded like she had on those rare nights when Toni was a little too tipsy to be left alone at a bar.

"For real?" Toni felt like the air was sucked out of her. "But the second one isn't even finished. I can't—"

"Preorders for Book Two are great," Emily said mildly.

"They're selling it before it's written . . . ?" Toni flopped onto her sofa, disturbing Oscar Wilde. "Can they do that?"

"There's a show greenlit, a bestselling book, and the sequel is in process," Emily explained patiently. "Greta is very optimistic. She—and I—have complete faith in you, Toni."

Oscar Wilde stretched out and jabbed his claws into her leg and then slunk off. Toni stared at her cat, wishing she could be as blunt in her discontent as he was.

"Toni . . . you have no choice on this. I shouldn't have let you weasel out of doing a launch event, but now? With the sales? The preorders? The show? You will go for the weekend, and you will stand beside that gorgeous woman and have photos taken to *promote your damn books.*" Em's tone of voice came through the phone with enough clarity that Toni could picture her taking off her glasses. Maybe on another day it would elicit guilt. Not today. Today was the anniversary of Anthony Darbyshire's death. The man who was solidly in the last place for Father of the Year perpetually.

"I hate publicity things," Toni said. "You know that."

And I don't know how to feel about seeing Addie since she's stopped replying to me, Toni thought.

Emily sighed in that way that made it seem like Toni was the difficult one. Maybe she was. Maybe she wasn't cut out for this job at all.

Finally, Emily said, "There is a promotion clause in the contract, Toni. You *know* that. They are exercising their right to have you promote the book at this event. You avoided having a launch event at Cape Dove, so now it's time to pay the proverbial piper."

"I don't have a Victorian suit." Toni heard the concession in her voice as clearly as Emily undoubtedly did.

"You do, in fact. I ordered some things for you when I sent you the invitation."

"Some *things*? Not a dress? Seriously, Em, there are lines and—"

"Exhale, sweetie," Emily interrupted. "Right now, you might think I'm a monster for not figuring out how to get you out of upholding one of your *contractual* obligations, but I'm not about to try to force you into a corset or bustle." Emily chuckled. "Give me a little credit."

Toni closed her eyes. "What did you order?"

"Best friend before being your agent, sweetie. I know you. Tails. Vest. Several interchangeable pieces. You'll look like the most dashing Victorian gentlewoman that Cape Dove has ever seen." Emily's voice softened as she tried to point out the upsides of this damnable Victorian-immersion weekend.

"Hat?"

"But of course!" Emily laughed. "I'm really looking forward to the publicity photos, you know. I think we ought to use one on the back of the second book. There'll be a photographer there to take some shots of just you if you cooperate. Honestly, if you like the look, we could order a whole Victorian wardrobe for promo events for future books."

"I can't think about another contract, Em. Let me finish the *second* book and . . ." Toni hadn't planned on the first one succeeding like this, so she'd accepted that two-book deal. Instead, she'd already paid off the worst of the debt, and with careful planning and a bit of belt-tightening, she could live off the rest of the incoming money for literal *years*. "What if Book Two sucks? What if the show fails? What if tastes shift and lesbian detective books are not viable and . . . I can't sign a new contract to write a third book, too, Em. I can't."

"There's a name for this panic, you know," Emily said, cutting through the rising flood of fear that was filling Toni just then. Lightly, Em added, "Imposter syndrome. What you're feeling is normal."

"Em."

"Toni." Emily mimicked her tone. "You need to face facts when you feel this way. Your book has legs, Toni. It's back on the List this week."

"The List," spoken with a capital letter, meant *The New York Times* bestseller list. This, in publishing speak, was said the way "tenure" was spoken by the younger members of an academic department. Of course, tenure came with long-term job security, and the List simply meant that publishers wanted to buy more books— preferably of the same genre and success level.

I can't guarantee the same success level. In fact, I'm pretty certain it won't match this.

"Can we argue about this later?" Toni sank back deeper into the sofa, trying to focus on the here and now. Tangible things. The moment. Doing that was one of those grounding techniques she'd read about. The sofa was everything Toni had dreamed of when she fell in love with the Victorian era—but with one critical update. It might *look* like a stiff, gaudy purple-and-gold fainting couch, but it was deceptively plush.

A paw swatted Toni's ankles before she was able to get clear of the fuzzy menace. She let out a muttered word and added, "I'm going to sell you, beast."

"Oscar Wilde's awake?" Emily asked.

"Whatever possessed me to get fringe on the edge of the damn sofa?" Toni was grateful for an excuse to change the subject. She had accidentally created what Oscar Wilde considered his own personal den, so the sofa was a bit of a war zone between them. So far, the cat was losing, but Toni's ankles were rarely left naked thanks to the claws that flashed out when she disturbed his "curtains."

"I'll come down to feed him while you're away." Emily's offer to take an almost three-hour train from Manhattan to Washington, DC was enough to say how important this weekend was. "That way he's not alone, and I can be there to debrief when you get back."

"Thanks. Do you want to crash here?" Toni offered, flopping back into the sofa.

"Planning on it. I could use a Smithsonian day."

"Fine. Visit the cat and paintings instead of me. I see where I rank. Just don't let him convince you to give him extra food. You can't ply him with treats to win his love, no matter how much he claims otherwise. He's just fur and claws."

"Oh, I'm used to besties with claws."

Ignoring the jab, Toni said, "I have grading to do. Go away."

"So about Addie . . . ," Emily said casually, bringing up the topic

Toni still wasn't sure how to address. "Have you talked to her since LA?"

"No. Like I said, friends with no strings," Toni said, just as casually.

Emily paused a few beats too long. "You didn't text or call, then?"

Grumbling to herself, Toni stretched her feet out on the sofa to protect them from the monster under the fringe. "I had a book to write, essays to grade, events—"

"You will need a date for a few promo things coming up, you realize. Maybe Addie—"

"No. That's like asking for public speculation now that there are cameras aimed at her. Whatever I do with her is behind closed doors—"

"Unless it's for the show! These promo photos sound fabulous," Emily interjected.

"Fine." Toni refused to think about seeing Addie, about having a chance to be near her and talk to her. Clearly there was something wrong with Toni that the idea of *talking* to Addie was almost as appealing as getting her naked again.

Friends. Friends talk, Toni consoled her inner panic.

"Sweetie?" Emily prompted, pulling Toni away from dangerous thoughts. "I'll be at your place if you need me to talk about whatever happens when you see her."

"There's no need. She's a casual friend, and this is a work event. That's it. You'll do just fine for any promo events where I need a date. Agent or bestie, either way you can be my arm candy." Toni let out an *oomph* as Oscar Wilde crept out of his fringed den and landed on her chest with his sizable self. "It's you or Oscar Wilde, and he's grumpier than I am most days."

"Oh, twist my arm." Emily chortled. "You'd think ranking only above that adorable cat would be an insult, but I know you, Toni. You want my moral support, and I'm here for it. Always have been. Always will be. And who knows? Maybe I'll meet someone at these events."

"As long as it doesn't get in the way of you being my plus-one," Toni said. "Maybe you ought to come this weekend. The last thing I need is to do something newsworthy at one of these things because you're not there to manage me."

Emily paused for a moment. "They are sold out. Maybe I could room with you. It'd be just like high-school sleepovers."

Toni looked away. "I am hoping to have Addie in my bed for the weekend."

"Right . . . Should I be worried about you and Addie this weekend?" Emily asked, no longer joking at all. "Your self-control where she's concerned hasn't been the best."

"I haven't even texted her, Em. I'm sure I can manage one weekend without doing something foolish." Toni sighed. "I had an itch, and she had a curiosity. That's all it was."

"Uh-huh."

"I want more, but right now, I doubt she'll even want to come to my room. If she does . . . I have it under control." Toni certainly had hopes of spending whatever free time she had naked with Addie, but that's why doors had locks. She knew how to be discreet. That one incident in the garden was a bit indiscreet, but she'd had terrible news that night, and she slipped up.

"You can call me, you know," Emily said. "If you need to talk . . ."

"I'm fine, Em. Nothing to worry about," Toni reassured her. These days she had to think about being a public figure, as a professor and a writer, and both meant that Toni was not doing anything to risk tarnishing her reputation.

Nothing will go wrong, Toni thought. *Some publicity pictures, a little book-signing, and then I'll have Addie alone. We'll talk out whatever made her go silent, and if I'm lucky, she'll be naked and in my arms again.*

What could possibly go wrong?

Chapter 23

Addie

Addie knew that Marcela Gibson, the power who had made the show happen, was basically her boss. This was *her* show, and every detail seemed to cross her desk—even things that were not strictly her purview. More than a few people thought she was a micromanager, but Addie thought she was brilliant. They'd clicked, though, in part because of Marcela's almost maternal protectiveness.

"Are you all set for the weekend then?" Marcela asked from the doorway of the room. She kept her distance, never being in a closed room with the young star of the show. There were fewer powerful women in the industry than men, but sometimes Addie thought that being a powerful woman made Marcela more of a target.

And if Addie was right about Marcela's private life, she was doubly likely to be targeted by people who wanted to see her fail. Actors could be bisexual or lesbians and still build a flourishing career, although admittedly it was still sometimes a delicate path to walk. For people on the production or directing side, there was still more of an old-boys thing going on.

"I'm nervous," Addie admitted, looking over the dresses hanging on the rack in front of her.

"About the event? You've handled everything gracefully so far."

"This is different. You aren't there, the show writers won't be—"

"The writer is there, though," Marcela corrected with a pointed look.

Addie smiled. "Yes, the novelist, but none of the show people. It's just weird."

"The event wants the character and her creator." Marcela shook her head. "We're working with the publishing team on this one. They're keen to have you there."

"The *character,* you mean, not me." Addie looked at the dresses again. She had selected several dresses from the show, *after* Marcela and the costumer, Frederick, had narrowed her options down to a dozen gowns. "I worry about spilling something or ripping something or—"

"It's a work event, Adelaine." Marcela shook her head. "You aren't borrowing clothes for a date. You will dress in character, and act in character, and the press that's present will eat it up. You're good in your role, and the costume is part of that. If the dresses have a mishap, we'll have them fixed."

Her pointed pause made Addie not look away from the dresses she'd selected: three day dresses, two evening dresses, and two ball gowns. Publicity had a list of the events and had made arrangements for travel, and costuming had taken care of the necessary adjustments so Addie could dress without help. She had a corset that hooked in the front, and she would be going corset-free in the ball gowns. She had a bustier that made her breasts somehow larger, but there was no help for it.

Toni would like it. Not that it matters, but . . .

"Should I worry about your past with the author?" Marcela finally asked bluntly, interrupting Addie's thoughts about the author. "Because even though we haven't discussed it, I saw the interplay between you when she was on set."

"We're *friends.*" Addie met Marcela's gaze. "Off the record, we met at a bar in Scotland, and we hit it off. We . . . decided to be friends, though. I respect her."

Marcela said nothing at first. Then she walked closer, looking at the gowns Addie had selected. "If any of my friends looked at me the way Toni Darbyshire looks at you, I'd go with this dress instead."

"It's not like that," Addie protested as she brushed a hand over the jewel-toned silk. "This is a promo event for the show and therefore for her book. I'm just a prop, for the book, for the show. I'm not there as anything else, no matter what I might want. This is work."

Marcela didn't argue, and for that, Addie was grateful.

Then Marcela stepped into the room, pitched her voice low, and warned, "Just be careful, Adelaine. Your reputation is still a blank slate, but you have talent and drive. Some people will want to quash that. Don't think I haven't noticed how Philip looked at you when Darbyshire rebuffed him. She didn't want to talk to the two costars. She only wanted to talk to you, and Philip noticed it."

"He wasn't officially cast yet," Addie said weakly. "Toni just—"

"Wanted to talk to you. Everyone noticed. Philip intimated that he thought you seduced her for the role."

"Me? Seduced *her*?" Addie's mouth gaped open briefly. "I was the person *you* cast in the role before she even knew I was auditioning. You chose me!"

"I know. So does he, I'm sure. Maybe he's just power-driven, or maybe it's homophobia. I can't say. I'd think the former, since the story and the author and the lead actor are all lesbian. If he was a homoph—"

"We dated. Briefly. Philip and me. I thought it was nothing, but Philip says I embarrassed him by ending it. I think he just doesn't like me much after I left him, and now he probably saw the sparks with Toni," Addie said, pointing out the very obvious truth. He'd been a jackass when they met again, and he continued to seem determined to belittle her in any way he could.

"You should have disclosed that. Both of you." Marcela paused. "Any other relationships to disclose?"

Addie sighed. "Toni and I . . . we . . . we *met* in Scotland. I said that. We aren't dating. I spent two nights with her, but that was more significant than a month or so dating Philip. He and I barely kissed."

"I see. Well, I've spoken to his manager about his tawdry remarks on set," Marcela said mildly. She glanced over at the still-open door. "He's a talented actor, and you spark animosity with him, so the conflict between you sizzles. The camera captures that . . . but Philip saw this as a breakout role. He expected to get the attention, and he *wants* to be the bigger star."

"It's a book about Adelaine Wight." Addie stared at her boss in confusion.

"Oh, Addie! You and I know that, but Philip wants to be the heart-throb, the star who gets the attention, and use the show to launch into bigger roles. Just watch your back with him, and . . . be careful with Darbyshire. I had my team do a deep dive into her life. She's had exactly no relationships to the best of my knowledge."

"I know," Addie said quietly. "I have no expectation of being the person to change that. I just *like* her. I didn't mean to, and when we met, I wasn't in her show and she hadn't sold the book."

"If I knew that you and Philip had a prior relationship, I wouldn't have gone with him for the role," Marcela said with a sigh.

"It was less than a month of casual dates, not a relationship or even a hookup, for goodness sakes! I didn't think it mattered. It wasn't like I had sex with him," Addie blurted out.

Marcela cracked a smile at that. She nodded at the dresses Addie had chosen. Then she walked over and slid the rich blue dress next to them. "Might as well add an extra dress. You'll photograph well in this. There'll be some promo shots of you and Toni."

"Okay."

"Addie, she couldn't take her eyes off you. Just be careful, please. There aren't many shows about our sort of women, and I don't want this one to get mired down in bad press. Try to make nice with Philip, and keep whatever is going on with the author discreet."

"We aren't dating." Addie wasn't sure what else to say. She rather desperately wished that there *was* something still going on, but Toni hadn't so much as texted or called once.

"So you say." Marcela paused for an extra beat. "There's a lot that isn't 'dating' that can create bad press, too, and whatever you do or don't do, keep it away from your costar. He's cast now, but his anger over not being sent to this event was . . . pointed."

"Does it get easier to be in this business as a lesbian? Or even as a woman?" Addie asked softly.

"It will. Maybe not for us, but for the next generation of women, I hope. That will happen only if we continue to push boundaries." Marcela gave Addie a sad sort of smile. "There have been a lot of years with a lot of closed doors for us. We had Dorothy Arzner directing films in 1927. The first lesbian book, *The Price of Salt,* with a somewhat good ending was in 1952. Even in sports, where we think of a larger out population, things are recent. There were a few scattered players who came out like New York Liberty's Sue Wicks in 2002, Sheryl Swoopes in 2005, and Brittney Griner in 2013."

Addie felt unsure, realizing her own sense of history was thin. *I bet Toni knew all of that, though. I bet she knows more, too. She is a history professor.*

"You and me? We're a result of the progress they all made possible, and doing this show is about making *more* progress," Marcela declared. "What we do now is always about moving forward or giving them an excuse to push us back."

"I'll do a great job. I swear," Addie said.

"Of course you will. This show. This book. Those are steps forward. Remember that when you feel self-doubt." Then Marcela turned and left.

Addie was still standing there when one of the costuming staff came in with Marcela's assistant. They had clearly been waiting in the hallway. Marcela was cautious like that, keeping her people nearby so there was never even a hint that there had been a moment where something improper *could* happen.

"I'll pack up some costume jewelry, shoes, and hats for each dress," the first woman said. "I'll check the bible for options."

The bible, in this case, was the costume director's binder.

"Great," Addie managed, overwhelmed by the sense of history

she hadn't really considered and by the importance of her role in the show and, under it all, by the desire to do right by the woman she couldn't stop thinking about despite the way they'd left things.

After she left the room, she found herself walking around the set. It was starting to feel like home in a way that Addie couldn't quite explain. She was walking around a Victorian manor, detailed as much as Toni's book. She was in her character's study, where she would be pouring over ledgers and trying to find out who was behind the theft soon.

She heard a noise and turned. "Hello? Who's here? Hello . . . ?" She looked around, realizing that the set was mostly deserted. If anyone was here, they ought to be a member of the team.

Which means they ought to answer.

Unless they're wearing earbuds . . . ?

Addie felt uncommonly vulnerable. Then she heard footsteps. Marcela walked in. She startled, looking at Addie.

"Were you in here a minute ago?" Addie asked.

"No. Why?"

Feeling foolish, Addie shrugged. "I thought I heard someone, but no one answered. Maybe I'm getting *too* into character." She laughed nervously.

Marcela frowned. "Well, just to be safe, make sure you let someone know if you're coming onto set. Being careful needs to become second nature, Adelaine. The show is poised to make you recognizable. Sometimes, fans or antifans can be dangerous, especially in a show that's already getting some pushback from conservative corners."

"Sorry. I started out with Method acting, so I wanted to walk around fake-Addie's space to get into the mindset before I fly." Addie looked around the set again before shaking it off. "I guess I got too into character."

Marcela jabbed something into her phone. "I'll have security do a sweep just to be sure." She smiled at Addie. "And you, my dear girl, need to get home. Tomorrow's your flight, correct?"

"It is."

"Why don't you take the new episode's script to the author, since you'll see her?" Marcela motioned for Addie to follow her. "I know she'll frown at a few liberties, but maybe if you read some of your lines, she'll be more receptive."

"Sure." Addie inwardly winced. She didn't really want to be a go-between, but it would give her some excuse to have a private moment with Toni, and she wanted very much to have Toni away from curious ears when she asked her why she hadn't called, especially since Addie left her out-of-office up to encourage Toni to reach out for real.

But Toni hadn't called. She hadn't even texted. Whatever her reason, Toni had withdrawn almost completely, and Addie was not sure if she wanted to chase after her again.

Or wait.

I was patient for a year. Waiting. Hoping. And for what?

Chapter 24
Toni

The next day, Toni was in the Dulles airport headed to Rhode Island. She felt fancier than she did in her day-to-day teacher attire, not that she was dressed *that* differently. Trousers, blazer, and shirt were her go-tos for most things these days. She wore that for teaching, for events, for interviews. Maybe this was a nicer blazer, one she'd splurged on, and maybe her shoes were some designer brand that made her feel like she was walking on clouds.

It's just comfort. It's not as if I'm trying to impress anyone.
Especially Addie.

Toni had been driven to the airport in the usual black town car, and she had that weird feeling she got when she was doing any book events—as if she were living someone else's life and any moment a stranger would call her out as a fake.

There had been several midweek events lately now that *The Whitechapel Widow* had hit some sort of nebulous sales plateau that publishers never explicitly shared. In fact, Toni had been sent to another morning television interview in the wee hours midweek. *That* had been a hellish teaching day.

But the entire department knew about her success, especially since Harold had proudly put his autographed copy of her book on the corner of his desk, where everyone saw it. So far none of her students had brought it up, but several of her colleagues had mentioned reading it. All told, it was not the reaction she'd feared. It was . . . nice.

Going to book events still felt like Toni was slipping on a mask, though. She had to embrace a new persona: A. M. Darbyshire was a *New York Times*–bestselling debut novelist. More approachable than a professor but not too casual. It was a peculiar line to walk.

"Where to?" the TSA officer asked as Toni approached with her identification and ticket.

"Rhode Island."

"Vacationing?" The question was mere small talk, but Toni simply nodded. Vacation was a lot easier than saying she was headed to an immersion weekend where she'd dress in period costume. Maybe the hatbox might give it away, but she suspected few people realized that it was a hatbox she carried.

She moved through security, which was easier as she hadn't brought any electronics other than her phone and e-reader. No laptops were allowed at the manor. Technically, no e-readers were either, but there was only so much socializing Toni could manage before she became prickly.

Just in case Addie is no longer interested, I can read, Toni thought. *Maybe she didn't text or call because she met someone.*

That thought made Toni want to cancel the whole weekend. Sooner or later Addie would meet someone who was more suitable. *Not that they'd deserve her either!* Addie was too brave, too insightful, too beautiful to settle for Toni for long, and once the show was out, Toni had no doubt that Addie would be swimming in potential suitors.

Maybe we ought to discuss red flags so she knows what to watch for. Toni paused midthought. *Telling her "avoid anyone like me" feels like stabbing myself in the eye, though.* Toni was fairly sure she was a walking red flag. She might be financially solvent now, maybe even objectively a "good catch," but her genetics were a ticking time bomb. *One day I'll be in memory care like Lil.*

Not to mention the fact that Toni had exactly zero ideas for continuing her writing career into the future, or that she had no template of what a healthy relationship ought to look like, or that she had taken a year to *still* not even tell Addie her surname.

Would I have if she hadn't been at the audition?

Toni was capable of friendship. She could offer that. It made sense, since the thought of someone hurting Addie made Toni as surly as the thought of anyone hurting Emily. That was a side effect of friendship. The added desire to chase away Addie's potential future suitors was illogical, but surely that was because Toni was hoping to find herself happily tucked away in her most recent happy place—the inviting juncture of Addie's thighs. Toni was just protective because they were friends.

And because I'm not ready to let go.

She would be. Eventually. One night didn't erase a year of celibacy, though. Toni wanted a lot more of Addie before Toni surrendered to her own bleak future.

Despite that, Toni had respected Addie's silence. When Addie hadn't texted or called or emailed after the flowers, Toni reminded herself that filming had to be exhausting. It wasn't a rejection. It *couldn't* be. But when September turned to October, and there was still only silence, Toni was a little more upset than she wanted to admit.

I won't need a book to read, Toni promised herself. *I'll be with Addie.*

Still, Toni had hidden her e-reader in a case that, at a glance, looked like an antique book. It felt oddly Victorian, despite the anachronism of it. The Victorian era was built upon being one thing on the outside but another thing entirely on the inside. Modern people—aside from history aficionados—thought of the Victorians as prim and proper. On the outside, that was true, but the paper she was intending on presenting next week was a discussion of all the ways the middle-class and upper-class Victorians were incredibly debauched.

Toni's thoughts drifted back to the contradiction that was Adelaine Stewart, innocence and bluntness, sex and sweetness. *She really is perfect for m—the character,* Toni corrected mid-thought. *Addie is perfect for portraying my character.*

Sex, money, and power: Addie could ooze them. She could draw every eye in a room, and she acted like she didn't notice. She was remarkably Victorian. Such grace and confidence being a part of her success wasn't all that different from the modern era.

Unlike me.

What most people knew—and what Toni had written about so far—was the upper crust, and despite the book-sale royalties that Emily had said to expect, one successful book wasn't going to turn a tattooed, suit coat loving, lesbian history professor into aristocracy. Her tailored suit would not have been the sort of thing that a woman like her would have been allowed to wear as a Victorian woman. Women *did* wear pantalets and bloomers in the Victorian era, but not at the sort of event that Cape Dove Manor was mimicking. Trousers weren't even *legal* for women in the States until the 1920s.

Addie will be dressed like the sort of woman the character is: feminine and innocent on the outside and ripe for debauchery under those elegant skirts.

For all that Toni loved history, she never forgot that the rights that she had as a lesbian in the present were far superior to the ones she'd have had in her beloved Victorian era. And that was part of what Emily couldn't quite understand about Toni's resistance to this immersion weekend: it was one thing to study the era, to fictitiously represent it, but to go to this event meant facing attendees who would be faux-scandalized by a lady in trousers—or perhaps they would be legitimately offended and take the historical excuse to voice that outrage.

Let them be scandalized.

Toni wasn't about to forsake modernity for anyone's comfort. At the end of Sunday's dinner and dancing, Toni would leave the Victorian dress and manners behind. She'd go home. Her biggest joy at being at the weekend was that, while she was there, she'd hopefully find temporary love in the arms of a willing woman. She would not, however, forget that in the *real* Victorian era, she'd likely be forced to wear a dress and marry a man.

A few hours later, the driver brought Toni from the airport to the end of the drive at Cape Dove. "Miz Darbyshire, I apologize, but they don't allow anything of 'this era' to enter their grounds. I have to stay outside the grounds with the car."

He pulled the town car up to a group of horse-drawn carriages, all in bright colors and excellent condition. To the left were a clarence carriage and a brougham. Both were glass-fronted, enclosed carriages, but the larger clarence would allow four guests to ride while the brougham was a one-horse, two-guest carriage. Beside the brougham was a landau, a versatile four-person carriage that could be enclosed or open-air. The landau was folded down, but in need, the two-part hood would fold up to protect any guests from the weather. Behind those were a pair of hansom cabs, two-person carriages with the driver in the back.

The one that caught Toni's eye, however, was the phaeton. Open-air, designed for a single driver or a driver and passenger, and typically an excuse to show off the finest of your horses. If money were no option, Toni would have a reproduction phaeton and pair of horses worthy of it. It was also one of the only ones with no horses at the ready.

The town-car driver came around to open her door, but Toni was already out and taking in the small crowd in the gravel lot. The driver closed her door and offered to take her carry-on and hatbox.

"Thank you." Toni always felt a little foolish handing her things over; it was quite the step to go from broke-ass grad student to having people try to do things for her. On the day-to-day, she opened her own doors and carried her own things, so these random one-offs still seemed unnecessarily awkward.

On the other hand, in this moment she wanted to study the

carriages waiting there in front of her. It wasn't *quite* authentic to have all of them parked here waiting, but it was close enough that most guests would be charmed. *I'm charmed,* she admitted to herself.

The Cape Dove carriage driver was already loading her very modern bag into one of the hansom cabs. *At least they didn't require historical luggage!* The line between studying history and wanting to live in it wasn't one Toni often crossed.

She looked longingly at the phaeton. That, however, could be an exception. She wanted to *drive* it, not sit idly at the driver's side. Instead, she walked over to the hansom cab.

The carriage driver offered her a hand to steady herself as she climbed into the carriage, and this time, she accepted. Getting in and out of cars? That was easy enough, but carriages weren't always as steady, what with the live animals at the front and the significant step up into the carriage.

"I'll need to take you round back, miss. The back stairs are for those not already dressed for the event."

"That's fine." Toni looked out at the few other early guests on the ground, searching for one particular woman, but also enjoying the rainbow effect of the women in Victorian dress. What modern people would consider garish colors were popular in the 1800s. While the 1840s had muted hues, those were followed by a rainbow of vibrant shades including oranges, red-violet, crimsons, emerald, and even iridescent dresses. Decorations were as varied as bows and ostrich feathers, beads and tassels, ribbons and lace. While none of it was Toni's taste in clothes to wear, she certainly appreciated the rainbows of beauty that such a wide swath of time offered.

Several clutches of women were already in period dress, complete with hats with sumptuous feathers. The event allowed 1845 to 1899 dress, so there would be considerable variety, and as a writer and historian, there was something lovely about seeing it—though she'd typically rather see it via streaming video. Distant observer, that was the historian's way. If Toni wanted to immerse herself within a group, she'd have been an anthropologist.

Still, Toni took it all in as the hansom cab carried her toward the rather impressive manor. She'd read enough to know that Cape Dove wasn't *strictly* historically accurate. It was a reproduction of a Victorian country manor, initially built in the Gilded Age by one of the ostentatiously wealthy men who dominated that era, but in recent years, it had been fitted with modern plumbing and, most likely, a very modern kitchen. The lights and heat were visibly crafted to still look historical, but the house had the benefit of modern electricity, too. In all, it was as Victorian in spirit as most Victorians had been in that the current façade was quite a bit removed from the truth.

The manor house was better suited for a bed-and-breakfast or hotel than the home for one couple, as it initially had been. Enormous pillars, looking like they belonged on a Grecian temple, sat in front of the house like a statement of arrogant excess. A structured garden outlined an oversized fountain, and a round drive snaked between fountain and house. The entire scene looked like it could've been lifted from Toni's book.

The driver drove the carriage down the long gravel drive, slowing briefly as they crossed directly in front of the enormous house. The house itself had that Vanderbilt Gilded Age feel to it—complete with towering stone arches over the front windows and more architectural excess on the second level. She could picture this as a setting for her series.

Then he drove around the back. He stopped at what looked like a servants' entrance. Massive azaleas framed the steps to the door.

"It's beautiful, innit?" the driver prompted as he helped her down, clearly expecting a level of gushing that wasn't that far off from Toni's thoughts. She was, of course, a historian, and most of history was museums and documents—not actual costume events and carriages that were able to be touched. She'd have to apologize to Emily. There was a distinct possibility Toni might actually enjoy this far more than she expected. The idea of physically walking through history always left her contemplative.

If only there weren't all the people!

"Very beautiful," Toni admitted. "Obviously, the owners take care to create the illusion of stepping back in time."

"That they do, miss. That they do. The inside is even more lovely."

"And the carriages . . ." Toni shook her head. "What I wouldn't give to take that phaeton out!"

He laughed. "The hansom turns beautifully, too. It's a pleasure to drive them, but they don't hire them out for guests."

"Shame."

A man dressed in green-and-gray livery—undoubtedly the uniform of the Cape Dove Manor—bowed and carried her bags inside. Toni saw no option but to follow. She paused to take in the marble floor, the gilt ornamentation that accented the molding around the ceiling, and the immense crystal-and-bronze chandelier that glistened as if it were polished just that morning.

"Miss Darbyshire!" A fit woman wearing a sharp day dress approached as Toni stepped inside. The woman paused awkwardly at the sight of Toni's modern dress, but then quickly smiled and said, "Welcome to Cape Dove Manor. I'm Lady Dove."

"Thank you for the invitation." Toni bowed her head, not overly deep, but enough to show respect to the feigned aristocracy. Strictly speaking, she didn't need to bow, but it appeared that the proprietress of the manor was in character already.

"Will you be needing a lady's maid for your dress?"

Toni heard the question under the question: *Will you be wearing a dress? You appeared to have just bowed as a man would.*

"I'll be wearing a suit, Lady Dove. Period appropriate, of course." Toni smiled and hoped that the answer was acceptable, all while silently cursing her publicist for not clarifying that detail in advance. "I'm ill-suited for corsets and gowns. You, however, look absolutely lovely."

Lady Dove paused. "And will you be addressed as Lady Darbyshire or Lord?"

Toni relaxed at the question, which was as close to a Victorian version of asking her pronouns as possible. "Darbyshire is fine. No need to muddle the guests."

"Will you take whisky with the gentlemen after dinner?" Lady Dove pressed, but it felt more like she was trying to avoid missteps than making a point.

"At least one night, but I prefer the company of the ladies . . . after dinner on the other." Toni let the pause between words linger to make things as clear as she could without being vulgar.

Lady Dove laughed cheerily, and her Victorian persona slipped a little as she said, "Well, Darbyshire, if it's the *company* of ladies you prefer, I suspect drinks with the men both nights would be the more appropriate choice, now, wouldn't it? We don't want any impropriety."

Relieved by Lady Dove's good spirit over Toni's revelation, Toni grinned as if chastised. "Indeed, Lady Dove."

"I'll have Tomas take you to your room, then. He'll be your valet. This is the 1800s, after all, and it wouldn't do to have one of the lady's maids put in a compromising position."

At her word, a man, no older than twenty, appeared from another room up and said, "If you'll follow me . . ."

"Darbyshire." Lady Dove curtsied again and swept away, still smiling.

As Toni followed Tomas up the well-polished back stairs, slightly wider than servant's stairs would be, Toni figured that this had worked out as well as it could, given the circumstances. Her pronouns were she/her, but since she wasn't going to bow to gender constraints by dressing in corsets and curls, she'd been socially sorted with the men for the weekend.

So be it.

At least it would be a statement to anyone wondering whether or not she was available to or interested in male attention. The idea that this wasn't addressed in advance was a bit awkward. Her character was a woman who was solely interested in women, so it wasn't that much of a stretch to think that Toni was "writing what she knew" on that front.

Obviously not every aspect of a novel was a case of "write what you know." She was also writing about murder in the books, and she had no experience with that. Her books were, in fact, fiction, but she wrote stories about a character she could relate to—a lesbian who sometimes felt ostracized by a society that wasn't always sure what to do with her.

Stories, plural. I'm really writing another book, she thought. The second wasn't yet finished, but it was getting closer. *Who would've imagined that I'd pull off writing a second one, too?*

Toni allowed herself a small smile of victory. Maybe the weekend could be a bit of holiday, a reward for working too many hours the last month or so. A bit of whisky and billiards sounded like a fine reprieve after dinner, and it paved the way for dancing with women at the Saturday evening ball.

Dancing with Addie, Toni's libido filled in.

"Your room." Tomas opened the door, bowed, and waited for her to enter.

While she took in the lavish room, Tomas hung her suit coats and trousers in the enormous mahogany wardrobe with a full mirror in the center of the three pieces. The bed, an equally heavy wooden antique, was an intricately carved French rococo piece with an embroidered footboard.

An ornate painted trifold divider hid a corner of the room. The design was decidedly Victorian; extremely crowded images of feathers and swirls that were vaguely fleurs-de-lis covered the material so thoroughly as to be clashing with themselves.

Tomas caught her gaze. "A dressing area for if a guest has a spouse who wishes privacy."

He walked to the side of it and grasped the glass doorknob. "And your necessity room." He paused awkwardly. "The house has modern plumbing, so the water no longer needs to be heated and brought up. And the"—he gestured at the toilet—"also is modern."

"Marvelous."

"Will there be anything else?" Tomas asked.

"Will someone call us to dinner or . . . ?" Toni was peopled out already, and it was not yet mid-afternoon.

"The schedule." He pointed to a packet on the nightside cabinet. "But if you need me to fetch you, I can."

"*You* specifically? Are you the only one on staff right now?"

"No." He squirmed, and Toni wasn't quite sure why until he recited, "'Aristocracy without a lady's maid or valet will be assigned one.'" He shrugged. "You're *someone* here, probably out there, too, if you're who I think you are. Novelist with a television adaptation. I was assigned to assist you in dressing, refreshments, answering questions, retrieving a book, or showing you to the library."

"I will *not* need help with my dressing—"

"Thank Victoria and Albert." He grinned.

"Direction to the library later, but for now, all I require is a tea tray with hot chocolate or coffee or tea and a timely reminder when I need to dress." Toni paused, not wanting to get him in trouble. "And, you know, when no one's around you don't need to sound quite so much like we're in the 1800s if you want."

"*Awesome.* The job pays well, and tuition isn't exactly free. . . ." He sighed and admitted, "I'm not great at the acting, though. Chem major, not history or drama."

"History prof," Toni said, pointing at herself. "I mean, the novelist part is true, but either way, I still would rather not sound like I live in the 1800s."

He laughed, and somehow, Toni felt better. In a light tone, she said, "At least I was assigned the best valet. . . ."

"Ha! I'll grab your tray, Darbyshire."

Tomas left, and Toni kicked off her shoes. She had a few hours to relax before she had to be wearing both a Victorian-era persona and an author persona, and Toni was going to hide out in her room and relax for every possible moment.

Chapter 25
Addie

Addie stared at the enormous house. It looked like it belonged in England, complete with the fountain out front and the creeping vines that trailed across the stone front. Honestly, Addie thought she might want to talk to Marcela about on-site filming possibilities. There wasn't an excess of Victorian mansions in Los Angeles. New England, however, had more than a few. Perhaps having the show film here was what Cape Dove Manor was angling for, considering their persistence on offering to host promotional events for the show.

I wonder if they offered that to Toni, too.

Every thought somehow led to *her*. Addie could argue that in *this* case, it was logical, but everything tied to Toni. Addie felt like her life was permeated by the woman who hadn't even called since they had sex. Now, Toni would be here, inside this house. Maybe she was even here already. Toni, who sent two bouquets and not a single text or call. Toni, who seemed to be perpetually on Addie's mind. Toni, who had made Addie quiver and beg.

I'm not interested in casual sex, though, and if that's all I was to her . . .

Or maybe she was just busy and—

"Miss?" The driver was extending a gloved hand to her. "We're here."

Addie descended from the carriage, absurdly grateful for her practice on the set. These dresses were no joke to walk in, sit in, travel in. When the publisher suggested she arrive in costume, Addie had delayed answering. Part of her said no. Another part thought wearing her historically accurate drawers made perfect sense.

Not that I'm going to sleep with her.

We need to talk before anything like that is even remotely possible.

Addie was stung that Toni hadn't called once. She hadn't texted even to say she looked forward to seeing her this weekend. Admittedly, Addie had been busier than ever in her life. Filming a show—as the lead character—was exhausting. They had filmed for the last three weeks nonstop, and then an order for more episodes came in. The eight-episode order for the show was now twelve, and there was talk that they might even expand to twenty episodes. The studio bigwigs liked what they saw in the initial episodes.

Does Toni know yet? She must.

Addie had just found out when she was told to take the weekend off—and go to a promo event. So the weekend wasn't "not work" in reality; technically, she was only required to be here Sunday. Still, she told them she'd fly Friday. If she was going to have two days off, why not fly out early and confront her absentee lover?

Should I have emailed her the show news? Or that I was arriving early?

"Miss?"

Addie startled as she stared up at the front of the house, where a servant in livery waited. Then she glanced behind her.

The servant asked, "Do you have a bag?"

"A bag?" She stared at him. "Oh. Right. My *trunk*. Yes, if you could fetch my luggage . . ."

Is "fetch" the right word?

She was fine with a script, but her Victorianese was not as good off set. Addie pondered how much of that she'd need to master as she walked up the steps to the main door. *Surely, most events wouldn't expect that of me!* Another servant darted forward to open the door before Addie could touch it.

She nodded. Trying to think of the rules without a script was feeling more than a little outside of her skill set. *Where's Toni when I need her?* Addie stepped inside, where she was greeted by a woman whose dress was in what Addie thought was 1800s: front slit, visible bustle, and an excess of ornamentation.

"Name?" the woman asked, staring at a list.

"Lady Adelaine Stewart."

The smile was even wider then. "Of *course!* The actress! Stepped right from the pages of Darbyshire's book, then. I heard . . . well, never you mind." The woman turned and said, "Tomas! *Lady Adelaine Stewart* is here. Please show her to the suite. We'll swap the two on Sunday when the other one arrives. I best tell my sister."

"The suite?" Addie was increasingly confused. "I didn't book a s—"

The woman patted Adelaine's wrist as if they were acquainted. Then she hustled away to answer a question about dinner and left Addie with another servant.

"The misses Dove are always quite lively people, best just to say your bit, and quickly at that," he said conspiratorially. He led her up the stairs and opened the door, bowed, and once she entered the room, he closed the door behind her.

Feeling unsure of everything, Adelaine glared at the door. Her luggage wasn't here yet, and she felt out of sorts about the whole event. They seemed unsure of her room at first, but now she was in a suite.

I wonder what that will cost? Will the studio pay for the extra nights?

Addie turned around to look at her suite. There was someone here, in the bed, back to her. "Oh, I'm sorry, I—"

"Room service? Not what I expected here, but—" The person rolled over, and the voice stopped dead.

Toni's voice.

Addie gaped at *her.* Toni. Only this time, she wasn't wearing one of her blazers. She had on her underwear and a racer-back tank top. That was all. And she was stretched out in a rather rumpled bed.

Briefly, Addie looked around the room, wondering if there was another woman here. *Someone Toni is with now that she's over me.*

"Again in Victorian costume," Toni murmured as she stood up and walked up to Addie, who backed up so she was leaning on the door.

I ought to open it and flee.

Toni's bare limbs were on tantalizing display. She was as calm as if she had seen Addie the night before, as if there was nothing amiss. "I wake from my nap and here you are," Toni said. "Am I dreaming you? Are you real?"

Addie glanced at Toni's bare skin despite her attempts at propriety. Her hands practically itched to trace the ink that stretched from shoulder to forearm. She folded her fingers into tight fists to resist that temptation.

"Hello?" Toni said when Addie stayed silent.

Bad idea, Ads. Addie channeled her sternest voice. *Don't give in.*

"Not a dream," Addie managed to say.

"You look amazing," Toni said hurriedly, not reaching out with anything but her gaze. "No matter what you wear, you're always gorgeous. I swear those promo pictures for the show are designed to torture me."

Addie stepped away from the door, closer to temptation. She'd expected time to get her mind clear and brace herself to see Toni, but here they were. "Really? You liked them?"

"Yes, really. You are magnificent."

"I didn't mean to be in your room," Addie whispered. "They brought me here by mistake or something."

"Oh . . . ?" Toni reached over to a chair and grabbed a dressing gown of some sort of boldly toned silk and slid it on. Her voice was cooler as she asked, "Do you need me to get Tomas back?"

"I don't know." Addie started to shake. "This is your room, though. Not mine. I was to be in a regular room, and one of the Sisters Dove sent me here and . . . Should I go?"

Toni shook her head, voice even more reserved now. "I'm not kicking you out, Addie, but if you want to be somewhere else . . ."

Addie shook her head. How had she gone more than a literal decade without being tempted by sex, but seeing Toni for all of a minute made her want to be stripped bare?

"You're already dressed for dinner, but I'm not. So if you want to go find your room . . ." Toni gestured toward the door as if it didn't matter to her what Addie did, and the dismissal stung like a slap.

"*This* was to be my room, according to Lady Dove. I gave her my name, and she sent me here . . . unless there are two suites? Why would she direct me *here*? To you? Were you expecting me?" Addie felt her cheeks flush at the thought.

Toni stared at her, not quite replying. A slow inviting smile eased over her. "Expecting? No. Hoping? Yes."

"I liked the flowers," Addie blurted out. "Both bouquets. I would've texted, but . . ." She shrugged. "I lost your number."

"Okay." Toni stared at her. "And my email?"

Addie wasn't sure what to say to that. She was far too aware that Toni was wearing next to nothing under that robe, and it made Addie's mind all muddled. Toni's very presence made Addie's brain slow to a halt.

After the silence dragged on too long, Addie finally said, "I was busy with the show and didn't have anything I wanted to say."

"Right . . . well, let me dress, and then we can find your room," Toni said, sounding a lot less friendly again. She was hot and cold, and Addie was over feeling jerked around.

Toni added, "Maybe it wasn't Lady Dove, and you were sent to the wrong room. We'll get it sorted out."

Addie nodded. This awkward stiffness wasn't what she wanted, but damn it, she was hurt. She needed to think clearly, and that was not working well with Toni standing there beside a rumpled bed.

"Did I do something to upset you?" Toni finally said.

"You left."

"Job."

"Left *without a word*," Addie amended.

"I tried. Hell, I kissed you goodbye," Toni admitted.

"Really?" Addie's voice squeaked slightly on the word.

"Really." Toni shrugged. "And you said some version of 'let me sleep, Professor.'"

Addie's cheeks burned. "Oh."

"Ah, so that's what you call me in your fantasies then . . . ?" Toni stepped closer finally, robe gaping open now.

"Maybe." Addie closed her eyes against the tempting vision in front of her. "You hurt my feelings. Generic note. Another generic note with the flowers. And then back to . . . closed up in your email."

"You felt rejected," Toni summarized.

Addie's opened her eyes. "Friends aren't cold. You *withdrew*. I get that you don't like being vulnerable—"

"I didn't say tha—"

"I *see* you, Toni Darbyshire. I see how buttoned-up you are. I watched you withdraw. I watched you close down even after sex." Addie felt like her voice was going to break. All the pent-up hurt was boiling over. "You don't get to say we're friends and be my lover and then talk to me like I don't matter. *No one* gets to do that to me."

"I didn't mean to hurt you," Toni said.

"But you *did*," Addie countered. "Do better, or stay out of my life."

"I *missed* you," Toni admitted, holding Addie's gaze as she explained, "I wanted to email. I did email, more than once, but I kept getting that out-of-office and . . ." She made a little growling noise of what Addie surmised was remembered irritation.

"I missed you, too." Addie caught the edge of Toni's robe and tugged her even closer.

Self-control be damned.

For a moment they stood there. Beautiful Toni in her silk robe, waiting for more of an invitation or permission or something. So Addie blurted the only thing she could think. "I understand why they wore those drawers. I can't bend or anything."

Toni stared at her for a second before she laughed. "I really did miss you, you know?"

"Good. If I could, I'd . . . ," Addie started, but she didn't quite know the words for what she wanted as Toni stared at her like she was starving.

"What would you do, Lady Adelaine?" Toni challenged.

"Touch you. Show you that I missed you."

Toni stepped around her and locked the door and turned to face Addie again. "What if, since I'm not trapped in a corset, you just stand there and look gorgeous for me? Would that work? Will you let me make you feel good, Addie?"

For a moment, Addie felt like it was the first night all over again. She trembled as Toni took her hand and led her to the wall farthest from the door. A chair was there to her side as they stepped around a privacy screen. "In case someone comes looking for you after they realize you aren't in your assigned room . . ."

Toni slid her robe off as she stared at Addie, and then she took two hands full of Addie's dress and heaved them upward. "Hold this a moment."

Addie did so, and Toni knelt on the floor. She stared up at Addie. "You're going to want to lean against that wall, love." She shot her eyes to the chair. "Hold the top of the chair if you need it for balance."

"How? The dress . . ."

"Trust me." Toni gripped Addie's calf and lifted her leg, so it was draped over Toni's shoulder. The tank top had such narrow straps that Addie's bare thigh was touching Toni's bare shoulder.

That shouldn't be sexy. It's a shoulder.

"I fucking love these drawers," Toni said, her breath hot against Addie's skin.

"I wore them for you," Addie confessed.

"May I put my mouth on you, Lady Stewart? Finally?" Toni asked, staring up at her now. "Show you exactly how much I missed you?"

Addie trembled at the thought. They'd touched, but this . . . this was more. It was a different sort of intimate. Even when she'd been angry at Toni, Addie had thought about this, and she wanted it.

Toni said softly, "If you aren't ready—"

"You don't have to . . . do that," Addie interrupted.

Toni kissed Addie's thigh. "I *want* to, Addie. I have wanted to go down on you since the moment you walked into the bar like my very own fantasy come to life. I want to taste you, smell you, drink you. If you aren't ready, I can wait, but if you are ready . . . I would love nothing more than having my mouth on you." She licked Addie's thigh. "Say the word. Yes or no, love?"

Addie was almost embarrassed by how wet she was already. She nodded.

"Say the words for me," Toni ordered.

"Please, Professor . . ."

"Please what, Lady Adelaine?"

"I want your mouth . . ." Addie's words faltered as Toni nipped her thigh. "Your mouth . . ."

"Mmm?" Toni murmured as she kissed Addie thigh a little higher.

"I want to imagine being at a ball with you under there hidden . . . ," Addie managed to say, even as her entire body felt like it was on fire.

"Such a wicked lady," Toni whispered, her breath brushing over Addie's bared sex. Her tongue darted out briefly.

The noise Addie made was desperate. There was no other word to do it justice. Raw need ripped through Addie, and she said, "Toni. I need . . . you. Your mouth. Your tongue, your hands. Please?"

"I want you to think about this later," Toni ordered. "Me right here where no one else has been . . ."

Addie heard the question in those words. "No one. Just you. Still. Only you."

"That's my good girl." Toni licked her again. "Shall I give you a reward for being such a wickedly good girl, Lady Adelaine?"

Addie bit her lip and nodded as Toni suckled her clit, and Addie threw her head back in impossible bliss. *I was wrong. I was so, so wrong to not do this sooner.* There was nothing like this feeling, nothing like having a talented mouth on that bundle of nerves.

She swayed on her feet at the sensation, and Toni paused, looking up, face wet from Addie's own body. "Lean on the wall, love. I'm just getting started."

Then Toni pulled Addie's skirt over her head, and she set to proving exactly why Addie hadn't been able to come up with an excuse not to come to Cape Dove Manor. There was something surreal about the feel of Toni hidden under her skirts. Addie couldn't grasp any part of Toni, couldn't see her; all she could do was feel Toni's hands, her lips, her tongue.

Third time's a charm, Addie thought. *Please don't let her leave without a word at the end of the weekend.*

That was her last rational thought. Her head back against the wall, hand clenching the chair beside her, Adelaine was lost. Nothing in her life had prepared her for being at the mercy of Toni's attention.

Chapter 26
Toni

Role-play had never really been Toni's thing, but as she was hidden under the voluminous skirt of a woman who was begging and whimpering for more, Toni decided this was about to become her top fantasy for lonely nights at home.

Memory, not fantasy.

Under the thick fabric, Toni was grateful that she was nearly naked. It was sweltering, dark, and the scent of a woman was enough to make her wish she had a free hand to ease herself to the orgasm that was only barely out of reach already. *Ambrosia.* The scent and taste of a woman was as close to divine as any experience in her life, and right now, right here, with *this* woman, Toni felt like a god. Addie was saturating all of Toni's senses, and Toni could no longer remember any reason she'd want to be anywhere but right here.

"Toni . . . so . . . right . . . *yes.*"

Toni gripped Addie's hips as Addie found her release. *Does this count as makeup sex?* Toni held her steady for another moment before freeing herself from Addie's heavy skirt. Toni was on her knees staring up at the woman who had filled far too many hours of Toni's thoughts.

Toni wiped her chin as she sat back on her haunches and looked up at her. "Thank you."

Addie gave her a languid smile. "I think that's my line."

"I enjoyed myself, Addie. Trust me on that. I would start every day with my mouth on you if that was feasible." Toni didn't want to think too long about the weight that slipped from her shoulders when she'd realized that Addie hadn't rejected her—or the truth in her own admission. It was absurd, really, but Toni consoled herself in her panic by reiterating to herself that they had become friends. *Sometimes naked friends, but just friends.* That was why she was off-kilter now. No one likes fighting with a friend.

Especially friends who say "really?" in that breathy, hopeful tone that Addie does when she's surprised, Toni mocked herself. *Or friends who haunt your dreams naked but listening to you tell them your every worry and panic.*

Toni wasn't about to let anyone have the kind of power over her that came from a relationship.

But if I did . . . it would be her.

Addie reached down and cupped Toni's face between her hands. "Come up here. I still can't bend well."

Toni stood, and Addie all but fell into her embrace.

"I don't want to get your skirt all wet." Toni tried to pull her hips away a little.

"Oh?" Addie's went wide.

"I enjoyed that," Toni stressed. "A lot. If your skirt is up against me, I'll leave a wet spot."

Addie stepped back and looked down at Toni's damp underwear. "Oh."

Toni couldn't repress the laugh that bubbled out of her. "I told you I wanted to . . ." Her words faded as Addie slipped her hand into Toni's underwear.

"I can't bend at the waist or anything, but my hands work fine." Addie made a throaty noise when she discovered just how much Toni had enjoyed being on her knees. "I want to try that on you. You could teach me how."

"Okay" was all Toni managed to say. Between Addie's fingers and the image of Addie's mouth of her, Toni was not anywhere near articulate.

"Can you move to the side and put your foot up on the chair I was holding?" Addie asked, frowning slightly. "I want more access."

This time, Toni didn't try to hide her groan. She did what Addie asked, watching as Addie parted her lips and sighed. The angle meant that Toni could see herself in the dressing mirror. "Addie."

"Do you like seeing yourself?" Addie's free hand curled around Toni's low back, as if she was afraid Toni would step away.

"I like seeing you touching me," Toni said. "Your expressions."

"I love the feel of you right here," Addie said guilelessly as her fingers glided over Toni's slick flesh. "And knowing you're so wet from . . . touching me, I like that, too."

"From licking you," Toni correctly. "Tasting you."

"Teach me." Addie stared at her. "Teach me how to make you feel like that."

"Like what?" Toni prompted, wanting to hear the words Addie would use to describe her first time having oral sex.

"Desperate." Addie's fingers moved faster. "Like I would do anything for you, for that feeling. Like there are stars exploding inside me." She leaned closer. The hand on Toni's back slipped down to cup Toni's ass. "Like I will die if you stop. Like my own touch will never be this good. No one else will ever compare. Just you."

Addie's fingers slowed down.

"Don't stop," Toni urged.

The smile Addie gave her was feminine power personified. "Why?"

And Toni almost whimpered. "Because I need . . ."

"What? Ask me," Addie insisted. Her voice trembled slightly, but she still said the words. "What do you want from me, Toni?"

"Touch me, Addie. Harder. Faster. *Now.* Please?" Toni turned her head and kissed her softly, and when she pulled back, she whispered, "I need *you*. Not someone else. *You*."

Addie smiled and gave Toni what she desperately needed in that moment, fingers flying faster and faster until Toni reached a level of bliss she'd rarely found.

Toni buried her face against Addie's throat.

"You destroy me, love," Toni whispered, hoping that Addie didn't realize exactly how true those words were. She was in too far, interested in Addie far too seriously, and as Toni stood there in her sodden underwear, she couldn't fathom how she'd let Addie go after this weekend.

Or ever.

"I missed you," Addie murmured. "I wanted to tell you about filming every day, but I *couldn't* . . ."

"I didn't call or keep emailing because I thought you didn't want to hear from me," Toni confessed. "Even when I sent flowers, you said nothing, so . . ." She shrugged awkwardly, as she had her arms around Addie, who was making no move to put distance between them. "I would've loved to hear how things were going out there."

"Or to talk to me about how the book is going?" Addie said in an obviously insecure voice.

Toni pulled back, so she could stare at her. "Yes. Maybe we can talk on the phone or video chat after the weekend."

Addie blinked like she was going to cry. "I thought you left without a word because you were disappointed or didn't enjoy—"

Her words were lost as Toni covered her mouth in a kiss. When she pulled back again, Toni said, "Not at all. I overslept because some lovely creature kept me up all night, and I had to get through several stock signings before my flight home."

"Oh. What's a stock signing?"

"I stop at a store, sign the copies of *The Whitechapel Widow* that they have in stock, meet the booksellers. Repeat at the next store." Toni gave Addie a look. "My agent had to buy me perfume because I went to the lobby smelling like your delicious—"

Addie clapped a hand over her mouth to end Toni's words. "Oh. My. Goodness. She must think I'm awful."

Toni licked Addie's palm, making Addie let out a yelp that resulted in one of those deep belly laughs that Toni so rarely had. "Yep. I smelled like overpriced perfume all day because I didn't want to turn on the shower and risk disturbing the beautiful woman who grumbled at me in her sleep."

When Toni stepped back, she felt the loss of Addie's presence instantly. Without thinking, she reached out and twined her fingers around Addie's. "Emily was thrilled, actually. Not about my being late, but I am apparently worse than an angry bear when I'm celibate."

Toni briefly debated telling Addie that Emily sent the first bouquet of flowers, or telling her Emily was so grateful to her that she spent her own money to send them to Addie, but Toni was fairly sure that would sound rude, so she said, "Did you like either of the bouquets?"

"Obviously!" Addie said. "I was so hurt the first time, though . . ." She glanced away. "And the housekeeping staff woke me that morning, and I just felt—"

"I'm sorry." Toni cupped Addie's face in her hands so she could stare into her eyes. "I didn't think you'd sleep that late, and I left a note. . . ."

"One my dentist could send," Addie grumbled.

"You have sex with your dentist?" Toni teased, biting back a flicker of absurd possessiveness.

Addie swatted her arm. "Perv."

"That's a no?"

For a moment, Addie simply stared at her, and Toni felt completely ridiculous. "Yes, Toni, it's a *no*. Just you. Have I mentioned that? I was fairly sure I had."

"You did . . . I think I might like hearing it." Toni paused before she admitted, "So maybe I'm a little more possessive than I realized."

"You think?"

"I don't want you in anyone else's bed while we are . . . together," Toni finished the sentence awkwardly. There wasn't an exact word for what they were. "Fucking" sounded crude. "Friends who get naked" might be offensive. "I like hearing I'm the only one touching you."

Addie stared at her and said firmly, "Only you, but I was untouched by any hand but my own until you. . . . You, however, have had a long string of lovers. So *I'm* the one who probably ought to be worrying here."

"No worries. You've been the only one in my bed since the night we met." Toni cleared her throat awkwardly. "Maybe we can set a time to talk after the weekend? Make *sure* you don't lose my number again . . . ?"

"Honestly? I deleted it because I was upset," Addie blurted out.

"I figured that out, Addie. Maybe next time I piss you off, we can try to talk first?" Toni suggested gently. "I was in a bookstore signing my books, and there were too many people around to say anything personal to you."

"Did I mention that I'm a little impulsive in both good ways *and* in my temper?" Addie asked with a sheepish smile.

"Worth it." Toni turned away as she said it, though. Admitting just how much she liked Addie was a danger she couldn't allow. Addie was precious, and Toni was certain she'd end up hurting her if she tried to get too close.

After a long quiet pause, Addie asked, "Want to go explore the grounds before dinner?"

Toni glanced at her as Addie unplaited her long hair and began to re-braid it, transforming her from disheveled woman to proper lady. Toni felt like she froze that image in her mind, and suddenly understood why the Victorians had invented photography.

Addie was so at ease, so natural, so beautiful.

And in my room.

"Exploring works," Toni said, sounding raspier than she liked. Luckily Addie didn't comment. There was something about Addie that made Toni imagine things that were impossible. The flicker of the idea of seeing Addie getting dressed in Toni's home was a weird temptation, but Toni wanted her. Not just her body. Toni wanted Addie's presence, her laughter, her bluntness, her ethereal charm.

As Addie braided, Toni pulled on clean underwear and trousers. She left her black tank on, but then she added the stiffly starched shirt over it. Then a low vest—cut to accommodate her smallish bust without having to have buttons bulge—and over that a tailed dinner jacket with burgundy trim. She was silent up until she added her burgundy cravat.

Then she stood in front of Addie, feeling uncharacteristically awkward, and asked, "Well?"

"Can I unwrap you later?" Addie asked in a voice that made Toni feel both like she was altogether willing to be "unwrapped" right then and like she owed Emily a thank-you gift for sending the suit.

Insecurity fled at the look on Addie's expression and the tone of her words.

"Yes. Most definitely, yes," Toni agreed.

"You are gorgeous," Addie said, gaze sweeping Toni from head to toe and back again. "Smart, bold, beautiful, possessive . . . and talented. I am obviously already the luckiest woman at this event. Probably in the whole state."

"Just the state?" Toni teased.

"And you're so deliciously arrogant," Addie continued with a small laugh. "Did I mention that I like a confident woman?"

Toni hadn't felt arrogant over the last few years. Something about her professional mien and busy schedule had kept her from catting around as much, and the release of *The Whitechapel Widow* had brought out all of her old insecurities about being judged and found lacking. Addie made her feel like she was worthy of attention; she'd reminded Toni that the weight of her family obligations didn't define her.

As they left the room, Toni offered her arm to Addie.

"Thank you," Addie whispered. "Sometimes, on set, I worry about tumbling over with the corset and small bustle. I think about the character—and about me—having to fight someone or run, and I think *someone* ought to talk to the studio. You know there was a very popular show that did away with corsets?"

Toni nodded. "I'll talk to the producer. The last thing I want is *any* woman being limited, especially on a show for my book."

They walked into the foyer where the woman waiting, Lady Dove, smiled at them. "Well, aren't you just a picture!" She held up a mobile phone. "May I?"

"Only if you send us both copies," Addie said firmly. "There were contracted terms about photography, as I'm sure you recall. Only preauthorized photography of anyone involved in the show." She flashed a smile that softened her words, but only just. The sternness was still there even as she added, "You and the second Lady Dove ought to have signed the paperwork the studio sent over. Every guest should *also* have done so with their reservation. Have they?"

Her smile implied that *she* had no voice in the matter, that she was relatable and understood how difficult they were. Toni shot her an admiring gaze. Like Em, Addie had a way of managing people that seemed so natural.

Maybe I ought to ask for pointers there.

A few photos later, Toni summarized the room situation. She ended with, "I think Miss Stewart was shown to the wrong suite."

"That was Nelly, my sister. The other Lady Dove," *this* Lady Dove explained calmly, hands folded over her belly like a statue. "The note said that there was a person coming about the book, but your publisher only reserved the one room, Darbyshire."

"Where am I to go?" Addie's far-too-blue eyes filled with tears.

"The rest of the manor is full," Lady Dove pointed out. "They failed to communicate—"

"Yes, I suspect there was a miscommunication," Toni said, already mentally spinning the idea of their shared quarters as simply practicality. She couldn't exactly have the star of the show left sleeping on the billiards table or somewhere else.

As if I'd allow that.

"No worries, Lady Dove. Miss Stewart can take my bed. I can sleep on the floor or a cot or something," Toni cut in. As far as she was concerned, the matter was solved.

Addie's hand tightened on Toni's arm, but she remained silent, seeming content to let Toni resolve matters.

Toni, obviously, had no intention of sleeping anywhere other than at Addie's side, but there were still appearances to consider.

"That simply won't do," Lady Dove said with a shake of her head.

"I can go to a hotel and travel back and forth or something," Addie offered.

"Hush." Toni patted Addie's hand.

"Darbyshire," Lady Dove murmured softly. "I assume you will introduce Miss Stewart as your intended bride if you'll be sharing a room. Cape Dove Manor is not the place for inappropriate acts, and as you are not dressed as a woman—"

"She is! Women can wear trousers!" Addie interrupted with a scowl, eyes flashing, finger suddenly shaking like a furious governess. In a blink, the meek woman who had waited for Toni to handle things was gone. In her place was a fierce do-not-cross woman.

"Do you have *any* idea how many women actually wore split skirts?" Addie demanded.

Lady Dove nodded toward Toni. "*That* is not a split skirt, and respectable women do not wear suits in the Victorian era." In a voice that was not open to negotiation, Lady Dove added, "We make allowances for those who would have had Boston marriages. Darbyshire has a valet and is wearing trousers. I don't care what you have inside your drawers. To each her own, I say, *but* you cannot be the sort who *compromises* women and share a room with a woman."

"But it's not *actually* the 1800s!" Addie retorted, releasing Toni's arm and stepping closer to the older woman.

"It is in this house." Lady Dove's chin tilted like she was ready for a fight.

"So I should call the studio?" Addie said in a tone that sounded exactly like the threat it was.

And Toni was torn between the thought of bad press—which could hurt Addie—and the fact that Addie had defended Toni. It made something in Toni's chest tighten in unfamiliar ways.

Foolishly, Toni offered, "Let's have a wedding for the guests then.

Turn the inconvenience into something fun." She tucked Addie's hand back in the crook of her arm. "That way there's no hint of impropriety this weekend."

Lady Dove smiled widely. "That's a *capital* idea. We do have a reverend on the grounds."

"Toni?" Addie whispered.

"This is fine, love." Toni patted Addie's hand where it again rested on Toni's arm. "The guests will be happy to participate. Lady Dove? Would you mind terribly if we imposed on the houseguests for an impromptu wedding? It would be a lovely chance for photographs, pending studio and publisher permissions, of course!" When Lady Dove agreed, Toni smiled wider and then added, "I know my lovely bride was not prepared, though. Is there a veil of some sort? A coronet of flower blossoms for her hair?"

Addie looked flabbergasted, verging on alarmed as Toni pointed out, "You have your engagement ring. Is there anything else you need?"

"You. Only you."

"Scandalous creature," Lady Dove chastised. "Why don't we do the ceremony after dinner this evening? I'd hate to see poor Miss Wight be debauched."

Toni didn't look away from Addie. "You aren't invited to watch. Propriety, Lady Dove. You will upset my bride with such scandalous speech."

Addie giggled.

Lady Dove *tsk*ed and walked away with a huff, calling to someone. "Fetch William for me. Tell him to get out the ministerial garb. We are to have a wedding tonight after dinner."

When they were alone, Toni lifted Addie's hand and kissed the air just over her knuckles. "Walk with me somewhere private? As we are engaged, Miss Stewart, I see no harm in it . . . unless you worry for your virtue."

Addie gave a single nod.

They stepped outside, descended the stairs, and stood for a

moment in strange silence, but a servant appeared. "The gardens are that way, Darbyshire."

Toni led Addie to a remarkably well-maintained garden. The last of the year's roses and a few other flowers still blossomed, even though leaves were turning and there was a definite chill in the air. Wrought-iron benches were scattered around. In all, it was lovely, even if Toni's flower identification skills were only adept enough to declare the flowers "roses" and "not roses."

"Do you mind fake-marrying me?" Toni asked after a few moments. "We can spin it as a promo event, and then note that in reality I slept on the floor."

"Fake-marrying . . ." Addie echoed.

"I should've asked you if you minded. Do it up right." Toni decided then and there to make a show of it. "May I borrow your future engagement ring?"

Mutely, Addie slid the opal off her finger and gave it to Toni, who dropped to a knee and held the ring out.

The shiver Toni felt was surely just because of the October chill. That was all. It wasn't anything more.

"You're the first person to warm my bed over several states and two continents, the only woman in the last year and a half, and I *like* you, Adelaine Stewart." Toni felt a flicker of panic at just how real her words were. "You're brave and beautiful, smart and unforgettable. You're funny, and you're a wonderful lover. Will you do me the honor of being my bride for the weekend?"

"I will," Addie whispered. Her hand shook as Toni slid the fire opal onto the spot where her wedding ring would belong.

Toni stood, realizing that they had watchers, and in a low voice, she said, "I fully intended to ravish you, fake bride of mine, but we're in the 1800s today, so I can't even kiss you the way I want to right now."

"I am yours, Lord Darbyshire. Wholly and completely yours," Addie said in a regular volume. Her voice quavered as she added, "You have protected me from the moment we met while abroad to this moment, and nothing would make me happier than spending my life with you."

Smiling at how well she'd resolved their room problem, Toni offered Addie her arm. Speaking lowly, she praised Addie, "You role-play beautifully, love. I look forward to spiriting you away after our fake nuptials."

After their walk, they were directed inside for dinner. Their absence from predinner mingling had been excused with murmurs of "young love."

Dinner itself was a tedious affair with too many courses, many of which were not historically authentic. An opener of fresh figs draped with prosciutto and parmesan cheese was followed by a cold soup, which was followed by an appetizer of asparagus branches, and then the first entrée was presented: seared salmon with a lemon-dill sauce and accompanied by roasted root vegetables.

In all it was far more food than Toni ever ate, and that was before the dessert—jelly cakes, strawberries, and cream. After that was the dessert wine, Madeira from Portugal or sherry from Spain.

During the entire meal, Toni was in a strange blend of professor and author persona, answering writing questions and sharing historical tidbits, but through it all, she couldn't stop staring at the ring she'd slid onto Addie's finger.

It's not a real engagement.

It was her ring already.

It's a fake wedding.

But when Toni was a kid, marriage between two women was illegal, and it felt strange to even pretend to marry Addie. Not that Toni *wanted* a real wedding, of course. She wasn't built for that, and Addie deserved someone who could give her the sort of whole-hearted love she deserved.

But I can pretend for the weekend.

The thought of it made Toni feel a tightness in her chest. This was the only wedding she'd ever have, and it felt right to have it with Addie. *She* felt right.

It's not real. Toni needed to remind herself of that more than she expected. The truth was that Toni wasn't built for forevers. She was not going to ruin anyone's life the way her father had—especially if that someone was as wonderful as Addie.

As everyone rose from dinner, the elder Lady Dove announced, "We have a bit of a surprise tonight! If you would all join me in the ballroom."

She marched out of the room, bustle waggling like a honeybee leading them to pollen.

"Are you really okay with this?" Toni asked Addie as the group adjourned to the ballroom for what was about to be their wedding.

"I am."

"We could leave," Toni blurted. "Call in sick or—"

"Toni." Addie looked up at her. "I'd have said yes even if it was a real wedding."

Toni tripped over her feet. "What?" She backed away a step. "You know I think you're great. You're funny and sexy and . . . I mean, I'm sure you'll make someone an amazing bride, but—"

"I know this is a fake wedding," Addie cut her off. "I just want you to know that I *care* about you." She looked around to be sure they were alone. Then she stepped closer, leaned up, and caught Toni's mouth in a soft kiss, and when she pulled back, she said, "If marrying you meant I had two nights in your bed, I'd have said yes."

At her words, Toni relaxed. "You really missed me, did you?"

"Marry me, and I'll show you exactly how much," Addie teased.

Chapter 27
Addie

The fact that Addie's heart swelled at the thought of marrying Toni was daunting. In those few brief moments when Addie thought it was a real wedding, she'd had *zero* hesitation. Would she have done it for real? Hell, yes. She was increasingly certain that whatever else was going on, the connection between them was as real as they were.

But the wedding was fake. Without a marriage license, a wedding *couldn't* be real. It could be a commitment ceremony, but that was all. And for them it wasn't even that.

The vows were fake.

She doesn't love me.

This is pretend.

She looked terrified at the thought.

Addie had to repeat reminders in her mind a few times because the way Toni stared at her in general felt awfully real. The way Toni stepped up repeatedly to rescue Addie—whether from lecherous strangers or the lack of a room of her own—was real. The way she confided in Addie and listened to her? Still real.

So Addie sat perfectly still while strangers fastened roses in her hair. Pink and red roses. The scent of them was dizzying . . . or maybe that was the corset she needed with this dress—*the dress I wore when Toni was under my skirts.*

The weight of the dress and the tightness of the corset made sitting less comfortable than standing. Addie sat in a stiff chair while her hair was done.

"We could pin it—"

"Loose. She wanted it left loose," Addie insisted. "So no."

On set, they did her hair and makeup before she was laced into a too-tight corset. Here, she was already dressed. The effect of which was that her breasts were already lifted up like they were on a serving tray. The fact that Toni spent half of dinner glancing at them and then at the ring made Addie feel confident that she wasn't alone in her feelings. Toni was in denial, but that didn't mean that she couldn't see what was happening between them.

The fact that Toni spent an equal amount of time catching Addie's eye made her feel something else. Something softer, fragile, and altogether wonderful. Toni might not use the words to say so, but her actions made it quite clear that she felt something more than desire.

Not that she lacked that.

Thankfully.

"All set, my dear." Lady Dove stepped back. She held up a mirror so Addie could see the delicate roses in her hair. Several flowers were braided into long but narrow braids that met at the back of her head. "Might I take another photo or two?"

"Same rules, Lady Dove," Addie said firmly. "Nothing posted without studio approval."

"Of course, dearie." The older woman nodded, and then she took a series of photos. "Up you go. Pretty little thing, aren't you? No wonder *that one* stares at you like the wolf spying an innocent lost in the forest."

"I would *strongly* recommend not speaking ill of her," Addie warned. "I'm not unlike a rose, Lady Dove. I might look sweet, but I have thorns aplenty. I *also* have enough influence to make you extremely unhappy, which I will do if you insult Dr. Darbyshire."

Lady Dove looked stunned. "Well, excuse me for calling you an innocent."

"Not that part. Don't ever insult Darbyshire, and we'll get along beautifully." Addie smiled sweetly. "I'm simply a vicious sort when someone I care about is insulted."

"So you knew her before the show?" Lady Dove gave her a sly look. "Were you friends or dating her then? I'd think you'd need to be if you're wanting to share her room."

Silently, Addie straightened the fall of her skirt, weighing the questions. *What are we?* Addie wasn't even sure. "Dating" was the wrong label, but so was "just friends." She was increasingly hopeful about what was growing between them; she couldn't imagine it possible to fall in love after a few brief conversations and a few orgasms.

Although the conversations were so personal.

And the intimacy felt like everything.

And we spoke for a year over email. We aren't really *strangers.*

And in all my life, she is the only person to touch me.

What they already had might eventually blossom into love. Perhaps it *was* blossoming already.

If so, this wedding is a dress rehearsal!

Addie decided to ignore the questions. She smiled at Lady Dove. "Let's go out there. She's waiting."

"That she is, Miss Stewart. That she is." Lady Dove pulled back the curtain separating them from the rest of the ballroom, and Addie saw Toni standing at the front of the room.

She'd stared at Toni as she'd dressed earlier in the suite. This brilliant, beautiful woman in her custom-tailored suit was *hers* right now. Addie felt like this was a lot closer to real than she could admit, even to Toni.

And seeing the vulnerability in Toni's eyes only highlighted that.

Addie had seen Toni mostly *un*dressed before that. She'd felt Toni under her skirts, and then on her knees again but this time to slip a ring on Addie's hand. Somehow, though, seeing her waiting in front of a minister with all the guests watching was different. There was a tightness in Addie's chest that she was unprepared for.

I want this. Her. Us. For real. I want her looking at me with that sort of wonder, and I want this wedding to be real.

Music began, and Addie faintly realized that there was a cello, a harp, and a piano in the corner to the left of her.

"Go on then," Lady Dove urged.

An adorable young girl, no more than eight, skipped forward spreading rose petals everywhere. She tossed handfuls of them toward guests, and Lady Dove sighed and muttered. "My granddaughter is a menace."

Addie said nothing. Her gaze—unlike those of the guests, who were now watching the rose-flinging child—was fixed solely on Toni.

The fact that the gorgeous woman in front of her wanted to even fake-marry her felt outstanding in ways Addie couldn't, *shouldn't,* admit.

"Go *on,* girl." Lady Dove again motioned her forward. "She's waiting."

Addie took as much of a breath as the corset allowed, and then she started walking toward Toni—who now watched her walk forward like this was real. The anticipation was raw and evident on her face, and whether or not Toni admitted anything, there was no way Addie could believe that she was the only one moved by what was happening here.

This is a fake wedding, Addie reminded herself. *It's a ploy to share a room.*

Then Toni smiled, and Addie felt like she had to blink away tears.

I'd have said yes for real.

Veilless, Addie walked toward Toni as slowly as she could. She half expected that the roses twined together as a crown atop her loose hair would fall, that the whole moment seemed silly to the audience, but the look on Toni's face made the rest of it all matter very little.

She looks like someone just gave her a gift.

Like I'm the gift.

Briefly, Addie ducked her head to hide the joy she felt. She didn't want to scare Toni with how excited she was.

Addie's hair fell forward over her shoulders. With her braids loosened, her hair had a wave to it, and she could smell the wafts of the few stray flowers tucked into those waves. Someone had carefully cut the thorns from roses and twisted the thornless stems into the circlet that now sat precariously in her hair, even though Addie had her eyes fastened on the petal-strewn floor.

When she reached the front, Toni's hand was there, extended to take Addie's hand in hers.

Addie looked up as Toni touched her cheek with her other hand. "Okay?"

"Yes. Very."

"Still ready to marry me?" Toni teased quietly.

The minister cleared his throat as Addie simply stood and stared at Toni.

Addie managed to say, "Yes, please."

Then the minister started in with the very modern, "We are gathered here tonight, last minute, to join these two people, Miss Madeline Wight and Lord Toni Darbyshire, in matrimony."

He had managed to get both her first and last name wrong.

"*Adelaine* Stewart," Addie whispered.

"Right." The minister swayed, and Addie caught a whiff of gin. She wasn't sure what was accurate and what wasn't, but a last-minute wedding by a drunken minister made her have to resist a giggle. Maybe that was how women could have gotten married in the 1800s? Drunken ministers. She bit back another giggle at the thought and looked at Toni.

Toni was staring at her like this was as real as it felt to Addie. "You're sure?"

"I am. I would. I do." Addie took a quick breath and added her actual truth, "You're *The One* for me, Toni Darbyshire."

Toni looked panicked at that, but they both said their official— *but fake!*—vow of "I do."

The minister hiccupped loudly after Toni took Addie's hand and made her vows, causing a ripple of laughter in the room. But Addie was certain Toni had been trembling in that moment.

In a few short moments, the minister said, "You can kiss her now.

You're all wed. Legal and proper. Why else would anyone do that if not to get the reward?"

It was a cold, drunken statement, but Addie shrugged it off because Toni had her arms around Addie before "now" was even out his gin-soaked mouth.

For a moment, Addie leaned in, forgetting their audience, forgetting that this was to be something they could use later and explain away as a publicity stunt if they wanted. Then Lady Dove cleared her throat loudly.

"The guests are retiring to their drinks and gossip." Lady Dove rested her hands on her stomach and looked between them. "Most creative solution to rooming problems I've seen in all my years . . ."

Toni's arm slipped around Addie's waist, and Addie could swear that the palm of her hand was fire through the dress and underlayers. She bit the inside of her lips to keep any inappropriate noises in her mouth.

"I had a few of the photographers here," Lady Dove added. "Since you couldn't look away from your bride, I wasn't sure you noticed, but I'll send photos to the studio and your publicist on Monday, Darbyshire. They can decide if they want to use any of the images or not."

She glanced at Addie but had no words to go with the curious look she gave her. Then she was off, leaving Toni and Addie alone in the ballroom.

"Take me to our room, Toni." Addie stared up at her. "If I'm your bride the next forty-eight hours, I believe I deserve a fake honeymoon."

Toni chuckled. "It just so happens that I have a suite at a manor house. . . ."

"Lead the way." Addie paused before adding, "I've been in corsets for weeks because of you. It's about time you removed one."

"With pleasure." Toni motioned her forward. "Better to follow you up the stairs, love, in case you topple backward."

"I would like to be naked before you topple me backward," Addie said in her primmest voice. "I have wifely duties, and I cannot manage them with this damned corset."

They reached the suite door a few moments later, and Toni said, "I feel like I ought to carry you over the threshold."

Addie laughed and stepped around her. "How about we skip that, and you start freeing me from this costume? Unlike yours, mine isn't cut for comfort."

Toni locked the suite door behind them, silent as she stalked toward Addie in the dimly lit room.

Trying not to react, Addie looked around. She saw her trunk had been delivered and set to the side, noted that the bed had been turned down, noticed the rising moon outside. She swallowed against nerves that made no sense. This wasn't their first night together, and the wedding wasn't real.

Publicity stunt.

Fake.

Then why does this feel so real?

Toni didn't say a word as she unfastened the bodice of Addie's dress. She took a moment to stare as she removed the bodice. She paused, looking at Addie's chest. "You have the most perfect breasts I've seen." Toni sounded almost reverent. She kissed the overflowing swell. "For all that I write about the 1800s, I cannot imagine the challenge of seeing such sights and being told loving women was wrong."

Toni let the skirt pool at Addie's feet and removed the tiny bustle—leaving Addie in only a corset over her underwear.

"Loving me isn't wrong," Addie whispered. That was exactly what Addie wanted: Toni's love, forever and always.

"Thank heavens." Toni stepped behind Addie. "You are a vision."

Addie glanced over her shoulder at Toni, whose arms now wrapped around her. Toni slid her hands over the swell of Addie's breasts. Even though removing these last layers had seemed essential for hours, Addie moaned at the position she was in.

Briefly, Toni's eyes closed as if she was praying for mercy. Her lips ghosted over Addie's neck as she unlaced the corset with one hand.

Her other played over Addie's nipples like they were an instrument to be plucked.

By the time her undergarments were stripped from her, Addie was shaking with need, but she pulled away. "Fair play, Toni. You don't always have to wear the metaphorical pants."

Toni said nothing, still, as Addie stripped away her elegant cravat, jacket, vest, and shirt. However, Toni was clearly not used to being passive; she reached for Addie a few times, tracing her hips and sides.

Addie didn't resist, and Toni got bolder by the moment.

Addie divested her of her shoes, trousers, and very modern underpants. Then she pointed to the edge of the mattress. "There. Sit, please."

When Addie knelt on the floor, Toni tossed a pillow down, ever considerate woman that she was. Addie slid it under her knees, and then she leaned forward. Gently, she bit her fake wife's inner thigh, sucking to leave a bruise that only Toni would notice.

"What are you doing to me, Adelaine?" Toni murmured as her hands tangled in Addie's hair.

"Making love to my bride," Addie answered before leaning to lick the moisture beading on Toni's sex. Addie gripped Toni's thigh tightly, thumb on the bruise she'd just left, and Toni moaned.

Addie's suspicions had been right. Toni's prior remarks on liking it rough extended to a bit of bruising in soft places.

"Tell me what you like, Toni." Addie looked up at her. "I've never done this."

Toni let out a shuddering breath.

"I'm an innocent on her wedding night, yours to debauch. . . ." Addie trailed her tongue slowly over Toni's slick flesh. "Teach me how to please you, Lord Darbyshire."

This might be only a fake marriage for the weekend, but Addie wanted to prove to Toni that she someday wanted to make it real.

Chapter 28
Toni

Seeing beautiful Addie kneeling between her legs made Toni feel complicated feelings. She wasn't used to being the person women knelt in front of, especially almost innocent ones. There had been years when she was figuring out what she wanted, who she was, and she'd tried giving over control a few times. It had never worked out well.

"I need to touch you first," Toni tried to explain.

"You did." Addie tilted her head. "Earlier . . ." She motioned to the privacy screen, but she stayed where she was, kneeling while sitting back on her heels. "You put your mouth on me."

"I did." Toni reached down and cupped the curves of her wife's breasts in her hands, thrilled as Addie leaned up. "I'm not sure I can do this. . . ."

"Which part?" Addie asked, sounding more curious than hurt.

"Let go of control this fast." Toni felt self-conscious admitting it.

"Ah." Addie rose up on her knees. "I've noticed that."

"Let me make you feel—"

Addie stood up and kissed Toni, cutting off the words she was about to say.

They weren't untrue words, but they weren't the whole truth. Toni felt vulnerable, feelings exposed and public as she'd watched this incredible woman walk toward her.

It's an act. She's an actor.

But it hadn't felt like an act. The way Addie had looked at her made Toni feel like there was a truth there, a yearning for something Toni couldn't have—or give Addie. What that meant was that Toni needed to put this thing between them back on familiar grounds. She needed to have control, to have Addie, to give her the only thing she could offer a woman: satisfaction.

Her arms wrapped around Addie as they kissed.

Then abruptly, Addie pulled back. "You feel overwhelmed," she said astutely.

"It's silly, but—"

"It's not," Addie interrupted, staring down at her. "I did, too, you know. Seeing you looking at me like that, and all those people watching."

Toni rested her face on Addie's chest. "Yes."

"And you want to feel in control," Addie finished softly. "I get that. Can we try something?"

Toni kissed the space between her breasts and leaned back. "Like what?"

Addie walked away and opened one of her bags. Toni watched her sort through clothes and pull out a small box. Addie straightened and looked over at Toni before she opened it. She walked over to the bed, and Toni felt her own vulnerability fade as Addie sat down on the edge of the bed instead of kneeling. There was a beautiful, naked woman who wanted Toni, who accepted her—hang-ups and all.

Addie's cheeks were reddened as she held the box with both hands. "So I wasn't sure if you'd . . . if we . . . I knew I'd want you, but after you didn't call, I thought I'd be on my own."

"I'm sorry. I swear I'll call next—"

"I thought I'd be left to my own *devices*," Addie said louder.

Hearing the emphasis on that last word, Toni stared at the box. "Oh?"

"So I went shopping," Addie said. "I haven't used it yet." She held the box out. "It has a remote."

Still reclining on the bed, Toni opened the box, looking at the bright-purple vibrator and the discreet little remote control. "Who were you going to hand the remote to?"

"Myself." Addie didn't look away. "I thought it might feel more like someone else was in control if it was a remote. It has a music setting, too, so you cannot know when or how much it will vibrate."

"I love your mind, Addie." Toni stared at her with a small smile on her face. "Are you going to give me the remote?"

"Only if you let me touch you while you have that control . . ." Addie tilted her head slightly, challenge obvious in her expression. Her voice wavered as she said, "I want to have my mouth on you like you did with me. You can have this if I can have you."

Toni felt a wave of desire that reminded her of how bold Addie was, and how much she'd craved that. *Craved her.* She looked at the vibrator again. "Did you wash this already?"

"I did." Addie stared at her. "I wasn't sure how long I'd be willing to wait after seeing you."

Toni stared at her in awe, unable to think of words to explain what she was thinking and feeling in that moment. Addie's admission that she was as overwhelmed by this yearning between them made Toni's chest tighten.

Tentatively Addie suggested, "I could use it on you if you would rather—"

"No." Toni shook her head. There were rules, limits that she hadn't allowed anyone to cross. She wasn't opposed to being touched, and sometimes she felt okay with having a woman's mouth on her cunt. Reaching *okay* often required a bit of whisky or a longer friendship. Toni was used to giving, not handing over control. And a vibe? Controlled by someone else? That was a step too far for her comfort, even with Addie.

"Your plan is good. . . . The first plan, I mean."

"It's okay to say no to things," Addie said softly, taking Toni's hand in hers. "Sex isn't about just what one of us wants, you know? If you aren't comfortable with my mouth on you . . . because I don't know what I'm doing or for whatever reason. It's okay to tell me no."

"I just need a moment, Addie. I want this, though," Toni admitted.

"Tell me what you need." Addie stroked her thumb over Toni's hand, and there was no way to pretend in that moment that this was just casual sex. There was affection here, on both sides. Toni trusted her, wanted to please Addie, but she also wanted to feel Addie's touch, mouth, whatever *she* wanted.

Stop this. Stop the whole thing.

Toni stared at her. "I need to touch you until I'm . . . until . . ."

"Comfortable?" Addie filled in.

When Toni nodded, Addie put one bare foot on the bedpost and leaned back. She watched Toni as she widened her legs. "I trust you, completely and wholly. If you are willing, I would like to put my mouth on you tonight. I want you to teach me how to please you, but if that's not tonight, there will be other nights, I hope. So for right now . . ." She gestured at her body. "I believe you fake-married me so I could be right here. Do with me what you will, Lord Darbyshire. I'm yours tonight."

Toni put the box to the side and stared at Addie. "You might just be the perfect woman, Lady Adelaine."

Addie smiled up at her, and it felt different. Everything about tonight felt different.

This is what I wish I could have, Toni admitted to herself as she sat upright so she was facing Addie's bare chest.

Toni shoved her traitorous thoughts away and touched Addie—her thighs, the delicate curve of her breast, the hollow of her collarbone, the swell of her hip—and everywhere her hands explored, her mouth followed.

Addie arched and twisted, but she let Toni have the control she needed. She didn't grab her or try to reverse their positions, even as Toni pulled Addie onto the bed and slid down her body until her mouth found its way to Addie's bare sex again.

"Toni . . ."

"Yes, love," Toni asked.

"You have *all the control*," Addie swore. "You know that, don't you? You have complete control of my body every time you want me. Give me a *little* back."

"You don't want me to keep going?" Toni asked, unused to a lover who was so determined to find equality in the bed.

"I want to learn your body," Addie half asked, half begged. "I want to know what *you* taste like."

Toni continued licking Addie leisurely, not fast enough to push her too near the edge but enough that Toni felt her own body grow wetter and wetter. There really was nothing quite as heavenly as the taste of a woman. The only things that compared were the scent of a woman's desire and the sound of a woman in the throes of passion.

As Toni continued to taste Addie, she reached out to the box she'd left on the mattress. *Addie's vibrator.* Toni slid it over Addie's bare hip and toward the juncture of her thighs. "Shall we try this, then?"

"I've never used one with anyone." Addie breathed the words. She stared at Toni. "Only you. Everything I have tried is with only you."

That possessive thing flared up inside Toni again, and she knew that Addie was aware of it, and that she liked it. Addie was clever enough to realize that her words worked, and she used that freely.

She's perfect for me.

Carefully Toni slid the still-motionless vibrator inside Addie's dripping body. Then she brought her mouth back to Addie's clit, suckling and licking until Addie was writhing. Toni paused and said, "Are you sure you want me to stop?"

"Pause," Addie gasped. "Just pause so you . . . I want you to . . . feel good."

Toni sat upright. "Pull your legs closed. Just like that, so the vibe stays where it is."

Addie whimpered as she obeyed.

"Slide over," Toni directed. "On your side."

Once Addie did so, Toni moved so her legs were straddling Addie's face. "Just do what you think would feel good if you were . . ." Toni's words faded as Addie parted her folds and licked. Toni added, "Yes. Just like . . . that."

Toni fumbled for the remote, as Addie devoted herself to making Toni unable to think. Addie's moans felt as good as her tongue. Then Toni managed to find a setting that had Addie arching her hips.

Addie looked at her from the open frame of Toni's legs and said, "No wonder you like this. Every time you moan, my body answers."

Toni turned the remote to a faster speed.

"Please, Toni," Addie begged. "I want to . . . get . . . *you* . . . offfff."

But Toni couldn't reply. She couldn't tell Addie that seeing her coming undone, hearing her gasps and moans, having her slide her fingers faster and harder inside Toni as her mouth was busily trying to keep pace was almost on the edge of too intense.

When Addie's orgasm started to wash over her, Toni felt herself arch against Addie's mouth, and she followed her into completion. In a lifetime of women, Toni had never trusted anyone enough to be in a situation like this: mutual orgasm, mutual satisfaction.

"You're fucking perfect, Adelaine." Toni moved and pulled Addie up to rest on top of her.

Addie slid the tiny device out of her body and collapsed like she had no energy left to move herself. "You, too, Professor."

Toni kissed the tip of her nose. "Sleep?"

"Soon," Addie agreed. "Not just yet, though. I want to hear about everything I've missed the weeks we weren't emailing."

Toni's heart tightened uncomfortably at the intimacy of the request. This wasn't a nameless one-night stand, and no matter how often Toni tried to shift it into that box in her mind, Addie repeatedly dismantled that illusion.

"Classes are going well, and my new TA is phenomenally capable," Toni said as her hand idly traced up Addie's spine.

Addie propped her head up and listened as Toni talked. If not for the naked part, it would be the sort of friendship that Toni cherished. If not for the friendship, this would be the sort of sex that made Toni consider another night. The combination of the two, however, was vaguely terrifying.

Chapter 29
Toni

Toni woke in the middle of the night when tendrils of Addie's unbraided hair all but smothered her. She hadn't braided anyone's hair in a lot of years; her own hair hadn't been long enough for such things since elementary school, but she had the general thought that it was easy enough to do.

Carefully she divided the mass into three chunks and started trying to plait them together.

A giggle was her only warning before the woman attached to the cloud of hair looked back at her. "I've heard of fairy knots as a kid, where the wee creatures put knots in horses' manes and ladies' hair, but you look a bit big for a fairy."

"Your hair tried to strangle me," Toni started. "I'm just defending myself."

"It's not sentient." Addie rolled over. "I can braid it so you can sleep."

Toni pulled her closer, so Addie was curled against Toni's chest. "You got to hear about my life before you distracted me again. Since you're awake now, tell me the things we would've talked about if you hadn't lost my number."

Addie snuggled in before saying, "Well, the big thing is that they expanded the show. We are up to twelve episodes now, but you probably heard."

Toni started to absently thread her fingers through Addie's un-braided hair. "Twelve is good, right?"

"Even more would be better, but it means that the pilot was well received by the money people," Addie explained.

"All the buzz put *The Whitechapel Widow* back on the bestseller lists, you know?" Toni offered, still stroking Addie's hair. "We sold more overseas translations, too."

"Same with the show. It will air in more places than originally planned," Addie told her. "So the real question is how are *you* coping with all of it?"

Toni was surprised. Most people saw only the bright part of success, and that part was great. The crushing imposter syndrome—and the panic that everyone was staring at her, hoping she failed—was there, too, though. She confessed, "I'm not sure I *am,* honestly. I mean, I'm happy with the sequel so far, but I feel like a big fraud with every interview. They act like it's something huge—"

"It is," Addie interjected.

"Okay, but I sold it to pay a bill. I was hoping for a few dollars, so I didn't have to rent out my guest room." Toni took a pause, realizing what she was about to say.

No one but Emily knew the whole story. *Addie is my friend. It's safe to tell her the whole truth.* Before she could change her mind, Toni said, "I know I told you the small version, but the full story is that the night I met you, I'd found out that my deadbeat of a father had left my mother *hundreds of thousands* of dollars in debt, and Lil—my mother—needs to be in a memory care facility. I was panicking. I have to make sure she's safe, but I can't go to work to pay for things *and* move her into my place. She can't be left alone. She and I aren't close, but she's my mom. . . . It was a lot of upheaval."

"Your poor mother!" Addie stared up at Toni. "And poor you! No wonder you were at the bar that night."

"This may come as a surprise to you, but I haven't traditionally had great coping skills." Toni gave her a wry grin. "Liquor and ladies."

"So you were there looking for . . ."

"Exactly what I found." Toni hated the flash of guilt she felt as Addie winced. "But I didn't expect to meet a *friend* or the actor who'd be my character. Hell, I hadn't even thought the book would sell. Em suggested I try writing, and I admitted I had written a book. . . ."

"I met you as a broke college professor, then?"

Toni chuckled. "Painfully so."

"And your mom . . ."

"She's getting the care she needs now. We've had our issues over the years. I was a tomboy, very politically outspoken, and a feminist lesbian . . ." Toni paused, weighing how much to admit. "If you could letter in sex, I'd have been a star athlete in high school. My mother was mortified. I was not a *wanted* pregnancy, and I wasn't a wanted child."

"I'm so sorry." Addie squeezed her, a hug of sorts. "Did you end up closer to her as an adult?"

Toni snorted. "No. I fought with her, mostly about my louse of a father, but he had her wrapped around his finger. She had a hit song before she got pregnant. Did a little touring. Then he wanted her to be a fifties-style homemaker—which was painful. She was a terrible cook, could ruin laundry randomly, and was just *miserable*. And my dad? Gambled away her royalties every time they came."

"He's gone, though?" Addie prompted after a few quiet minutes.

"Yes, but he took a loan against her house, credit cards that she cosigned, and ran up so much debt that even with selling the house, she was deeper in debt than I could pay off in a decade. . . ."

"Until the book deal," Addie filled in. "You *saved* her, Toni."

The awe in her voice made Toni feel marginally better about telling her everything. "I did what I had to do. That's all. I paid her bills, and since he's gone, he can't make new ones now."

"Have you told her about the show?"

"No. She's not a big fan of lesbians, or rather, she never used to be." Toni wasn't sure she'd told anyone this much about her childhood in years. Possibly ever. Here or there, things came out in conversations, but straight-up telling someone was new. "Anyhow . . . so I wasn't expecting all of this to happen, but it's erased Lil's debt. And I met you."

"My parents are a different sort of mess." Addie shook her head, tickling Toni's chest as the tendrils of hair slid around.

"You told me some in LA." Toni couldn't imagine anyone not getting along with Addie or feeling lucky as hell to know her.

"Right, well, they project their drama onto me. I guess the good news is that I think I became an actor as a result. I had a lot of practice pretending to be *perfectly okay* with whatever their latest drama was." Addie huffed in remembered irritation. "At least they encouraged my career. Mom took me to auditions, and I did a few commercials as a kid. That money is what I've been using to offset bills until I got my big break."

"I like the idea that my book was a part of that 'big break' for both of us, financially," Toni confessed.

"Me too." Addie yawned. "We probably ought to sleep, as much as my body is starting to have other ideas. We have photos tomorrow."

"And luncheon, and a book signing."

"Open to the public?" Addie clarified. "They shipped photos from the show for me to sign, too. I've never done anything like that, and I'm nervous."

"Sticky notes. That's the secret. That way you can see how they spell their name." Toni kissed the top of Addie's head. Then she froze. It was a little gesture, but not exactly a friends gesture or friends-who-get-naked gesture. But Addie didn't react. Instead, she sat up, pulled her hair over her shoulder, and braided it with far more speed and ease than Toni could ever have managed.

Then she met Toni's eyes. "You are the best thing that's happened to me this year, you know? Whatever this is between us, I like it."

"I do, too," Toni confessed. "You make me feel safe and like I want to protect you."

"Same. I couldn't do the things we did without that," Addie said quietly. "If I don't have any comfort with someone, I can't let them touch me."

Toni nodded. "I need to be . . . hella aroused usually. I'm okay touching people, but there's a . . ."

"Vulnerability," Addie supplied.

"Yes. That. I don't let everyone I take to bed touch me, and if they do, it's often just hands." Toni couldn't remember ever sharing these sorts of details with a lover. "I've never let anyone do to me what I did with you. . . ."

"The vibe?"

"Yes."

"With your control issues, that makes sense," Addie said simply.

Toni chuckled. "To you."

"Maybe someday you can," Addie said lightly. "It felt really good. Or maybe you can try something else new. I'm pretty game to try new things *with* you, but only ones we both want. I don't want you uncomfortable just because I'm so excitable."

She sounded so earnest that Toni felt like her heartbeat was erratic. "I like how excitable you are."

"Only with you."

"Well, I like that, too."

"I noticed." Addie snuggled in against her side.

And Toni could only pull her closer.

They fell asleep like that, and Toni felt an unfamiliar sense that everything was finally going to be smooth sailing in her life. It was a rare feeling, one she'd never had in her childhood home or in her academic career. Life was about precarious moments, but tonight, she had a career—two, actually—and she had financial security, and a friend who made her feel like everything was sunny.

Chapter 30
Addie

After a successful wedding breakfast, they were settled at a table for a book and photo signing. Unlike the majority of the furniture in the antique-laden house, this was a foldable table. It was dressed up with a tablecloth that was decorated with arrangements of fresh flowers. Between Toni and Addie was a tea set, fortunately filled with black tea that someone kept pouring into her cup.

The initial line was daunting, but now that they were done, Addie had a moment to look over at her new (fake!) spouse. For all that Toni claimed not to love her author responsibilities, she was both gracious and charming. There was no doubt that the attendees were invested in the success of the show and the book series.

"It seems like a lot of effort for a small group," Addie murmured in a lull between people.

"Sometimes it's about the news coverage." Toni pointedly looked at the photographers. "This event will result in interesting photos and articles both on the books and the show."

"Oh."

"Part of that is because of you." Toni stared at her, and the intent way she did so made Addie positive that the cameras were now zeroed in on them. "You are a beautiful star, and the buzz for the show will mean that these photos are sent to assorted outlets.

"And the money from the tickets goes to charity," Toni added, not looking away from her.

"Which creates more coverage." Addie smiled over at the photographers.

"So jaded, so soon," Toni murmured. "I picked the charity. It was my condition for being here."

"Alzheimer's?" Addie guessed. "Or a queer organization?"

Toni glanced at her. "Both."

"Good." Addie smiled up at the next group of Victorian-gowned women with books and asked, "Are you enjoying your weekend?"

They'd developed a system of sorts. Toni signed and said "thank you" or answered some historical question. Addie made small talk. Most of her headshots were pre-signed, and few people wanted those personalized. They posed every so often for photos—*that* sort was preapproved for all attendees—but mostly, it was a book signing.

In the second hour, the signing was opened up to the public, and that was a different sort of thing entirely. There weren't as many historical questions from the signing line, but there were a lot more lesbians and queer folks. The crowd took on an unusually vibrant mix as the hue of boldly dyed Victorian dresses mixed with a smattering of rainbows and vibrantly dyed hair, along with older women in mundane dress.

"This is your audience," Addie whispered. "This eclectic group."

"Your audience, too," Toni pointed out. "You're *their* Adelaine Wight."

Addie felt herself studying her future audience. These were the book people, the crowd that put Toni's book on bestseller lists, and her job was to add to their number. She'd swell their ranks by her work in the show. *Hopefully.* And they'd buy Toni's books, too. There was talk of a show-related reissue for the paperback with one of the stills from the show.

I'd be on the cover of the book she wrote.

She couldn't repress the smile that stole over her at the thought of that bit of peculiarity. They were in this together, and Addie's success would become more success for Toni, too. That made her want to do better, not just because she loved *The Whitechapel Widow* and the career possibilities but because of how much she liked Toni.

"We're going to have to do this again after the show launches," Addie said lightly, smiling at the fan who had both an advanced copy and a hardcover copy of Toni's book.

"Excellent. Then they'll only want your autograph, and I can hide in the background," Toni teased as she accepted the books and the Post-it with the reader's name on it.

"Hush." Addie looked at the line of people. "This crowd is here because of your book. They won't vanish because of an adaptation."

As the day wore on, Toni was obviously peopled out, but aside from her surliness over the post-signing promo photos, she hid it well. The rest of Saturday was a blur. Dinner. After-dinner drinks.

"No weddings tonight," Lady Dove tittered. "We do, however, have accompaniment for a dance."

Toni offered an arm to Addie as they were all herded into the ballroom. "Like sheep to a shearing," she muttered.

Addie smothered a giggle.

"Our guests of honor will start the dance," the second, sterner Lady Dove announced. Her gaze met Addie's, and she nodded toward the floor.

"Do you mind?" Addie asked quietly. "I can refuse if—"

"I never mind having you in my arms." Toni led her to the center of the floor, glanced at the musicians, and gave a solitary nod.

The music started, and for the next minute or so, they were the only people on the floor. Addie felt transported. Never mind that this was a fake historical setting, and she was in a fake marriage. What mattered was the fire in Toni's gaze, the command with which she led Addie, and the certainty that Addie was the luckiest woman alive in that moment.

"What's that smile about, Lady Adelaine?" Toni murmured as they flowed across the room. Other couples were filling the floor now, so she had to be alert to those dancing or walking by them.

"I'm happy," Addie confessed. "Being here in your arms makes me feel incredible. I suspect it would be the same if we were wearing jeans and flannels. It's not the dress, or the music, or the room. It's just you."

"So I'm not a terrible fake wife," Toni teased.

You are exactly what I want in a wife, Addie thought.

All she said, though, was "You're doing a fine job of romancing me, Lord Darbyshire. I bet half these women will fantasize about being in my place."

Toni laughed loudly, seemingly relaxing into the moment. "I doubt most of them would want to be around the real me. I'm moody, short-tempered, introverted—"

"Clever, funny, giving," Addie interjected.

"You bring out the best in me," Toni said lightly, twirling her past the women in their dresses and the men in their suits. Today, with being open to the public, there was a sea of unusual costumes as well as Victorian ones. It also meant that they weren't the only pair of women dancing together.

Their brief waltz made Addie feel like a princess at a ball—or a Victorian at a ball that was historically inaccurate for its tolerance of the suit-clad author who swept her around the room. The ballroom was as stunning as the rest of Cape Dove Manor. The attention to detail in every corner of the mansion was breathtaking, and the musicians playing 1800s compositions only added to the ambiance. Still, it was the joy of being in Toni's arms that made Addie feel like swooning.

Parts of history are amazing; parts of modernity are, too.

The music paused as the song ended, and Toni released Addie. She bowed briefly. "Thank you, Adelaine."

"For dancing?"

"For everything, love. The dance, the smiles, being in the show. You are a . . ." Toni shook her head. She looked incredibly serious, and Addie wished she knew what Toni was thinking. All else Toni said was "I am grateful."

Impulsively, Addie leaned forward and dropped a kiss on Toni's cheek. "I like you, too."

Toni stared at her for a moment before cracking a smile. "Come on. We have photos with fans next in the library, and then I can show you how *much* I like you. . . ."

By the time they'd retired for the night, Addie was fairly certain that she wasn't the only one who would be a little heartbroken to return to their regular lives. She was struck with the fantasy of life in such a stunning setting, dancing in Toni's arms, spending night and day together. Instead, she'd be returning to her tiny apartment on the other side of the country.

Far, far apart.

This togetherness with someone who made her smile was what Addie wanted for the rest of her life, and she was starting to think that she wanted it with Toni. That night, they spent as much time talking as touching, and the thought of leaving was obviously weighing on both of them.

"It would be nice if we lived closer together," Addie said lightly at one point.

Toni paused. "I have to be in DC for teaching, and you need to be in LA for your job."

"I know, but it would be nice to see you more often."

"You'd get sick of me if we lived closer." Toni squeezed her hand. "I'm more fun in small doses."

Addie didn't argue, but it was a legitimate question to ponder. She had wanted this career forever, and Toni had her mother and the college keeping her on the East Coast. Was something *more* impossible? How could they click so naturally but be unable to be together?

Although Saturday night was bliss again when they were naked together, Toni continued to be a bit hot and cold, withdrawing into herself when they were not having sex or after she answered a too-personal question, but she also opened up more and more.

Addie shoved away the bigger issues of long-term impossibilities. In the short term, the worst thing since arriving for the weekend was the realization that Toni was a cover thief. When Addie woke to an alarm far too early Sunday morning, she made a mental note that she might have to get up and get dressed in the night after she had sex with Toni. The alternative appeared to be waking up freezing every morning.

"You're lucky you're cute, fake wife." Addie shivered as she slipped out of bed in search of a robe or something. "You're a cover thief."

Toni blinked up at her. "What?"

"I'm freezing—" Addie tugged on Toni's shirt from the night before. "—because *you* are a cover thief."

In fairness, Toni looked guilty. "I don't usually do sleepovers, Addie. So I don't have a lot of practice at sharing my bed with friends. You'll have to adjust, or we can see if—"

"You better not say 'if there is a second room open,'" Addie shook a finger at her. "I fake-married you!"

"I was *going* to say 'if there are spare blankets.' I like having you in my bed."

"Awww." A warm flush came over Addie as she realized that she wasn't the only one with a few firsts. "I guess we'll figure it out when we see each other."

Toni's sudden discomfort was as obvious as a flashing sign. She might not be screaming in panic, but the expression wasn't hard to read. Addie hadn't missed the way Toni used the word "friend" like a shield, but the wide-eyed look on her face when Addie commented on "seeing each other" was frustrating.

So Addie continued, "The good news is that, most of the time, I'll be in my cozy bed without fighting for a corner of the blanket, but maybe if we are at the same promo thing or you are in LA or . . . Oh! New Orleans! We're filming the outside bits in New Orleans because it has that 'historic streets' thing. You should come!"

Toni got out of bed. "Maybe . . ." She walked into the bathroom, leaving Addie there feeling like she'd crossed an invisible line. The only time Toni truly opened up was during sex or if no mention of the future was made. At all.

While Toni was in the bathroom, Addie pulled out her phone to check email. Supposedly it was a no-tech weekend, but today they would return to the real world. Next week, after the studio vetted all the photos, there would be a deluge of promo publicity—and already there were undoubtedly photos from the signing.

Addie's news alerts—which, yes, she still had set on Toni's name but now also included her own name, the book, and show title—had exploded. Addie's eyes skimmed them in growing horror.

SURPRISE WEDDING?

VICTORIAN MYSTERY WRITER WEDS STARLET

NEPOTISM? THE BRIDE WAS CAST IN HER NEW WIFE'S SHOW

Addie sank back on the bed as she kept scrolling. These were not the social media posts she expected. Signing photos? Sure. Wedding pictures out of context? No. Footage of the two of them getting married? Definitely not that.

"Toni? I think you need to come here." Addie's voice sounded shrill, but she was panicking a little.

Toni came into the room, toothbrush still in hand. She met Addie's gaze. "What's up?"

"The wedding . . ." Addie held out her phone. "Check your email. I need to call Marcela. Fuck."

Toni stared at the headlines as if she couldn't process what she was reading.

Definitely not a morning person.

"Hey?" Addie put a hand on Toni's arm. "Get your phone. Email or call your agent or your publicist."

"It was a fake wedding," Toni muttered.

"Yes." Addie clicked on a headline. "That's really you on one knee, though." She scrolled. "That's really me with flowers in my hair. That's actually us kissing."

"But the *wedding* was fake." Toni pulled out her own phone. "Like the whole weekend. It was all just pretend."

Addie knew what Toni meant, but the words still made her wince internally. She snapped, "Not *everything* was fake. The sex certainly felt real enough, and the conversations we had, and—"

"You know what I meant." Toni pulled on her trousers hurriedly, as if she were dressing for battle. She said nothing comforting to Addie; she didn't acknowledge the real parts. "This is a fucking disaster."

And Addie pointedly did not stare at the beautiful woman in nothing but her trousers. It wasn't fair that Toni looked that good even as she said such heartless things. Toni glanced at her, said nothing else as she grabbed a bra and shirt. Then she went into the bathroom with her clothes and phone.

The *snick* of the door sounded louder than it should, and Addie felt like they were having an argument.

I didn't do this.

I didn't make her stage a proposal.

I didn't force her to sweep me around the ballroom.

I didn't make her fake-marry me or . . . look at me the way she does.

Those were the pictures that made everything seem real: the way Toni had looked at Addie in the proposal and wedding shots. Well, that and the ones of them kissing. They could explain the wedding as a publicity stunt, but there was no doubt that at least some part of the story was true.

Addie turned her back and flipped over to her private email. Her parents had emailed repeatedly, and they'd undoubtedly called, too. She'd get to that. *And Eric.* For now, her reputation, the show's reputation, had to be her first priority.

From: Marcela
To: Adelaine Stewart
Re: Wedding??

Call me. ASAP. 818-555-5555

Marcela

That was the email Addie had to address. She took a breath and tapped the number. While she was waiting, she closed her eyes and made a wish that this was not a disaster.

"Addie?"

"Um, hi?"

"You *married* her?" Marcela sounded as if she wasn't sure whether to yell or cheer. "What happened to *friends*?"

"I can explain," Addie said. "There was a room shortage, and the owner said we couldn't share and—"

"You didn't think to call?"

"No? The photos and this video of the wedding weren't to be shared unless the studio vetted them. Just like the dinner," Addie said weakly. "It was fake, Marcela. We can make a statement that the wedding isn't real."

"Addie." Marcela sighed, and Addie could picture the tightening around her eyes.

"It was as real as the period clothes and carriages," Addie offered. "The whole thing was make-believe. We issue a statement—"

"It's not that simple. She isn't looking at you like it's fake. And that kiss looks damn realistic. . . . You're obviously involved with her, and I'm not going to issue a lie. Was that a real minister?"

"I don't know, but . . . the *wedding* wasn't real," Addie said weakly. "We didn't have a license, so it's not a real marriage, right?"

A voice in the background said something.

"That's her people calling," Marcela explained. "Go speak with her. We'll come up with a plan on our side, but for now . . . go back to Washington with her while we sort this out. There will be a ticket waiting for you at the airport. Stay off socials until you hear from me."

Addie was staring at her now-silent phone when Toni walked back into the room. She looked up as Toni scrubbed her hand over her hair.

Awkwardly, Toni said, "I guess you're coming to DC."

"I guess." Addie looked up at her, hoping that they could laugh this off, hoping that Toni wouldn't withdraw into herself.

Instead Toni walked over and started packing. She said nothing for several minutes, and then when she finally spoke, all she managed was, "It was a stupid idea. The wedding."

"It was to be a tech-free weekend," Addie pointed out. Her voice was a little shrill as she added, "Other than the approved photographers, it was to be tech-free."

Toni gave her a look that made Addie feel like she was a fool. "I didn't want there to be bad press about you sleeping in a hotel off-site, and I wanted you with me, so I thought— You know what? It doesn't matter what I thought. I'm sorry this happened. We can find you a hotel in the city while we sort it out."

"I thought you had a guest room . . . ?" Addie felt her temper fray.

"I do, but—"

"So you don't let friends stay with you?" Addie snapped.

Toni pressed her lips tightly together, like she was trying to trap words. She failed, though, as she said, "I don't bring women I fuck to my condo."

The words hit Addie like a slap. "Well, luckily for you, it turns out you aren't *fucking* me anymore. So I'll be staying in your guest room while the publicity people figure out the next move. Either of us staying in a hotel will add fuel to the fire, *or* I'll be forced to hide out in my room the whole time, so no one knows I'm there alone. What do I do, Toni, live on room service in my historical dresses and a hotel robe?"

Tears slipped over her cheeks. She hadn't created the spectacle. She hadn't leaked the photos. And she wasn't the one currently being a bitch.

But I am the one they're saying got the role on my back, and not because of my acting skills. Philip accused me of that when he talked to Marcela. Is he involved? He wanted to come here and . . . Addie didn't bother sharing any of that. *What does it matter?*

Toni closed her eyes and took several breaths, but she didn't reply. Addie hated this, hated everything about the fact that yet again she was pushed away.

Neither woman spoke as they packed and headed to the airport.

At least we won't be seated together. . . .

Chapter 31
Toni

The entire checkout and ride to the airport, Toni kept replaying the conversation with Emily in her head. This mess wasn't Addie's fault, or Emily's, or . . . well, it was the fault of someone at the event, and Toni had no idea which person that was. Someone leaked it, and, of course, Toni herself caused it. She wanted Addie with her, so she set out on a stupid plan—just like her father had done so often. Toni couldn't believe she'd screwed up so badly already. She thought about Emily's words again.

"*If you try to say it was fake right* now, *you'll come out looking like a predator.*" *Emily's voice was gentle, as if that would offset the horrible words.*

"*A predator?*"

"*You aren't looking at her like this is fake . . . and you aren't an actor,*" *Emily said bluntly.* "*You are looking at her like she's everything, and she's younger. An unknown actor.*"

"*She's in her mid-twenties, only four or five years younger than me at most,*" *Toni argued, as if age was the real issue.*

"*I'm aware,*" *Emily said dryly.*

"*It's not . . . I'm not like that . . . you know me, Em.*"

"*I do, and I think you have far more feelings for Addie than you are admitting, even to yourself.*" *Emily took a breath.* "*If it looks like you seduced her and paid her off with the role . . . sweet,*" innocent, younger actor . . . that's some MeToo fallout we don't need."

"But when we met, I hadn't even sold the book." Toni closed her eyes. "There wasn't a show to even get a role in—"

"Yes. So in this situation, closer to the whole truth is better. I know you like your privacy, but you created this mess. You can either look like a monster, or admit you have feelings for a woman you met before selling The Whitechapel Widow. I'm talking to Greta and publicity, and I have a call in to Marcela. What I need you to do is take your bride home, and be the fucking charismatic woman you can be the entire time you are in public. You're the one who has a lot to lose here, Toni. If she decides to go to the press and say you pressured her or—"

"She won't." Toni looked toward the closed door. "I know her, Em. She's not like that."

"I hope you're right," Emily said ominously before disconnecting.

Toni understood the worries, but she trusted Addie. Even though she was currently angry, Adde wouldn't lie. She was a good person, one who deserved more kindness than Toni had shown her today. It wasn't Addie's fault that Toni felt embarrassed by having feelings.

They walked through the airport side by side, but Addie was not so much as glancing at Toni. She was again dressed in regular clothes, but slightly nicer than average. Jeans and a blouse. A scarf and sunglasses. Bright lipstick. Jangling bracelets. She looked like a hippie with some extra cash to spend on her appearance.

"You look amazing today," Toni said in a low voice. "You always do."

"You were an asshole." Addie stared straight ahead. "Complimenting my clothes doesn't undo that."

Toni sighed. "I didn't cope well."

"Right, because having everyone think I *fucked* my way into the role is great. That must be why I lashed out at you." Addie shot her a scathing glance. "Oh, wait . . . that's not what *I* did, is it?"

After a moment of cycling through guilt and embarrassment,

Toni opted to be honest about her reaction. "Em says that if we deny it—us, the wedding—I look like a predator."

Addie was not having it. "Oh, I can see how that excuses your bullshit today, because it looks so *great* for me. I simply love that it looks like I earned this role on my back."

Toni flinched visibly. "I'm sorry."

"The wedding was your idea," Addie reminded her.

"I know."

"And the pictures . . ." Addie sniffled. "You can tell them it was an act."

"I'm not an actor," Toni said weakly.

"Then tell them you were just *fucking* me. Tell them you were pretending you care about me." Addie bit out the words as tears spilled.

"Addie, I wasn't *pretending* to care." Toni wasn't going to overtly admit how deep her feelings were or that she was terrified seeing the proof of it in those pictures. And she sure as hell wasn't going to admit that this had stirred up her feelings about being just like her dad.

I won't ruin your life like he ruined my mother's, Toni promised silently.

"You look like you actually like me in those pictures. *Really* like me. Like I matter to you." Addie pulled off her sunglasses finally. "I looked at the pictures."

Toni sighed. "I do like you, Addie. We both know that. We're friends, aren't we? We spent a year emailing. Friends care, right?"

"I don't know. My *friends* wouldn't refer to me as a woman they fuck," Addie said coldly before wiping away her tears and putting her sunglasses back on.

They were silent as they walked to the gate. Addie's steps were sharp, as if she were trying to stab the floor with each footfall. Anyone who thought dating women was easier than dating men hadn't ever dealt with an angry woman.

Not that we're dating! Toni's brain filled in quickly. *We're friends who ended up in a situationship sort of thing. That's all this is.*

Toni had been a lousy friend today, though. That detail was indisputable. She reached out and took the handle of Addie's carry-on. "Let me take this for you."

Addie shot her an unreadable look, but she cooperated. It wasn't much, but Toni felt relieved by it. Eventually, Addie's rapid steps slowed to an almost normal walk. She'd walked her anger off to some degree, or maybe her temper relaxed with enough time. Whatever it was, Toni was grateful.

By the time they reached the gate, Toni's phone buzzed. She glanced down, bracing for another disaster.

"Upgraded" was all it said.

"We need to stop at the desk," Toni murmured when Addie gave her a curious look. "New boarding passes."

Addie made a sort of agreeing noise, but she said nothing. She stayed at Toni's side as they stopped at the gate.

"We need to pick up new boarding passes," Toni said, pulling out her ID and handing it over.

After a moment of digging in her bag, Addie held hers out, too. She stayed silent as the woman printed the updated passes.

"Here you go." The cheerful gate agent handed the passes and IDs to Toni with a smile and a few other pleasantries Toni barely heard because Addie had walked away.

"Sorry," Toni murmured to the gate agent before following Addie.

Addie picked a seat in the corner, as far from the others waiting for the flight as she could be without leaving this gate. When Toni sat next to her, Addie held out a hand for her pass silently.

"We're in row two now," Toni offered, handing over the boarding pass and Addie's driver's license.

"I didn't plan to sit next to you. I don't think I want to either."

"I'm sorry for my choice of words earlier," Toni said as quietly as she could. "I was upset."

"So was I." Addie stared out the window at the planes lined up at their jet bridges. "And yet I wasn't an asshole. . . ."

"Addie," Toni tried.

Addie continued to stare out the window, but now her foot was tapping in the air.

"I was wrong," Toni added. "I handled my shock poorly, and I was wrong to word it that way."

"I'm staying in the guest room." Addie glanced over. "Not a hotel."

"Yes." Toni bit back the temptation to suggest she could share her bed. That was what had gotten them in to this mess. They had to step back, reassess, think this through clearly. She nodded. "That makes sense."

"And you *know* this wasn't my fault, so being an asshole to me isn't fair." Addie's eyes were bright with unshed tears, and her voice was wobbling with some combination of anger and sorrow.

Angry women, crying women: they were hard to face. *Justifiably* upset and angry ones were worse. Knowing it was entirely Toni's own fault was the absolute worst, though.

Toni held open her arm to invite Addie closer. "I was wrong. You should yell at me when we don't have an audience. I was completely out of line, and I'm sorry I spoke to you that way."

"You hurt my feelings."

"I'll do better," Toni promised.

Addie practically threw herself into Toni's arms, despite the seat arm between them. PDA was far from Toni's comfort—at least this sort of PDA. The occasional exhibitionism she could support, but Toni was not generally a fan of nonsexual affection with people in public or, honestly, in private. This hugging, cuddling thing that Addie liked was not Toni's usual way of acting with women, even those she was sleeping with, but Addie was upset right now.

And it's ultimately my fault, so I have to fix it.

"It'll get sorted out," Toni said. "And while it does, I swear I'll do better."

Addie sniffled. "You better."

Someone nearby snapped a picture, flash making the moment impossible to ignore. This was their reality now, apparently. The press for the show all featured Addie's face—for obvious reasons—and Toni's picture took up half the back cover on dust jackets.

"Don't overreact," Addie whispered before settling back in her own seat. She put her sunglasses back on and stared out the window.

Toni decided she was less okay with the fellow passenger taking their picture than she'd expected. She angled her body, putting her back to everyone there and blocking Addie partly from sight—and from any more photos. When Toni glanced down at Addie, she noticed her slight smile.

"My hero," Addie whispered.

There was no way to reply to that. Toni was a lot of things, but hero wasn't one of them. They were in the news because of her mistakes. They were fake-married because of her. And Addie was stuck in DC because of her.

Toni was certain that she was nowhere near a hero, but it felt good to have Addie look at her that way all the same. It was a helluva lot better than the hurt and anger she'd aimed at Toni earlier. The worst part, though, was that the sight of Addie's forgiveness made Toni want to tell her that she wasn't misinterpreting the way Toni looked at her in the photos. Toni was feeling things that would only lead to pain for Addie, and it made Toni want to run. She needed time to think, space to rebuild the walls Addie had destroyed.

Instead I'm going to need to cope with having her in my home without letting myself think we could last.

That was the real reason Toni didn't want Addie in her home. Toni was already falling for the vivacious, talented women shooting her secretive smiles. Having her in Toni's home was just asking for trouble, complications, *feelings* that couldn't last. . . .

Addie's life was in LA; Toni's was in in DC. Addie was healthy and wanted love; Toni had a not-insignificant chance of ending up like her mother. This thing between them would end. It *had* to.

Chapter 32

Addie

The flight was blissfully short, but Addie had noticed several passengers looking at them. *Do they know something? Recognize us?* The average American only read a few books a year at most. The show, however, had ads on billboards and on the sides of buses. Addie had no idea whether they were looking at them because of the scandal, the show, the fact that they looked like they were together, or just the fact that they were women in first class—which typically was filled with far more men than women.

"Are you okay?" Toni asked as the plane bounced along the runway.

"Fine." Addie had on the smile she wore around her parents and men who aggressively hit on her. It didn't look anywhere near real, and she knew it.

Toni opened her mouth like she was about to reply, but she didn't. She closed it and stared at the flight attendant until it was time to stand to deplane. The people in row one grabbed their bags from the overhead, and Addie tried not to flinch as she took in the tense set of Toni's jaw.

Addie wasn't sure what to say. She wasn't about to admit that she felt self-conscious deplaning with Toni. She didn't admit that she'd never flown first class, although the flight was short enough that it didn't matter that much. She thought about mentioning that it was nice to be up front, where fewer people were able to stare at them—but she didn't really want to talk about the media debacle anymore.

Addie glanced out the window once more before saying, "I've been here once."

"DC?" Toni looked back at her.

"I was a teenager." Addie shrugged. "We did the usual monuments and museums tours."

Toni stepped into the aisle and retrieved their carry-ons from the overhead. Then she looked at Addie. "After you."

Addie tried to remind herself that being charmed by basic courtesy ought to not be a thing, but her dating experience was thin enough to not need all of her fingers to count the people who had taken her out more than a few times—and none of those people had been like Toni. There were a few attempts at dating boys, including that mess with Philip, and then a couple of sort of friendshippy-date-things with women. Then her. Toni.

Without letting any of those words out, Addie stepped in front of Toni. She held out a hand for her bag, but Toni ignored her. For someone who claimed they were friends, Toni sure acted like they were dating. That would be the case even without the sex. She was considerate in ways that no friend had ever been.

Other than that crass remark. Let's not forget that. She said I was a woman she was fucking.

Addie kept her spine straight and her pace quick. Toni caught up once they were off the jet bridge and stayed at her side, silent as they walked. Her behavior continued at the baggage claim; she loaded Addie's giant luggage onto a trolley. Then instead of a car service or rideshare, Toni pointed. "This way."

They walked through an underground walkway to a parking garage, and Addie felt a little bad that Toni was pushing the trolley with all the luggage.

"I feel like I ought to do something," Addie admitted.

Toni scowled briefly. "About?"

Addie gestured. "You're carrying everything and—"

"You're wearing heels." Toni glanced at Addie's feet. "This is faster."

After that, Addie kept her mouth shut and trailed behind her until they reached a bright red Jeep. Toni loaded the bags into it, paused, and asked, "Do you have clothes that aren't from another historical period?"

"What I'm wearing." Addie shrugged. "I wasn't expecting to need more things . . . but maybe I'll be able to go home quickly?"

Toni sighed. "Do you want to stop at a store?"

"The store? Like for shopping?" Addie blinked at her. "You want to go *shopping* with me . . . ?"

"No, but I can't imagine you want to wear corsets all week if you're stuck here."

"I have regular underthings, and I can wash these." Addie gestured at her underwear and bra. Although they were covered by her jeans and top, Toni's gaze fixed on Addie's chest for a long moment.

"Do you have spare jeans? Or pajamas or whatever?"

Addie sighed. "Can I borrow maybe a T-shirt or sweater or something? Hopefully I'll only be here a day or so. . . ."

Toni's expression tightened.

"So no sleeping at your place or wearing your clothes?" Addie guessed. "Is that what this is?"

Toni was silent at first. Then she said, "No. You can wear some of my things. That's not the issue. My jeans and my shirts just won't fit you. You're shorter, for one, and you have a lot of . . . your chest is . . . You have *curves,* Addie. I like them, but my clothes aren't going to fit you right."

"Your blazer fit. I can wear a larger T-shirt or tank top and maybe one of your jackets . . . ?"

"Or we could stop and pick up a few things. There's an outlet mall called Potomac Mills about thirty minutes away we cou—"

"No. What I have is fine," Addie insisted.

She felt like she was being absurd, but she was not interested in going clothes shopping with Toni. Something about it felt too personal, and Addie already couldn't handle that with the way Toni was acting. She'd called her someone she "fucked," and then treated her like she was a delicate sort of wife. Toni carried bags, walked so that Addie was sheltered from anyone who might bump into her, and in general was as chivalrous as the ideal spouse—but she claimed they were "friends" and referred to what they were doing as fucking.

How am I to make sense of any of this?

"Fine." Toni started the Jeep and headed out of the parking garage. She didn't say anything else, and the silence dragged out until Addie decided that she wasn't going to bother trying to talk to her.

DC's traffic was no worse than LA's; it may even have been better. Riding with Toni felt different than car services or rideshares, though. Toni was an aggressive driver, which ought not have been a surprise. What was a surprise was that Addie found it stupidly attractive. She darted a glance at Toni, who was sliding her Jeep in and out of the, what? six lanes of traffic currently, but doing so with the sort of comfort that Addie could not fathom. If she had to drive in traffic like this, her knuckles would be white and her jaw would be clenched.

"You're staring," Toni said, not looking at her.

"You're an arrogant driver." Addie didn't mean it as an insult or a compliment. It was a statement of fact. "It probably shouldn't surprise me, with your control issues."

Toni laughed. "You're more of a passenger princess?"

"Better that than a pillow princess," Addie quipped.

"I'm okay with those." Toni kept her eyes on the road. "You're only the second passenger in the Jeep, though."

"Oh?"

"Em."

"She seems protective of you." Addie wasn't jealous of Toni's agent. Maybe she ought to be, but it was obvious that she'd totally misread them in Scotland. Now that she'd seen them in LA, Addie realized that the two were the sort of friends who were more siblings than potential lovers.

"We've known each other since middle school," Toni said. "A lot of years."

"I always wanted a sister. I have Eric, but . . . he's like a brother. Literal cousin, but close like a brother." Addie relaxed as they started chitchatting again. This was closer to normal.

Their conversation drifted in and out as Toni drove them to her place. She keyed in the gate code and drove to a numbered spot. For a moment, she didn't move. She turned off the engine, glanced at Addie, and said, "I'm really trying not to be weird about this."

"Being fake-married?"

"Yes, but . . . bringing a woman home. I know there's no way to say this without it sounding like I'm . . ." Toni shook her head. "I've never been great at letting people into my home, and I *just* moved here. I bought it. My first home that I *own*."

"So more of a garden-and-hotels sort of woman," Addie teased.

"Yes."

Addie reached over and squeezed Toni's arm. "I figured that out a while ago. I'm your *friend*, Toni. I'm not judging you for whatever you did before me." Addie couldn't bring herself to add "or after me" because she didn't want there to be anyone else. "But you're my friend, and we're in this together, and we were already tied up together because of the show. . . ."

"So you think I'm overreacting," Toni surmised.

"Yes." Addie climbed out of the Jeep. "So I'm visiting a friend in DC today. I promise I don't require special avocado toast or bedtime stories. I just need a place to be while our publicists figure it out, and because of what's going on, it makes more sense if that's here with you."

Toni nodded. "You're right. You are. I know that. I just panicked."

Addie went to the back of the Jeep and got her carry-on. "Lead on. I can come back for my trunk after I'm not trying to guess where I'm going. . . ."

"I'll come out and get your trunk." Toni took Addie's carry-on from her hand again. "Come on."

Without another word, Addie followed Toni to the front door. The condo was an end unit that had a standard New England, red brick, colonial vibe. Addie took in details as Toni keyed in a security code and turned the key in the door.

The windows she could see all had blinds, and the building itself looked like new construction.

Inside Toni put their bags down in the foyer and motioned to the steps. "The living room is that way. Bathroom to the left. Guest room and office are down here. Another bathroom here that will be yours. I'm going outside for the other things."

Then she left Addie there to make her way deeper into Toni's home.

Addie kicked off her shoes, setting them to the side and headed upstairs. The view was lovely. A simple room. Minimalist in style. A few photographs: landscape, not family. The kitchen, to the right, was spartan. In all, it could've been a generic model home or vacation rental—except for a plush purple sofa with gold trim and fringe. That stood out as an unusual flash of difference.

"Wow." Addie stepped closer. The sofa looked like it could be on the set of the show. Victorian. Over-the-top. Plush. Addie ran a hand over the arm before looking back to see Toni coming up the steps with her trunk.

"Watch out for—"

"Ouch!" Addie leaped back, stumbling over a coffee table, as something scratched her ankles. "What was *that*?"

A thump sounded as Toni dropped her bag and darted out to steady Addie. Toni's arms wrapped around her, and instinctively, Addie nestled closer. There was something perfect about being in Toni's arms, and after spending Friday night, Saturday day, and Saturday night in those arms, it had felt unsettling to have such distance between them all day.

"My cat," Toni finally finished. "He's territorial about his den." Her smile was indulgent. "The fringe has somehow become his door. . . ."

Addie giggled as a pair of fuzzy paws stretched out. The rest of the attacker's body followed in a flowing stretch, like he was some great lion or panther. He was an oversized fluffy cat of indeterminate breed—at least to Addie's eye. Maybe someone who knew more about cats would have a better guess. Her answer was that he was a fluffy-breed kind of cat. She hadn't ever had a cat, but the one in front of her managed to be both regal and daunting.

"He's gorgeous," Addie said.

"He knows it, too." Toni watched the approach of the cat. She was grinning at the furball with a disarming kind of openness that made Addie bite back a sigh.

She's even lovelier when she's relaxed.

Toni looked down as if the cat understood her and said, "Don't give me that look. I know you had plenty of love and food, Oscar Wilde. Emmy spoils you."

The cat let out a noise that was somewhere between a meow and a yawn before sitting down, tail wrapped around his feet like a fluffy cloud, and staring up at them.

"This is Addie," Toni said, introducing her to the cat as if that was normal behavior. "Addie, meet Oscar Wilde." She glanced at him again, smiling affectionately. "Em was cat-sitting this weekend, so no matter what he says, he's not been neglected in the least."

Addie squatted down and reached a hand toward him, figuring he could either reject or lean into her hand. "Hello, Oscar Wilde. I'm Toni's friend."

The fluffy creature took one step forward, pressing his head into her palm.

"Aren't you just the sweetest thing?" Addie whispered as she gently petted him.

"Lies," Toni muttered from behind her. "Moody and arbitrary beast. Terrible manners."

Addie looked over her shoulder. "I've heard animals resemble their humans."

Toni rolled her eyes. "I am not going to dignify that barb with a reply, Miss Stewart."

When Toni walked away, Oscar Wilde pranced after her like a joyful downy cloud, and Addie took the moment to settle her feelings again. This situation with the faux wedding had brought up a lot of complications—not just the viral photos.

Addie looked in the direction Toni went, and she had to fight back the urge to follow her.

She is not great at emotions.

Don't pressure her.

It's pointless anyhow. She has a life here. I have a life in LA.

Instead of following Toni, Addie stood and walked to the guest room, alone. She closed the door while she looked for something to wear for the night. On the bed was one of Toni's shirts, and Addie forced herself not to pick it up and sniff it.

This is not just a fling, not for me. I'm falling for her.

Chapter 33
Toni

Toni struggled to sleep that night. She waited in the living room for Addie to reappear, but Addie stayed away. Toni, objectively, couldn't blame her. It wasn't often that Toni was that insensitive, but her default reaction when women tried to get too close was not kindness. Cold words and exit: that was the strategy that had always enabled her to stay commitment-free.

I want to spend time with her, *though.*

Addie was settled in the guest room; fortunately Emily had washed the bed linens and tossed them in to dry before she took the train back to Manhattan. A part of Toni could admit that she was being ridiculous about pushing Addie away again, but she wasn't sure how to undo that without getting in deeper.

They weren't really dating, and honestly, if they weren't on opposite sides of the country Toni would have ended it by now. Hell, she hadn't even shared her last name over the year they emailed. Maybe the illusion that there was a distance, literally and emotionally, was why Toni let Addie get this close.

I should stay away from her.

Two nights in a bed ought not be enough to miss the feel of Addie next to her, and inviting Addie to sleep in her actual bed was different than sharing an anonymous hotel bed. That was commitment territory, and Antonia Marie Darbyshire wasn't commitment material. So she was alone in her bed with the woman she wanted out of reach, even though they were under the same roof.

Toni flopped over again, picturing the woman she'd trusted enough to talk to like a friend *and* spend two nights in a row with. Addie was remarkable. Funny, even at seemingly odd times. They'd laughed during sex, and that was always a sign that a person was a great match. Sex ought to be fun. It ought to make you feel like all the stress in the world has temporarily vanished.

And she defended me.

Toni wasn't used to that. Her aunt. Her bestie-turned-agent. Only a short list of people had ever taken the time and energy to stand up for Toni. She was implacable, tomboyish, and smart-assed. Most people interpreted that as impervious to insults or slights. That wasn't accurate, but for the most part, it was the image Toni let stand. Addie saw through it.

And I rewarded her with a scandal. If I hadn't suggested that fake marriage . . .

Toni told herself that she was simply solving a problem, but there was more to it. She wanted the illusion. She didn't need to stage the proposal, either. She had wanted the whole lie, though: the proposal, the wedding, the feeling of being with Addie. She'd basically declared that they were involved, as if what they did at Cape Dove was not going to matter when the weekend was over.

But it does, and now we need to figure out how to fix that instead of thinking about whatever it is we're doing.

Addie made Toni think dangerous what-if thoughts. She had never believed in marriage, imagined that perfect woman, pretended she was a bride during playtime, or flipped though wedding magazines. Marriage was an institution that allowed her father to destroy decades of her mother's life—while he catted around with married women.

And those are my genes.

Addie deserves a better woman than me.

The condo was quiet, which was usually what Toni preferred, but after two nights of falling asleep to the sounds of Addie breathing, the silence felt oppressive. Toni checked her phone yet again, as if there would be news from publicity in the middle of the night. Admittedly, publicists seemed to exist on little sleep, overworked as they were, but it was after midnight on the East Coast.

After she finally fell asleep, Toni spent the night waking from odd nightmares that Addie hated her, that the publisher wanted the money back, and that all of it had been a dream: the book deals, the teaching job, the TV show, meeting Addie again in Los Angeles.

Come morning, Toni was grateful that she had a coffeepot with an automatic timer. It was one of her favorite indulgences. Being home meant waking up to the smell of fresh-brewed coffee. She thunked the alarm to turn it off, looking for the normal morning patterns. This was typically when her cat showed up to say good morning.

"Oscar Wilde?" Toni looked around her bed. It looked like she'd been alligator rolling all night, but there was no fuzzy menace buried in the covers.

She sniffed, smelling onion and peppers instead of just the usual coffee. That had never happened. Em wasn't a fan of cooking in the morning, and no one else had stayed over.

Grabbing a robe and pulling it on, Toni wandered toward the kitchen. Her cat wasn't present, and from the smells, Addie was cooking. Toni glanced at the clock again. Six o'clock in the morning. *Who actually cooks at this hour?* Toni was more inclined to grab a bagel or banana, maybe a yogurt with granola if she had the time.

By the time Toni made her way to the kitchen, she realized that she was not prepared to see Addie there. Instead of being irritated that Addie was making herself at home, Toni felt a strange feeling in her gut at the sight that greeted her. There shouldn't be, but there was a rightness to seeing Addie making herself at home—and to realizing that Addie was wearing Toni's clothes.

That flare of affection was unexpected, but the hunger wasn't. Addie was wearing one of Toni's well-worn faded sweatshirts. The hem came down past Addie's hips, but if Toni didn't know better, she'd think that Addie had nothing under it. If this had been Saturday or even Sunday before the stupid photo debacle, Toni would have felt comfortable checking.

Along with the shirt, Addie had on a pair of oversized ankle socks she'd borrowed. They ought to have looked silly, but instead she looked like a vision of everything Toni couldn't keep. *Didn't deserve.* Addie was bare from the curve of her bum to her shins, and she wasn't self-conscious at all.

"I didn't touch your coffee." Addie glanced at the machine. "I was making an omelet. I found sun-dried tomatoes, an onion, and part of a pepper. Want to split it?"

"I need to go to the grocery." Toni tried and more or less managed not to stare at Addie's legs—at least while Addie was looking at Toni, expecting an answer.

"This worked." Addie shrugged. "I wasn't sure what time you head to campus, but I figured the coffee kicking on was a clue."

Toni poured her coffee. "Do you want a cup?"

"I want tea or juice, but I guess that's not—"

"That cupboard. There are a few tins of teas." Toni gestured, feeling inordinately pleased by Addie's little sound of joy. Toni hadn't done anything to earn that sound. She pushed back her reaction to that noise, the memories that accompanied it, and focused. "Do you have a plan for the day?"

Addie filled a tea ball and dropped it in a mug. "Read? Nap? We aren't filming today, so if I were home, I'd probably go to the gym. Here. I'm on my own."

Toni rinsed out the teakettle and filled it while Addie divided the omelet onto two plates. The whole thing was a kind of comfortable domesticity Toni had never shared with a woman she'd taken to bed. Mornings after were rare enough, but to linger and share a meal was almost unheard of. If it did happen, it was at a coffee shop or maybe room service.

This isn't a morning after, Toni reminded herself. She'd slept in her own bed last night.

As Addie carried the plates to the table, she paused to eye Oscar Wilde, who was flicking his tail at her. "I gave him more cat kibble and some water."

"He's waiting for his soft pouch." Toni released her coffee mug long enough to give him the cat food, and then she washed up again and grabbed her coffee. Glancing at the clock, she wondered how much off her schedule would be with sitting down to eat. She wasn't behind yet. Mornings included coffee and wake-up time, especially if she was going to drive.

At the table she pulled up a Metro map on her phone, snapped a screenshot, and started to edit the photo—marking where the college was, the museums, and the condo. Then she texted it to Addie.

Her phone was apparently near the living room sofa, if the chime was accurate, so Toni showed her the image on her phone. "This square is us."

"And the . . . is that an *eyeball*?"

"Museums, things to see." Toni grinned. "The 'A-plus' is the college, like on an essay."

Addie looked like she might be trying to resist smiling. "You're funnier than you admit."

"You're just biased." Toni looked away. Being with Addie for breakfast, chatting with her, this was far too nice, too cozy, even. Toni cleared her throat and took another drink of coffee. "You can take my spare key or just leave the bolt undone and use the code. It's a safe area."

"Says the lady with multiple locks."

Toni rolled her eyes. "The only time they're all locked is when Em visits. She tends to use them all."

Neither of them had mentioned the reason Addie was here in DC, or publicists, or the gossip, but ignoring it wasn't going to do them any favors. Toni said, "You'll let me know if you hear any news from the LA team?"

Addie sighed. "So far, nothing but the idea is that we just need to let it blow over. There's always something new and juicy. The attention will die down."

"Okay." Toni nodded, and they ate in silence. Finally when it really was getting to the point that Toni had to get ready, she said, "It's nice to see you longer. I mean, not necessarily under these circumstances but . . . if you wanted to visit again . . ."

"I need to think," Addie said softly. "You were a jerk to me, even though I didn't do anything to deserve that. I didn't send pictures or plot this or—"

"I know. I apologized," Toni reminded her.

"And then you tensed up about me being here, and overreacted at the thought of me borrowing a shirt. . . ." Addie plucked at the shirt. "I thought we were friends."

Toni sighed. "We seem to either misunderstand each other, or I screw up—"

"Or we get along great and have mind-blowing sex," Addie interjected. "I know the first time was me misunderstanding and overreacting."

"This PR mess was my turn to overreact, I guess." Toni stood, finished her coffee, and carried her plate to the sink. "Would you mind people knowing we were involved?"

"Not at all. I am not ashamed. Are you?"

"No. I'm . . . private." Toni met her gaze, determined to fix this. "I didn't think it through when I suggested the wedding. I just wanted to spend the weekend with you."

"I know."

"Do you want to meet for lunch? I really do want our friendship to work, even if it shifts to a friendship without sex." Toni glanced back, then washed her plate and fork. "I'm free at one."

"I'll text." Addie smiled, but it didn't quite go all the way to her eyes. She crossed her arms over her chest. "I need a little time to think, Toni. I get that you have baggage, but you hurt me."

There was nothing else to say to that, so Toni refilled her coffee and said, "You can text if you need anything else, too."

And then she tried not to let her face show how much Addie's withdrawal stung. It wasn't like Toni could give her a real relationship, but she wasn't ready to call this quits. Eventually, she'd have to, but right now, Addie was here.

In my home. Wearing my clothes. Cooking me breakfast.

How was Toni to keep her at distance? How was she to resist her?

Later, when there were thousands of miles between them, they could go back to emailing. Right now, Toni wanted to cancel her classes and take Addie to bed. What was the harm? Publicity would sort out the marriage mistake. It wasn't even a legal marriage, so it ought to be simple enough to get in front of this.

Why not enjoy the honeymoon she supposedly was on?

Chapter 34
Toni

Walking out of her condo and leaving Addie there was one of the most unexpectedly difficult things Toni had done that year. Worse than starting a new college position. Worse than a book tour. This was something in her belly that felt like fear, as if she'd turn around and discover that Addie was already long gone. *But I didn't want her here in the first place,* Toni argued with herself. *I should be okay with this.*

Toni hadn't expected that sense of panic or worry that she was losing something before she even had it, but there it was—and she was steadfastly not thinking on it. Instead, she got in her Jeep and dialed Emily.

"I always know you're panicking when you call before ten," Emily said.

"What's the situation?" Toni steered out of the lot.

Emily sighed. "There are a couple photos that went viral, and they're still climbing in visibility. You two look great together, and there are memes now. Plus, of course, the period dress. The show. The bestselling book. It was basically a perfect storm of reasons, and now you have this viral, buzzworthy moment."

"What does that even mean?"

"Millions of views, Toni. It means millions of views. And that means that people are noticing."

Toni listened, trying not to panic. "Right, well, what's the plan? How do we make it go away?"

"We don't. You make a smart couple, and even though gossip stuff doesn't pay as much attention to authors, your book is a phenom, and Addie is stunning." Emily sighed. "There are wedding gifts from a few foreign publishers. I think some of it is trying to be seen being pro-LGBTQ. Some is the network. Anything film or TV is always more buzzworthy. This could have turned into a MeToo moment, but instead it's looking like a good thing . . . unless Addie makes a statement to counter that."

"I want to issue a statement. Point out that Addie's casting wasn't because of . . . me? That this is a lie." Toni flinched at the word. It was only partly a lie. She was involved with Addie. She wasn't pretending . . . but the *wedding* itself was fake.

"No statement. You're sleeping with her, Toni, so saying it's all a lie would actually *be* a lie. Do you see the problem?" Emily paused like she expected a blowup that didn't come.

"Fine. I want to make a statement that we are dating casually, but that Addie was living in Scotland, and we met before the book and that I had no idea she was auditioning."

"Are you sure?"

"I don't want her reputation to hurt because I wanted her in my room for the weekend," Toni said.

"She went along with it."

"Em."

Emily sighed. "Fine. Draft a note, send it to your publicist, and we'll pretty it up. But Addie should still stay there for a few days, and then she can go back to filming. That gives it time to be less exciting, and then . . . well . . . people will eventually move on." Emily sounded forcibly cheerful as she added, "Maybe don't do anything else newsworthy this week."

"That shouldn't be too hard."

Emily's laughter wasn't encouraging, but Toni was optimistic. Her week was filled with lectures, meetings, and, if she was lucky, getting things back to a solid friendship with Addie. They weren't doing to do anything newsworthy. She was sure of it.

While Toni drove, Emily chattered. Then a few moments later after they'd seemingly moved to lighter topics, Emily said, "How are you coping?"

"With all the news? I keep my phone off and—"

"No, sweetie. How are you coping with having Addie in your condo?" Emily had the speaking-to-feral-creatures tone now, but Toni couldn't truly blame her. Emily knew Toni better and longer than anyone ever had.

Until Addie. She understands me already.

"She stayed in the guest room." Toni slid between a couple of cars and switched lanes. "I pissed her off, and . . . I said some things."

"Are you okay?" Emily was the definition of loyal. They both undoubtedly realized that *Toni* was in the wrong, and yet Emily was still asking about her feelings.

"I like her."

"Yes, that part is very obvious. I knew that before seeing you looking smitten in every viral picture," Emily said dryly.

"No, Em. I *like* her. I liked waking up with her this weekend, and I like having her in my house." Toni took the exit toward campus. "If I wanted a relationship—"

"This *is* one. Just because you don't want forever doesn't undo what it already is." Emily sounded more frustrated than usual.

"Did something happen with you, Em? That sounded . . . I don't know."

She sighed. "I want what you have with her, and you are running from it. Sometimes life isn't fair. It's not your fault, but I wish it was me. I wish I found *my* person. You found the perfect woman for you, and you're being a dumbass." Emily paused, as if there were more things to say.

When Toni didn't reply in that long silence, Emily added, "I'll check in later today."

And she disconnected after stilted goodbyes.

Toni hated that Emily was upset, but she had no good words, no defense for her reticence to enjoy what she'd found with Addie. How could she give in? Her genetics were a soup of dementia and gambling. Plus, even without that, Toni's life was here on the East Coast, and Addie was steadfastly in LA right now. How could anything work with those sorts of issues?

Not to mention my abject terror of failing her.

Addie deserved more than a half-relationship with someone who would either screw everything up or forget everything when dementia struck. Toni wasn't going to ruin Addie's chance of a career the way her father had ruined Lil's.

By the time Toni got to campus, she had convinced herself that things were best off with this being the end of her dalliance with Addie. It was briefer than Toni wanted, but this was ultimately for the best. *Why drag it out?*

Even when *The Whitechapel Widow* hit the List and Toni went on tour, no one other than Harold had really mentioned the book beyond polite congratulations and small talk about how busy she was, and so there was no reason to expect that today would be different. The history department was a place of decorum and serious study, albeit with a distinctly quirky sense of humor.

So when Toni walked into Tulip Hall, she was not expecting to see her office festooned with decorations more suited for a preschool birthday party. That was not what she'd been expecting—pretty much ever in her life. Streamers and balloons were taped to her office door, and a CONGRATS! sign was stretched diagonally over the door.

Toni stood there, not quite processing what the right response was.

"You're here. I wasn't sure if you would be," Harold said as he walked toward her. "I expected an email requesting someone cover your classes this week."

"Because?"

"Your wedding." He gave her a frown before asking, "Are you registered anywhere? Just tell Gabe, and he'll let the department kn—"

"I'm not really married, Harold. It was a promotional event, and there was a bad decision because they were short on rooms and then some pictures went out that shouldn't have and . . . it's become a whole *thing* now." Toni batted away a balloon so she could open the door. Several people passed in the hallway, low murmurs of their conversations creating a familiar pleasant home. Here. Here was where she felt more secure. She couldn't lose this.

"Well, that's awkward." Harold stood at her office door, not stepping inside or backing away. "You really looked . . . happy in the pictures. Truly not married?"

Toni gave him a tired look. "Yes. Very much so. The rumors are a mess."

"I'll head off any drama with the college. I can just pop over to see the dean . . ." Harold had his serious face on now, and she was once again reminded that this was the place she'd wanted to teach for more reasons than its location and salary. There were good people here.

"So everyone knows?" she asked.

"A few people know." Harold smiled. "You have a *great* book that's selling well and becoming a television show, and the general critical reviews are flattering. It's not anything but wonderful, Toni. We can certainly use some more positive representation, especially as the moment we stop being activists the damnable politicians start harping that we're groomers."

For a moment they were both quiet, and then Toni added, "Doomed to repeat history because enough people aren't studying it."

"Too true, my dear. Too true." He sighed loudly. "Well . . . as they say, *Illegitimi non carborundum!* Even if the bastards trying to grind you down are your own fears."

"Intellectually, I know that. I swear I do." She paused, trying to figure out how to admit her crushing fear of failing very publicly, her panic that came from years of living in a household where big wins were always followed by massive losses. She settled on, "My dad was a con artist, a gambler, and nothing good ever *lasted*. We were a step away from homelessness more often than I want to admit."

"So your fears are that *you'll* fail because he always did," Harold surmised.

"On some level . . . and the scrutiny terrifies me. I remember it from school, and when these pictures got out, I felt like an awkward teen all over again. *Ugh*. There are people suggesting that Addie used me to get the role, or that the role was payment because I slept with her, and—"

"People gossip, Toni. Are any of those things true?"

"Well, no. I met her before I sold the book, and I had no idea that she even auditioned until after she was selected for the role—or that she even knew that the show existed because I hadn't told her about the book." Toni squirmed at her admissions. "We talked all the time, but I didn't tell her about the book, so she didn't tell me about the audition."

Harold smiled like a much younger boy then. "Ah. So the real problem is that you *like* her. Worried about her reputation, too?"

"You're awfully personal for an administrator," Toni dodged.

He chortled. "I think of my faculty as family, Toni, and you just blurted all that out, which means you need a shoulder. Ergo, I am here. Surely you realize the difficulty people like us had creating families when I was your age." He opened his arms. "This is my family. We have a bond here, and I am glad to have you as part of our family."

"Well, you can't screw up more than my actual father, so I guess it'll be easier than that." Toni dropped off the things she didn't need and looked at Harold. "I've got a class to teach."

"You're an asset to the department, dear. Now we just need *you* to admit that you're fantastic and ignore the naysayers." Harold gave her a surprisingly steely look. "Don't underestimate me, Dr. Darbyshire. You'll come around to seeing that I'm right."

"Have you ever considered a backup degree in therapy?" Toni muttered as he moved to let her out of her office.

He laughed again. "My brother's the shrink. I'm just a mild-mannered history professor."

When she stepped out into the hall, Harold asked, "Where is Miss Stewart, by the way?"

"At my condo."

"Hmm. Why don't you skip the committee work this week? I can't excuse you from all your classes, but I can ease the workload. I'll have your TA . . . I think Kaelee Carpenter is your TA, right?" He glanced at Toni, who nodded. "I'm sure Kaelee would be glad to take a couple of the lectures for you. She's a driven woman. Maybe she can do a note review if she can't use your lecture notes. . . . Truly, my dear, you ought to at least show your wife around the city, don't you think?"

And Toni couldn't think of a decent excuse to refuse. She *wanted* more time with Addie, despite it likely being a terrible idea for her already rebellious heart. So Toni offered, "I'll look at my schedule and see if I have any lectures I can have Kaelee cover."

First though, she had to email a note her publicist. She waved goodbye to Harold, who walked away, whistling like the meddlesome friend he had become.

Chapter 35

Addie

Addie stared at the article. Clipping, really. It was just a clickbait social media post that led to photos from the weekend. She wasn't expecting to end up as the source of gossip, not for something as innocuous as a kiss. If she'd gotten caught in that garden in Edinburgh with Toni, that would be different. This was a costumed weekend of make-believe. Plenty of people online were making that exact point, but that adoring look in Toni's eyes, the way her gaze was fixed on Addie, those were hard to explain away.

If I knew who sold or shared these pictures, I'd kick their asses.

But all Addie knew in this moment was that the wedding was apparently officiated by a real minister. Was it legal then? He'd muddled Addie's name, but he'd also been a real wedding officiant.

We had no marriage license, though.

Addie read the snippet again. It read like they were stealth marrying without telling the guests it was real. The pretense, according to this spin, was that it was a real wedding right under the noses of the guests.

MODERN VICTORIAN BRIDES?

Ingenue Adelaine Stewart was recently cast in the adaptation of her new wife's book—and at a Victorian ball to celebrate *The Whitechapel*

Widow's success the two tied the knot in an elaborate "costume" wedding. The twist? A real reverend! The author wore a custom tailcoat in a ladies' cut and the actress wore a lovely 1892 dress. From invisible to married in mere months, this couple knows how to make a statement.

So Addie forwarded the link to the studio publicity team and to her manager, June, with a question. "Am I actually married?"

She stared at the email after she hit SEND. Would it be so bad if it were real? She cared about Toni, and she was certain she'd be in love if not for the walls she kept erecting to protect her heart. They talked, laughed, enjoyed both dates and intimacy. In all the ways that Addie could imagine, they fit. They both had their own careers, so no one could be accused of stealing the other's money. They were building trust—in and out of bed. Marriage would be a bit hasty, but on the other hand, they'd spent a *year* exchanging email.

Toni doesn't want *a wife, though. She might want me now, but not forever.*

And I don't want to give up my career for anyone.

That was the crux of the problem. Toni didn't want a commitment, and Addie wanted a career. On the other hand, she'd watched her parents find ways to respect their desire to be together but not necessarily in all the ways that seemed "traditional." Maybe there was a compromise to be had here, too. . . .

Only if we both want it, though. And she doesn't.

Addie had washed the few not-Victorian clothes she had with her, and she'd decided to ship the others back to LA. The dresses were studio property, so after she'd sorted out her personal things from the studio property, she had a shipping service pick it up.

"Releasing promo photos and video teaser today," June texted. "Riding wave of viral photos by releasing useful things."

Addie rolled her eyes. June was as subtle as a brick with her remark on "useful things." It wasn't as if Addie intended the photos to leak or be misconstrued. At least some of the responses were focusing on the costumes and on the show—and by extension on the book.

"Live morning show request," June's next text said.

That one, Addie couldn't ignore. "Where?"

"Several. One in Chicago, one in Richmond. Both of you. First on Wednesday."

"What happened to saying nothing?" Addie frowned.

"Publisher sent a statement. Darbyshire admitted that you are dating, but the wedding was simply part of historical weekend not real. No marriage license. No legal wedding."

Toni admitted it? Addie read and reread that message again. *Toni admitted that we were dating. In writing. In media.*

"Details?"

The text included a screenshot:

The author notes that they met in Scotland, and that she "named the character after Adelaine." She was unaware that Miss Stewart had moved to the States or had auditioned until the actor was cast. She strenuously objects to any implications of impropriety in casting. Will reword her expletive laden note on the topic and admonishments that anyone viewing the show will be clear of Stewart's talent being why she was cast. Author notes that they are casually dating. Press release to follow as per author's insistence. Please ask Miss Stewart to use these talking points.

"Agree to appearances?"

"Yes but only me," Addie replied. "Toni is teaching."

The trio of little dots flickered as June typed, presumably erased, and typed some more. When her reply came, it only said, "Checking with her people if that will work for her."

There was no way Toni was going to Chicago, and honestly, Addie was fairly certain she didn't want her to come—although that statement was impossibly sweet. Addie reread it. Toni might admit they were involved, but she clearly needed time to figure out what she thought about the increased intimacy between them, and having an interviewer poke at her feelings was likely to make Toni back up more.

I'll sacrifice the promo for her happiness. It wasn't just Toni's happiness at risk. Addie wanted Toni in her life, as permanently as she was willing to be. That meant that the interviews were a terrible plan.

Addie pulled on her clean underwear and jeans. She'd need to shop after all, especially if she had a couple live TV spots. She'd done enough media training to know that nothing she had here would be suitable, and she'd already shipped her costume dresses back. She could've used one of those. This time, however, she would make a statement. Polished. Professional. Abundantly clear that she was an actor—and that speculations about her personal life were off-limits.

She picked up her phone and emailed June, cc'ing Marcela and the publicity team, a message that said: "I need official talking points for interviews. I can make them work."

Then she looked at the map and decided to see Toni rather than find interview clothes. She texted: "Going to be near campus. Lunch?"

Toni didn't reply, but Addie figured she could still be in class or meeting students or something. Addie hadn't pressed too much about Toni's schedule, because when she asked questions, Toni seemed to retreat. Addie was fairly sure that, given the option, Toni would hide most things about herself. She was intensely private to the point that asking about her teaching schedule felt like prying.

Another reason we can't work, Addie thought.

She put a few odds and ends in her bag, borrowed a cardigan Toni had included in her pile of clothes to use, and headed toward the Metro. After being in Europe for a couple years, it was more natural to use public transit than rideshares, but as Addie walked to the station, she saw a huge image of herself, one of the promo shots taken on the set. She looked back at the larger-than-life Addie Wight staring out from a bus before quickly ducking her head. She might not be as private as Toni, but Addie was not sure how she felt about her ability to avoid being unnoticed. Her privacy seemed to be in peril—but honestly, the way she looked as Addie the *character* was so different. There, her hair was primped, her face painted, and her bosom lifted like it was screaming "notice me." The real version of Addie was wearing thrift-store jeans, well-worn boots, and a sweater she'd tossed on over a borrowed T-shirt. She looked like a student.

A stray thought of pretending to be a student with Toni had Addie's cheeks burning when the innocent thought quickly went off-track. . . .

Addie stared out the grimy dark window of the Metro car, buffeted by a weird mix of the ozone-ish smell that permeated the train car and the underlying scent of sweat. At least it was warmer in here than it had been in the short walk to the station. Addie had apparently adapted to LA weather again, because DC felt cooler than she'd expected.

Is it normally this cold in October?

The car wasn't very crowded at midday, which helped Addie feel less conspicuous. She got off, walked the short distance to the college, and looked at the campus map she'd screenshotted.

A glance at the time told her she was going to be earlier than planned, but better that than late. *Hopefully Toni checked her messages and knows I'll be there.*

Addie felt at ease on the campus, students darting from place to place with backpacks on their shoulders. A surprising number of pay-as-you-go scooters rested against old-fashioned lamp poles, and the buildings themselves could've been modeled on Edinburgh's architecture.

She found Toni's office building with its shiny brass plate declaring it Tulip Hall and joined the crowds heading through the building. The map said it connected to other buildings where classrooms were held, so she couldn't blame the students for cutting through it to avoid the chill outside. While it wasn't winter, the air had a sharper bite today—one her light cardigan wasn't exactly repelling.

One door was decorated like a child's party was about to erupt, and Addie felt a sinking sensation. That had to be Toni's office. Maybe she hadn't replied because she was mortified.

"You're Dr. Darbyshire's surprise wife, right?" a young woman asked. Addie hadn't even noticed her until that moment. Very queer style—undercut, masculine trousers, and button-up Oxford. In a weird moment, Addie realized her overall look and style was similar to a slightly younger Toni, one who had not yet adopted vests and blazers. The woman looked like she was loosely Addie's age, late twenties, but far more Toni's build.

"I'm Adelaine Stewart." Addie held out her hand to shake. "I'm here to see Toni."

"Uh-huh." The woman, who was possibly older than Addie, smirked. "Aren't all the pretty ladies here to see her?" When Addie didn't reply, the woman added, "I'm Kaelee. English department, but I'm TAing for Toni this term. I teach a few of her classes and do note reviews, help with grading."

"That's nice." Addie smiled and waited.

"So you're the one in the book."

"Well, I'm not really a Victorian lesbian detective, but yes, I'm the actor in the role." Addie looked around, noticing a few other students looking at them. There was a weird sense of not wanting to be an asshole because this was Toni's space—her college, her students—but Addie wasn't a fan of violating Toni's privacy.

"She's a lucky woman." Kaelee looked Addie up and down with the kind of gaze that was far from subtle, and Addie started to think she ought to walk away. Addie wasn't unaccustomed to being assessed and found attractive, especially as an actor, but Kaelee was a *student,* one who worked with Toni.

"Kaelee?"

The girl looked up; guilt flashed over her face.

"I suspect that Miss Stewart is here for me," Toni said in a friendly voice. In a lower voice, Toni added, "She is not available for whatever thought went with that look on your face."

Kaelee laughed. "So you really got married? Wow. I thought the rumors were lies."

"I'm not married, but that doesn't mean I like you looking at my friend like you are planning on trying to get her into bed." Toni sounded perfectly calm, but also possessive enough that Addie's pulse thrilled at the territorial vibe of it.

"No poaching intended," Kaelee said, glancing over at Addie briefly with a friendly smile. Then she continued, "I was just keeping her company while I waited on you. I wanted to talk to you about—"

"Not today," Toni interjected.

"You're usually free after your ten thirty," Kaelee pointed out. "I can email for your notes, though."

"Good idea." Toni darted a smile at Addie. "Luckily for me, I am not free today."

Then, surprisingly, Toni reached out a hand. Instinctively, Addie took it, and Toni pulled her close. She brushed a kiss over Addie's cheek. "Hello, dear."

Addie was grateful that her back was to Kaelee, because her eyes widened in shock at Toni's greeting. Toni was acting incredibly familiar, and Addie hadn't expected anything of the sort. "Hi," she managed.

"I have office hours posted, but outside of appointments, I'm not going to be free this week. If you could tell my classes that, Kaelee, I'd appreciate it. Addie only has a few days before she has to go back to LA." Toni didn't release Addie's hand even as she unlocked and opened her office door.

"Right. Send me the notes. I can pick up your Tuesday Thursday 386 section, too. Let me know if you need anything other than class coverage," Kaelee offered.

"Thanks. I'll email you later." Toni didn't even glance at her. She simply pulled Addie into her office and shut the door.

Once she released Addie, Toni looked a lot less confident.

"Thank you for being patient with Kaelee." Toni looked like she'd peeled off a mask. "She's a great TA, but she's also finishing a book and so she has a lot of questions about publishing. I'm not role-model material, and—"

"Really?" Addie interrupted. "Successful, accomplished, sexy? You seem like a pretty impressive role model to me."

"Ignoring that." Toni smiled at her, nonetheless. "She has alternated between asking about the publishing world and trying to be my friend. I told her I couldn't read her book until after she's not my TA." Toni sighed. "I'm new to the professor thing, and she is a good TA, but . . . I feel like her friendship is awkward when I'm a professor. I mean, I get the drive to go to the bar with a friend and meet . . . err, people."

Addie felt a bloom of jealousy, but it was quickly quashed when Toni added, "It's not like she's interested in me, but I haven't felt much like being at the bar since I've been seeing—I mean since you and I . . . are whatever we are."

"Well, I can make the sacrifice of kissing you in the hallway when I'm in town, so she understands you aren't going out on the prowl as her wingperson," Addie teased. "Maybe that would clarify matters for her. . . . Maybe it will clarify some things for you, too."

"I wouldn't say no to a kiss."

Addie reached for the door. "Shall we step outside? Kiss for your reputation? To protect you from your fan club?"

Toni pulled her into her arms. "No. I want a kiss just for me. I hated when you were mad at me."

"Who says I'm not still angry?" Addie said, sounding far too breathless to be even a little convincing. She'd thought a lot that morning, and she wanted to move forward. She could accept that this was temporary. It was for the best for both of them. All Addie had to do was keep her feelings in check.

"Are you angry?" Toni stared down at her.

"Depends. Where am I sleeping when I visit you?" Addie wasn't going to keep letting Toni push her away, only to pull her closer when she wanted to talk or have sex. "Are you going to treat me like your *actual* friend?"

"My friends don't share my bed, Addie."

"Well, this one does. Your bed. Your body. I want to be able to be with you, Toni. I'm not asking you to write me sappy poetry, but I want you to admit that I matter to you."

"You do."

"And you like having sex with me," Addie prompted.

"I do."

"And since people already think we're together, and more will after that statement you sent the publicists, so there's no harm in being around each other in public." Addie stared at her, bracing for Toni to flinch.

"True . . . Can I kiss you yet? Now that we've negotiated the terms of my surrender," Toni teased.

"Yes. Then I want lunch." Addie didn't wait for Toni, though. She stretched up on her toes, kissing Toni and leaning into her until Toni took a stumbling step backward, and they ended up leaning against a file cabinet. There was a loud thunk, but Addie didn't stop kissing her. And thankfully, Toni didn't seem to care about the noise, the knock on her door, or the ringing of the phone.

She did pause when Addie reached toward Toni's trousers' button. Her hand caught Addie's wrist. "No sex in the office, love. I'd never be able to concentrate in here afterward."

Addie pouted exaggeratedly. "Fine. Then I need lunch, Professor. And I'll go home and take care of—"

"I have the afternoon off. Kaelee is covering my class," Toni said. "I was thinking we could go out, but if you'd rather—"

"I like going out," Addie said quickly. A flush of warmth that wasn't sexual washed over Addie. "You canceled your work because you wanted to spend time with me!"

Toni didn't admit or deny anything about the very obvious date-like plan she'd already arranged. All she said was, "There are a lot of great museums in the city. Obvious ones like the big three: American History, Natural History, and Air and Space. There's also the Library of Congress, African Art, the Portrait Gallery, the American Indian— they're also a great spot for lunch. So is the National Gallery."

Addie brushed a kiss over Toni's lips. "Sounds like museums and museum café for lunch?"

"If you want." Toni shrugged, but she was smiling and added sort of sheepishly, "Did I mention that my degrees are in history?"

"I happen to like history enough that I could be convinced to visit a few times to see everything with the right tour guide," Addie said lightly. "Interested? The position has no pay and only the slightest of benefits."

Toni gave her an appraising look. "Can I sample the benefits later?"

"Depends on how good the tour is . . ." Addie shrugged. "Tips are earned."

"Well, let's get going then." Toni gestured toward the door. "I apparently need to prove my worth."

"Thank you," Addie said, putting her hand on Toni's wrist. "I saw the note you sent—well, a summary. I guess the original was 'expletive-laden.'"

"Not right for your reputation to take a hit," Toni said, looking away.

"I appreciate you coming to my rescue again."

Toni met her gaze. "That's what I should've done from the start. I'm sorry. I'm not a fan of my private life being public. I reacted poorly."

Addie kissed her lightly and then said, "I'm honored that you'll admit we're casually dating."

"I didn't know what else to call it." Toni heaved a sigh. "Can't get her out of my mind, would chew glass for the chance to touch her again, think she's fucking amazing . . . that seemed too wordy."

Addie giggled. "Just so you know, I like you, too."

"Thank goodness." Toni pulled her closer. "Come on. We have museums to see."

Chapter 36
Toni

After lunch, museums, dinner, and an impromptu show at the Kennedy Center thanks to an impulsive ticket purchase, Toni felt like she'd been on a marathon date—and she liked it. They were walking back to the Jeep, just another couple in the post-theater crush, when Toni admitted to herself that she could get used to everything about this, get used to having someone at her side. Not forever, of course, but maybe for a while.

Only if that someone is her.

They reached the row where the Jeep was parked, and Addie let go of Toni's arm. "That was wonderful." She spun out into a sort of pirouette. "Excellent tour guiding."

Toni stared at her for a moment before she pulled Addie closer, turning them so that Addie was against the Jeep, and slanted her mouth over Addie's. They'd spent one day and one night without sex, and then barely touched today—so far—and that felt like an eternity.

Addie made another little noise, and Toni pulled back.

"If we don't leave, I'm going to have my hands on you here in the parking lot." Toni took a steadying step away from her.

"Exhibition is on my to-try list," Addie said in a quiet voice.

Toni shook her head. "Not in the theater parking garage, Addie.

I promised Em we weren't going to do anything newsworthy this week, and it's too cold out here for any part of you to be exposed."

Addie pouted, jutting out her bottom lip. "So next trip then. I'll wear more skirts. I bet that would make it eas—"

"Hush." Toni reached past her and opened the door. "Get in the seat, Addie."

"Yes, ma'am." Her voice made quite clear that hers was not an accidentally chosen reply, and just in case Toni had missed it, when she got into the driver's seat, Addie asked, "With your control issues, do you like being called ma'am or something else?"

Toni refused to answer. She reached over and hooked Addie's seat belt. "Stop talking and flirting, so I can drive us home safely."

When Addie gave her a single nod and then primly crossed her ankles, Toni relaxed slightly. She wasn't far from tossing caution to the wind and moving the Jeep to the darkest corner of the garage, and she was fairly sure Addie would agree if she suggested it.

There are probably cameras somewhere, her common sense insisted.

Instead of risking it, Toni joined the flow of traffic inching out of the garage. "I had fun today."

"Same."

"I had fun at the beach in California, too." Toni paused for an older man in a Lincoln who apparently had decided that backing into the traffic queue and expecting everyone to move out of his way was better than waiting for an opening.

"Sounds like you like spending time with me," Addie said in her already-familiar intentionally casual voice.

"I do." Toni wasn't going to deny the obvious. "I didn't think that was a secret."

Addie grew quieter. "I'm afraid you'll pull away again the moment I leave. I'm afraid that you'll be heartless with me again. Insensitive because of something that's not my fault."

"What if I try not to do that?"

Addie stared out into the lot around them. "I'd like that, but Toni"—she looked over at her—"I'm not going to forgive the same thing over and over, you know?"

Toni thought of her parents. "You shouldn't."

The car behind them honked, and Toni eased forward again. They slipped into faster-moving traffic, and Toni made a note that they ought to do this again in the spring when the doors could be off. *And I bet she'd like seeing the cherry blossoms.* Her stomach squirmed, and she quickly reminded herself, *Thinking a few months ahead isn't the same as a relationship. Casual. We're casual bedmates and friends.*

But when Addie reached over and rested a hand on Toni's leg, it didn't set off the alarms it should.

Just a few months, Toni's inner devils whispered. *She knows this thing between us is temporary. Maybe we can last until the new year? Maybe spring?*

Addie gave her a smoldering look when they parked the Jeep outside the condo. "I'm pretty sure you owe me a staycation-style honeymoon. Theater and dinner was a good start. Any other plans?"

Toni opened Addie's door and held out a hand. "Might I invite you to a seduction for the evening? Local spot. Cover theft afterward . . . and I can promise a potentially hissing cat at some point."

Addie stepped out and melted against Toni's side. "Oh, I do like a seduction."

There was no way to resist the laugh that bubbled up at Addie's exaggerated earnestness. She made Toni laugh and smile more than anyone had ever done. That alone was reason to keep her in Toni's life.

"Do you think I could get a drink before the seduction?" Addie asked as they walked to the condo door. "My date tonight was lovely, but I had to deal with this surly woman yesterday. It was vexing."

Toni pushed open the door. "*Vexing?* You poor dear."

"She has a marvelous figure, and she's really quite clever. That helped, but"—Addie leaned in so that her breasts were smooshed against Toni's arm—"*she* didn't even invite me to a seduction. She had terrible manners."

"No," Toni gasped in faux outrage. "I bet she slept terribly."

Addie giggled. "I do hope so. I was left having to . . . well, I don't know if I can tell you what I did after that." She widened her eyes, lowered her voice, and stretched up so her lips were almost touching Toni's. "I touched myself right there in her guest room. All by myself . . . it was . . ." Addie made a moaning sound. "Well, it was good, but I wanted more."

"You're trying to kill me, Miss Stewart." Toni fumbled to open the door and tugged Addie inside. She swept her arm out. "Welcome to your temporary home."

Addie sighed. "I only have two days, you know. I have an interview in Richmond because *someone* issued a press release that she was dating me, and then I have another in Chicago, and then it seems silly to head back to LA, so I'm going to just go direct to New Orleans, where we're filming the next scenes."

Something in Toni's heart that was misbehaving took a tumble. "So you leave in two days?"

"Thursday, technically, but I have a live TV spot in Richmond Wednesday. I could stay there, but—"

"No need. You're fine to stay here. It's not a terrible commute down there, so if you are okay with that . . . ?"

Addie put a hand in the middle of Toni's chest. "So you don't mind me being here after all?"

"I could get used to a few days of you around here," Toni admitted. After an extended pause, she added, "I like you, Adelaine. Far too much, in fact."

"Same." Addie smiled.

Toni tried to tell herself that having Addie here was no different than the few times she spent a few days in a nameless hotel with women or that one unexpected cruise ship, but she couldn't lie to herself. She liked having Addie in her home. She liked it far more than she wanted to admit.

By the time Toni drove Addie to the airport three days later, she was exhausted. When she wasn't grading or teaching or dealing with book things, she was with Addie. And while it was possible to teach and write or to write and be with Addie, trying to juggle all three was exhausting.

But waking up to the knowledge that Addie was leaving wasn't doing wonders for her mood. She'd rather be exhausted than without Addie.

Toni had glowered at everyone the day prior when Addie was in Richmond for an interview on morning TV, but by evening, Addie was home. While Addie was away, Toni had managed to squeeze in a nap, order delivery, and get a few chapters of her new book revised. She even caught up on email. If Addie was busy part of the time, Toni thought she could juggle everything she had to do.

Not that it matters. I live here. She lives in LA, and neither of us can move.

Toni's anxiety twitched down to her very marrow realizing that she was considering a future in which Addie was still in her life. That was impossible even if she did want it. Addie wasn't going to stop acting, and Toni wasn't going to stop teaching. That meant opposite sides of the country.

She glanced over. "Do you think I have been overreacting to . . . things with us?"

Addie made a noise that sounded a lot like a snort.

"That's a yes." Toni kept her attention on the traffic. The DC Beltway was never anything other than chaotic, and Toni enjoyed the adrenaline of it when it was moving. Not rush hour—well, rush *hours,* if one was honest; no rational person enjoyed the stop-and-roll hours of the Beltway.

"You've already fake-married me, and if you *really* don't do relationships, I'll be the only chance you get to try one. Plus we live on opposite sides of the country, so you have plenty of time without me." Addie stared at her, even though Toni refused to look her way.

"So you think we should . . . date?"

"We *are* dating, Toni. You're just calling it other things in private. You even admitted it in a press release." Addie huffed. "Are you afraid of being wrong? Afraid you might actually fall for me if you admit that we're dating?"

"No." Toni was pretty sure she would fall hard if she stopped resisting, but she wasn't going to give in to that. "I want us to be friends, even after we stop having sex someday."

"You're an idiot, you know. How about we focus on *right now* instead of borrowing trouble from a future that might not happen? Can we focus on next week? Do you like seeing me? Being naked with me? Or are we done when I get on this plane?" Addie sounded exasperated. They'd gone on several great dates, and the last couple nights—plus the weekend and the night in LA—were all satisfying.

"I like you, and I like kissing you and sex with you. That's all I'm able to give anyone. You need to understand that," Toni said carefully. "I can't give you more than this."

"I like this. So why can't we keep doing *this*?" Addie asked. "Why are you complicating things instead of enjoying what we have now?"

Toni weighed the thought of it. It sounded so simple. She'd get to spend more time with Addie. They were friends, and the sex was good. *Where's the harm?* She could date her fake wife without developing impossible romantic feelings.

"There's no future, though," Toni added, glancing over at her again.

"So you say." Addie gave her a smile that would have been suitable for the greatest temptresses in history. "I'll forgive you if you're wrong, and if you're not, I hope we stay friends no matter what else happens."

Toni dodged the question as she parked in short-term parking and cut off the engine. "So Chicago, then New Orleans . . ."

"Then either back to LA or . . . I could stop here." Addie shot her a hopeful look. "Or you could come to New Orleans for the weekend."

"Let's play it by ear." Toni hopped out and went around to open Addie's door. "I can't make any long-term promises. I need you to be okay with that."

"Two to three weeks is long-term?" Addie scoffed. "Friends, Toni. That's what you said, right? Friends who get naked and go on dates. Surely, *friends* can talk about plans for the next month."

"That's still new territory for me, love."

"I'm not trying to scare you," Addie whispered. "We're both busy, and I like being around you, so a little planning is going to happen or I won't be able to see you at all. Don't throw out something good because of what might happen later."

Toni shoved her panic deeper. "Let me see what I can do. I can't promise anything."

The problem wasn't that she didn't want to make plans. Hell, she'd be on board with going to all the places Addie went just to fall asleep with Addie in her arms. *That* was the real issue. She could see a future together, and she was starting to crave that, but Addie deserved more. She deserved someone who could give her everything.

She deserved a better person than Toni.

Chapter 37
Addie

The interviews were fine. The flights were fine. Everything was *perfectly fine*. And Addie was still blue. Aside from her glum mood from knowing she'd be alone in a hotel on Halloween night later that month, Addie's life was as normal as it ever was.

And I miss Toni.

Over the last week and a half, she had exchanged calls with Eric and with Toni. She texted a few times with her mother. The reality of it was that she was lonely—but she was torn between wanting to go out and sadness that there was no one in the city to go out with. She and Eric had lived together for years, so they always went to a party or a bar or something. Addie had actually debated flying home for Halloween.

But filming was in New Orleans right now, so she didn't fly back to California or to DC, although both sounded good. There was something disconcerting about having left her life in Scotland behind, and now being away from her new life in LA.

And away from DC, where my heart is, too.

Addie's frequent email refreshing was proof enough that she had made exactly no progress in keeping her heart safe. She waited for each message with the impatience she'd felt after they first met. A part of her thought the yearning to talk to Toni ought to have eased after fifteen months. Reality was that she had to force herself not to reply the moment she read each email.

Mostly, she managed to wait at least an hour before replying. Tonight, though, she was failing that.

From: History Toni
To: Addie

How's the filming? How are you? Call tomorrow?

Toni

Briefly she replied:

From: Adelaine
To: History Toni

The French Quarter is lovely. It's a wild place here with Halloween coming in a week, but I'm in my hotel too tired to go out. Wanna come spend the weekend? YES, on the call.

Addie

Toni didn't wait an hour before she replied:

From: History Toni
To: Addie

I wish I could, but work is backed up. Some gorgeous woman kept me occupied the other week. I'm almost caught up, but I don't think I can take the weekend off.

Toni

This time, Addie replied instantly. If Toni was going to reply that fast, maybe it was okay.

From: Adelaine
To: History Toni

I guess I'm going to be left to my own devices. . . .

Addie

Or maybe they ought to switch to text? Addie took a picture of her vibrator on the bedsheets and sent it to Toni over text. It was the closest she'd come to phone sex.

Is text sex a thing?

Toni replied over text: "Damn it, woman. You test my self-control."

This time, Addie sent a picture of her hand holding the vibe, angling it so her bare legs were visible.

The phone rang instantly. Addie repressed a smile as she answered, "Hi."

"Hi yourself." Toni's voice sounded like she did when they had been alone and intimate. "Are you serious?"

"About what?"

"About what you're doing there?" Toni asked.

"Eventually. Since you aren't here . . ." Addie felt her cheeks warm, embarrassed by her own boldness.

"Let me see you."

Addie paused. "I'm not sure that sort of picture is something I ought to be sending. Not that I don't trust you but—"

"Video?"

Her heart sped at the thought, but Addie wasn't sure.

"If you don't want to, that's fine, too." Toni had her soothing voice now. "I can listen over the phone or not . . . whatever you want."

"I want you," Addie confessed. "Right here. In this bed. I want to come back from filming and have you here."

"We are often not going to be in the same city or state, love. You know that." Toni sighed. "Try this with me. If you don't like it, I can hang up. Or if you want to try video . . ."

Addie didn't reply, but she grabbed her laptop and opened up a video-chat app. "Is this a thing you do a lot?"

"Never tried it. No need. Usually I don't keep in touch after sex." Toni sounded matter-of-fact, but the admission was not without weight, and Addie suspected they both knew that.

"Answer your video chat," Addie finally said.

The phone disconnected, and Toni's face appeared on Addie's laptop. At first she didn't say anything, but her expression was telling. Her gaze raked from Addie's chest to her face, and the look she had as she stared at Addie was not simple lust. Whether or not Toni admitted it, there was a sort of relief in her eyes as she looked at Addie.

"I really like seeing you," Toni said quietly.

"I wish you could come to New Orleans, but this is nice, too." Addie smiled. They'd been emailing for almost a year and a half, texting for a few months, calling occasionally, but this video thing was new.

"I guess it's only fair since I got to watch you in Los Angeles," Addie murmured.

"Watch me do what, love?" Toni said softly.

"Masturbate," Addie said, trying not to blush.

"Such a technical term . . ." Toni teased.

"Are there other words you like?" Addie asked, feeling more curious than she expected. "You are the writer."

"Words for that?"

"Sex words." Addie managed to hold Toni's gaze as she said it.

Toni was walking through the apartment, and when she paused, Addie could see the bedroom behind her. "I think it depends on the person I'm with."

"Me," Addie pointed out, a little possessively. "You're with me, Professor."

Toni laughed. "Would that I were, love. I like all sorts of words." She smiled and added, "'Pussy.' 'Cunt.' I like those best. I couldn't tell if you would find them too crass, though."

Addie swallowed. "Maybe. Maybe not."

Toni nodded. Then she pulled back the bedspread and sat cross-legged on the sheets. "I see you kept my sweatshirt. What else are you wearing, love?"

"Jeans. Underpants. A shirt and a hair tie."

"No bra?" Toni asked.

Addie stared at the camera and pulled her shirt—well, *Toni's* shirt—over her head. "Nope."

Toni made a low noise of appreciation. So Addie crawled across the hotel-room bed, set the laptop on the nightstand, and unbuttoned her jeans. She said nothing as she slid them and her panties off.

"Take out the ponytail." Toni was still fully dressed and already giving orders.

"If you take your trousers off," Addie countered.

Toni matched Addie's bedside position and did so. She left her button-up shirt on, though. Apparently, she required specific instructions.

Addie stretched out on her bed, facing the laptop, and rolled onto her side. "Buttons undone, please."

As Toni complied, Addie plucked her nipples, pinching them as Toni liked to do.

"Such a very good girl," Toni murmured. "Move your leg, so I can see your pussy when you touch yourself. . . ." Her words faded as Addie obeyed instantly.

Addie smiled. "I think I like that word when you say it. Say the other one."

Toni rolled onto her back, half seated, so the camera was not showing anything but Toni's chest and face. "I love the taste of your cunt, Addie. The feel of it, the smell of it, the way you arch against my mouth so I can lick you."

"I . . . want to hear that when you're with me," Addie said. "I like how much it sounds like you crave me."

"I *do* crave you, all the time." Toni stared at her. "What else do you like?"

"I like the way you're looking at me right now," Addie confessed.

"How's that?"

"Like you are struggling for control," Addie told her. "It makes me feel powerful when I watch your expressions, and you look ravenous."

Toni's gaze was riveted to the hand that Addie had lowered to her sex. "Do you mind if I don't lower the camera?"

"I want to see you watching me."

Toni's voice was increasingly hungry as she asked, "Are you wet?"

Addie shifted so she was on her knees. The camera was capturing only the center of Addie's body now—belly, hips, parted thighs—and her hand. "Do you see?"

"Yessss." Toni's hand was out of the frame, which now only showed her gaping shirt and face, and her voice coming through the connection was breathier.

"Are you touching your . . . self?" Addie whispered.

"Yes." Toni's lips parted. "Seeing you . . . like this for me makes it impossible not to."

"Only for you," Addie reminded her as she lifted the vibe and flicked it on. The low hum sounded loud in the room, and seeing Toni bite her lip as if to repress a moan made Addie feel like she was wetter than she could ever get when she was on her own. Watching Toni watch her wasn't as good as being able to touch Toni, but having her reactions onscreen made it much better than masturbating alone.

Addie didn't say a word as she angled the device and slid it along her body. She said nothing as she held it to her clit. She kept as silent as she could so she could hear the sounds of Toni's hand moving against herself.

"Faster," Toni breathed out. "I know it turns up higher than that."

So Addie increased the speed and held the vibe against her clit until she was shaking. Seeing herself in the camera—hips moving, body trembling—was surprisingly sexy. Seeing Toni's reaction to it, though, was *more*.

"I want to see your face, love," Toni said. "Can you move so I can watch your expression?"

Addie thought she might bite through her lip at the feeling of joy that request brought. She dropped back to the bed, angling the camera so it was aimed at her face. And Toni caught her gaze instantly.

"I want to look at you as you come for me," Toni said.

And that was all it took for Addie to do just that. Tremors rolled through her body, and Addie let out a muffled sound. In the next moment, Toni's expression was sheer bliss. Eyes flickering up, and neck tilted as if a live wire ran through her.

The silence that followed was heavy. Addie stared at her through the camera, and Toni looked back at her like she was a revelation. After a long pause, Toni said, "I could get used to that when you're not in town."

"I wish you were here, though. I want to be in your arms now," Addie said, feeling exposed but closer to Toni despite the physical distance between them.

"Same." Toni's voice was so quiet that Addie almost thought she'd imagined the admission. Then Toni grinned and added, "Even if your hair is trying to murder me in my sleep."

Addie smiled. "It's self-defense. I had to tuck the covers under me the last night I was there, just so I didn't freeze."

Toni looked away. "I ordered a larger top sheet and comforter for when you visit."

Inside, Addie was squealing at the thought of visiting often enough that she'd need that, but outside all she said was, "That does sound better than sleeping in clothes. Although I *did* get this new sweatshirt. . . ."

"You're going to end up with a collection of my clothes at this rate. Blazer and my sweatshirt, too?"

"Come and get them," Addie challenged.

Toni chuckled. "I wish I could. I have a late class on Friday, though, and I'm *so* close to wrapping up the new book. I'll see if I can pull off Halloween. No promises, love, but I'll see. The book is already later than my original deadline."

Addie mock-pouted and sighed. "Fine. Be responsible."

They chatted about life until Addie had to crash lest she be raccoon-eyed on set. Makeup seemed magical, but it still had its limits.

Chapter 38
Addie

Everything felt more natural the next day when actual filming started again. Interviews and fittings and reading script changes hadn't taken up nearly enough time to push away her disappointment that Toni wouldn't be there that weekend. She loved her job, but right now she'd rather be in DC with Toni. She'd rather be *anywhere* that Toni was.

For the first time, though, Addie was glad that Toni wasn't a social media user. The pictures of the two of them had become the base of several memes, and while most of the buzz was positive, a few montages about wanting Toni to "be their teacher" were the sort of things Addie was fairly sure Toni would hate. Addie had turned her own account over to her manager because she mostly wanted to either defend Toni—or agree with random users that *yes,* she was incredibly sexy, and *yes,* Addie was a "lucky" person. The low-grade envy was uncomfortable, though. She didn't think Toni was incredible just because she was gorgeous or wealthy or talented. Toni, the real woman, was so much more than that.

Addie resolved to stay off socials, and when strangers recognized her in the lobby or the street, she just smiled and waved. What else could she do?

Filming went well the first few days of the week, and by Thursday, she was busy enough to not think about Toni. *Much.* Maybe what she needed was a hobby, a distraction, maybe she could volunteer or take a class or—

"Well, that's one way to steal the spotlight," Philip said as he came over beside her. They were waiting for some cords to be better hidden. The streets near Jackson Square were cordoned off, and elements of modern traits had been removed. The excess of ghouls and skeletons was also not present in this small section of the city. Outside of their filming area, it was like the holiday had exploded over the city.

Addie looked at him. "Excuse me?"

"Sleeping with the writer. I knew you were desperate when we dated, but oof." Philip kept his voice low. "I don't think I've ever sunk quite that low for attention . . . or to get a role."

"Fuck off." Addie smiled at him as she said it, feeling awkward that anyone on set might overhear. She didn't want a reputation as hard to work with or anything else. *Be nice. Be polite. Be soft-spoken*, she reminded herself. It wasn't her default setting, but she wasn't going to ruin her working environment just because her costar was a prick.

"Quick moves, too. I wondered why you insisted it was just you at the event in Rhode Island." His gaze raked over her. "I thought you just wanted all the attention."

"I didn't insist on going alone. The *publisher* made the call." Addie glanced around to be sure no one was nearby to overhear. "You've done your share of promotional things, too. You're in a lot of the promo photos, considering that it's a show about a lesbian detective."

"That's right. And conveniently, you're now a lesbian. I knew the whole lesbian thing was a way to get attention, Addie, but this? Did you blackmail her to get the role?"

That exact accusation showed up a lot on socials, Addie realized. Obviously Philip was following the news closely since that was his first volley.

Addie turned and gave him a scathing look as her temper edged forward. She stepped closer to him for privacy. "Maybe you ought to ask yourself why the character and I have the same name?"

He glared at her. "Is that how someone gets past your frigid exterior? Offer you some fame?"

Addie opened her mouth to reply, but someone called out, "Places!" and Addie had to slip back into character. In the show they were in the city where Philip was to introduce her to several of his friends as potential suitors, and her character was secretly there to meet a witness to a crime she'd been investigating.

The screenwriters had changed the nature of the crime twice already because the higher-ups hadn't loved the original version. Not sexy enough. Not controversial enough. This part was still the same, though. Addie would be meeting a witness—one who would be set up as a potential love interest, although that wasn't in the book.

With the cameras rolling, Philip walked through the city streets quickly enough that Addie had to cling to his arm. That part was in the script. The revulsion she felt at touching him was, too, but Addie didn't have to struggle to portray that particular emotion. Neither did she have to pretend as her character looked at him and declared, "I would gladly fake a swoon and topple you into the way of oncoming carriage wheels."

"Try it, Adelaine. You make a mistake in forcing me to be your enemy," Philip, as Cousin Colin, said in a dark tone. It felt incredibly honest as he looked at her and declared, "I could ruin you and sleep like an innocent babe the same night."

The flicker of fear in Addie's heart was far too real. He wasn't bad at acting, but he wasn't *this* good. The threat was real. Regardless of what else happened, Addie made a note to herself that her costar was an enemy she could not dismiss lightly.

"Cut."

Addie relaxed slightly as things were reset and cameras moved. This was a job, one she'd worked toward, and she wasn't going to let any man—any person at all—ruin her joy. She'd keep alert, but that was common sense anyhow.

"Attention whore," he muttered as he stopped at her side.

His smiles were still constant, but they felt laced with threats now. *Do I tell Marcela? My manager? Toni?* Addie wasn't sure of protocol when one's costar was a jackass. He wasn't saying things that she couldn't also read on socials, but it felt different when he was on set—and in the same hotel with her.

By the time Addie returned to the hotel, she was ready to scream. The entire day had been peppered with Philip's whispered and muttered jabs. It was as if he wanted her to make mistakes. Addie kicked off her shoes and slipped into a pair of hotel slippers.

A glance at her socials made her wonder whether Philip was behind them or just parroting them. Sure, there were a lot of romantic ones, but there were others accusing Addie of being a "desperate dyke" and suggesting that it was suspicious that someone with no credits was cast in such a major role when other experienced actors were interested in it. A few even suggested that she'd blackmailed the publishers—as if they were involved in casting.

Even though Addie knew better, she worried and debated if she should say something to Toni. For now, she took a few screenshots and emailed Marcela with a note asking, "Do we need to make a statement about how casting works? Maybe a sort of behind-the-scenes from book to screen?"

Room service was at least thirty minutes away from arriving, so she left the stress of strangers castigating her, Toni, the studio, the publisher, and probably their parents, too. People could be so vicious. *Not all of them.* There were still plenty of people who said lovely things. Sometimes hate sounded louder than kindness, though.

Instead of letting it add to her anxiety, Addie checked her email—smiling when she saw the message.

From: History Toni
To: Addie

I liked waking up to breakfast with you when you were here. Oscar Wilde misses you

Kaelee stopped by the office. She spent several minutes telling me how fabulous you were. She's not wrong. I saw the second teaser from the show. You are even more fabulous than I could hope. If this show succeeds, it's because of you.

Toni

Briefly she replied:

From: Adelaine
To: History Toni

Just Oscar Wilde? I miss you. Should I be longing for the cat to cuddle instead of you?

And I think the source material is why the show exists, or did I misunderstand that detail? Maybe some of the credit goes to the talent of the author.

Addie

Not five minutes later, Toni emailed again.

From: History Toni
To: Addie

Fine. The cat has good taste. I miss you too. I don't cuddle though. I simply hold you after your bones are sufficiently melted. It's part of the package. I wish I could've held you the other night after our video chat.

I'm nearing the end of the Widow's Curse, incidentally. I think a few days of trying not to think about what I'd rather be doing has made me productive. Halloween looks iffy. How's work?

Toni

From: Adelaine
To: History Toni

I think you protest too much, Cuddlebug.

I am struggling to decide if it's a conflict of interest to complain about work when work is about the adaptation your book. Pretend I'm on a different project. My co-worker says I slept with you for the publicity. They either cast Cousin Colin really well so he's Method-acting or he's just a bloody nackle-ass. I guess it's partly my own fault. I went out on a few dates with him, so I guess he's still sore about me ending it.

Addie

This time, Toni called rather than emailing again.

"You went out with your costar?" Toni said instead of "hello."

"I did. I wasn't sure if I . . . I thought maybe I needed more in common to feel attraction, so I went out on a few dates with actors. Turns out, I'm simply not straight," Addie said. "Also hello."

"When?"

"When what?"

"When did you go out with Philip?" Toni sounded tense.

"Before I moved to Scotland." Addie glanced at the clock. She had about ten minutes until dinner arrived. Maybe they'd be sharing a meal at a distance. Foolishly or not, Addie was excited by the thought. She was a social creature, so having a dinner companion—even one who was not in the same room—was preferable. Having *Toni* as that companion was even better.

"Oh! You thought I meant recently?" Addie shook her head, even though Toni couldn't see it. "Seriously? You have massive trust issues."

"No shit." Toni paused, before she said lightly, "Historical swearing? If I wasn't worried about Philip's behavior, I might think you're flirting with me by calling him a nackle-ass."

"It can be both things," Addie said, stepping onto the balcony. From here she could see the vibrance of the French Quarter, and she wished that Toni were here in person. "Just like both you and that fluffy demon are missing me."

"True."

"I'll take that as an admission," Addie teased, relieved that Toni was done panicking over infidelity. *Would it have been infidelity if we aren't committed?* Addie had no desire to date anyone else, least of all Philip, but she found Toni's reaction telling. *She really likes me, whether or not she admits how much.*

They caught up on the minutiae of their lives for a few moments before there was a knock at the door. "Room service is here. Can you hang on a moment?"

"I can let you go," Toni offered.

"Or you can have dinner with me," Addie countered, opening the door to find not room service but Philip standing there. She was at such a loss that she simply stared at him. "What are *you* doing here?"

Through the phone, still against her ear, she heard Toni. "Addie? What's going on? Addie!"

"I thought I'd come rekindle old flames," Philip said. He stepped forward like he intended to come into her suite. As he did, Addie caught the unmistakable scent of some sort of liquor. Philip stared at her. "Hang up."

"No."

He glared. "I thought you'd get a hint when I released the photos. . . ."

"*What?*"

"An old friend was there. He sent them to me, asked why I wasn't there, too." Philip shrugged. "I figured if you're going to whore yourself for the role, everyone might as well see the truth."

"Fuck off, Philip."

"Addie? *Philip's* there? What's going on?" Toni's voice sounded harsh. "Talk to me."

"If I hang up, call hotel security," Addie told her, staring at Philip. "There's an unwelcome guest at my door." She looked back at him. "I wasn't interested when we tried dating the first time, and I'm not interested now. If you think you can intimidate me, you're stupider than I thought."

He narrowed his eyes. "Dyke bitch. I don't know who you think you are, but—"

Addie cut him off. "Go sober up."

A man in a hotel uniform appeared then, wheeling a tray toward the room. "Excuse me, sir."

Philip turned to leave, and the room-service attendant paused, glancing after him as he wobbled away. "Are you okay, miss?"

Addie affixed a professional smile. The last thing they needed was more drama attached to the show. "Coworkers, right? I think he just took a wrong turn. Everything's fine." Addie stepped to the side and the young man rolled the table in. "Right over here would be great. I'm glad dinner arrived when it did."

Through the phone, Toni was obviously not calming down. "Are you okay?"

"I'm fine," she said quietly. When the room-service attendant glanced at her, she gestured toward the street, where women in tall heels were clinging to their dates and laughing. There was some sort of party nearby, but she was starting to think that was a permanent state in the French Quarter.

Smiling at the room-service guy, Addie said, "It's such a vibrant nightlife down there."

"That it is," the young room-service guy said. He gave her a kind look. "Do you need anything else? A manager maybe? *Anything?*"

"Addie." Toni's voice was still in her ear. "Are you okay?"

"Let me sign this slip," Addie said as cheerily as she could. Then she answered both of them. "Everything is just peachy here. I'm fine. An awkward moment with a drunk coworker isn't going to ruin my night."

It wasn't fine. Not really. Addie wasn't sure what Philip was there to do. Was he just going to insult her some more? Threaten her? Worse? He was drunk, and drunk logic was never quite predictable—especially when mixed with anger.

Chapter 39
Toni

Toni felt a surge of fear that had her hands shaking. *What if Addie had been alone?* She was, in truth, but the room-service timing and the phone call meant there were witnesses. *What if she hadn't had anyone listening or interrupting?*

As she waited for Addie to finish talking to the room-service attendant, Toni flipped open her laptop and fired off an email to Harold.

From: Toni Darbyshire
To: Harold Ellis, Department Chair

I swear this won't become a problem/habit, Dr. Ellis, but I need to go to New Orleans for the weekend regarding trouble with the show. Could I get coverage for Friday's class? Kaelee is more than able to teach it. If not, I will be canceling class. Emergency.

T.D.

Then she flipped over to a new email and started to draft a message, cc'ing both Marcela and Emily.

I will be in New Orleans for the weekend. Philip just

appeared at Adelaine's hotel room and called her vulgar, homophobic terms. He was the photo leak, too. He needs to be replaced. ASAP. I won't be silent if that sort of person is associated with the show.

T.D.

Before she hit SEND, she waited to hear Addie's version of what had happened.

"I'm back," Addie said. "Sorry about that. Who had 'drunk costar at the door' on their bingo card?" She laughed awkwardly. "As if him being a jerk all day wasn't enough."

"Did I hear him call you a 'dyke bitch,' Adelaine?" Toni said as calmly as she could.

"He was drunk—"

"Addie," Toni interrupted. "Did I hear that correctly?"

"Yes."

"Are you okay?" Toni's tone was softer, even though she felt certain that there were coils of lava rolling through her veins.

"It's not the first or last ugly thing someone will say to either of us," Addie said lightly. "He saw the show as a star vehicle for him, and he was drinking, and all the buzz is either about me or about the marriage. The new clips were something like ninety percent featuring me, and then the photos—"

"Which he leaked," Toni interjected. "He admitted that, right?"

"Yes. He wants more publicity, and apparently, he can't fathom how I'm the star. Lead named character, but my success is because of you." Addie sounded both hurt and frustrated.

"Ignore him, please. The clips are about you because it's a show about a female Victorian detective," Toni pointed out. "And because you're amazing."

Toni clicked SEND on her email. There were plenty of actors they could recast, and the team wasn't so far into the filming that he couldn't be replaced or written out of the show. If necessary, she'd kill him in the book. That would create a huge plot hole, but she'd figure it out. She wasn't sure what the options were, but keeping him on the show wasn't one of them. Of that, she was certain.

Addie sighed. "He admitted the photo leak, Toni. The whole media thing. He thought it would ruin me. I'm so, so sorry."

"Addie! Why would I blame you for his actions?" Toni asked.

Plus, he gave me extra fodder to insist they fire his ass.

"I know you're an introvert, and you hated your life being in the media." Addie sniffled. "It was my fault."

"No. It was his fault, and honestly"—Toni sighed—"the media wouldn't have been so extreme if I wasn't staring at you like you were the answer to every prayer I've ever had."

"Really?" Addie's voice was tremulous.

"Really. I admitted as much when I emailed the publisher. They said it in more polite terms than I did, but the sentiment is the same. What I should've added was that you were my muse, Adelaine. My good luck charm. I named a character after you once the book was written, but this sequel exists because you returned to my life."

"You don't have to say that."

"I'm not just saying it. It's true. New topic," Toni said, rather than arguing. "Do I need my own hotel room? Or can I stay with you?"

"You're coming after all? I thought you said it was unlikely?" Addie sounded like someone had just given her a new puppy. Her ability to switch moods was beautiful in that moment.

"I am coming to New Orleans." Toni clicked on available flights. There was one leaving at 5 A.M. She glanced at the clock. "I ought to get to bed soon, but I wanted to let you know. I made it work."

"You mean . . . tomorrow? Not on Saturday but tomorrow? Halloween?"

"I do mean exactly that." Toni pulled out her wallet and a credit card she used for business expenses. *It's a business expense if it's for the show, right?* Foolishly or not, she swapped that card out for her personal one. Seeing Addie wasn't business.

"I'm filming until midafternoon," Addie reminded her.

"So I'll nap in your bed, if that's okay," Toni countered. "Unless you don't want me to be in your room . . . ?"

"No! I mean yes." Addie let out a joyful squeal. "Yes, please. Stay with me. Come see me. I'll ask for a spare blanket at the front desk."

"Or you could just sleep on top of me and then you don't need the covers," Toni suggested, only half joking.

"So that's the trick? I just stay in your arms all night?" Addie teased. "What time do you arrive?"

Toni finished buying the ticket and looked at the receipt. "I land at eight ten. I have an open invitation to the set. . . . Would you mind if I came by? I don't want to make you uncomfortable, especially with all the wedding talk still buzzing around."

While there wasn't as much drama as in the initial forty-eight hours, it was still enough that Toni wanted to cringe away. Her fear of being judged had kept her off social media, off news sites, and Emily filtered everything. *She isn't a student or fan, though. She is a beautiful woman I met before the book even sold.* Maybe admitting that was the wrong move, or maybe she ought to accept an interview and clear the air.

"I'm not embarrassed that people think you'd choose me as a lover," Addie said.

"So I can come by the set without making you uncomfortable?" Toni pressed.

"Depends on what you mean by 'uncomfortable,' and it probably depends on how you greet me when you arrive." Addie's voice was light, but she sounded more serious, more anxious, than Toni wanted to hear.

"Last time, I crawled under your skirt and put my mouth—"

"Toni!" Addie laughed. "I'm fairly sure that isn't a public act."

"Says the woman who suggested sex in my Jeep at the Kennedy Center parking garage," Toni teased. "And tried to seduce me in my office."

"So no sex at work? Either of our places of work?" Addie said, still sounding like she might laugh.

"What about phone sex tonight? Or video again?"

Addie's breath caught. "Maybe, but I thought you had an early flight."

"I'll sleep better if I know you're resting and relaxed," Toni pointed out. She stopped herself then and added, "I didn't like hearing you afraid and vulnerable, love. I'm on edge now."

"I'm safe. I swear." Addie paused. "There are two locks on the door, and I'm on the second floor staring down at the French Quarter."

Toni sighed. "Can I ask that you also lock the balcony before I hang up to sleep?"

Addie was quiet for a moment. Then she said, "Done. You don't need to worry, though. I'm not worried. He was drunk, and I should've looked through the peephole and—"

"He is angry, drunk, and homophobic." Toni forced back her temper. Men like Philip expected a level of entitlement just because they were cis, het, white, able-bodied, reasonably attractive men. When she was a child, she used to believe that there was fairness at some point.

If she was educated enough.

If she was strong enough.

If she wasn't poor.

If she didn't look *so queer.*

If she didn't flinch at their rudeness or sexism or homophobic jokes.

Now she realized that for some people, there was never a point at which they would become tolerant. Their fear was permanent—from discomfort with drag shows to book bans to trying to legislate away women's bodily autonomy. Some people would always let their baseless fear drive their actions.

But that doesn't mean that Addie ought to have to face it alone. No one should, really, but Addie, especially, Toni wanted to protect.

And while Toni couldn't protect everyone, she was damned if she was going to let her . . . whatever Addie was be at risk.

There ought to be a word for people you like to spend time with and have sex with. More than "lover." Her brain filled in: *There is a word, and you know what it ought to be. "Girlfriend." "Woman." "Partner." "Beloved." Pick one.*

Toni couldn't sit still. She shoved that series of dangerous thoughts away and started throwing assorted clothes into a bag. She paused and filled up the cat's autofeeder and autowaterer.

"I'm not okay with Philip's behavior, love," Toni said softly. "I'd feel that way if I didn't know you. I'd feel that way if you were any actor who had the lead in this show."

"So it's not personal?" Addie asked quietly.

"Damn it, Addie. Of course it's also personal. You're mine, and you shouldn't have to suffer for that." Toni's temper had always bubbled up like a geyser, but she'd spent the last decade learning how to control it.

Until Addie.

"Yours, huh?" Addie replied, voice soft and sweet.

Toni could kick herself for the slip. "My friend, the actor in my show . . ."

"Your lover," Addie filled in the space.

"Yes." Toni closed her eyes, trying to keep the other words from spilling out her lips. She wanted that for the first time in her life, but it wasn't what was best for Addie. Instead of the other words that curled at the back of her tongue, Toni said, "I don't ever want to cause you problems, and because you were with me—"

"Toni," Addie interrupted. "You were my first and my only, but if I was not with you, there would still be someone else eventually. I was still a lesbian before we were in bed. So . . . just don't borrow trouble that's not yours."

Toni switched the topic to resist the reaction she had to the idea of someone else touching Addie. She said, "You've used that phrase before, you know, about borrowing trouble."

"One of my therapists said that a lot, because my parents were such a disaster, I took on blame that wasn't mine. I was borrowing other people's baggage, basically. I think about that a lot. I guess I use it a lot." Addie sighed. "The point is that I don't need you to carry *my* baggage, Toni, and I *won't* carry yours."

The words felt like a warning, and Toni had a fleeting thought that her baggage was eventually going to be the cause of their end. She could only hope their inevitable parting would be mild enough that she could keep Addie as a friend at the end.

What if I can't? What if she hates me? What if occasional days together stop being enough?

"Halloween in New Orleans," Toni said, pushing her flare of panic away. "Shall I pack a costume for you, too?"

Addie laughed. "I *do* have a few Victorian dresses. All I'm missing is a woman in a good suit. Know anyone who might be willing to escort me?"

"Incidentally, I have just such a suit." Toni wasn't sure how she'd gotten this lucky. Addie was everything Toni didn't think could exist in one person, and she continued to be a historian's dream woman.

My dream woman.

Maybe we could keep this up at least until the show's season is filmed . . . or maybe until they decide about a second season.

Before disconnecting, Toni said, "Promise me you'll be careful, Addie. The thought of something happening . . ." Her words trailed off, because Toni couldn't even pronounce the rest of that thought. "Security can escort you if you go anywhere. I can pay them for—"

"You're not my sugar mama, Toni. I don't need you to pay anyone or do anything. Philip was a drunk jerk. That's all." Addie sighed. "I'm not your responsibility."

But I want you to be, Toni admitted to herself. *I really need to get my feelings in check because I want you to be, Addie. And I want to be yours.*

Aloud, though, all she said was, "I'll see you in the morning, love."

Chapter 40

Addie

Knowing Toni would be on the set today had left Addie with goliath moths in her belly. She was fine when the cameras were running, but when they were between takes or between scenes, Addie felt like her head was on a swivel. She scanned the people in the streets, hoping to see Toni.

She ought to have been here by now.

"We have an idea that we may want to run with," Marcela said as she approached Addie midmorning. "I wanted to bounce it off you."

Addie looked her way. "You're the boss."

"Yes, but I don't want to spring anything awkward on you."

Her tone made Addie pause. "Okay . . ."

"We wanted a cameo with Toni," Marcela continued. "So I was thinking we can have her alongside the witness you meet. Can you do that without . . . complications?"

Addie felt like she was glowing. "Of course."

"Without grinning the way you are right now? It would look odd if you were all wide smiles through the whole scene," Marcela added in a teasing voice.

"I will definitely try."

"It'll be good promo footage to have her in the shot," Marcela added, glancing to a commotion across the street. In a lower voice, she muttered, "And hopefully keep her from punching Philip."

"What?" Addie stared at Marcela. "How did you—"

"Later," Marcela said. Then louder, she called, "Someone bring me Darbyshire." She pointed to where Toni was talking to a security guard at the perimeter.

"I'll go!" Addie turned to head across the street.

And all Addie could do was force herself to walk toward Toni, trying to be mindful of the fact that her heavy dress was not meant for speed—even without the corset. Thankfully, Toni had argued that Addie and the rest of the cast be free from those if they wanted.

Toni was in a Victorian suit, not the same one Addie had seen, and she was stalking across the street with a sort of focused purpose that made Addie's chest as tight as if she were still wearing a corset.

"Adelaine," Toni said as they met in the street.

Addie stopped a foot from her and stared at her. "You're *here*."

The look in Toni's eye was not just the usual fondness or desire; she was studying Addie. "Are you well? Safe?"

From behind them, Addie heard, "Cut."

"What?" Addie turned back and scowled.

"Improv, but it'll work. We can use that as a brief scene, a setup," Marcela said. "Excellent chemistry, Toni and Addie. Hopefully, the viewers don't beg me to give you a role."

"I can guarantee you that *that* won't happen," Toni muttered. She wrapped an arm around Addie's waist as she said, in barely a whisper, "Do you want me to try to have that deleted? I didn't know they were doing that. I was told I just had to sit in a room and stare at you adoringly."

Addie put a hand to her mouth, as if she could hide the laugh that wanted to bubble up. "I am perfectly fine with that improv scene *and* still want that other scene, if you're willing. . . ."

"Fine, but I need sleep after," Toni said. "I have plans tonight."

"Yes, ma'am."

Toni shot her a quelling look, and this time Addie did start laughing. After a moment, she took Toni's hand and dragged her over to

Marcela. "You need to let her see that scene before you use it." She shook a finger at her. "You're tricky."

"And you two were splendid." Marcela gave them a long look. "Fake marriage, my ass. My eyes still work, you know."

"We're dating," Toni said simply. "That part is true. I've said that, and Adelaine has done interviews. The wedding was . . . part of a historical weekend. You *know* that. The wedding itself was not real. There was no marriage license."

"Are you willing to do an interview together?" Marcela asked. "That footage, the interview . . ." She drifted off, obviously plotting. "The sound bites would be amazing."

"Fine. One interview with both of us. You can come chaperone if you want," Toni added.

"I'll set it up." Marcela smiled gleefully.

Addie stayed there silently, contentedly holding Toni's hand in hers even as she knew that Philip was nearby glaring at them. *At me.* She could feel his gaze on them without looking, and she knew that last night's rage was still simmering there.

Toni's next words drew her attention, even though her voice was too low to be overheard. "And the matter I emailed about?"

This wasn't the tender side of Toni that Addie had grown accustomed to hearing, or even the professorial one she'd watched online and in person. This was something more forceful.

"I'll need about three weeks," Marcela said evasively, speaking as quietly as Toni had been. "I spoke to Ms. Haide and to the studio. I share your opinion, Toni, but you know there will be repercussions."

Toni nodded once. Her voice was still pitched low as she said, "Good. I will expect security in those three weeks, and the interview before that because I will not be able to be polite if asked directly. I can be cooperative, but only if Adelaine's safety is prioritized."

"Toni . . . ?" Addie had a sinking feeling that she knew exactly what the topic was they were discussing. *Philip.* It had to be about him. "I'm okay."

Toni squeezed her hand. "We'll talk about it tonight, love." Then in a louder voice, Toni said, "Shall we get this cameo filmed so I can head to the hotel? I'm not a morning person, and today's flight was earlier than I like."

Filming the cameo was harder than Addie expected. She wanted to go to dinner, lunch, drinks, walks, anywhere with *only Toni*. She didn't want cameras on them.

Honestly, it wasn't even that she wanted Toni naked in bed. Addie wanted to explore the city with her. They weren't filming the next day—weekends were free—so she had already been looking forward to exploring the city. Today's work hours seemed to have been dragging already, and now she was in a shop—supposedly in the 1800s, thanks to creative work by the team—talking to the woman who was to be a witness . . . and the woman's companion.

Adding Toni to the scene was a minor script modification, but Addie was struggling to keep her eyes off Toni. They were to be former lovers in the new scene, so Addie was "allowed" to shoot her a heated look.

Between takes, Marcela politely said, "Think of your character, Addie. You are a bit lacking in subtlety. More pining, less 'I want to ravish you.'"

"My character has been without affection for months. I think a bit of lust is appropriate," Addie argued.

"Less of it, unless Toni is planning to take up a role on the show." Marcela crossed her arms and looked at them.

"Addie? I could use a nap. Can we get this done?" Toni said in a low voice. "As the queen supposedly once said, 'Lie still and think of England.'"

Addie giggled, recalling a video of Toni talking about that tidbit as Queen Victoria's answer on how to endure sex. It was not *actually* what the queen said, but it had become a fun catchphrase, and Toni had used it in her book, too.

Once they finished the scene with the cameo, the crew hustled to get ready for the next scenes of the day. Addie had a few moments to talk to Toni, but before she could do so, Philip walked up to Toni.

Toni shot Addie a smile and continued toward the barriers

As Toni walked away, he pursued her, not quite hurrying, but Addie knew he was trying to reach Toni before she left the set. "Miss Darbyshire? Toni?"

Addie winced internally when Toni pivoted to meet his gaze.

"*Dr.* Darbyshire," she said, correcting him.

"Right." Philip straightened, as if he could rebuild himself, or maybe he was trying to stand as her equal. He was technically taller, but he looked small as Toni stared at him. "I just wanted a chance to meet you and—"

Toni cut him off. "Why?"

"What?" Philip stared at her, frowning now.

"*Why* do you want to meet me?" Toni prompted. "You called my girlfriend a dyke . . . which means that you likely have no respect for me either, as I'm the dyke who wrote the book."

"I don't know what she told you, but—"

"I was on the phone, Philip. She told me nothing. *You* did, when you uttered that slur." Toni looked at him. "I could kill you, you know. No one would mind that much."

"*What?* Did you threaten—"

"In the *book,* Philip, I could kill your character off, and no one would miss you." Toni leveled a look at him that would make sensible people retreat, and Addie realized that Toni had intended it as a threat against his livelihood, but she undoubtedly *also* realized exactly what he'd hear in her words.

He stood there, gaping at her. "I had no idea you were on the phone or—"

"And since you seem confused, let me clarify. I've known Adelaine since well before the book," Toni said, voice carrying clearly. "She didn't fuck me for the role, as you have so charmingly suggested. We dated before I sold the book, and I didn't even know she'd auditioned until after she was chosen by Marcela for the cast. She kept it a secret until the day I met both of you. If *anyone* benefitted from her being cast in the show, it was me."

Toni's voice grew louder as she continued, "She makes the show better, and I have the pleasure of seeing her more often because she auditioned. *Marcela* hired her without me knowing. So if anyone is benefitting here, it's not Addie. I'm the one benefitting from her presence in my life and on this show. She's the one gracious enough to audition, to accept the role, and to allow me some of her free time. She's an amazing, gorgeous, talented, kindhearted woman, not someone who has to lie or connive to succeed."

Toni didn't look at Addie the whole time, but Addie was well aware that Toni knew she was watching. She knew Addie was listening—as was half the crew.

And yet, Toni still said those things, those ridiculously flattering things.

Addie wanted to go over and kiss her until they were embarrassing themselves. She wanted to point at Toni and say, "Do you hear that? She *likes* me." She wanted to melt from how hot her cheeks were burning. Instead, Addie just watched Toni in awe.

"Next time you decide to make a homophobic slur . . . actually, just *don't*. She's succeeding because she's talented," Toni said to him, more gently now. "And honestly, Philip, who accepts a role in a show *written by a lesbian about a lesbian detective* and makes a comment like that?" She shook her head. "I have already told my team that I won't sit at any events with someone who calls a woman a 'dyke bitch.' And if the powers that be try to insist, I'll explain *in public* why I refuse. Let's see how that affects you getting cast in anything else."

Finally she glanced at Addie. "I'll be at the hotel."

Then she turned and left. And Addie couldn't quite wipe the shocked look off her face. It wasn't just that Toni had outed Philip for his homophobic remark, but she had also just publicly said she was dating Addie.

She called me her girlfriend!

Chapter 41
Toni

When Toni woke in Addie's bed alone after a good nap, she was tempted to head out to explore the French Quarter. It had been years since she'd been here, and the last time was for an academic conference, so it had not been exactly the sort of free time she had this weekend.

But I want to explore with *Addie.*

There were a few museums of note, and Toni was a historian. The Presbytère, The Cabildo, and the 1850 House were all near enough that she could walk there in the time she had. *Leave a note for Addie, and . . .*

Toni pulled out her laptop instead. *The Widow's Curse* was coming along well, and there was no need to go wandering without Addie. The last thing she wanted was for Adelaine to be here alone and have to deal with Philip. If they filmed the final scenes with him, they could let him go in a matter of weeks. A few weeks. That was it.

How secure is Addie's LA apartment?

The thought popped up intrusively. Toni wasn't even sure she wanted to think about that. Addie in LA, vulnerable. *Maybe I should go stay with her.*

The thought wasn't even fully formed before Toni reminded herself that she had obligations in DC—to her job and to her mother. *Addie needs someone in her life who can be there for her.* She shoved the thought away.

First crisis first.

Toni fell into the story of a late-night Victorian world with its gas lamps and gardens; in some ways it wasn't too dissimilar from parts of Edinburgh or New Orleans, if one ignored the modern elements that crept in. Of course, her character was hunting a killer while vulnerable on the danger-filled streets. The initial plan had been that Cousin Colin would have a personality evolution and become an ally. Now, Toni needed a new plan.

Or they can recast Colin?

She made a margin note to talk to her editor, Greta. Changing the story for the sake of the show seemed extreme, but if there was another character—a bastard brother? an old friend of her deceased husband? the brother of an ex-lover?—who could fill that role, Toni would like it. *A gay man, ideally. And the role cast with a gay man. . . .*

Her note-to-self grew longer as she started adding what could be an exciting plot shift.

By the time Addie texted—"Done in a few. See you at the hotel?"— Toni was ready for a break . . . or maybe she just missed Addie. She'd spent most of the last few weeks writing when she wasn't at the college or the gym, and she was far enough along on *The Widow's Curse* that she could turn it in *before* her extension due date.

"Meet you at set," Toni texted before she grabbed her wallet and opted for a jacket-free day. Unlike DC, where the autumn weather was chilly, New Orleans today was warm and humid enough that this wasn't jacket weather.

Toni was grateful that the hotel was near the filming site *and* that she had a basic grasp of directions. The streets were filling with tour groups, drunken tourists, and locals. A plethora of costumes covered most of the crowd. The French Quarter was already a thriving mass of revelry. Fake spiderwebs, bones, and beads seemed to be festooning every possible surface. Unlike the historical accuracy of the Cape Dove Manor weekend, this was a chaotic blend of everything under the sun.

By the time Toni reached the filming area, she was wishing she'd taken the time to dress in her suit. When Toni walked up to the steel barricades that lined the perimeter, she had to catch the attention of security. She flashed her access badge, and the man checked his clipboard. Apparently, they had taken extra precautions as the day went on. She couldn't blame them, though. The crowd milling around the streets seemed to have quadrupled since morning.

A remarkable number of people wore semi-historical costumes, and the streets were as interesting as the decorations on the buildings. A wedding party in black lace twirling black umbrellas danced by in a parade of beads and booze, accompanied by a jazz parade and what appeared to be at least three Baron Samedi look-alikes— one in a dress.

The set, however, was deserted in comparison to earlier. Most of the actors and crew were gone. Toni looked around in confusion. Inside the small space was a veritable oasis of peace. And in that oasis was Addie, who was dressed in a scarlet gown that was far from her character's usual modest ensemble. Her chest was on abundant display, and ringlets were falling around her face—although the majority of her hair was pinned up like a proper Victorian woman. Dainty boots peeked out from under heavy skirts that were a shade too short. Rouge and dark-red lipstick completed the outfit.

"Damn. I'm not sure where to look, love. You are a vision." Toni took a step back to fully appreciate the ensemble and woman wearing it.

"We shortened the skirt to keep it out of the streets," Addie said.

"The length of your skirt was not anywhere on the list of what I was admiring," Toni said.

Addie turned her neck where two bright marks showed as if she'd actually been bitten. "Costuming did me a favor." She executed a small spin. "I was actually done an hour ago, but I thought—I mean, when in New Orleans . . ."

"You are magnificent." Toni took her hand and gave her a small bow. "And I am here to volunteer as your willing victim."

"They offered to give you a pair of fangs for the night," Addie blurted out hurriedly. "A couple people waited after your whole monologue earlier, and I was thinking you could be a vampire since I have the bite."

Toni laughed. "You know what? Why the hell not? Lead on."

A short while later, Toni had a period suit and her prosthetic fangs, and they were walking through the crowds pouring out of bars and restaurants. It was a crush, with music and drunks and costumed partiers everywhere. They had been photographed by staid tourists as they worked toward the restaurant on Royal Street.

"You tell me if you change your mind on photos," Addie repeated.

"They're fine. It's just tourists who like the costumes, and who can blame them?" Toni's gaze swept over Addie again. "I am being accompanied by the most beautiful woman in the city."

"Who is under your thrall," Addie said cheerily.

They arrived at The Court of Two Sisters and were seated. *Thank goodness for Marcela pulling strings on a reservation.* Toni had already ordered a drink for both of them when Addie looked at her and said, "I feel like I *am* sometimes, you know."

"Like you are what?"

"Under your thrall." Addie blushed under her exaggerated costume makeup. "I swear I didn't know people thought about sex this often until I met you."

Toni looked at her, weighing just how honest to be, before saying, "You know it's not just sex for me, don't you?"

"I don't want to presume," Addie said quietly. "I'm never sure . . . you are confusing sometimes. I know you want me, and I think you feel . . . the things I do."

"Addie . . ."

"It's just hard to know what will make you run." Addie smoothed the napkin in her lap. "I don't want you to push me away or run. That's getting tedious. If it keeps happening . . ."

"I'm here with you right now," Toni said, reaching out for her hand.

Addie gave it to her, and they sat there like that for a moment.

"I want to be here," Toni said. "Not just for sex. I accept it, Addie. We're dating."

"You sound sad about it," Addie murmured.

They were still sitting in silence, hand in hand, when the server arrived and took their order.

Once the server left again, Toni looked at Addie and said, "My dad loved my mother with his everything, but he was a bastard. He would gamble away her royalties. She gave it all up for him . . . for me, really, too."

"I'm not after your money," Addie started, pulling her hand away.

Toni caught it. "I'm not worried about *that*. What if I'm like him? He destroyed everything he touched, and Lilian, my mother, was miserable. What if I ruin your life?"

"Toni . . ." Addie's eyes glimmered like she might cry. "Your mother must be a very strong woman. I'd love to meet her next time I visit."

Toni visibly flinched at the thought of taking Addie there. Her mother was likely to look at Addie and think she was one of the women Toni's dad had seduced. Toni could admit in the privacy of her mind that Addie was definitely his type. They hadn't shared too many things, but this was one thing they had in common: a love for beautiful, curvaceous, hyper-feminine women.

"No one meets Lilian," Toni managed to say. "I just don't see that happening."

"Right." Addie's expression went carefully blank. "So that's the fear? Being like your dad? Hurting someone you . . . care about?"

Toni nodded. "Or what if I'm like *her*? She doesn't know who I am. I don't know how long it had been going on before he died, but she was already failing before I even knew. She's in memory care, and all things considered, she's doing well. But . . . she's lost in her mind. I don't know whether to be angry with him for dying or forgive him because it's hard enough for me to handle when she doesn't even know my name. She thinks I'm my aunt or maybe that I'm one of 'his floozies.' Who could deal with that? What if I end up like her? Or turn out to be a drunken selfish bastard like him?"

At first Addie said nothing, but after Toni looked away, Addie said, "So you can't have a relationship because your parents sucked at it? Is that the issue?"

Toni looked back at her, but then the server dropped off their drinks.

Once the server was gone, Addie let out a loud sigh and took a gulp of her drink. Then she looked at Toni. "Did they write novels?"

"What?" Toni scowled at her.

"Since you have to be just like them, which one was the novelist?" Addie stared at her. "Or the lesbian? How about history professor?"

"I see what you're doing," Toni managed to say. "It's not like I think I'll be like them in all ways—"

"Just the one that gives you an excuse not to fall in love with me?" Addie said calmly.

"If I fall in love, I can't continue to see you." Toni stared at her, willing her to understand. "I won't let my feelings make me ruin your life."

Addie took another drink. "Well, what happens if I fall in love with you? It doesn't actually matter as long as you don't love me, does it?"

Toni stared at her. "You'd tell me if you were . . . ?"

Addie smiled cheerily. "I love spending time with you in and out of bed. I like being in your thrall. And you don't love me, right? There's absolutely no reason to end something if it works for both of us. Honestly, it's not like either of us is considering ending her career to move across the country. Are you?"

For a moment, Toni just stared at her. She couldn't ask that of Addie, which she knew, but she couldn't quit her job and abandon Lil either. Carefully, she said, "I can't move to California. I have a contract."

"Good thing I didn't ask you to, then, isn't it?" Addie crossed her arms. "Honestly, if the sex wasn't so good, all your hang-ups would be a major red flag. I guess they still are."

"So we're both okay with dating?" Toni said carefully. She'd just confessed the things that were keeping her from giving her heart to Addie, and Addie's response felt like she was saying she could accept it.

"We are," Addie said.

This was a turning point: Addie had given them permission to continue on as they were.

"I'm relieved. I would hate for this to end," Toni confessed, and while she was at it, she added, "I came here because of what that asshat said, you know. I bought the tickets while we were on the phone."

Addie shook her head. "I bet lots of friends do things like that. If someone threatened Emily, you'd be in New York, right?"

Toni paused. "I would."

Addie shrugged with one shoulder. "No big deal then, you coming here."

For a moment, Toni was certain that something was wrong, and she was missing it, so she asked, "So you're okay with the fact that I can't love you, and you can't love me, and we will have to end this if either of us falls in love?"

"Yes." Addie stood. "I need to run to the ladies' room."

Toni stood quickly. She wasn't going to dress like a "gentleman" and not treat Addie correctly. "I'll be right here waiting for you."

Addie leaned close and brushed a kiss over her lips, and then she was gone.

Chapter 42

Addie

Addie stood in front of the sink with tears threatening to bubble over. "Damn it. I'm in love with a fool."

An older woman exited the stall and looked at her. "Aren't we all? What did he do?"

Addie gave a watery laugh. "Well, *she* says we have to break up if either of us fall in love."

"*Hmph*. And folks say going gay is easier," the woman grumbled with a heave of her sizable bosom. "Do you love her already then?"

Addie nodded. "Yes. I think I do. I didn't realize it until . . . now. Today. There's no future, though." She paused and sniffled. "I can't give up my career, and she . . . won't even think about a future. How do I love someone who doesn't want my love?"

"You tell her yet?"

"No." Addie accepted the tissue the woman held out and dabbed at her eyes. "She flew here to be with me this weekend because some guy from work showed up at my door and called me a rude thing."

"*Hmph*," she said again. "The sex good? With your lady?"

Addie's cheeks flamed. "Very."

"Least they were right about that when they said it was better to date women." The woman touched up her lipstick, and then looked at Addie in the mirror. "So don't tell her. Enjoy your weekend, girl.

Once that show of yours airs, everyone and their mama will be wanting a bite of you if you act half as good as you look."

For a moment, Addie just stared at her. "Oh."

"Your face is on the side of my daily bus, child, and even if it wasn't, I pay attention when shows film in my city." She sounded gentle as she spoke, as if she was afraid she'd spooked Addie. She reached into her giant bag and pulled out a pen and a receipt. "Can I get your autograph since we're here?"

Addie accepted the pen and paper and wrote, "To the wisest woman in NOLA, love Adelaine Stewart."

The woman chortled. "I'm going to frame this, Miss Adelaine, and then I'm going to hang it on my wall and host the next book-club meeting."

At that, Addie laughed. "Thank you for the advice and for cheering me up."

"You get back out there and show her how fabulous you are, child. Then if she's fool enough to let you go, you don't let her know you're hurt." The woman patted Addie's cheek. "Go on, now. Enjoy our fair city. I've yet to see a heart that can't be fixed by the music in this city. At the least, it'll ease what's ailing you."

And Addie decided that it wasn't a bad plan at all. She was in New Orleans for Halloween, wearing a lovely costume, out to dinner with a stunning woman. There was music on the street and pouring out the door of every bar she'd passed when she'd gone walking. Why shouldn't she make it a night to remember? A weekend to enjoy?

When she returned to the table, Toni stood and pulled out her chair. "Everything okay?"

Addie gave her a bright smile. "Why wouldn't it be?" She trailed her fingers over Toni's cheek and jawline. "No more gloomy subjects, though, okay? You made me cry, talking about your mother's life."

Toni gave her a strange look, but then she nodded and seated Addie at the table. When she took her seat she regarded Addie again. "You're sure? Are *we* okay?"

For a moment, Addie debated coming clean, but all that would do was ruin their weekend. And this time, Addie wanted a whole weekend together with no drama. If it was going to be the last one, she wanted it to be perfect.

It has to be the end, though, or I have to lie about my feelings. I can do it for two days, but after that . . .

So Addie smiled and said, "Let's explore, drink, dance. Tomorrow museums. Between them, I want to be ravished, Lord Darbyshire. Debauch me."

Toni swallowed hard. "Well, okay, then. I can do that if that's what you want."

"What are friends for, right?" Addie glanced at her from under lowered lashes. "Shall we play a game?"

"You make me nervous with that tone, Adelaine." Toni took a drink. "What do you have in mind?"

"Dealer's choice. Show me what you can do with those fangs, or you can take a stroll to the ladies and take my purse with you." Addie handed her the bag. "There's a surprise in it."

Toni took her bag and looked inside. "For me?" She looked up at Addie. "Are you sure I should be the one wearing that?"

The tiny bullet vibe had a remote control that Addie had hoped to hand to Toni, but now? Now Addie wanted the control. Once. Before this was all over. Addie wanted the power. So she pushed. She taunted, "Unless it's too intimidating for you to give me control . . . ?"

Toni shut the handbag and put it on the empty seat between them. "Any other options on this list of yours?"

"Maybe tomorrow," Addie said lightly.

"After dinner." Toni closed her mouth as the server delivered their meal. She looked over the table and pronounced, "Both."

Once the server left, Toni gave her an odd look. "I can't concentrate once we start playing games, and right now, I want to talk to you, Addie. You *matter* to me, so I want to know about your week, the filming, where all you want to go this weekend. I was thinking The Presbytère, The Cabildo, and the 1850 House. Dating me requires a lot of museum trips, if you're willing."

Addie bit back a sound. She was willing. She was willing to do all the things, touristy and not, with Toni. All she had to do was hope that she could pretend not to be in love with her for two days—and hope Toni was deep enough in denial to not realize she was there, too.

And then I can fall apart over things ending already. Toni had only just admitted they were dating, and it was already the end. *I can do this. I can enjoy the weekend and then let her go.*

"Can we shop a little, too?" Addie asked as they started their meal.

"There's a lingerie store I passed earlier," Toni said lightly.

Addie giggled. "I was thinking about a bookstore. . . ."

"Fine." Toni fake-sighed. "Drag me to look at books. Don't complain when I take hours."

"Tonight, though? Dancing!" Addie eyed her between bites. "There's supposed to be a whole bunch of bars with great music on Frenchman? Frenchmen? Something like that."

"Another scandalous waltz, perhaps?" Toni teased. "Maybe I can practice a bite on the other side of your throat to see how secure these fangs are."

"I was thinking somewhere a little more southerly," Addie said without even a quaver in her voice. "Unless that's too—"

"It's not too anything," Toni said. "Not at all."

Addie smiled at her before continuing her meal. *This is enough. It has to be. Enjoy what we have right now, and then let her go.*

Toni was a fool. Addie was certain of it, but this would have to be enough because the alternative was losing her tonight. Despite the lies she'd offered, Addie was, in fact, very much in love. *And so is Toni, whether or not she admits it.* So she'd take her last weekend with her beloved and make it unforgettable. There was no other option. Addie wasn't going to throw her career away on anyone, and Toni would run away if she realized Addie loved her.

Whatever this could have been, it's over now.

Sometimes love wasn't enough. Sometimes clicking perfectly,

great sex, laughter, and all the rest were still not enough. They had separate lives on separate coasts, and Toni didn't want Addie's love.

Briefly, Addie considered trying to talk, but what was there to say that she hadn't already said? Toni had once again decided *she* made the rules, and Addie wasn't interested in putting everything—her career, her self-respect, and her heart—on the line for someone who refused to even try.

Chapter 43
Toni

When Toni woke before dawn to leave New Orleans on Monday, she felt like something was still off between them. Addie had been cheerful, fun, and adventurous the last two days. They'd laughed and enjoyed their time, and they'd talked about their dreams for their jobs—and unusual "get to know you" topics from favorite drinks to cities they wanted to visit. On the surface, it was good.

And yet as Addie kissed her goodbye in the pre-dawn hours and said she was staying in bed rather than walk downstairs or even walk to grab coffee before Toni left, Toni was certain that she wasn't imagining it.

"Did I do something wrong again?" Toni asked.

"Why would you ask that?" Addie stared up at her from her cocoon of blankets. "I have a few hours until I need to be on set. It's cold, and I don't want coffee. You can go early, or grab one at the airport."

"If I do that, I could stay a little longer," Toni mused. She leaned down to kiss Addie again. Maybe they had time to—

"I need sleep, Toni. We said goodbye last night," Addie interrupted the thought before rolling away from Toni. She waved half-heartedly over her shoulder. "Go to the airport."

Toni was out of ideas. She couldn't force a conversation, and there was no mistaking Addie's actions. Toni was being dismissed.

She rolled her bag to the door, paused, and looked back, and then she headed to the waiting car. They'd been intimate all weekend, and they'd talked a lot. Toni made sure to hold Addie as long as she wanted, even when they hadn't just had sex. She pondered every detail as she headed to the airport.

She texted Addie:

> It was great to see you. Next time, D.C.?

After a moment, Addie's reply came in:

> I'll check my schedule.

Toni read it, reread it, and scowled. She was *definitely* being dismissed, and she had no idea why. Finally, she looked at the clock. It was an hour later in New York, and Emily was a disgustingly early-morning person.

Toni texted Em:

> Are you awake? What does it mean when a woman rolls over and ignores you? And then says "I'll check my schedule" when you try to plan to see her?

Emily called. "What did you do?"

"Nothing." Toni stared out the window. "We had a great weekend. That asshole showed up at her door drunk, so I flew down and—"

"I'm on that, by the way. Continue." Emily sounded businesslike. "What went wrong?"

"I have no idea. I thought we were doing great," Toni muttered. "She didn't want to get coffee today. And when I texted, she said she'd check her schedule. That's not normal."

"Was she . . . content? Did you ignore her? Fail to get her off?"

"*Obviously* not, Em." Toni thought back to the weekend, to Addie's very obvious pleasure. "I don't fail in that area."

"So you said or did something wrong," Emily surmised. "Did you give her the 'we're friends with benefits' talk?"

"No." Toni squirmed as she admitted the next bit. "I actually referred to this as *dating*."

Emily laughed. "Sweetie, you don't need to say it like it's a vulgar word."

"I like her, and I told her I had missed her, and I suggested that she come to DC to visit me." Toni thought back over the weekend. Since their awkward conversation about Toni's parents and her hang-ups on Friday, everything had been great. She told Em as much, including Addie's suggestion that she could visit Lil.

Em stopped her there. "She wanted to meet Lil?"

"I told her no. Who knows what would happen? Do you remember the nurse with the Betty Boop figure?" Toni thought back to the way her mother had launched herself at that poor woman. It had been terrifying. There was no way Toni was going to subject Addie to that sort of risk. "Speaking of Lil, I missed my visit this weekend because I was out of town. I need to stop on the way to campus. It's early but . . ." She wondered if it was too early. "Maybe I should go this evening, but I was hoping to talk to Addie tonight. Find out what has her acting so weird."

"You know, if you didn't care about Addie, you wouldn't be so worried that she was upset." Emily had slipped into her dealing-with-difficult-people tone. "Do you think maybe we should discuss *that*?"

"No." Toni felt panic curdle her stomach. It felt that way every time she thought about what it could mean that she missed Addie, that she was making excuses to extend their friendship-dating-situationship. Abruptly, she said, "I'm almost at the end of the book. I'll probably be done by the end of November."

"You have December if you need it," Emily reminded her. "Probably early January. Everything in publishing shuts down in December anyhow."

"I'll be done before winter break. *My* break, that is. At the college." Toni watched the driver take the exit for the airport. "Hey, I'm almost here. Thank you for talking. I'll call you this week, okay?"

"I wanted to ask you about your TA," Emily said.

"Kaelee? She's great. English major. Wrote a book. I haven't read it." Toni frowned. "Why?"

"She queried me, and she referenced working for you." Emily paused. "So many people reference you, but this one said she was your TA."

"She is," Toni said. "Kaelee's smart. Driven. A little too much like me, probably, but I know nothing about her book. We're pulling up at the airport . . . unless it's urgent? I can call you back after I get through security."

"Tomorrow is fine. Fly safely," Emily said.

By the time Toni got to Dulles, she was ready to call Addie again. She'd hoped that there would be a call or an email or something. Instead, there was only a text message from Kaelee asking if Toni wanted her to cover the noon class.

"Headed to nursing home. Will be into campus by eleven. Should be there to teach unless traffic accident or etc," Toni replied via text.

Honestly, for all that Toni had protested, she thought Kaelee was great. She was juggling her PhD in English Literature, although her Master of Arts was in History, and was TAing for Toni—all while querying agents. If not for the fact that Kaelee technically worked for her right now, Toni would be glad to call her a friend.

By the time Toni collected her bag and was in her Jeep, she was down to roughly an hour at the memory care center before she had to get to campus. She parked over by the sign for the home, walked in, and signed in.

"Lil's been in a funk the last few days," one of the staff caregivers said when she saw Toni.

"Did something happen? Did she fall or—"

"No. She's been concerned that your father hasn't called or visited." The woman gave Toni a sympathetic look. "Grief is so much harder when you have to keep experiencing it as if it's fresh."

Toni didn't want to repeat that it wasn't his death that was the issue; it was all the horrible things he did in their life together. So she left it at, "I'll see if I can talk to her."

"She's in her room," the woman said.

Toni always braced herself for seeing her mother, and she was already on edge today. She tapped lightly on the door before going in. As she did, she had to duck. Her mother threw a shoe at her.

"Lil!"

"I thought you were your dad," Lilian said. It was not an apology. At best, it was a half-hearted explanation.

Toni stepped into the room, taking in the pile of used tissues on the table next to her. Beside that was—

"Why are you drinking coffee?"

"Because I wanted to. I had one of the neighbors smuggle it in." Lilian looked proud of herself. "The nurse refused, so I went around her."

"Mom . . ." Toni leaned down and dutifully kissed her mother's paper-dry cheek. As she was doing that, she took the cup from her mother's table. "It's bad for your heart."

"So's your father, but I didn't dump him down a drain. Maybe I should've. I landed in a prison anyhow." Lilian gestured around the tiny room. "Least we'd have something in common if I ended up in the hoosegow."

"The *what*?"

"The joint. The slammer. The pokey." Lilian grinned at her, a flash of her still pearly white teeth. "Instead, your dad tried to convince everyone he died and stuffed me in the old people jail. Do I look old to you?"

"You're beautiful, Mom." Toni smiled. "He's really gone, though. He died over a year ago, and the house was too much for you."

"Huh. Gambled it away, did he?" Lilian shook a finger at her. "You can't lie worth a damn, Toni. Never could. Too much like me."

Toni was always at a loss when her mother had windows of clarity . . . or near clarity. In a lot of ways, it was easier when Lil thought she was talking to Aunt Patty.

"Well, sit down. You make my neck hurt having to crane it up at you. Too tall for a woman," Lil grumbled.

Toni tentatively sat in the chair across from her mother.

"Is he actually dead?" Lil asked after a drawn-out pause. There were tears in her eyes.

"He is."

"And you're stuck taking care of me?"

"I'm not stuck—"

"Don't lie to me." Lilian gave her a glare that was as infuriating now as it was growing up. "We have never been close enough for you to care about my feelings. Don't pretend you like me now."

"You're my mom." Toni knew she had a mirrored expression of her mother's. "And you weren't *bad* to me. We just clashed. I love you, so yeah, I found you a safe place to live."

"I love you, too." Lilian looked around her sitting room. "Posh for an old folks' home. Did you do something reckless?"

Toni squirmed. "I wrote a novel, and it sold well. There's a, umm, television show coming out, too."

"Really?" Her mother's expression was awe-filled. "All I did with my life was write a few songs."

"Good songs. You still make royalties on them, you know," Toni assured her. "Plus, you convinced me that the arts were worth a try."

"Gambler's spirit, right there."

"No," Toni objected quickly.

Lilian leveled her with a stern gaze. "If I wasn't willing to bet on the impossible, I wouldn't have sold those songs, or gone on stage, or kept my baby, or married your father. Sometimes, you have to take ridiculous chances if you want to win big. Your dad and I had that in common, you know? Gambler's hearts. You never saw it, though, did you? He and I had that in common. No one else saw that side of me. Just him. He *saw* me, you know? Warts and all, and he loved me."

Toni felt like she was having a long overdue conversation, and she was inordinately grateful for her mother's lucid window. "Even though he did all those things that hurt you? You *still* don't regret it?"

"We had a lot of fun, and I wasn't always a picnic myself. I think Patty took you with her the first few times because of my temper." Lilian looked a little sheepish. "I cut the crotch out of all his trousers the one time. Told him if he couldn't keep his pecker in his pants, I might as well make it easier. That was an expensive choice."

"If you could do it all over—"

"I'd still pick the life I had, bad times and good. I had you. I still sang. And I had a man who made my toes curl every time he kissed me," Lilian said. "It wasn't always easy, and he made mistakes. But I did, too. Love's worth it, though. Nothing in the world feels like that."

Toni shook her head.

Lilian continued, "Have you ever been in love? Felt like you might just die if you have to wait much longer to see your person? Like your heart might thump right out of your skin when you see them? Like you don't care what other people say or think or do? Like the sun is inside them, and you feel warm and happy and safe in their arms? Like you are *invincible* because they believe in you?" Lilian stared off with a small smile. "That was how your father made me feel every day, even when we fought. I never wanted a life that wasn't with him. The hard times were worth it because of the good times."

And it occurred to Toni in a horrible flash of clarity that she knew *exactly* what Lilian meant. She understood every word her mother had said, and with each question, she thought, *Addie*.

Toni swallowed, trying to deny the clarity she'd been running from, trying to push this far down to wherever delusions lived so she could not lose Addie. *I can't love her. I won't. I don't.* Toni wasn't sure when or how it happened, but it had. She was in love with Adelaine.

"Patty?" Lilian reached out. "I forgot what we were talking about."

Toni gave her a strained smile. "My brother."

Lil laughed. "He's ridiculous. Do you know he bought me a sapphire as big as a baby's thumb? We'll end up pawning it when he gets in too deep, but . . ." She shrugged. "What can you do?"

Toni tried to think of something to say, but her words were dry. She nodded, and she wasn't sure whether her mother's mental shift was a blessing or a curse in that moment. Lilian was laughing and telling stories now, and Toni was left reeling from her own epiphany.

What do I do now? I love Addie.

When she came out of the home, Toni had a distinct disjointed feeling at seeing Kaelee pacing beside her Jeep. Her mind was on Addie, not her job.

"Kaelee? Is everything okay?"

"Did you ask Ms. Haide to sign me? I mean if you did, thank you and all. I just want to make it on my own." Kaelee crossed her arms over her chest tightly. "I'm not trying to be disrespectful. You know that, right?"

Toni stared at her. "Slow down."

Kaelee nodded.

"Haide as in Emily? My Emily?" Toni prompted.

"Yes. Your agent." Kaelee held out her phone. On it was an offer of representation from Emily. "I want her to be my agent, but if it's just because of you—"

"It is not." Toni stepped closer. "I'm not going to recommend your book if I haven't read it."

"So you didn't make her offer to repr—"

"No one could *make* her offer representation," Toni interrupted. "Hell, she wouldn't have offered it to me if she didn't like my book, and I've known her since I was a kid."

Kaelee looked like her knees were going to buckle. She stared at Toni and muttered, "I think I have an agent. Holy fuck." She swayed.

Quickly, Toni wrapped her arms around Kaelee. "Whoa! Don't fall."

Kaelee hugged Toni tightly. "I think I might puke. I should stay here until I'm safe to drive."

"You can get your car later." Toni steered her to the passenger door of her Jeep. "You will not puke. I'm going to drive us to campus now, and you will *not puke in my vehicle*. Do you hear me?"

Kaelee nodded. "I'm an author. This is my thesis, and Ms. Haide is going to sell it."

"Right, well, hook your seat belt." Toni pointed.

As she turned, she saw a man with a camera, thought about the photos of her and Addie, and promptly decided she was being paranoid. No one knew her mom was here, and if they did, they couldn't get past security.

Once she was at campus, she was going to call the front desk of the memory care home anyhow. She didn't care about a lot of people, but she wasn't going to have her mother splashed all over the media. It was hard enough when someone had dug up her music. The renewed interest meant royalties for Lil, but the invasion of privacy sucked.

That's what Addie's life was always going to be, too. Media. Toni already hated her own career's lack of privacy. She didn't want her life analyzed by strangers—and yet it was.

No wonder my fake wedding was such a story.

The wedding might be fake, but I'm actually in love with Addie.

Toni could figure this out. She had to—or she'd lose Addie, and Toni wasn't ready to do that.

Maybe I can hide it.

Keep from telling her.

The thought of lying to Addie hurt almost as much as the thought of losing her.

Chapter 44

Addie

A week passed in which Addie simply didn't reply to Toni. She set her phone to Do Not Disturb. She turned her out-of-office responder on for email, and she replied to texts only after a few hours had passed. When Toni replied instantly, Addie still waited at least three hours before replying. Then she moved on to waiting a day between replies.

Addie wasn't trying to be rude. She simply didn't know what to say.

The comments on socials had taken a turn; so many people were making crass remarks or baseless accusations, mostly making everything seem tawdry. Several accounts had started to ask for proof of Addie's age, implying that Toni had done something wrong. One interview request suggested that Addie had been Toni's student. Another suggested that Toni had "turned her" into a lesbian, revealing that Addie had dated men including Philip. She was fairly sure he was behind that leak.

From: June
To: Adelaine Stewart
CC: Marcela Gibson
Re: Interview

We need to get in front of the noise, Addie. What's the
plan with the joint interview? Do we need to loop in
the publisher on this to get it on the calendar?

June

Addie winced. She knew she had agreed to the interview with
Toni, but she wasn't sure she could pull it off. Not now.

She dialed June. "Hey."

"What's going on? Have you seen the latest?" June sounded
strained. "This is bad press, Addie. You *need* to do the joint interview."

"Why?"

"Why? Because she was seen with another woman," June said.
"Have you talked to her?"

Addie felt tears burn. Apparently pushing Toni away for a week
was all it took for her to move on. "We aren't really married. You
know that. Let's do a release saying it was a scene for the show that
was misconstrued. Could we use it? A fake wedding that the character remembers?"

June was quiet. "There is footage that works. I'll call Marcela.
Let me see what I can do."

Addie hung up and opened her laptop. There it was, Toni and her
TA. Addie knew it wasn't what the media was saying, but what stung
was where they were. Clearly, the building—a memory care home—
was where Toni's mom was, and Toni was okay taking someone else
there. She could take a random student to visit her mother, but not
Addie.

"You let *her* in," Addie muttered. "Not me, though."

She clicked away from the photo and opened her email. She read
all of the messages straight-though. The last one was about the photo:

From: History Toni
To: Addie

I swear the pictures are not telling the story they claim to. I
was visiting my mother. I wasn't there with Kaelee. I swear,
Addie. You can email Kaelee if you need proof. I said I
would be monogamous with you, and I meant it. Please
stop ignoring my calls and messages.

Toni

Addie had no doubt that Toni had kept her word on monogamy.
She'd heard Toni's pain over the fact that her father was unfaithful.
Toni might be a fool, but she wasn't a cheater.

From: Adelaine
To: History Toni

I know you aren't sleeping with your T.A. That's not why I
haven't replied.

Addie

Not two minutes later, the phone rang. Addie didn't have to look
to know it was her. She ignored it. Her email chimed again.

From: History Toni
To: Addie

Answer the damn phone.

Toni

This time when Toni called, Addie answered. "Do we need to do
this?"
"Do what?"
"Talk about things?" Addie sighed. "Can't we just . . . I don't
know . . . not?"

Toni was silent for a long moment. "I don't understand what happened. We had a great weekend. I didn't do anything I can think of—"

"I think we just took this as far as it can go," Addie said, cutting her off.

"I don't understand. I did all the things you said you wanted. I held you, and we talked. I just don't fucking get it." Toni sounded frustrated, veering toward either anger or panic. "What did I do wrong this time? You were feeling upset, and I dropped everything and flew there. Christ, Addie, I'd come to you any time you needed me. Anywhere."

"What if I need you every day?" Addie asked quietly. "Forever."

"Addie . . ."

The sob she was holding in escaped. "We talked for a year, Toni, and you couldn't even share your last name. We did things together . . . *beautiful* things, and the moment there was a crisis—one we should've faced together—you didn't even want to let me into your home. I feel like I'm constantly waging a siege on your walls, and you still don't want to let me in."

"I care. You know I care. I've admitted it repeatedly."

"But you don't *want* to care," Addie snapped. "If you or I fall in love, this has to end. That's your rule. Who cares what I want? Who cares how *fucking lucky* we are to have found each other? Or how well we fit? Or any of it? All that matters is that you have decided that you don't want anyone to get close to you."

"You *are* close to me, Addie," Toni insisted. "More than anyone I've ever so much as kissed. You. Only you."

"What if I fall in love with you?"

"You can't," Toni said. "I can't . . . we can't *do* that. I'm not going to ruin your life by—"

"By loving me back?" Addie finished. "Maybe it doesn't even matter. What are we even doing? I can't give up my career, and you can't leave DC, so what are we even doing? This is a mistake. We had fun, and it's over now. I won't be like my parents, living my life with half a relationship. This was a mistake. I had a *plan*, Toni, and this? It's not it."

"Can't we just do what we've been doing? We're good together," Toni cajoled.

Addie swiped at her tears. "No."

"I don't understand why—"

"Because I already love you, Toni," Addie blurted out. "And since *you* decided that love means we're done, we're done. Your rules, Toni. It was your call. From the first moment, it always has been, though. Hasn't it? I was just here, letting you set all the rules, and I'm not that person. I can't do this anymore."

"That's not fair, Addie," Toni started.

"So we're just glossing over the fact that I said I love you?"

Toni sighed. "You *can't* love me. It's just that I was the first woman to—"

Addie disconnected. She wasn't going to listen to Toni argue that she knew Addie's feelings, to try to talk her out of feeling what she felt, to argue that she mistook lust for love. *I know what I feel.* She would focus on her career; maybe she'd get a new therapist, try a few dating apps.

Tears streamed down her face. She had to prioritize herself. No one else was going to do that. The woman she loved certainly wasn't willing to do it.

Chapter 45
Addie

The next few weeks were chaotic. Addie ignored social media, ignored her email, ignored her phone. She had to set her phone to only allow Favorites, and everyone else was on Do Not Disturb.

Prioritize my own well-being.

By the end of the month, she felt together enough to face her family. Still, Addie had outright lied to her parents that she couldn't be there until Thanksgiving evening. "Leftovers and pie is perfect," she'd told them. Eric was driving up north with her, and honestly, a part of Addie was looking forward to the long drive and a weekend off.

Toni had finally stopped calling and texting. She had sent an email that basically asked Addie to come to DC for dinner. Any other time the last year, Addie would've done so with hope in her heart and a skip in her step. This time, she'd replied with, "I love you, so no."

To that, Toni hadn't replied at all.

I don't want crumbs.

That was the crux of it. She had a life here, her bestie, her parents, a career, and she wasn't ignoring it for a few crumbs and lies. Toni wanted her to either pretend not to be in love or lie or who knew. Addie wasn't going to pretend, and Toni ought to know better than to ask it—even inadvertently. For someone that lectured, literally lectured at conferences, about authenticity, she was being a hypocrite.

Today, Addie was on set. Eric had rented a car and was going to meet her here for the drive north. The actual drive to visit family was probably the best part. If they left late enough, they could make it in under eight hours, traffic permitting. If not? They'd grab a hotel and drive tomorrow when everyone else was at wherever they were having their family meals.

There were other people still at the studio. A career in film or television meant long hours. Marcela was working late, and Addie had just finished up talking to costume. But for reason of sheer foolishness, Addie was walking around a Victorian manor that had been designed based on the book created by the woman she loved.

A book with my name in it.

A sequel I inspired.

A scene in New Orleans.

How do I let her go?

Addie heard footsteps and looked behind her. "Marcela? Hello . . . ?"

At first no one replied, but then she heard the steps come closer, heavy, shuffling slightly. Addie wasn't sure that speaking again was wise. She slipped off her shoes so she wouldn't make a sound, and then she backed up slowly until she was in the sitting room.

Maybe she was overreacting, but when no one replied to her, she assumed there was a reason. If it had been Marcela or security or someone on staff, or if Eric was early, they would have replied.

Addie crouched down behind a settee, brushing away the fleeting thought of another Victorian sofa, that one with a surly Oscar Wilde under it. Thinking about Toni wasn't helpful. Thinking about much else wasn't helpful. Not right now.

When she saw the shadow of a man on set, she bit back the fear that Philip was here, drunk and angry again. He had showed up at her hotel room. He had been hostile on set. He had leaked photos and lies about her.

Maybe it's Eric, early.

Maybe it's the new security guard or—

"I know you're here, *Adelaine*." Philip sounded a few steps past drunk, and as he stalked around the set, she could see the shadow of a bottle in his hand.

Drunk. Angry. Alone.

She just had to hope that he wouldn't see her or find her.

"Come out, come out, wherever you are, you venomous bitch." He slurred his singsonging, but it didn't make him less frightening.

Maybe he'll pass out.

Please let him pass out or leave!

"Do you know what I just heard?" Philip continued as if they were having a conversation. "My *fucking role* was cut. I'm gone before the whole season even airs. We filmed all the scenes I was going to still be in. I guess my character is being sent off on some colonialist boat or war where I'll die." He laughed harshly. "Whatever solution that lesbo bitch likes best."

Addie flinched both at his words and the virulent hate in his tone.

"But guess what?" He leaned over the sofa to stare down at her. "I'll land on my feet. Nothing *you* can do will ruin me."

"Philip . . ." Addie straightened and backed away from him.

He reeked of liquor and sweat, and any sympathy she might have felt faded as he stalked toward her.

Loudly, she called out, "Is anyone here? Hello!"

"'Is anyone here?'" he mimicked. He reached out to grab her, and she swerved, trying to put the settee between them. "You could've told me she was on the g'damned phone that night. I'm not a bad guy. I'm actually nice, Addie. I'm like Colin. Misunderstood."

"Then stop saying rude things and walk away right now," Addie countered, voice shaky.

"Let me make it up to you, and we can be friends." Philip lurched over the sofa to grab her. "We can be the great love story. Costars date all the time. Leave her. Date me. I can pretend to like you. . . ."

"No!"

She hit her head as the sofa fell on her, and then something jabbed her in the back of her shoulder as she fell. Addie screamed.

The sound was muffled by Philip shoving his hand over her mouth. He was leaning down, body pressing the sofa onto her. The weight was forcing whatever jabbed her shoulder deeper into the skin.

Suddenly, Philip stopped, eyes wide, expression horrified. He backed up, all the while staring at her with his mouth open like he was saying something.

Then he dropped the bottle. It rolled over the settee and spilled cool liquid all over Addie. The scent of alcohol was harsh, and her shoulder burned as the liquid hit her.

That doesn't make sense.

Why would liquor burn my arm?

"Damn," Philip breathed. He turned and ran, stumbling into the darkness.

Addie was pinned, or maybe it was whatever she'd landed on, but her shoulder was throbbing. She fumbled at her hip for her phone. Her arm screaming in objection, she lifted it up. She couldn't get her arm to move right, though, so she had to lift her head and squint.

She tried to jab Favorites and call Eric, but when she saw Toni's name, she called her instead.

Chapter 46

Toni

"Toni?" Addie's voice sounded wrong, and it felt like a punch to the heart.

"Are you okay?"

"Not really." Addie made a strange noise. "I'm at the studio, and there's a sofa on me."

"A *what*?"

"Sofa. And my arm feels funny," Addie continued. "I need help, Toni. Can you send someone here to move the sofa? I can't get up, and it hurts."

Toni stood up, pacing like there was a solution that didn't include hanging up on Addie. The best she could think was a conference call. "I don't know if I'm going to do this right. Let me try to call Marcela."

"Don't hang up!"

"I'm not planning on it," Toni swore. "I'm going to try a conference call. Add her to the call." She looked at her phone and jabbed ADD CALL. She tapped Marcela's name, and in short order, she had her on the phone, too.

"Addie's at the studio and hurt."

"*What?* Where?" Marcela sounded like she was in her car.

"I'm pinned under the sofa. Philip flipped it, dropped . . . liquor on me, and my arm feels funny," Addie said in a burst. Then she gasped. "I thought . . . I thought he was going to . . . I don't know. I backed up and—"

"Let me call security. I'll be right there, but there's security on site." Marcela disconnected.

"Are you still there?" Addie asked.

"I am. Let me get a flight out, and I'll be there," Toni started.

But Addie cried louder. "I don't want you here. I don't want to see you."

"Addie . . ." Toni didn't want to upset her, but she sure as hell wasn't going to stay away when Addie was hurt. "Listen."

"No." Addie sniffled. "Someone's coming. I hope it's not Philip."

Toni's stomach twisted at the thought of Philip hurting her again. This was Toni's fault, insisting he be fired. He wasn't to know until Addie was gone for Thanksgiving. "Who's there? Is it him?"

"They're here. Security." Addie made a whimpering noise. "I'm going to go shower and maybe get a sling for my arm. Just . . . thank you for sending help. Stay away, please, Toni. My heart already hurts too much even hearing your voice."

Then she hung up, and Toni was left staring at her phone in shock. *She's safe now. She said so.* But she was hurt. That homophobic jerk had hurt Addie. Toni's fist curled into a ball, and she realized she was shaking.

Addie was injured, and of all the people she could call, she picked Toni.

And then she said not to come.

Toni wasn't even sure whom she could call for updates. Marcela was driving, and Toni didn't have Addie's roommate's number. Or her parents'. Or her . . .

What about her manager?

Before the thought was fully processed, she called Emily. "I need Addie's manager's number. She's injured, and I need to know what's happening."

"Call Addie then."

"She won't talk to me, Em. It's been a month. I have been trying to talk to her every damn day," Toni blurted out.

"Why?"

"Because she won't answer, and now she's hurt and—"

"No. Why do you keep calling?" Emily asked. "It's obviously not about the show, and if she won't talk to you, there are plenty of other women who will."

Toni flopped onto her sofa. "Em . . ."

"Have you told her?" Emily asked gently.

"I don't want to hurt her," Toni said helplessly. "You know me. I can't be what she wants. I can't move to California. I can't ask her to give up her career. I watched my mom suffer because—"

"Addie isn't Lil, and you haven't even tried," Emily pointed out. "You couldn't get a PhD or write a bestselling novel or a sequel or . . . handle your mom's care. You can't do a lot of things if you don't even *try* it. You're being a coward."

Toni realized she was crying when Oscar Wilde headbutted her face and came away damp. She swiped at her cheeks. "I need to know she's okay."

"Because?"

"Because I love her," Toni whispered.

"I'm fairly certain she feels the same way," Emily consoled her.

"She does. That's why she ended things. I said if either of us fell in love we had to stop seeing each other, and she said she loves me, so . . ." Toni's words faded.

"Go to LA, Toni. Make it right. Don't be a scaredy-cat. *Go* to her, and be there with her." Emily sounded like she was trying very hard to be patient—and about to fail. "Buy a ticket and go there. Now."

Toni held on to Oscar Wilde. "What if I fuck it up?"

"You are almost guaranteed to fuck up sometimes," Emily said bluntly. "You love her, though, and she loves you, and you are *happy* with her. You'll figure the rest out together."

"What if I get like Lil?"

"Old and beautiful?" Emily countered.

"Em."

"Sweetie, there is no way to know if you'll develop dementia in the distant future, but refusing to let yourself love Addie and be loved by her because you *might* develop an illness decades from now is cowardly. Refusing to try is impressively stupid. And, honestly, it's not just your decision. Let Addie decide if you're worth the risk. Hell, she might leave you in a year."

"She won't," Toni said.

"Then stop being a coward." Emily sighed. "Go tell her you're a fool who loves her before someone who isn't this obstinate sweeps her away."

"Will you watch Oscar Wilde if I'm not back by Monday? His feeder is full, and his new litter boxes are self-cleaning, but he'll be lonely."

"Yes." Emily sounded like she was smiling now. "I know this is scary, sweetie, but I think she's lucky to have found you. Go see her. Show her that you won't run away when you get emotional or afraid. Tell her what you were afraid of."

Toni already had her laptop open. Finding a last-minute ticket the night before Thanksgiving was neither easy nor cheap, but that was exactly what Toni was going to do. She was going to fly to California, tell Addie how she felt, and beg for forgiveness.

They could figure it out . . . if it wasn't too late.

If Addie's okay.

She has to be okay.

I can't lose her.

Chapter 47
Addie

Addie blinked as the stage lights came on. Two security guards came in and lifted the sofa off her. Everything was blurry. *Maybe whatever Philip spilled got in my eye?* She was confused, but she knew something was wrong.

"We've got you," one said. "Try not to move."

Addie tried to move her arm to push herself upright, feeling embarrassed to be found under a piece of furniture—no matter how heavy it apparently was. "I'm in a puddle of someone's spilled liquor. I'm going to get up."

"Ma'am, there's broken glass, and you're bleeding from the . . ." He gestured at her shoulder where tiny brass tips were poking up from a hole in her blouse.

"Oh." Addie turned her head and saw that there was a puddle of blood, pinkish as it mixed with the liquor puddling around her.

"The paramedics are almost here," the other guard said. "Miss Gibson says we have to wait on them. Take pictures and then wait."

"I can put a blanket over you," a third guard, this one a woman, said as she approached. "Are you cold, Miss Stewart?"

"Addie. I'm Addie," she said, staring at the woman with the blanket. Tears were streaking over her temples and into her hair, which was bloody and liquor-soaked. *Tequila, from the smell of it*. And the woman calling her "Miss Stewart" was not Toni.

She wasn't sure how much later it was when Eric came in, accompanied by Marcela. The paramedics were there almost simultaneously.

"I think there are scissors in my arm," Addie said. "Embroidery shears? I'm not sure what they are really. Sharp things. They're definitely sharp. The points came all the way through me."

"Well, that's no good, is it?" said a woman in some sort of uniform.

"Cuz . . ." Eric was staring down at her. "Should I call my mother or yours? Fuck. I don't know—"

"Let's get her to the ER before we go asking her to make any decisions," the uniformed woman said. "Do you know how long you were here?"

"He just got here," Addie whispered loudly.

"Right you are." The woman smiled. "What about you? When did this happen, Miss Stewart?"

"Today." Addie glared at the scissors in her arm. "The scissors weren't there before today." She frowned. "I think I hit my head when the sofa fell on me. . . ."

The next thing she knew, they had moved her carefully onto a stretcher and were carrying her to the ambulance. Addie looked at Eric. "Can you call Toni? Tell her I'm fine?"

He took the phone she had been clutching. He frowned. "Sure, if that's what you want."

"It is. Tell her I'm sorry I messed up filming and—"

"Because you meant to be attacked?" Eric bit out. "No, I cannot tell anyone that. Was it that homophobe?"

"He was upset that he lost his job, and he blamed me and . . ." Addie's words faded as they went down the steps. Even as careful as they were, they had jostled her slightly, and it hurt.

Because there are scissors in my arm.

"I have this, Ads." Eric squeezed her hand. "You go to the hospital. I'll be there as soon as I can."

Marcela gave her a smile and patted her wrist on the uninjured side gently. "Everything will be fine, Addie. Let's get you patched up."

The ride to the hospital and the exam were a blur. All Addie could say for sure was that she was in an operating room, and then she was breathing and counting backward.

When she opened her eyes again, she was in a recovery room with Eric at her bedside.

"Ads!" Eric jumped to his feet, brushed back her hair, and kissed her forehead. "I am going to quit my job and follow you everywhere. We should hire a bodyguard, too. I'm not great at violence."

"Hush. I'm okay. Fill me in," Addie managed to say the next time she opened her eyes. "Where's my sweater?"

It was Toni's sweater, the cardigan Addie had taken home when she left DC. Although it no longer smelled of Toni's cologne, the worn-out sweater had been a security blanket of sorts. Addie slept with it beside her.

Eric draped it over her, and she pulled it up toward her face with her good arm. She closed her eyes for just a moment.

Her next clear memory was Eric saying, "You'll be fine, Ads. Are you staying awake this time?"

"I think so . . . ? Sorry to delay the trip," she said. "You can go and—"

"As if." Eric stared at her like she had suggested a heinous crime. "You're stuck with me, at least until the professor arrives."

"Toni? She's not coming." Addie scooted backward, wincing at the pain in her arm. "She doesn't want to see me."

Eric hurried to help Addie as she tried to prop herself upright to force herself to stay awake. "What do you need? Do you need a nurse? Or—"

"Answers." Addie leveled a look at him. "Why do you think Toni's coming? We ended things."

Eric gave her a long appraising stare. "She's flying out here. You said to call her. I did."

Addie closed her eyes. "That doesn't mean I want to see her."

"Well, how was I to know that? You were in an ambulance, and before you left you said call, so I thought you two had made up. Again." Eric let out a frustrated noise. "I cannot keep track of where you two are on the reject-her, love-her, run-away process. Don't be angry with me because—"

"I'm *not* mad at you," Addie said. "At least she doesn't know which hospital or where I live—"

"Actually." Eric looked sheepish. "You can't blame me. You said to call her."

Sighing, Addie looked at him. "I don't blame you. Let's get me released and . . ."

Eric held up both hands in a defensive gesture. "Ads. You hit your head, have bruised ribs from a sofa on you, and you had to have surgery for a tear from being stabbed. You're here overnight."

"Damn it." Addie blinked away tears, and then a nurse—or maybe she was a doctor? Addie had no idea—came to check on her.

A short while later, someone else was wheeling her entire bed to her room. Eric stayed at her side. "I called Aunt Marlene. Gave her a modified version."

Addie winced. "Are we being invaded?"

"Sorry, cuz." Eric squeezed her hand. "I can tell her not to come until Friday. That's the best I can do."

With a sigh, Addie said, "Phone." She took the phone, grateful it was hers so the numbers were preprogrammed, and jabbed her mother's name. "Mom? Yes. Hi. I—"

"You could've died," Addie's mom wailed, dragging the word out in a cry.

Addie downplayed it. "It was a pair of scissors. Set accident. I'm—"

"I hope he lost his job. Eric said it was a man on the set," her mom said. Then she started crying. "You're my baby, and I know this is a nice job but . . . you need to move home. I talked to your father. He can move in with me, and you can have his half of the house."

Eric gave her an empathetic look.

Addie's dad obviously took the phone. "Temporarily, Addie. Temporarily." He lowered his voice. "I love her too much to live with her long-term, even for you."

Addie laughed, wincing with pain as she did. Her ribs were sore. She pointed at them and mouthed, "Broken?"

Eric shook his head and whispered loudly, "Bruised."

"Bruce?" her mom asked, back in possession of her phone now. "Who's Bruce?"

"I'm *bruised*, Mom. No Bruces here." They'd reached her hospital room then, and Addie took it as the distraction it was. "I need to go now. I'm fine, though. You and Daddy can stay—"

"We'll be there tomorrow night. Eric will give up his room for the night. It's all settled, and then once you can travel, we'll get you moved back here to the Bay Area."

"I'm not moving," Addie insisted.

"We'll talk tomorrow," her father yelled.

"We love you, Addie." Her mom sniffled again. "We'll be there, and we'll discuss it."

When she disconnected, Addie looked at her cousin. "At least *you'll* be able to have a drink when they're here."

"Well, you'll be on pain meds," Eric countered.

Addie laughed, hand coming to her sore ribs again. "You could still run away and see the rest of the family."

He took her free hand and squeezed. "I'll be staying here. I have to intimidate your ex when she shows up at the apartment, anyhow. She tricked me into giving her our address."

"How?"

"Well, she sounded very nice and asked me." Eric widened his eyes. "I was completely blindsided."

"She has that effect on people."

"Do you want to talk about it?" Eric asked gently.

Addie looked at her phone and quickly texted Toni: "I'm fine. You don't need to come."

"Ads?" Eric said, drawing her attention back to him.

She glanced away from her phone, which was not showing any replies so far, and told Eric, "I don't want my heart to hurt more. I love her. She doesn't want me to, but I do."

"Then she's a stupid person," Eric insisted. "There are better women out there, Ads. And once you're healed, we'll find one of them for you."

Addie blinked away tears. "I don't want to see Toni."

"Then you won't. I'll stop her," he promised.

If the only way to get her to be by my side is to be injured, she isn't worth it, Addie thought before she closed her eyes again.

Chapter 48
Toni

Toni took multiple connections. One of the commuter flights out of Dulles routed her through West Virginia and then to Pittsburgh, where a fifty-minute layover was all she had before boarding a flight to Vegas. Although she preferred the tight-enough-to-have-to-run time to this indeterminable wait in Las Vegas.

A series of delays with mechanical issues and then the lack of a pilot had Toni with an eight-hour layover. *So far.* By the fifth hour, she was ready to rent a car and drive to Los Angeles, but she'd been awake most of the last thirty hours. Her three- to four-hour nap from Pittsburg to Vegas wasn't enough to make her confident that she could drive safely on Thanksgiving Day through the desert when she wasn't sure if service stations would be open—or that she could stay awake even with the amount of coffee in her system.

She read and reread Addie's messages as she waited. The last one—"I'm fine. You don't need to come."—cut deeper because Toni knew Addie was injured and still refusing to talk to her.

A month of trying to convince herself she could move on was resulting in exactly no progress. Toni had to fix this. She needed Addie in her life. There was no other answer. She sat in an airport looking up tests to see if she had the genes that meant she'd end up with dementia. *Maybe that would help.* Then she searched ways to decrease her odds of it. It was stupid, unscientific, but it made her feel less helpless. That was something, at least.

Toni finally got to LAX late afternoon on Thanksgiving, and since her only bag was a carry-on, she took a car straight to the hospital. She hoped Addie had been discharged, but she also wasn't going to go to her apartment in case she was still at the hospital.

"I'm here to visit a patient. Adelaine Stewart," she told them at the welcome desk just inside the lobby.

Toni got her room number and headed to the third floor. By the time she reached the third floor, Toni was fairly sure she was going to make a fool of herself. She had no idea how to have this conversation, especially after that last text from Addie.

I need to see her, though. I need to know she's okay.

But when she reached Addie's hospital room, Toni felt a wave of relief when she saw that Addie was wearing the cardigan she'd borrowed from Toni. Surely, that meant something, right? Addie was still wearing Toni's clothes.

"I told you not to come," Addie said, crossing her arms over her chest. "You don't need to be here."

"I do. You were hurt, and I *needed* to see you." Toni stepped into the room, staring at the machines. An IV was jabbed into Addie's hand, and a monitor showed her heart rate—currently escalating—and another showed her oxygen levels. Toni was familiar with all of this from when Aunt Patty was sick.

"I'm fine." Addie motioned at the bandage. "There were set scissors, dull enough to take effort to shove through my skin."

Toni winced.

"Dirty blades, though, so they have me on antibiotics and stuff." Addie shrugged with the unbandaged arm. "Bumped my head. Some minor cuts. I could've told you over the phone and saved you a flight."

"Four. Four flights." Toni dropped her carry-on by the wall where it was out of the way. Then she walked closer. She didn't want to sit on the bed and jostle Addie, but she needed to be nearer to her. Her hands fisted with the twin urges to cradle Addie and to find the person responsible. Instead, she asked, "Did you press charges?"

"What?"

"He hurt you," Toni said.

"So did you," Addie snapped. "Getting hurt happens to me a lot lately."

Toni dropped to her knees beside the bed. She was exhausted, and standing seemed too challenging when Addie was determined to cut her down. She wanted to take Addie's hand more than she had words to explain. She reached out, not touching Addie. "Addie, love, I was a fool. I never meant to hurt you—"

"And yet you did." Addie's tears streaked over her cheeks as she pulled her hands out of Toni's reach. "Loving me is so awful that it means that we have to be apart if you loved me or I loved you. That was *your* rule. You didn't even ask what I wanted. You expect that it's okay to worry about your reputation, your feelings, your career. Did you ask how any of that affected me?"

"I screwed up. I was wrong about so many things, love." Toni stared at her, trying to make the words make sense, but she had been awake for almost thirty-four hours now. "I'm so sorry I fucked up. I *know* I was wrong, but you can't just tell me you love me and then shut me out."

"Says who? Is this another Toni rule? You just made it up and I have to obey—"

"I love you," Toni blurted out. "I love you, Adelaine Stewart."

Addie was silent for a long pause, and then she asked, "When did you know?"

"November first," Toni answered. She knew the exact date and time when she'd realized it.

"Did you say it in any of the messages you left for me?"

"No." Toni felt a sinking pit in her stomach.

"So you knew for the entire last month basically, but . . . did you email it? Text it?" Addie pressed.

"No."

"Then why tell me now?" Addie asked in a deceptively calm voice. "Because honestly? I already knew you loved me when we were in New Orleans, Toni. I knew you were falling when I walked toward you in that wedding. Half the country knew when they saw the pictures."

"Addie . . . I never wanted a relationship," Toni started.

"Right. Do you think admitting this *now* changes a damn thing? I don't deserve to be merely tolerated. I am worth a lot more." Addie glared at her. "I stopped talking to you because of *your* rules."

"You are worth everything." Toni stared at her, imploring her to understand. "I want everything with you. I want you in my life and—"

"No."

"Addie . . . I have been miserable without you because I love you. I understand that now, and when you were injured, I felt like I couldn't breathe. I needed to see you, tell you, know you were safe."

"Well, you told me, and you saw that I'm doing better." Addie gestured toward the door. "You can go now."

Toni stared at her. "I don't want to go."

"Don't you have classes to teach?" Addie said, voice trembling.

"Monday." Toni took her hand, flipped it over, and pressed a kiss into her palm. "I'll be in LA for the weekend."

"There's probably a museum or something you can see," Addie said.

"I want to see *you*. Help you. Be here to take care of you," Toni explained. "Please, Addie."

"You don't want a relation—"

"I do. I want that with you," Toni stressed.

"I have a career in LA, and you live in DC. None of this even matters," Addie countered.

"You set the rules. You set the terms, love. Tell me what to do." Toni stared up at her. "You're in charge, Addie. What do I need to do to try this for real? I love you, and I want to make this thing between us work."

"Well, Addie," a man's voice came from the doorway. "Give the poor woman a break. She's already married you once."

"As if that matters," another voice, a woman's, said. "Marriage is a trap by the patriarchy to control women and—"

"Hi, Mom. Daddy." Addie squeezed Toni's hand. She whispered, "Get up, please."

And Toni turned to meet Addie's parents.

"Marlene. Lenny. This is my . . . this is Toni. She was just leaving." Addie's smile was brittle. "Toni, my parents."

Toni stood, stepped forward, and held out a hand to Addie's mother, who shook it, and then her father, who used it to pull her in for a hug.

"Don't give up on her," Lenny whispered.

Toni walked over to the bed and took Addie's hand gently. "I love you, Adelaine. Let me know when you're willing to talk."

At first Addie said nothing, then she shook her head. "I don't want to talk to you."

Toni smiled. "Then I'll wait until you do."

Then Toni left in search of a taxi to a hotel where she could collapse and sleep. Addie was going to be fine, and Toni was going to find a way to make *them* okay, too.

Chapter 49

Addie

For the next two days, Toni emailed, sent flowers, had meals delivered, and stopped at the apartment. Several times, Addie was asleep, but whether she was awake or asleep, Toni was turned away at the door. Addie's heart twinged each time, but she wasn't going to let Toni in so she could hurt her again.

By Sunday morning, Addie's father looked at Addie and asked, "Do you truly love her?"

Addie looked up at him. "Yes."

"Then stop this." Lenny sat casually on the opposite end of the sofa from Addie, watching her expectantly.

"She doesn't want to love me," Addie said. "I have plans, a life here, and . . . she only wants me because I was hurt. Then she'll get scared again and push me away."

"You had a fight, Addie. She obviously *does* want to love you. She's emailed you how many times?"

"Four or so times each day," Addie said.

"Are you done torturing her yet?" He gave her a look she'd seen him give her mother often. "I don't always understand you, but I always love you, muffin. Right now, I see your mother in you—and not her good side. Maybe try to not be like your mom on this front? Us poor fools who fall in love with angry women can only suffer so much before we quit."

"Do you ever want to quit?" Addie asked. This wasn't a topic they really had ever discussed.

"Not for more than a stray moment. She makes me happy, but sometimes I'm slow on the uptake and she gets pissed off because I'm not there yet. Sounds like your Toni is more like your old man. We get there, but you have to pause and let us catch up. You and Marl? You always know what you want and where you're going. Not everyone is like that." Lenny smiled. "Doesn't make my love any more shallow or incomplete. Slow moving, is all. Marl is like lightning. I'm the thunder. Little bit delayed, but just as real."

Her mother came out then, as if summoned by some silent signal.

Eric made a hand gesture like he was smoking and pointed at Marlene, as if she couldn't smell the proof that her mother had just had her pre–road trip joint. *Some things never change.* Addie repressed a laugh.

Marlene was staring at them with wet eyes, so Addie knew she hadn't overheard Lenny. "Eric says I can't legally make you come home."

"Kidnapping. I think it's a felony," Addie said lightly.

"Calling every day?" Marlene countered.

"Misdemeanor in California."

Marlene sighed like a deflating balloon. "You're a horrible, selfish child, refusing to let me fuss over you."

"I love you, too." Addie stared at her parents. She wasn't ever going to understand them, not her mother hiding in the bathroom to smoke weed or her father thinking that he was qualified to give relationship advice. She *did* love them, though. "I'm glad you're still together, you know?"

"Together?" Marlene scoffed. "He's just my neighbor."

"Uh-huh." Lenny rolled his eyes. "She lets me sleep over on weekends."

"He cooks. It's nice to not have to cook for myself." She leaned her head on his shoulder. "Look at her, Len. Cute as a little bumblebee. We made her."

He looped his arm around her waist. "Let's get you down to the car. Eric can bring the bag of dishes."

"On it," Eric called, a piece of pumpkin pie in his hand. "I was just transferring the last few into our dishes." He paused as they started down the steps. "I'm going to have them drop me off at the theater, so *if* you wanted to have any guests, you could."

"Not going to stay and threaten her?" Addie said lightly.

"She loves you, Ads. I can't exactly criticize that, and she summoned help when you were hurt. And, well, *you* love *her*. You two need to talk, either for closure or getting together." Eric counted each item down on his fingers. "If you want me stay, I can. I just think you might prefer I'm not here."

Addie said nothing. He was right. So was her father. She sighed and texted Toni: "I'm free now."

Toni's reply was instant.

To call or see?

Either.

On the way.

Addie wasn't sure what she wanted, but Toni likely had to leave that evening, so it was see her now or not at all. And Addie was certain that "not at all" wasn't the answer she liked.

When Toni arrived, Addie walked over to unlock the door. She opened it and was met with a face full of flowers.

"Why did you open the door?" Toni looked around the apartment. "Where are your parents?"

"They left with my cousin. I'm home alone." Addie went back over to the sofa. Her ribs were better today. Still sore but definitely better than the first day.

"Do we need to hire a nurse?" Toni moved a pillow onto a chair. "What if you fall?"

"Toni."

She looked at Addie. "Right. You can make your own decisions. Did I mention that I didn't cope well with you being hurt?"

"Yes." Addie sat back down with a grimace. "Better" did not mean "painless." She tried to get comfortable and then prompted, "You wanted to talk."

Toni opened her bag and handed Addie a printed list. As Addie skimmed it, Toni stood patiently, not pacing, but not sitting down either.

Rules To Court Addie:

1. Tell her you were wrong. Repeat as needed.
2. Tell her you love her. Every day. (How often is normal?)
3. Don't retreat when panicking.
4. Figure out how to make the schedule work.
   - Term Break: Either go away together or fly Addie to D.C.
   - Long weekend in January.
   - Spring Break in March.
   - Sublet LA apartment June 1-August 26th
   - Consult with Addie on all of this.
5. Grand gestures. How often? What sort would she like?
6. Couples trips. Where is her dream vacation? Go there. (Maybe for Spring Break?)
7. Check out proper schedule for declaring commitment levels. Schedule them. (There has to be a book on this.)
8. Discuss what she thinks needs added to this plan. Add it.
9. Give her keys to my place.

Addie looked up at Toni several times as she read. Then she set the list aside. "So you have gone from running away to . . . whatever this is?"

"I was wrong, and I love you," Toni started. She held out a key ring. "This is the key to my place. Any time you want to visit, you can just show up. I always want you there, and I have no secrets that would mean you couldn't stop in at any time." She looked at Addie earnestly. "Kaelee got an offer of representation from Em. That's why she was there at my mother's memory care home, and why I hugged her. She was freaking out."

"I know you—"

"No." Toni dropped to her knees. "I swear to you that I didn't—"

"I didn't think you were *seeing* her. I was upset because she knew where your mom was," Addie said. "You wouldn't take me to meet your mom, though. You wouldn't let me in, but you let a random stu—"

"I think Kae is my friend, actually. I was shoving that away, too, because she was my TA, but . . ." Toni rubbed a hand over her face. "Kae only knew where my mom lives because last year, before I bought the Jeep, my old car broke down, and I had to call her for a ride." Toni clutched the key ring in her hand. "It was mortifying. I had to call my TA to pick me up. I guess I could've used rideshare, but I hadn't been paid yet and . . . I don't tell people about Lil, and I didn't take anyone to meet her. I didn't tell Kaelee where Lil lives by *choice*, love. I swear."

"I want to meet your mom," Addie said. "Add it to your list."

Toni looked at the ceiling like she was praying, and when she looked back, she said, "My father had a type—gorgeous, very femme, delicate women with vivacious laughs. So Lil sometimes thinks women are there as his mistress, and . . . she has a temper sometimes. I was trying to protect you. Most of the time, she thinks I'm my aunt Patty."

"Oh."

"If it's that important, though, we'll find a way. I want you to see that I'm serious, love." Toni knelt there still. "Don't tell me it's too late for us, please."

"This kind of plan isn't *you*. What happens when you feel panicked next time? Or you need to retreat?" Addie shook her head. "This list is too fast. You can't go from 'don't love me' to 'here's a relationship.'"

"Which part is too fast? I can adjust it." Toni pulled out a pen. "I can't lose you."

"You are being ridiculous right now," Addie grumbled.

"You wouldn't let me talk to you, so I read a bunch of articles and skimmed a few novels and—"

"You researched." Addie didn't bother hiding her smile. "You researched how to . . . what? Win a heart? You already have that, Toni. You've had my heart for a year, maybe more."

"I researched long-distance relationships, commitment-phobes, and apologies," Toni said without so much as cringing. "Honestly, love, I knew I was falling for you when I left LA last time. When we spent the night together. I thought I could control it, but then when you stopped talking to me, it hurt."

"Oh," Addie said again.

"Maybe I knew even sooner. Addie, I named my series protagonist after you. I've been thinking a lot between research bouts." Toni sighed. "May I sit?"

"No."

"I thought—"

"This way." Addie stood and gestured. "Come with me."

Toni stood hastily.

Then she led Toni to her bedroom. "My ribs hurt, and I want to lie down."

When Toni stayed in the doorway, Addie added, "With you, Toni. I want you to hold me. I can't give you all the answers you want, but I love you and I was scared and . . . just come here."

Toni toed off her shoes and looked at Addie's lilac bedspread.

"Under the covers, please." Addie reached to pull the top cover back, but Toni was faster.

"I feel like you're trying to prove a point by ordering me around," Toni said after Addie sat down beside her. "Are you?"

"Not consciously." Addie rested so her injured shoulder, where the scissors stabbed her, was not next to Toni. "Hold me, please."

"I don't want to hurt you." Toni's hand hovered in the air, as if she was afraid to wrap her arm around Addie.

"My hips aren't bruised."

Toni adjusted her arm so her hand was on the curve of Addie's hip. "I mean it, you know. I want to make this work. I would like it if you seriously think about what you're signing up for if you are willing, though. My mother has dementia. It could be genetic, and I don't want you saddled with me if I get like her. That was half of my hang-up." Her voice broke on the last part of her confession.

"Oh, Toni, you're impossible sometimes," Addie whispered. "That's not a right now problem."

"Loving anyone is terrifying." Toni stroked her fingers along Addie's hip. "What if I fail you or get sick?"

"That's what *everyone* has to weigh," Addie pointed out. "Every relationship. What if I have a heart attack some day? Or cancer? Would you leave me?"

"No."

"Then you need to trust that I wouldn't abandon you, either," Addie said gently. "I'll accept every step of your list and keep your keys, if I can add one more thing."

Toni stared at her expectantly.

"You agree to see a therapist to talk about this." Addie held her gaze. "I love you, but I need you to understand that it's *okay* to be loved, to let me love you."

"Do I need to do that first before we—?"

"Make the appointment, and then we'll make a plan for winter break," Addie offered. "I'm not sure about all of it. Let's get through each step. No rushing. I'll work on my temper, and you'll work on letting me love you. I know I love you, but I'm not ready to start sharing an address or anything. My career is in LA, Toni. I'm not giving that up or asking you to marry me. I just didn't want you to be closed off to a *possible* future."

"But one day, you want . . . to be married?"

"That's always been my plan, Toni. A career I am proud of, and a woman I love. I'm not actually that complex," Addie said, closing her eyes as Toni held her carefully.

"Can I tell you that I love you now?"

Addie giggled. "You already did. Several times."

"I was so afraid, Addie," Toni whispered. "I pushed you away to keep you safe from me, and then you were hurt, and I wasn't there."

"*Loving* you doesn't hurt." Addie sighed contentedly as Toni started stroking her hair. "Being rejected does. Just let me in, Professor. That's all I've wanted from the very first night."

Epilogue
Toni

SIX MONTHS LATER

The last six months had been amazing. Once Toni stopped trying to pretend that she wasn't in love, everything was easier. The worst part was how often they'd had to live apart. Trips were great, but the more time they were together, the more time Toni wanted to be together. Between events for the book and for the show, they had filming and teaching. Toni wasn't ready to give up teaching, but she had decided to take the entire summer off. She'd still fly back to visit Lil twice a month, but that was okay. She wrote well on the long flights, and finding a nonstop flight from LA to DC was easy when it wasn't last minute.

They'd found an apartment in LA for the summer, but it wasn't going to be available until June first. When Toni got a call that she could move in mid-May if she wanted, she realized that she was more than ready to go. Come fall term, Addie would move to DC any time she wasn't filming. For everything that had seemed impossible, there were easy-to-find answers now that they were on the same page.

Classes had ended May tenth, so once the grades were in, Oscar Wilde and Toni flew to LAX. She was excited to take possession of the apartment a little early. Her Jeep was being delivered the next week, but for this week, she had a rental car. And really, since it seemed appropriate for Los Angeles, Toni had rented a little convertible.

If it happened to be Addie's dream car, that was just a coincidence.

She'd hired a company to deliver the essential things—litter box, linens, groceries, and fresh flowers. The special items were there already, too: a collection of loose rose petals, a premixed pitcher of lemon drops, and a discreet box from a local shop.

"This is it, Oscar Wilde. Your castle for the night." Toni locked him in the second bedroom, which would be her office for the summer, before she scattered the flowers in a trail from the front door to the bed. Roses weren't toxic to cats, but she couldn't trust him to not eat them. And cleaning up cat sick wasn't exactly the mood she was aiming for tonight.

She put the glasses and the lemon drops in the fridge to chill.

Then she put her boxes in the bedroom—one from her carry-on under the bed and one from the delivery in the nightstand.

When the doorbell rang again, Toni checked herself in the mirror and went to answer it. She opened the door but held a hand up. Addie paused, and Toni lifted her into a bridal carry and carried her into the apartment.

Addie laughed. "Almost a year late, if I recall the date of our marriage."

"Ten months," Toni corrected her.

"So you decided to come out to LA two weeks early? Any reason?" Addie teased.

"Oscar Wilde missed you," Toni tried and failed to say with a straight face.

Addie laughed. "I do love him. So are you leaving him with me so you can go back—"

Toni cut off her teasing by pulling her close and kissing her until Addie was pliant in her arms. That was something therapy had taught her: it was okay to be a little impulsive without it being a sign of being like her father.

When Toni released her, Addie saw the pink and red rose petals on the ground. "Oh my goodness, someone murdered roses in here!"

"They were sacrificed for a good cause." Toni chuckled. "They were last week's roses. Dropping their petals, so this is their final mission. It was this or the trash. I thought the florist was going to lecture me all day for my request. They're the same color as the ones you wore when we were fake-married."

"Thank you." Addie leaned up and kissed the side of her throat. "Shall I see where they lead?"

Toni held out a package. "Would you indulge me first? Put this on."

Addie looked inside the box, where there was a Victorian night-dress. Pristine white cotton with a ruffle at the ankles, it was as close a replica as Toni had found. Without a word, Addie did as Toni asked. She stepped out of the bathroom in it a few moments later, hair braided back. No bra. No panties, either.

Toni took off her blazer and offered it. "You shivered."

"Because of how you're looking at me," Addie countered. "I don't need to be covered up, though."

Toni held out a hand as if to shake. "I'm Toni Darbyshire. I'm a history professor. I was here in Scotland to give a talk."

Smiling, Addie took her hand. "Lady Adelaine Stewart. I was here to watch you, actually."

Toni poured them each a lemon drop. "Do you suppose I could kiss you, Miss Stewart?"

Addie took a sip and then looked around. "I have a thing for gardens . . . any chance these roses lead to one?"

"After you." Toni motioned her forward. Then she set her drink on a shelf outside the room.

At the doorway, Addie stopped. The bed and the floor were littered with roses. The room itself was fairly nondescript, but the petals were everywhere. "Toni!"

"I want you *always* with me, Adelaine. I want to wake up next to you. I want to go to sleep holding you. I want to come home to find you talking to Oscar Wilde."

"I want that, too." Addie looked at her, seeming a little uncertain. "I'll be here all summer."

Toni dropped to one knee and held up the little box she'd tucked under the edge of the bed. She opened it to reveal a marquise-cut emerald in a Victorian-style setting with four diamonds—one at each compass point—on a rose-gold band

"I was thinking a little more permanent than that," Toni said. "Marry me? For real, this time."

"Yes. Every time." Addie extended a shaking hand for Toni to slip the ring on. "We could have the same minister. Do it at Cape Dove Manor."

"I don't care, love. As long as you're legally mine at the end, it's perfect," Toni said.

Addie looked at the ring, and then she looked down at Toni. "You know, I thought with the nightdress and the lemon drops . . ."

"Go on."

"I was expecting to be ravished in this makeshift garden." Addie backed up until she was flush against the wall.

"I'm going to spend forever worshipping you," Toni declared. "My heart and my body are yours."

"Toni . . ."

"Hush, fiancée of mine. Words, then ravishing." Toni swept Addie into her arms and carried her to the bed.

"I love you, Toni."

Toni pulled Addie on top of her. "Good, because I'm going to marry you, you know."

"I do," Addie said, very seriously. After a pause, she asked, "Do you really want to? For you, not just for me but—"

"I do." Toni leaned up and kissed her gently. "I do. For real and forever."

Acknowledgments

People (including authors!) don't owe their private lives to anyone, but *oof, the search terms I've seen on my name.* I suspect the searches are because until recently I didn't write lesbian romances. To clarify, I've been "out" and dating women since the 1980s, when I started dating. In the late '90s, I was told I had a couple years to have a baby before I lost my uterus. I chose to enter an open marriage with a male friend. I *wanted* a baby, and he wanted a mom for his then-four-year-old. We remain excellent friends and co-parents.

Since I sold my debut book in 2006, I identified as bi in public, which a lot of people read as "used to date women." I didn't volunteer clarifying information because really, unless I was intending to date someone, my identity was no one's damn business, but I also chose not to write lesbian characters because I was living a life that often "looked straight," so I didn't believe that was my right.

Then I met Amber. As with the other women and men who had been in my life, I didn't mention her in public for *years*. But from the time we first went on a date, I've been in a monogamous, committed relationship—to the point that a few years ago I dropped to one knee and put a ring on Amber's hand. So here I am writing a contemporary lesbian love story.

Like the rest of my books, this book is *fiction*. Amber is an Army vet, worked in intel, and now does architectural design, and has a habit of hiking the Grand Canyon. She's not a professor or writer or actor. I get frustrated when people ask if she's in my books. Nope. It turns out I'm actually intensely possessive for the first time in my life.

Nonetheless, the *book* exists because of her. So the biggest thanks goes to Amber for telling me to write the book for myself even if no one ever read it but her.

Then I shared it with a few friends because it was *fun* to write.

My friend Sophie Jordan was a huge influence on this book ending up in your hands. I ran into the "but contemporary romance isn't what *you* write" response from a number of people, but Sophie was there saying all the right things. (I'm grateful you're in my life again, Sophie!)

On similar notes, thank you to Jeaniene Frost and Kelley Armstrong for your enthusiastic support when I shared the initial pages with you and for your words in the burnout years, when you told me not to stop writing.

Thank you to Monique Patterson and to Mal Frazier for the enthusiastic response. Mal, you said *exactly* the words I hoped to hear; for that, I am forever grateful. Monique, your notes made me blush. It's been a joy to be your author.

Thank you to Merrilee, for yet again selling a book outside my "brand." I know I keep doing this. I guess I'm not genre-monogamous either.

As ever, thank you also goes to my adult kids and Loch, who, along with Amber, will mind the wee one when I am traveling or toss food or coffee toward me when I am on deadline.

Thank you to all of *you* who have been reading my books for years.

Thank you to those of *you* who have been changing the industry by reading queer fiction, and to all the queer folks who wrote lesbian books so that the publishing world could see that we are here, and we are readers.

About the Author

MELISSA MARR writes fiction for adults, teens, and children. Her books have been translated into twenty-eight languages and been bestsellers in the US (*The New York Times, Los Angeles Times, USA Today, The Wall Street Journal*) as well as overseas. *Wicked Lovely,* her debut novel, was an instant *New York Times* bestseller and evolved into an internationally bestselling multibook series with a myriad of accolades. If she's not writing, you can find her in a kayak or on a trail with her wife.